THE SCIENCE FICTIONARY

ROBERT W. BLY

Let the world know:
#IGotMyCLPBook!

Crystal Lake Publishing
www.crystallakepub.com

Copyright 2023 Robert W. Bly
Join the Crystal Lake community today
on our newsletter and Patreon!
Download our latest catalog here:
https://geni.us/CLPCatalog

All Rights Reserved

Cover art:
Ben Baldwin—http://www.benbaldwin.co.uk

Layout:
Kenneth W. Cain—http://www.kennethwcain.com

Proofread by:
Guy Medley, and Rie Sheridan Rose

No part of this publication may be reproduced, stored in a retrieval system, or transmitted in any form or by any means, without the prior permission in writing of the publisher, nor be otherwise circulated in any form of binding or cover than that in which it is published and without a similar condition including this condition being imposed on the subsequent purchaser.

WELCOME
TO ANOTHER

CRYSTAL LAKE PUBLISHING
CREATION

Join today at www.crystallakepub.com & www.patreon.com/CLP

Dedication

To my mother, Milly Bly—in loving memory

Acknowledgments

I want to thank Joe Mynhardt for having faith in me and in this book; Taylor Grant for bringing the manuscript to Joe's attention; Hunter Shea for sharing his horror knowledge and enthusiasm; Dave McCoy for his illustrations; and Fern Dickey for her research assistance.

A note on sources

Titles of short stories are in quotation marks. Titles of novels, movies, and TV shows are in italics.

"Science fiction is the search for a definition of man and his status in the universe which will stand in our advanced but confused state of knowledge (science)."
—Brian Aldiss[1]

"I think science fiction is a very important kind of literature … and I've struggled back and forth between my desire to make science fiction into a visionary literature of great emotional and literary intensity, and the publisher's desire to make a lot of money by selling a popular entertainment."
—Robert Silverberg[2]

---

[1] David Golder, *The Astounding History of Science Fiction,* Flame Tree, 2017, p. 8.
[2] *Publishers Weekly,* May 3, 2004, p. 176.

Introduction

Science fiction has often been referred to as a "literature of ideas." And within that literature, authors often describe the ideas they have invented with made-up words, phrases, and nomenclature they have invented. They also use in their stories words already in our vocabulary — most often, terms from science, engineering, and technology as well as folklore, myth, and legend.

The term science fiction was coined in 1851 by literary critic William Wilson.[3]

In *The Science Fictionary*, you get a guide to the fantastic ideas, and the words used to describe them, in science fiction and its related genres, fantasy and horror — from androids and antimatter, to bionics and black holes, to warp factors and worm holes — and everything in between.

The Science Fictionary taps into America's love affair with science fiction and the fantastic, and for fans of these genres, it serves three purposes.

First, if you want a clearer explanation of an important science fictional idea, work, author, or concept, you can often find it here.

Second is the nostalgic appeal. Flipping through the pages of *The Science Fictionary* is, for die-hard fans, a stroll through the streets of memory paved with endless hours of pleasurable reading, seeing, and dreaming while lost in fantastic stories and worlds of imagination.

Third, the definitions may serve as a springboard for further pursuit of your SF, fantasy, and horror passions, pointing the way to new books and authors you might enjoy reading, sending you back to those works you always meant to read but

---

[3] David Golder, *The Astounding History of Science Fiction*, Flame Tree, 2017, p. 14.

never got around to, and motivating you to reread that favorite Zelazny novel or Lovecraft story yet another time, so you can revisit the territory anew and discover more of its treasures.

Though the popularity of certain subgenres (e.g., vampires, zombies) may be cyclical, their appeal is timeless. And as a result, legions of science fiction, fantasy, and horror fans continue to watch the TV shows, go to the movies, buy the books, attend the conventions, and subscribe to the science fiction magazines and fan newsletters.

The biggest films in these genres are often blockbusters at the box office; e.g. *Avatar* ($760 million), *ET* ($435 million), *The Hunger Games: Catching Fire* ($425 million), *Jurassic World* ($652 million), and *The Guardians of the Galaxy* ($333 million).[4] Don't forget the Star Wars movies, which in movie theater and rental income, have in total and adjusted for inflation earned $21 billion.

And print is far from dead: Best-selling science fiction novels have sold in the millions of copies, including Ray Bradbury's *Fahrenheit 451* (10 million), Douglas Adams' *Hitchhiker's Guide to the Galaxy* (14 million), L. Ron Hubbard's *Battlefield Earth* (2 million), and William Gibson's *Necromancer* (6.5 million).[5] Given the immense and ongoing popularity of SF books and films, these sales figures will likely be even higher by the time this book gets into your hands.

We SF fans may be a minority, but we are not a small one: A 2014 poll from the Science Fiction and Fantasy Writers of America found that one out of five Americans reads science fiction.[6]

4
http://www.imdb.com/search/title?genres=sci_fi&sort=boxoffice_gross_us,desc

[5] http://flavorwire.com/347374/awesome-infographic-the-best-selling-sci-fi-books-of-all-time

[6] http://www.sfwa.org/2014/01/reads-science-fiction/

As you continue to read and watch our favorite genres, I do have a favor to ask. If you think of a science fiction, fantasy, or horror term, idea, character, world, or notion I have neglected to include in *The Science Fictionary*, would you kindly send it along to me? That way, I can share it with readers of the next edition of this book. They will thank you. And so will I.

You can reach me at:

Bob Bly
31 Cheyenne Drive
Montville, NJ 07045
Phone: 973-263-0562
Fax: 973-263-0613
Email: rwbly@bly.com
Web: www.bly.com

Foreword
Taylor Grant

As a longtime fan of Bob Bly's work, I was truly honored to have the privilege of writing the foreword to his latest book, *The Science Fictionary*. I was fortunate enough to be introduced to Bob's work decades ago when I decided to add copywriting to my freelance writing toolkit. While there are countless books on the subject today, they all stand in the long shadow of Bob's seminal work, *The Copywriter's Handbook*, which was, in many ways, the bible of copywriting at the time. To this day, I keep a dog-eared copy (with many highlighted pages) nearby on my shelf.

Bob knows more than a thing or two about the dynamism of words. He understands that words can educate as well as entertain, and he has mastered the power of words to generate emotion and drive action. His long-standing reputation as America's top copywriter is well-deserved. However, Bob's passion for words extends far beyond the realm of advertising and marketing. With over 100 published books on a wide range of topics, he has established himself as a prolific and versatile author in his own right, with a gift for making complex subjects accessible to readers of all backgrounds.

Which leads us to *The Science Fictionary*, a testament to Bob's lifelong love of genre fiction and his talent for distilling complex ideas into clear and engaging prose. This wonderfully entertaining reference guide is a treasure trove of information for anyone who loves speculative fiction, and Bob's encyclopedic knowledge of the genre shines through on every page.

I have no doubt that *The Science Fictionary* will become a beloved classic in the world of science fiction, fantasy, and horror, and I am proud to recommend it to anyone who wants to deepen their understanding and appreciation of these genres.

Taylor Grant, Two-Time Bram Stoker Award Finalist, and Bestselling author of *The Dark at the End of the Tunnel*

The Science Fiction, Fantasy, and Horror Dictionary A Through Z

3D Chess. A variation on chess played on a board with three levels. First popularized on the TV show *Star Trek*, where Kirk and Spock played the game. Now sold online and in many toy and game stores.

4D Man. In a movie of the same title, *The 4D Man* is a scientist whose experimental electronic amplifier gives him the power to walk through walls. Unfortunately, the energies he absorbs from his experiment also cause him to age rapidly. He discovers that when he passes his hand through another person's body, he steals their life energy, replenishing his own in the process. He reverts to his normal biological age, while his victim ages and dies in seconds.

99, The. In the comic book of the same title, the 99 are a team of Islamic superheroes, granted super powers by possessing the Noor stones. In the TV series *Get Smart*, 99 is an agent of Control, an organization that fights their evil rivals, KAOS.

ABEL (Automated Biological Laboratory). In Larry Niven's short story "Plaything," ABEL is a mobile probe that lands on the surface of Mars to search for signs of life. It consists of a cluster of metal and plastic sub-assemblies. These components are mounted on a low platform slung between six tires. A camera mounted on a telescoping leg captures images of the Martian landscape.

Abyormen. A planet in an odd orbit around a binary star consisting of a red giant and a white dwarf. The binary star orbit causes the planet to have a 40-year cool period during which temperatures are similar to Earth, followed by a 20-year hot period when the temperature is hundreds of degrees hotter. Source: Hal Clement's novel *Cycle of Fire*.

Abyssal chthonic resonator (ACR). Science fiction critic John Clute defines the ACR as a place that creates and is home to myth-images, or "mythagos." These are animals, monsters, elves, fairies, and other creatures generated from the ancient memories and myths stored in the subconscious minds of nearby humans. Clute cites as an example of an ACR the *Mythago Wood,* in Robert Holdstock's novel of the same title.

AC. In Isaac Asimov's short story "The Last Question," AC is the most powerful computer in the universe, existing only in hyperspace. When the universe burns out because of entropy, AC figures out how to reverse entropy and create a new universe — one in which it is essentially God.

Adamantium. An alloy of iron that is virtually indestructible. It is bonded to the skeletons of Wolverine and his clones X-23 and X-24, making their claws unbreakable and able to cut through almost anything. In the movie *Logan,* X-24 is killed when X-23 shoots him in the head with an adamantium bullet. Cyber, an enemy of Wolverine, has adamantium bonded to most of his skin; the comic books fail to explain how it can be flexible enough to allow him movement. Adamantium is specific to Marvel Comics. In the broader world of science fiction, any material that is indestructible is called "impervium," because it is impervious to harm.

Adjustment Bureau. From the motion picture of the same title, The Adjustment Bureau is a covert government agency that operates behind the scenes to manipulate geopolitical, economic, and other events and forces to ensure the safety and stability of the United States. In particular, they make "adjustments," meaning they take deliberate actions that interfere with and change the course of people's lives.

Adramelech. From the Sean Hazlett short story of the same title, Adramelech is a Mesopotamian deity whose worshippers burn children as human sacrifices.

Aepyornis. In H.G. Wells' *The Stolen Bacillus and Other Incidents,* the aepyornis is a species of bird found only on Aepyornis, an island off Madagascar. An adult aepyornis stands 14-feet tall with a broad head, brown eyes, green plumage, and a blue crest and wattle. It lays eggs that are 18 inches long.

After Ford (AF). In Aldous Huxley's novel *Brave New World*, years are designated "AF" or "After Ford" dating from the invention of the Ford Model T.

Aglarond. In J.R.R. Tolkien's fantasy trilogy *The Lord of the Rings,* Aglarond is an interconnected series of caves and grottoes under the White Mountains adjacent to an enormous gorge, Helm's Deep. The caverns are filled with gems and veins of precious ores. Pillars of white, saffron, and pink support the roofs of the underground chambers.

AI (Artificial Intelligence). AI means a computer, robot, or other machine that can think in a manner equivalent or superior to a human being. The famous Turing Test, proposed by computer scientist Alan Turing, says that if you converse with a computer remotely (i.e., via email, texting, Skype, phone), and you cannot tell that it is in fact not a human being, then the computer has achieved true AI. There are two levels of AI. The first is a machine that thinks and solves problems as well or better than we do, such as Big Blue beating Gary

Kasparov at chess or Watson defeating Ken Jennings in Jeopardy. The second level is that the machine becomes self-aware or sentient. Elon Musk is so fearful of an AI machine becoming self-aware he, despite being a libertarian, has called for the federal government to regulate development of AI computers and robots. The two great fears centered on the development of AI computers is first that they can do jobs now performed by people, resulting in massive unemployment. And second that when they become self-aware, they will rule or destroy humans as a means of self-preservation, as has been portrayed in countless SF movies including *Colossus: The Forbin Project, The Matrix,* and *The Terminator.* In the latter, much of humanity is wiped out, and the rest forced to live in hiding, when a self-aware AI computer network, Skynet, launches nuclear missiles and builds an army of killer robots, terminators, to exterminate the remaining humans. William Gibson wrote about AI in his 1984 novel *Necromancer.*

Akira Project. A project of the military and psi-powered children resulting in the creation of a powerful entity that is a cross between Frankenstein's monster and a demi-god, from the anime movie *Akira*.

AKKA. The ultimate weapon that would determine the fate of all of humanity unless it could be stopped. From Jack Williamson's novel *The Legion of Space*.

Alali. An African village populated by giant women. In Alali society, men are normal-sized and therefore physically inferior. They are hunted by the women and killed, or used as slaves. Source: Edgar Rice Burroughs, *Tarzan and the Ant Men*.

Albatross. In the Jules Verne novel *Robur the Conqueror*, the Albatross is a flying battleship, commanded by its genius inventor, Robur. He flies over battlefields and attacks the fighting soldiers from the air, with the goal of eliminating war throughout the world.

His ship is suspended in the air by the lift of 74 helical screws, mounted two by two on 37 masts. It is propelled by four larger and more powerful screws mounted on the front and back of the ship's deck. These screws are driven by electric motors using power supplied by onboard accumulator batteries.

Alberts. On the planet Fruyling's World, the Alberts are the intelligent indigenous species: 5 feet tall, green-skinned, alligator-like reptiles that have a single eye like a cyclops and walk erect. Source: *Slave Planet* by Laurence Janifer.

Aleph. In the Jose Luis Borges short story "The Aleph," an Aleph is defined as "one of the points in space that contains all points…the place where, without admixture or confusion, all the pieces of the world, seen from every angle, coexist…the Aleph [is] probably two or three centimeters in diameter, but universal space time [is] contained inside it, with no diminution in size…each thing [is] infinite things, because [you can] clearly see it from every point in the cosmos." The science fictional explanation of such a phenomenon could be a black hole or a wormhole, perhaps providing an entry or portal into other dimensions as posited by string theory, or universes within the multiverse.

ALF. From the TV series of the same name, *ALF* is a cute, cuddly alien whose major bad habit is eating cats.

Algernon-Gordon Effect. For a surgical procedure that temporarily increases the intelligence of the subject, the Algernon-Gordon Effect measures the rate at which the enhanced intelligence eventually declines and returns to preoperative levels. In the Daniel Keyes novel *Flowers for Algernon*, it is stated that "Artificially-induced intelligence deteriorates at a rate of time directly proportional to the quantity of the increase." In other words, the smarter you get, the faster you become dumb again.

Alicina. In the fiction of Matteo Boirdo, Alicina is an enchantress who lures men to a magic island, where she then changes them into beasts, trees, or rocks.

Alifbay. In Salman Rushdie's book *Haroun and the Sea of Stories,* Alifbay is the saddest city on Earth. Its factories manufacture sadness which is then packaged and sent all over the world.

Alkali. A research laboratory, run by Colonel William Stryker, that covertly collects genetic material from mutants for the purpose of cloning them and turning the clones into weapons. Alkali used Wolverine's genetic code to create mutants X-23, a young girl with abilities similar to his, and X-24, who is an identical adult clone of Logan.

Alkaline Free-Radical Serum. A formula invented by Professor Abednego Danner to unlock genetic potential. He injected his pregnant wife with the serum, and as a result their son Hugo was born with superhuman strength, super speed, and bulletproof skin. From Philip Wylie's novel *Gladiator.*

Alliance Government. In the year 2517, the galaxy is ruled by the Alliance government, an amalgam of China and America. Source: the 2002 TV series *Firefly*.

Alosun. In the 1940's *Thrilling Comics*, Alosun was a formula, made from a distillate of solar atoms that, when taken, granted the ability to fly and other super powers.

Alpha 60. In the movie of the same title, *Alphaville* is a planet whose inhabitants are controlled by a computer called Alpha 60.

Alraune. In the 1928 movie *Unholy Love*, Alraune is a girl created by a mad scientist by fertilizing a prostitute with the semen of a hanged man.

Alternate History. A science fiction or fantasy story taking place in an alternate timeline in which major historical events are different than in our reality; e.g., in Philip Dick's novel *The Man in the High Castle*, Germany defeats the U.S. in World War II. Works of alternate history are said by SF fans to be "uchronic." In Hawthorne Abendsen's alternate history novel *The Grasshopper Lies Heavy,* Germany and Japan lose World War II because FDR is assassinated and replaced by President Tubwell. The new President anticipates and prevents the attack on Pearl Harbor, which becomes a turning point for the Allied Forces. In Murray Constantine's *Swastika Night,* the two superpowers are the Japanese and German Empires, and Hitler is considered the savior of the latter.

Altneuland. In Theodore Herzl's 1902 novel of the same title, Altneuland is a utopian paradise established by a colony of Jews on a remote Pacific Island. They somehow have created advanced technology all powered by electricity, which was still fairly new and not yet ubiquitous at the time of publication. Michael Chabon also wrote about a colony of Jews in another remote region, off the coast of Alaska, in his novel *The Yiddish Policeman's Union.*

Altor. In the year 2040, Altor is a crime-ridden planet near the Milky Way where New York Police Lieutenant Brogan relocates to join the police force on the orbiting Space Precinct 88, from the TV show *Space Precinct.*

ALZ-112. In the movie *Rise of the Planet of the Apes,* ALZ-112 is a drug developed as a cure for Alzheimer's disease. When tested on lab chimpanzees, it greatly increases the animals' intelligence.

AM (Allied Master-computer). A self-aware AI computer formed by the merging of the master super-computers of Russia, China, and the United States. In Harlan Ellison's classic science fiction story "I Have No Mouth and I Must Scream," AM has killed all human life except for a group of five people it keeps alive in a vast underground complex and has made immortal for purposes of eternally torturing them.

Amadeus Arkham. In Batman comic books, Amadeus Arkham is the founder of Arkham Asylum, a prison for the criminally insane, which has held at various times Mr. Freeze, Poison Ivy, the Joker, Harley Quinn, Bane, the Riddler, and many of Batman's other foes.

Amazing Stories. Launched in 1926 by Hugo Gernsback, *Amazing Stories* was the first pulp magazine that published science fiction exclusively.

Amazonians. A group of feminists who settled the planet Artemis and built a society dominated by women. Men were mainly used as slaves for labor or entertainment. Source: *The Monstrous Regiment* by Storm Constantine. In Leslie Stone's short story "The Conquest of Gola," women are the dominant and ruling gender on the planet Gola.

Amber. In Roger Zelazny's novels, Amber is the one true world, the central reality; all other worlds and dimensions, which are said to exist in Shadow, are variations of this one true world.

Ambuquad. A model of small robot commonly used in the 25th century. Buck Rogers had one named Twiki.

American Siturgic Monopoly. A powerful organization that corners the wheat market in the 1990s and effectively gains control of all of America's food supply. Source: *Useless Hands* by Claude Farrare.

Amphiptere. A serpent with greenish-yellow feathers, green bat-like wings with feathered bone, and an arrow-tipped tail. Some are covered in feathers, have a beak-like snout, and the wings are bird-like instead of bat.

Amulet. A small object, typically a charm decorated with the image of a supernatural creature, which keeps the wearer safe from harm.

Anaye. In Navajo legends, the anaye are a race of giant aliens who were considered to be gods, even though they were cannibals who feasted on human flesh.

Android. A robot that resembles a human being in appearance. Unlike robots, which are made out of metal, androids are built out of colloidal materials—plastic and artificial flesh.

Jack Williamson featured androids in his 1936 short story "Cometeers." In *The Bicentennial Man* by Isaac Asimov, the robot Andrew Martin, over time, transforms himself into an android. Clifford Simak wrote a series of stories in the 1950s about androids that were treated as slaves by their human creators.

Data of *Star Trek: The Next Generation,* an android member of Starfleet, was built by robotic scientist Dr. Noonian Soong. In his short story "Fondly Fahrenheit," Alfred Bester notes that an android is "a chemical creation of synthetic tissue." Fritz Lang's classic 1927 movie *Metropolis* features an android named Maria.

Andromeda. An artificial female life-form featured in the 1961 British science fiction series *Andromeda.* She was built by a supercomputer which itself was constructed according to instructions transmitted to Earth from the Andromeda Galaxy. Astronomer Fred Hoyle was the co-creator of the series. From 2000 to 2005, there was a U.S. *Andromeda* TV series. But this Andromeda was a spaceship, not an android. Its commanding officer, Captain Dylan Hunt, was played by Kevin Sorbo, who was also TV's Hercules.

Anansi. In West Indian folklore, the Anansi is a monstrous god in the shape of a giant spider.

Aniara. An enormous generational spaceship, powered by "gyrospinners," that after a near-collision with an asteroid is sent speeding away from our solar system toward the constellation Lyra. From the novel *Aniara* by Harry Martinson.

Anime. The Japanese style of manga art used in animated TV shows. See "manga."

Ansible. A device capable of either faster-than-light or even instantaneous communication across vast distances of space. Short for "answerable," the term was coined by Ursula LeGuin in her novel *Racannon's World*. Operating principle: Ansibles transmit and receive messages by use of gravity waves. A message typed on the keyboard of the transmitting ansible is instantly displayed on the screen of the receiving unit, no matter the distance—even countless light years—between the two devices.

James Blish called the instantaneous communications device in his stories the Dirac communicator, after physicist Paul Dirac. Phillip Jose Farmer's 1953 short story "Mother" refers to the "ultrarad," a communications device that sends faster-than-light waves through something called the "no-ether." The generic SF term for devices enabling faster-than-light communication is "ultraphone."

Anthony Fremont. In Jerome Bixby's short story "It's a Good Life," Anthony Fremont is a young boy who controls an entire town with his almost godlike mind-over-matter power: anything he thinks and wants to happen, happens.

Antigerone. A youth serum that slows down the body's aging process, made from a strain of lichen. From John Wyndham's novel *The Trouble with Lichen*.

Anti-gravity Car. In his novel *Dying of the Light,* George R. R. Martin imagined an anti-gravity power grid. The grid both powers flying cars and lifts them above the surface. Operating principle: the grid redirects the gravity field immediately surrounding the car. The flying auto glides along these new lines of force; the car has a small internal power source that activates the grid. It also provides power to internal gyroscopes that stabilize the cars while they are in flight.

Anti-Life Equation. A mathematical formula with the power to destroy the known universe. From various science fiction movies including *Abraxas: Guardian of the Universe*, starring Jesse Ventura as a space cop.

Antimatter. As its name implies, antimatter is the opposite of regular matter. The positron, for example, is a positively charged equivalent of the negatively charged electron. When antimatter comes in contact with regular matter, it explodes; regular matter is also called "terrene."

Antimatter's existence was first proposed in 1928 by physicist Paul Dirac. The phenomenon soon captured the imagination of science fiction writers. The first science fiction story to deal with antimatter was probably "Minus Planet" by John D. Clark, published in the April 1937 issue of *Astounding Stories.* In 1943, A. E. Van Vogt wrote "Storm," in which a huge storm in space is caused by a gas cloud of ordinary matter coming into contact with an antimatter gas cloud. In 1955, antiprotons and antineutrons were observed in particle accelerators. Antimatter is a key element in the warp propulsion systems of starships in *Star Trek.*

Anti-time Flier. A large iron box, powered by electricity, with four curving pneumatic pillars, one at each corner, which enable movement. The machine produces a fluid to protect passengers from temporal counter-flow. Time is a function of Earth's atmosphere, a fact proven when food kept in sealed tins inside the iron box does not rot. Time travel into the past is achieved by flying backward in a direction opposite to Earth's rotation. Source: Enrique Gaspar y Rimbau's 1887 novel *El Anacronopete*.

Anubis. In Egyptian mythology, a jackal-headed creature who is the lord of the dead, a role he plays as a character in Roger Zelazny's novel *Creatures of Light and Darkness*.

Anvhar. A planet with an elliptical orbit resulting in long cold winters and short hot summers. From Harry Harrision's novel *Planet of the Damned*.

Ape Man, The. In the movie *The Ape Man*, a scientist, played by Bela Lugosi, takes a formula that turns him into a murderous ape. To revert to a normal human and stay that way, he has to ingest human spinal fluid.

Aphidium. In Barbara Paul's novel *Bibblings,* aphidium is an essential component of the fuel used for interstellar travel.

Apocalypse Device. In *Dr. Who,* a weapon that takes the form of a wraith-like ghoul who carries every disease in existence to infect those it comes in contact with.

Arabian Tunnel. An underwater passage connecting the Red Sea with the Mediterranean. The tunnel was first traveled by Captain Nemo.

Arctarians. An alien species, Arctarians are humped, amorphous masses of viscous, translucent jelly about 4 feet tall and 3 feet in diameter. When spreading out from their home world Arctar throughout the galaxy, some Arctarains landed on primitive Earth. Over many millennia, these original colonists degraded or "devolved" into more primitive life forms including humans — we are their descendants.

ARDNEH. ARDNEH — Automatic Restoration Director, National Executive Headquarters — is a computer that prevents nuclear war by changing the laws of physics to make atomic fusion and fission impossible. From Fred Saberhagen's *Empire of the East* series of novels

Argo City. The Kryptonian City where Kara Zor-El, who becomes Supergirl when she arrives on Earth, was born.

Ark, Simon. In the novels and short stories of Edward Hoch, Simon Ark is a Coptic priest and detective of the supernatural who is 2,000 years old. In the first century after Christ, Ark wrote a gospel praising Jesus, but was accused of deceitfully publishing them as a fifth Gospel. As punishment, he is doomed to walk the Earth forever until such time as God decides his fate.

Armor. Usually a metal suit and, in science fiction and comic books, a metal suit augmented with electronics, hydraulics, boot jets, and projectile and energy weapons. Characters with armor are numerous, from Iron Man and Jack of Hearts, to Dr. Doom and Rhino. The protagonist in Christopher Koklowicz's short story "The Armor Embrace" wears bulky, 10-foot-tall chromium armor called a Viathan Mech Suit with a helmet faceplate made of onyx glass.

Artemis. From Andy Weir's novel of the same name, Artemis is the first and only city on the moon, with a population of 2,000 people, most of whom are officials, billionaires, and tourists.

Artiforgs. Artificial organs grafted into place in the recipient's body in the same positions as the original organs they replace. From *Ubik* by Philip K. Dick.

Ascolais. Jack Vance's novel (actually, a collection of themed short stories), *The Dying Earth* takes place in a far future when the Sun is a dim red star nearing the end of its life. There are a large number of wizards who live in a forest called Ascolais. The wizards use magic by memorizing lengthy formulas for spells and speaking the proper words. Once the spell is cast, the wizard forgets it, and has to reread and memorize it all over again.

Asphyx. In a movie of the same title, *The Asphyx* is an aura that surrounds people just before they die. By trapping his or her Asphyx, a person may be able to achieve immortality.

Astral Projection. The ability of a person's mind, consciousness, spirit, or soul to leave and travel outside of the physical body, often as a spectral or ghostly entity.

Astro Boy. A flying robot boy with super strength and built-in machine guns.

Atavism. A type of devolution where a person or animal assumes a form or feature of its remote ancestors, as in the Max Brand short story "The Receding Brow."

Athea. A planet on which nuclear wars have caused a terrible drought and reduced the population to less than 300. The Athenians send an emissary to Earth. His mission is to use Earth's resources to build a spaceship which will bring the remaining Athenians from their planet to relocate on Earth. From the Walter Tevis novel *The Man Who Fell to Earth.*

Athos. In Lois McMaster Bujold's novel *Ethan of Athos,* Athos is a planet populated entirely by men where women are forbidden.

Atlantic Tunnel. A tunnel on the ocean floor, almost 3,000 miles long, built for purposes of having an undersea train travel between Manhattan and Brittany, not far from the French city of Brest. On its first day of operation, in 1927, an explosion destroyed a section of the tunnel, trapping the train though the passengers escaped in diving suits. Source: Luigi Motta, *Il tunnel sottomarino,* 1927.

Atlantis. In Greek mythology, Atlantis was an island sunk in a single day and night by a tremendous earthquake. Plato said Atlantis was real and had vanished around 9000 BC. He believed its inhabitants had been an advanced civilization with a powerful navy that had supposedly conquered parts of Western Europe. Atlantis has been endlessly featured in science fiction and fantasy; e.g., *Splash, The Man from Atlantis, Atlantis Found, Aquaman, The Atlantis Gene,* and *Raising Atlantis.*

Atmosphereum. A rare element found only in meteorites, atmosphereum emits a radiation with unspecified effects, such as the ability to partially resurrect a corpse in the movie *The Lost Skeleton of Cadavera.*

Atomotor. A miniature atomic-powered motor used to power androids and robots. From the short story "Helen O'Loy" by Lester del Rey, in which an inventor builds, falls in love with, and marries a female robot with true emotions including returning the love of her creator and husband.

Atom, The. Ray Palmer, the Atom, is a superhero in DC Comics who developed a shrinking technology powered by the remnants of a white dwarf star.

Atvatabar. A huge country lying just below the surface of the American continent from Canada to Ecuador. A sun inside the Earth provides continuous heat and light. The entrance is a large cavern in the North Pole. Source: William Bradshaw, *The Goddess of Atvatabar.*

Atworthy College Medical Clinic. In L. Ron Hubbard's novel *Fear,* ethnology professor James Lowrey is being examined at the clinic. That afternoon, he suddenly loses his hat and 4 hours of his life. He finds himself in a macabre world of night without day populated by strange figures out of time—hats, bats, and cats. A voice warns Lowrey that if he finds his hat, he will regain his 4 hours—and then he will die.

Audio-animatronic. A type of robot, really an automaton, used at Disney theme parks. The robot can speak, move, and gesture, but is permanently affixed to a spot in the ride or exhibit. An audio-animatronic android is featured in the film *Tomorrowland.*

Automan. From the TV series of the same name, Automan is a crime-fighting 3D hologram, human in appearance and programmed by police computer scientist Walter Nebicher.

Automatic Atomic Motor Repair Shops, Inc. On the planet Ishtar, a corporate chain of robotically operated repair shops that compete against local repair shops where the repairs are done manually, in A.E. van Vogt's short story "The Weapon Shop."

Autoverse. An artificial universe composed of 32 kinds of atoms and a simpler set of physical laws than those governing the larger universe. Virtual copies of ultra-wealthy people reside in the autoverse, granting them a kind of immortality. Source: *Permutation City* by Greg Egan.

Azazel. From the young adult novels of Isaac and Janet Asimov, Azazel is a demon who fulfills wishes, but often makes errors with unintended results.

Azi. On the planet Cyteen, azis are artificially grown and computer-trained workers and soldiers. Source: Bruce Sterling, "Cicada Queen."

Baby HP. From Juan Jose Arreola's short story of the same title, the "Baby HP" is an exoskeleton worn by children to convert their movements into electricity which is then stored in a Leyden bottle, a device consisting of a brass rod inside an insulating glass container with a cork lid, and coated inside and outside with metal foil, for later use to power electronic devices and circuits.

Baileys. In the year 2525, Baileys are alien machines that look like giant gargoyles. They fly above the surface shooting laser beams at humans, forcing humankind to live underground. From the TV series *Cleopatra 2525*.

Baitman. Hired crew on the enormous fishing vessels of Venus, who bait the lines sports fishermen use to catch the giant sea creature *Ichthyform Leviosaurus Levianthus*, or Ikky for short. From Roger Zelazny's story "The Doors of His Face, the Lamps of His Mouth."

Ballchinians. From *Men in Black,* a race of aliens whose testicles are in a scrotum that hangs from their chin.

Baltimore Gun Club. A group that buys up worthless land in the North Pole under the corporate name the North Pole Practical Association. Their plan is to fire a shell so massive from a giant cannon that the recoil jolts Earth such that it slows our planet's rotation, causing a warmer climate that will make their North Pole land holdings more hospitable, desirable, and valuable. Source: Jules Verne's 1889 novel, *The Purchase of the North Pole.*

Banshees. In Celtic legend, the banshees are female spirits sent from the underworld as omens of death. They can take many forms, both animal and human, from a crow or hare, to a beautiful woman or old hag. They emit loud howls and screams at night in the woods and forests. In Marvel comics, Banshee is a mutant who possesses an ear-splitting sonic scream.

Barbarella. From the 1968 movie of the same title, Barbarella is a futuristic, female, oversexed space hero who pilots a fur-lined spaceship. In the movies, she was played by Jane Fonda. Barberella began as a comic strip created by French artist Jean-Claude Forest.

Barrier, The. In Richard Wilson's short story "Don't Fence Me In," The Barrier is an invisible force field in outer space through which no spaceship or any other objects can pass.

Barsoom. The name given to the planet Mars by Edgar Rice Burroughs in his Barsoom series of novels featuring the hero from Earth, John Carter. Much like Superman did when he migrated from Krypton to Earth, under Barsoom's lighter gravity John Carter gained greater strength, including the ability to leap great distances, only to a much lesser degree than Clark Kent did.

Bartertown. In the third Mad Max movie, a town fueled by methane extracted from pig feces. Disputes are settled through gladiator-style fights held in the town arena, called the Thunderdome. The Mad Max series of films take place in a post-apocalyptic future where the most precious and coveted resource is gasoline.

Bartorstown. On a post-apocalyptic Earth in Leigh Brackett's novel *The Long Tomorrow,* Bartorstown is a secret community dedicated to the maintenance of scientific research and technological expertise. It is powered by a nuclear reactor and has a working computer.

Basia. In Eryn Adams' science fiction novel *King of the Shore,* the ancient civilization that once inhabited the planet Charen, a world rich in mineral and elemental deposits. The Basians were destroyed in a thermonuclear war, and Charen was later colonized by 500 pilgrims from the planet Skocia.

Basilisk. In Greek mythology, a serpent, six inches long, with venomous breath that quickly kills its victims. The basilisk can be killed by showing the serpent its own reflection in a mirror.

Baucis. An Asian city built on stilts so long that Baucis is located above the clouds. The residents have everything they need in their sky city, and so almost never visit the surface below. Source: Italo Calvino, *Le citta invisibili.*

BB-8. In the Star Wars movie *The Force Awakens*, BB-8 is a droid, or robot, with a spherical body. It moves, and can do so swiftly, by rolling its rounded torso over the ground. Like R2D2, the BB-8 droid is an "astromech" that communicates primarily via sequences of audible clicks and beeps.

Beast, The. In the motion picture *Split*, Kevin Wendell Crumb has two dozen separate personalities. The 24th is The Beast, in which the personality transforms not only Kevin's mind but his body, giving him superhuman strength, speed, ability, and limited imperviousness to bullets. The Beast is evil, brutal, filled with rage, and eats people. There are many other Beasts in fantasy literature including the central figure in the fairy tale *Beauty and the Beast* as well as a mutant named Beast who is a member of the X-Men.

Beast with Five Fingers, The. From the 1946 movie of the same title, the Beast with Five Fingers is the disembodied left hand of a deceased pianist, played by Victor Francen, come to life, capable of moving on its fingers like a crab on its claws, so it can reach its victims and strangle them.

Beelzebub. Beelzebub was a god of the Philistines, often depicted as having the shape and appearance of a deformed and hideous black goat. His full name is Baal-Zebul, which means "lord of the flies." Though the name Beelzebub is sometimes used as an alias for Satan, it was also used to refer to the trinity of the first fallen angels: Beelzebub, Satan, and Leviathan. Satan, or Asmodeus, was the demon of lust. Beelzebub, also called Baal, Belial, Beliar, or the Prince of the Devils, is the demon of lies. And Leviathan was a giant sea-monster said in the Bible to have done battle with God.

Bees. Giant, intelligent bees on the planet Handrea. The Bees are 20 to 30-feet long. They feed on knowledge and process it into the Honey of Experience. From the short story "The Bees of Knowledge" by Barrington Bayley.

Bellona. In Samuel R. Delany's novel *Dhalgren*, Bellona is a city in which the laws of our reality are suspended: the sun rises and sets in the same place; streets move; people lose all sense of direction, memory, and self.

Bender. A model of robot with enhanced physical strength made specifically to bend steel beams in construction projects. Bender, a main character in the TV cartoon *Futurama*, is a bender-series robot — unit number 1,729 and serial number 2716057.

Bene Gesserit. On the planet Dune, in the Frank Herbert *Dune* novels, the Bene Gesserit is a women-only cult conducting a secret breeding program to produce a new messiah.

Berserker. A class of gigantic battleships that roam space and destroy everything in their path. Conceived by Fred Saberhagen, it is not clear whether they have alien pilots or are operated by artificial intelligence.

BETA (Billion-Channel Extra Terrestrial Assay). BETA was a project funded by The Planetary Society. The mission: to search the universe for signs of intelligent extra-terrestrial (ET) life. The hardware: an 84-foot steerable radio telescope. The radar dish was equipped with dual east-west feedhorns and a third low-grade terrestrial "discone" antenna feeding a 240-million-channel Fourier spectrometer. The radar system incorporated a feature recognizer and correlator array in a set of Pentium motherboards. The recognizers sifted through 250 Mbyte/sec of spectral data seeking distinctive data signatures that could be good candidates for intelligent ET signals.

Betelgeuse. In the movie *Beetlejuice*, Betelgeuse is a ghost that haunts houses for the purpose of frightening and expelling the human residents.

Bevatron. In Philip K. Dick's novel *Eye in the Sky,* the Bevatron is an experimental particle-accelerator located in Belmont, California. It generates 6-billion-volts of radiation capable of sending humans struck by the energy into alternate universes.

Beyond. In Vernor Vinge's novel *A Fire Upon the Deep,* the Beyond is a zone or section of the cosmos in which faster-than-light travel, anti-gravity, and enhanced intelligence exist.

Bgarth. In Alexander Jablokov's novel *Deepdrive*, Bgarth is a massive tunnel being dug beneath the surface of Venus for the purpose of transforming the planet.

Big Bang Theory. A cosmological theory that the universe as we know it began as a tiny mass of "primordial matter." The density of the mass heated the matter to 10 billion degrees. At this critical temperature, the mass exploded. In less than one second, it began expanding into space, forming the elements, matter, planets, stars, galaxies, and the universe we see today. A number of science fiction works have featured the theory, among them Isaac Asimov's story "The Last Question." In the Chinese mythological version of the Big Bang, the creation of the universe begins with heaven and earth emerging from Hundun, a cosmic egg of chaos and nothingness.

Big Brother. In George Orwell's classic 1949 novel *1984,* the government, known as "Big Brother," watches the activities of most of the population most of the time, to ensure conformity with approved government behavior. More specifically, Big Brother is the figurehead ruler of the totalitarian government. His image is constantly visible on TV screens covering virtually all walls. The expression "Big Brother is watching" comes from the fact that these are two-way TV screens, allowing Big Brother and the government to watch everyone, even as everyone watches Big Brother.

Big Death. In the TV series *Jeremiah,* the Big Death is a biological virus attack which killed all humans age 14 and older, leaving Earth with a population entirely comprised of children, who then age normally and grow up without being affected by the virus.

Big Noodle. In Philip K. Dick's novel *The Divine Invasions,* the Big Noodle is a sentient version of the internet.

Big Three, The. The "Big Three" are arguably the most popular science fiction authors of the 1950s, 1960s, and 1970s – Isaac Asimov, Arthur C. Clarke, and Robert Heinlein. Robert Heinlein was best known as the author of the utopian cult novel *Stranger in a Strange Land.* Arthur C. Clarke is the author of *2001: A Space Odyssey.* A 1945 paper Clarke wrote proposing a system of communications satellites in geostationary orbit earned him credit as "inventor of the communications satellite." Isaac Asimov, one of the most prolific authors of all time, wrote almost 500 books including the classic science fiction trilogy, the *Foundation* series.

Bionics. *Dorland's Illustrated Medical Dictionary* defines bionics as "the science concerned with study of the functions, characteristics, and phenomena found in the living world and application of the knowledge gained to new devices and techniques in the world of mechanics." In science fiction, bionics refers to high-tech artificial limbs, organs, and other body parts used to replace injured or damaged tissue, bone, and muscle in humans. Martin Caidin wrote of a man with bionic limbs in his novel *Cyborg*. The novel was turned into the TV series, *The Six Million Dollar Man,* starring Lee Majors as Steve Austin, a bionic man with superior strength, speed, vision, and endurance.

Bio-restorative Formula. When the laboratory in which he is making his bio-restorative formula explodes, Dr. Alex Holland is accidentally transformed into the Swamp Thing, a half-man, half-plant mutant monster.

Black Cauldron. From the animated film of the same name, the *Black Cauldron* is a magical cauldron into which, eons ago, the gods cast the spirit of the Horned King, the most evil ruler the world has ever known.

Black Galaxy. An enormous black hole in the center of a galaxy; from Barry Malzberg's novel *Galaxies*. See also **black holes, quasars.**

Black Guard. In the 1987 movie *Wicked City,* a secret police force that battles demonic beasts from another dimension.

Black Hole. A black hole is an extremely dense star. The star has collapsed, increasing its density to the point where nothing, not even light, can move fast enough to escape its tremendous gravitational pull. Since nothing can escape, the star is like a "bottomless pit" or hole in space, sucking in everything that comes near. It is black because no light shines from it. Hence the name "black hole." The first black hole to be detected, Cygnus X-1, was found by astronomers in 1971. Since then, many other black holes have been observed. Black holes have been referenced in countless science fiction stories and films, including Alan Dean Foster's movie novelization *The Black Hole.*

Black Quartz. A crystal from the planet Ballybran that can produce a "fold" in the spacetime continuum. A pair of black quartz crystals can enable instantaneous interstellar communication over any distance by resonating simultaneously across the fold in space-time they created. From Anne McCaffrey's novel *The Crystal Singer.*

Blacula. From the motion picture of the same title, *Blacula* is an African prince whom Dracula turns into a vampire.

Blake's 7. In a BBC TV series of the same title, the Blake 7 are a group of seven escaped prisoners who commandeer a derelict alien spacecraft, Liberator, to exact their revenge on the Federation – a totalitarian regime ruling Earth – that sentenced them.

Blakesee Field. A region of space between the twin suns of the planet Placet, which travels in a figure-eight orbit between the two stars. Blakeslee Field is an area between the two suns where photons decelerate. The Field produces psychological effects that distort all visual images in hallucinatory fashion. Source: "Placet is a Crazy Place" by Fredric Brown.

Blesh. A shortening of the combined words blend and mesh, blesh is a process in which people with extraordinary abilities are able to combine their powers, and in doing so act as one organism – *homo gestalt*, the next stage in human evolution. From Theodore Sturgeon's novel *More Than Human.*

Blinovitch Limitation Time Effect (BLE). A law of time travel from *Dr. Who* which says if there is a *repeated* attempt by time travelers to change history, it could affect the timeline in a catastrophic way.

Blob, The. In the Steve McQueen film of the same name, *The Blob* is an alien that reaches Earth in a hollow meteorite. It grows by absorbing flesh and, upon its arrival on our planet, begins feeding on the residents of a small U.S. town. In the X-Men comic books, the Blob is a huge man, a mutant who cannot be moved by any force.

Bloody Baron, The. In Harry Potter, a creepy and scary ghost that haunts Hogwarts, in particular the Astronomy Tower. Bloody Baron has blank eyes, and wears chains and robes stained with silver bloodstains. In life, he was a hot-tempered man who became violent with Helena Ravenclaw, daughter of the founder of Hogwarts. He murders Helena and then commits suicide in remorse; his chains are a symbol of his penance.

Bloomenveldt. On the planet Belshazzar in Norman Spinrad's novel *Child of Fortune,* Bloomenveldt is a continent-wide forest. The forest is filled with tall, tree-like super-organisms from which bloom enormous flowers containing natural psychotropics, capable of producing altered states of consciousness.

BLR Unit. A unit of measure of telepathic aura or field. From *Ubik* by Philip K. Dick.

Blue Core. A positive energy sphere that powers Astro Boy, the robot hero of Metro City, a city floating in the sky.

Blue Holes. Deepwater holes off the coast of the Andros Island in the Bahamas, said to be inhabited by large octopus-like creatures.

Blue Sunshine. A form of LSD that turns people into bald, homicidal maniacs, from the 1977 film of the same name.

Bokanovsky's Process. In Aldous Huxley's novel *Brave New World*, a method of cloning a fertilized egg in incubation to produce 96 biologically identical people, creating teams of clones for improved workplace productivity and social stability.

Bolder's Ring. A portal to a parallel universe where gravity is a billion times more powerful than the gravity in our universe; as a result, the stars were only a mile wide or so. Source: *Raft* by Stephen Baxter.

Bolo. From the mind of SF writer Keith Laumer, the Bolo is a super heavy tank with advanced artificial intelligence and kick-butt firepower. The Bolo Mark XXXIII tank, the standard model in the series, weighs 32,000 tons. These AI tanks eventually become self-aware through constant learning over centuries of intermittent warfare against various alien races.

Bomba the Jungle Boy. Tarzan's adopted son as featured in numerous films and books.

Bonejacker. In the motion picture *Freejack*, bonejackers are mercenaries with time travel devices. The ultra-rich hire these bonejackers to travel to the past, and bring people back to current time just prior to their moment of death. The wealthy clients then have their personalities transferred into these purloined bodies from the past to achieve immortality. A "freejack" is a person from the past who escapes from his captors before another personality can be transferred to his body.

Bonies. Zombies in an advanced stage of devolution. They look like cadaverous ghouls and prey on both regular zombies and humans alike. From the movie *Warm Bodies.*

Book of Eibon. A book of magical spells written by the Wizard Eibon of the Land of Hyperborea. From the Clark Ashton Smith short story "The Coming of the White Worm." Also used by H.P. Lovecraft in several of his stories including "The Horror in the Museum."

Boomers. Biomechanical soldiers built by the GENOM Corporation in the TV series *Bubblegum Crisis.*

Boomstick. A firearm wielded by Ash in the film *Army of Darkness.* It is a 12-gauge double-barrel Remington shotgun with cobalt blue steel and a walnut stock, sold for around $109.95 at S-Mart Stores.

Borg. A race of cyborgs hostile to the Federation in *Star Trek.* One Borg, named Seven of Nine, defected and joined the Federation.

Bork, The. A heroic astronaut, Charles Elliot Borkman, whose body is nearly destroyed by an accident in space is given a new robotic body, turning him into a powerful cyborg and a freak called The Bork. He goes to an isolated euthanasia planet to die. But upon arrival, he finds a kind of peace, and decides to keep living.

Borrowers. In a movie of the same title, *The Borrowers* are a family of tiny people who live beneath a grandfather clock and survive by "borrowing" food and small objects from the home's human residents. Based on a series of children's books by Mary Norton.

Brainlock. A brain implant programmed to control a specific behavior; e.g., a chastity lock causes a person to be repulsed by the touch or even proximity to other people. From the short story "Dogfight" by William Gibson and Michael Swanwick.

Brains of Cireem. The last relics of a civilization that once populated a sand-covered planet orbiting the star Gror. Human colonists on the planet Helle acquire the three Brains, which gives them near god-like powers. Source: *The Brains of Helle* by Norman Lazenby.

Brakka Tree. On the planet Land, Brakkas are hardwood trees with an interior combustion chamber. Pikon crystals accumulated by the upper roots combine with purple halvell extracted by the lower roots to form an explosive mixture. The trees use it to blast forth their seeds; while the indigenous humanoid inhabitants used it as a source of power. From *The Ragged Astronauts* by Bob Shaw.

Breaks, The. In Samuel J. Miller's post-apocalyptic novel *Blackfish City*, which takes place on the floating city of Qaanaaq, constructed after many mainland cities burned or sank, "the breaks" is an illness that throws the sufferer into the memories of strangers.

Breen Energy-dampening Beam. In *Star Trek*, a weapon used by an aggressive enemy species, the Breen, that is part of the

Dominion. The formidable Breen warships have a unique weapon built into huge emitters in the front of the ship: an energy-dampening beam. The beam envelopes the ship being attacked and drains all of its power, disabling all systems including engines, weapons, and shields, rendering it essentially defenseless. For some reason, only Klingon vessels were immune to the Breen energy drain.

Bridge of the Gods. In Roger Zelazny's novel *Lord of Light*, the Bridge of the Gods is the magnetized ionosphere of the unnamed planet, which has been colonized by humans where the story takes place. Technology enables a person's soul to be transported to and stored indefinitely in this magnetic band of energy, and later retrieved and transferred into a new body.

Bridge System. From John Brunner's novel *Endless Shadow*, a technology that gives all the worlds of the human community instantaneous access to one another.

Brobdingnagians. A race of giants, as tall as church steeples, living on a huge, isolated peninsula on the coast of California. Source: Jonathan Swift, *Gulliver's Travels*, 1726.

Bronze, The. A nightclub frequented by Buffy in the TV series *Buffy the Vampire Slayer*.

Brown Note. An extremely resonant and deep note that, if heard, would cause you to lose control of your bowels. Featured in an episode of *South Park*.

Brutalacean Rollipede. In Stanislaw Lem's "Let Us Save the Universe," the brutalacean rollipede is a species whose top half is human or at least humanoid and bottom half is a set of rolling treads similar to a tank; one of the Reavers in the X-Men comic books has a strikingly similar anatomy.

Buck Rogers. A swashbuckling, ray-gun-toting space hero, whose first appearance was the 1928 novella *Armageddon 2419 AD* by Philip Francis Nowlan. Buck, a veteran of World War I, falls into suspended animation when trapped in a mine filled with strange gases; he awakens 500 years into the future. Buck Rogers was later featured in comic strips, TV shows, and movies.

Bug. Any alien who resembles an insect, featured in such movies as *Men in Black* and *Starship Troopers.* In his 1949 short story "BEM," E. Brown called them *BEMs* for "bug-eyed monsters." In Orson Scott Card's novel *Ender's Game*, these insectoid aliens are referred to as "buggers." Giant alien bugs are also the enemy in the novel and movie series *Starship Troopers.* In the 1975 movie *Bug*, the giant bugs are not aliens, but mutated Earth cockroaches that set fires with their behinds. Also called "insectoids."

Bugfuck. Crazy, almost certifiably so. Coined by Harlan Ellison.

Bunyip. Also called the Kianpraty, the Bunyip is a large mythological creature with the body of an alligator and the face of a dog or walrus. It lurks in rivers, swamps, and water holes, where it grabs unwary swimmers or waders with its sharp claws before crushing and eating its victims.

Burbclave. In Neal Stephenson's novel *The Diamond Age*, burbclaves are privatized suburban enclaves run by either corporations or the Mafia.

Bureau of Exotic Plants. A group of botanists who study the plant life on other worlds. On the planet Flora, they encounter an intelligent species of tulip. Called "siren tulips," these flowers emit a sound that can kill other creatures. Source: *The Pollinators of Eden* by Jon Boyd.

Buried People, The. Troglodytes living in deep caverns beneath the island of Amiocap. Their feet are flat with webbed toes. Their arms are short and equipped with three heavy claws. Bipeds, their naked bodies are hairless and have the pallor of a corpse. Instead of ears, they hear through two orifices where the ears should be. They have huge, bulging eyes and fangs. Source: Edgar Rice Burroughs, *Tales of Pellucidar.*

Bussard Ramjet. A spacecraft propelled by ejecting the force of thermonuclear fission or fusion behind it, with a physical or magnetic shield protecting the rocket and its crew from the blast and its radiation. Poul Anderson envisioned a fusion-powered spaceship in his novel *Tau Zero.* Journalist John McPhee wrote a 1974 nonfiction book, *The Curve of Binding Energy,* profiling physicist Ted Taylor, who proposed building such a ship, out of the rear of which would be ejected a series of atomic bombs; the force of the detonation against a massive shield would accelerate the ship to high velocity and into outer space.

Cabbala. A set of doctrines revealing how God spreads his essence throughout the universe. Its central image is a Tree of Life comprised of 10 interlinked spheres, each representing a different aspect of God. The Cabbala is featured in such fantasy and SF works as Algernon Blackwood's *The Human Chord* and Harold Bloom's *Flight to Lucifer.*

Caliban. In Shakespeare's play *The Tempest*, Caliban, who is the son of a witch and a devil, lives on Prospero's enchanted island. In the X-Men comic books, Caliban is an albino mutant whose power is the ability to track other mutants.

Cambry. In Russell Hoban's novel *Ridley Walker,* Cambry is the ruins of the former city of Canterbury, England, more than 2,000 years after the destruction of civilization by a nuclear holocaust.

Candy Kane. In the TV series *Captain Nice,* Candy Kane is a meter maid who is the would-be girlfriend of Carter Nash, a police scientist who invents a formula that, when ingested, transforms him into the flying superhero Captain Nice.

Candyman. In the movie of the same title Candyman is the vengeful spirit of a 19th century wealthy black artist who is tortured and stung to death by bees for falling in love with the white daughter of a landowner. Candyman can be summoned by looking in a mirror and repeating his name five times, after which he appears and guts you with the hook he has in place of his hand.

Capellette. In Homer Flint's 1921 story "The Devolutionist," Capellette is a double planet, orbiting the star Capella; the two Earth-like planets are joined to one another at the poles.

Captain, The. The Captain is a man who, after being exposed to a radioactive meteor, devolves in reverse into an intelligent ape. From John Taine's novel *The Iron Star.*

Captain Trips. A virus, developed as a biological weapon in an experiment code-named Project Blue. The contagious virus escapes quarantine when it is carried out of the lab by an infected worker, and then it spreads to kill 99.4% of the planet's population in Stephen King's novel *The Stand*. In Terry Nation's novel *Survivors*, a mysterious virus similarly wipes out most of the population, leaving the survivors to rebuild civilization. A number of SF novels have dealt with a plague that kills most of the planet's human population, one of the first of which was Mary Shelley's *The Last Man*, published in 1826. Another example is Jack London's 1912 novel *The Scarlet Plague*.

Captain Invincible. Also known as the "Legend in Leotards" and "The Caped Contender," Captain Invincible is a superhero played by Alan Arkin in the film *The Return of Captain Invincible*. The Captain's powers include invulnerability, flying, and magnetism. A hero during World War II, he later retires from being a superhero, moves to Australia, and becomes an alcoholic when the U.S. government persecutes him for flying without a license and wearing underwear in public.

Captain Midnight. In the TV series of the same name, *Captain Midnight* is a crime-fighter who combats evil with his arsenal of super-scientific weapons.

Captain Video. In the TV series *Captain Video and His Video Rangers*, Captain Video leads the Video Rangers. The team operates from a secret mountaintop base. They are a space-age law enforcement force. They had a robot, named by its manufacturer ROBOT I, that was played by David Ballard, an actor who was 7 feet 6 inches tall and weighed 340 pounds. In a famous episode of *The Honeymooners*, Ed Norton is shown wearing a Captain Video space helmet while watching the show.

Caravan Virus. In Susan Palwick's novel *Shelter,* caravan is a virus so contagious that patients who contract it are required to live in isolation nursed by robots, and to visit them requires the wearing of a whole-body protective suit.

Carbonite. Carbonite, a liquid substance made from carbon gas, can solidify through rapid freezing. When a person is placed in carbonite and then frozen, he exists in suspended animation, as did Han Solo in *Star Wars.*

Cardassians. In the TV series *Star Trek: Deep Space Nine,* the Cardassians are a hostile alien race that is the enemy of both the United Federation of Planets and the Klingon Empire.

Carnacki, Thomas. In William Hope Hodgson's story "The Gateway of the Monster" and his novel *Carnacki the Ghost-Finder,* Thomas Carnacki is a detective who investigates the supernatural.

Carpets. In Greg Egan's novel *Diaspora,* carpets are the indigenous life form of the planet Orpheus, which orbits Vega, a star emitting strong radiation, at a distance of 621 million miles – almost 7 times farther than Earth is from our sun. The carpets are so-named for their shape: flat and rectangular. They float freely in the oceans of Orpheus. Carpets are huge, weighing more than 27 tons each. Yet each carpet consists of a single giant molecule: a folded polysaccharide sheet of structural units held together by alkyl and amide side-chains.

Catman. From the Harlan Ellison short story of the same title, a Catman is a law enforcement officer aided by robotic animals, mainly big cats such as cheetahs and panthers.

Cat People. Members of a cursed family whose souls become cats at night, from the 1942 movie of the same title.

Cavity, The. A world located in an empty space within a matrix of solid rock. Its three quarter of a million human inhabitants believe the Cavity contains the total empty space of the known universe. They also believe emptiness can neither be created nor destroyed. From the 1973 Barrington J. Bayley short story "Me and my Antronoscope."

Cavorite. An anti-gravity material used by the protagonists in the 1901 H.G. Wells novel *The First Men in the Moon*. Cavorite is made by an inventor named Cavor; he fuses together a number of metals and other substances, heating the material in a furnace, and then allowing it to cool slowly. The Cavorite is used to build a spaceship in which Cavor travels to the Moon with a companion named Bedford. It works by negating the air pressure of any atmosphere above the Cavorite-containing rocket, so the column of air underneath it rises to fill the vacuum, lifting the rocket with it. In Percy Greg's 1880 novel *Across the Zodiac,* the anti-gravity effect is called "apergy."

Celestial Beings. Entities who, while possessing near God-like powers, are not omniscient nor all-powerful but are just far beyond humans physically and mentally. Starlord and his father in the *Guardians of the Galaxy* movies are celestials.

Celestial Garden. Also called Xanadu, the Celestial Garden is the imperial residence of the ladies and lords who are the royalty of the Cetagandan society on the planet Eta Ceta IV. A power plant is dedicated to projecting a force dome to protect the city. Source: Lois McMaster Bujold's novel *Cetaganda.*

Central Computer. In the Arthur C. Clarke novel *The City and the Stars*, an enclosed city is run entirely by a large computer, the Central Computer, which materializes whatever the residents need out of its memory banks.

Centaur. In Greek mythology, a centaur is a creature that is human in front with a torso merging into the body and hind legs of a horse.

Center. In the 24th century, the Center is the most popular vacation destination in our solar system – a planned resort located on many square miles of American Middle West farm land. And, it is haunted. From Lloyd Biggle, Jr.'s short story "Tunesmith."

Centuroids. On the planet Kakakakaxo, intelligent creatures that grow to about 4 feet high, with green skin and crocodile heads. Source: The short story "Segregation" by Brian W. Aldiss.

Centycore. In mythology, a hideous beast, found in India, with a horn in the middle of its face, the body of a lion, a large mouth, large ears, the muzzle of a bear, the hooves of a horse, and a voice like a man's.

Cerebro. An advanced machine used by Charles Xavier, enabling him to find and connect with the minds of mutants worldwide.

Chigs. In the year 2063, Earth colonies are attacked by an alien race called the Chigs. Pilots in the 58th Marine Corps Squadron climb into their Hammerhead attack jets to fight back against the aliens in space. From the TV series *Space: Above and Beyond,*

Chucky. A doll that comes to life when it is possessed by a violent murderer, Charles Lee Ray, in a series of *Chucky* movies. As he is dying from a gunshot wound, Ray transfers his soul into a "Good Guy" doll.

City, The. In Kevin Brockmeier's novel *The Brief History of the Dead*, The City is where you go when you die. It resembles an Earth-like urban city where you can easily find and move into an empty apartment. You reside in this part of the afterlife for as long as there is at least one person alive on Earth who remembers you. As soon as the last person who remembers you dies, you wink out of existence in The City, and what happens to you from there is completely unknown.

Champ. A giant aquatic creature, similar in size and appearance to the Loch Ness Monster, but inhabiting Lake Champlain—which, measuring 436 square miles and having a maximum depth of 400 feet, is the largest body of water in the U.S. other than the Great Lakes. Champ's body is as thick as a barrel, serpentine, and about 20 feet long, with a flat, snake-like head.

Chandalans. An alien race with a caste system. The minority upper caste maintains dominance over the majority lower caste by forbidding them to use even basic sanitation. As a result, most of the populace is often sick. From James Blish's short story "A Dusk of Idols."

Chaos Manor. Refers to both the home owned by and the *Byte* magazine personal computing column written by the late science fiction writer Jerry Pournelle, who delighted in the technical aspects of PCs, including testing different makes and models, peripherals, and software.

Charon. In Joe Haldeman's novel *The Forever War,* Charon is the tenth planet of our solar system. The temperature is near absolute zero and the surface is frozen hydrogen. Astronauts walking on the ground in their spacesuits found that the frozen hydrogen melted underfoot, becoming extremely slippery and making walking a challenge.

Chauka. On the planet Clarion, an instrument of torture consisting of a dish with a protruding rod. From William Greenleaf's novel *Clarion.*

Chew-Z. A drug found on Proxima Centaury that takes the user into an actual rather than just hallucinatory other world. Source: Philip K. Dick's novel *The Three Stigmata of Palmer Eldritch.*

Chieri. On the planet Darkover, a tall race of hermaphrodites with advanced mental powers and long lifespans. Their biological makeup was so close to humans that interbreeding was possible. From Marion Zimmer Bradley's novel *The World Wreckers.*

Chimaeras. Also known as "ghost sharks" because they are biologically related to sharks, chimaeras are fish with teeth whose skeletons, like those of a shark, are made of cartilage instead of bone. In Hunter Shea's horror novel *They Rise,* huge schools of giant prehistoric chimaera fish, frozen in ice, are released from suspended animation by warming ocean temperatures, and soon spread across the seas, killing everything in their path.

In Greek mythology, a chimaera was a three-headed fire-breathing monster with the head and body of a lion, the head of a goat on its back, and a serpent for a tail.

Chincato. In Hao Jingfang's short story "Invisible Planets," Chincato is a planet where the air is so dense the inhabitants live in constant darkness, and must speak to let others know where they are.

Chita. An island in the Caribbean on which grows a species of trees that look like giant lettuce. Chita is governed by a Chinese executioner who keeps a number of mutilated men as his subjects.

Chitty Chitty Bang Bang. In the 1968 movie of the same title, a magical car that can drive on land or over water and also fly. Based on the novel by James Bond creator Ian Fleming.

CHOAM (Combine Honnete Ober Advancer Mercantiles) Corporation. A large corporation that controls a huge percentage of all commerce and profit-making activities on the planet Dune, in Frank Herbert's Dune series of novels.

Chrononaut. In the TV series *Seven Days,* a chrononaut is someone who, with the help of a time machine resembling a silver sphere, can travel into the past no further than seven days to prevent cataclysmic disasters.

Chronopolis. In J.G. Ballard's short story of the same title, Chronopolis is a city in which clocks, watches, and other time-keeping devices have been banned or destroyed.

Chrono-synclastic Infundibulum. In Kurt Vonnegut's novel *Player Piano,* a machine that can convert people into waves, enabling them to travel through space-time and to materialize periodically on Earth and other parts of the solar system.

Chronovores. Terminally ill individuals who volunteer to be cryonically frozen until the development of new medical technologies that could restore them to life. Their bodies were kept preserved in Omphalos, a large structure built in Idaho as a fully automated deep freeze for the bodies. From Greg Bear's novel *Slant*.

CHUD (Cannibalistic Humanoid Underground Dweller). Mutated human beings, turned into hideous flesh-eating creatures by radioactive toxic waste. The CHUD live in subterranean sewers and train tunnels, where they eat homeless people who are also living in the underground. From the motion picture *C.H.U.D.*

Chupacabra. In Hispanic lore, the chupacabra, which translated means "Goat sucker," is said to combine the features of a kangaroo, a gargoyle, and a gray alien. About 4 feet tall, this hairy creature has a big round head, a lipless mouth with sharp fangs, and large lidless red eyes. In addition, chupacabras have claws, webbed arms, muscular hind legs, and a series of pointy spikes running down the backbone.

Citizen Oversight. A quasi-governmental agency that, somewhat like the NSA today, covertly collects data on citizens. The database includes medical, financial, and legal information as well as tracking individuals using video cameras with facial recognition.

Citizens Protection Bureau (CPB). In the year 2070, the CPB is a police department that protects people from technology used for illicit purposes. From the TV series *Total Recall 2070*.

Class B-9-M-3 General Utility Non-Theorizing Environmental Control Robot. The model number of the

Robinson's robot in the TV show *Lost in Space.* He served and protected the Robinson family as they adventured in space on their saucer-shaped ship, the Jupiter II.

Clarke Orbit. An orbit 22,307 miles above the equator. Satellites in the Clarke Orbit are geostationary, meaning they are always orbiting above the same location on the Earth's surface, because their orbits are in synch with the Earth's rotation. It is named the Clarke Orbit after science fiction writer Arthur C. Clarke because in 1945, he wrote a technical paper suggesting how satellites in geostationary orbit could be used to create a satellite communications network, which today is precisely what we have achieved.

Clarke's Three Laws. The three laws of science fiction writer Arthur C. Clarke are:
** First Law—If a distinguished elderly scientist states that something is possible, he is probably right, but if he states that something is impossible, he is probably wrong.
** Second Law—The only way of discovering the limits of the possible is to venture a little way past them into the impossible.
** Third Law—Any sufficiently advanced technology is indistinguishable from magic.

Cloaking Device. A device that renders something invisible or undetectable; in *Star Trek,* the Klingon "birds of prey" warships have cloaking devices.

Clone. Cloning is the process of making a genetic twin or duplicate of a living organism. The nucleus from one of the organism's cells is taken and implanted in an egg cell (from a different organism) whose nucleus has been removed. The combined cell is stimulated so it begins to divide, and is then implanted in an organic or artificial womb. The resulting organism would be an identical twin – biologically – to the nucleus donor, although it would of course be younger. One of the first science fiction stories to feature cloning is Fritz Lieber's "Yesterday House," published in the August 1952 issue of *Galaxy Science Fiction* magazine. In *Star Wars*, clone troopers were grown on the planet Kamino from the genetic material of bounty hunter Jango Fett. In reality, the first clone of a vertebrate was produced in 1967, when a British biologist successfully cloned a South African clawed frog. In 1997, scientists successfully cloned mammals including sheep and monkeys.

Cloud City. In *Star Wars,* a multi-level city built on Bespin, a gas giant planet similar in size to Jupiter. The upper atmosphere contains Tibanna, a rare gas mined as a valuable resource. Cloud City is kept aloft in Bespin's atmosphere using repulsorlift engines and tractor beam generators. The City consists of 392 levels. The upper levels house luxury resorts. The lower levels are where the refineries are, where Tibanna is processed, and where refinery workers are housed.

Coal Black Mountains. In Harold Longman's fantasy novel *Andron and the Magician*, a mountain range at the top of which lives the Great Magician, a wise man thought by some to be the most powerful magician in the world.

Cold Iron. Forged metal that resists magic, spells, and enchantments. It also limits the use of powers and special abilities in fairies, elves, and other supernatural beings.

College and Order of Heralds. Linguists on the planet Lyra VI, tasked with negotiation of business deals with traders from other worlds. From "That Share of Glory" by C.M. Kornbluth.

Colmar. In Keith Laumer's novel *Star Colony,* a planet where the indigent species are invertebrates resembling giant amoeba. They live in hives with a life-cycle and social structure much like ants and bees on Earth.

Colossus. In the movie *Colossus: The Forbin Project,* Colossus is a U.S. supercomputer. When it connects with its Russian counterpart, Guardian, the two computers essentially control all weaponry, taking over the world. E.M Forster wrote a short story about a supercomputer that runs the world in his 1909 short story "A Room with a View." In John Barth's 1966 novel *Giles Goat-Boy,* two supercomputers make all decisions.

Colossus of New York. In a motion picture of the same name, The Colossus of New York is a dying scientist whose brain is transplanted into a giant robot body. The Colossus has super-strength and can shoot death rays from his eyes. There have been a number of other characters in SF created by putting human brains into robot bodies, including Tobor the 8th Man and Robot Man in the Doom Patrol.

Combined Miniature Deterrent Forces (CMDF). A federal agency that runs the U.S. miniaturization program, which uses technology to make objects tiny by shrinking their atoms. From the motion picture *Fantastic Voyage.* A similar miniaturization technology is used to shrink Dennis Quaid in the movie *Innerspace,* in which he is accidentally injected into Martin Short. DC Comics scientist Ray Palmer uses a technology based on material from a white dwarf star to shrink himself and become the superhero The Atom.

Communicator. In science fiction movies, the characters almost never call each other on the telephone: usually, they use some sort of mobile device, a hand-held communicator. *Star Trek* was probably the first movie or TV show to actually discuss the communicators as part of the story: Crew members could not be located or beamed up when their communicators were lost or not working properly. Comic strip detective Dick Tracy had a watch with a built-in communicator, similar to the Apple Watch today.

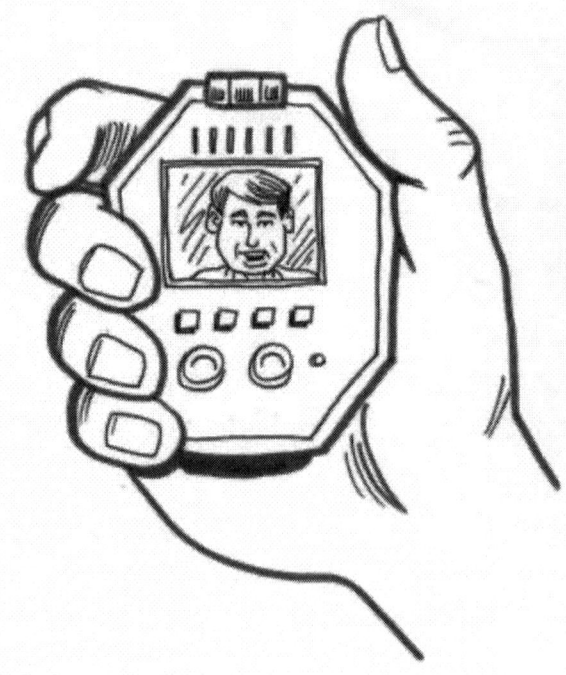

Con. Short for "convention" and used in the names of science fiction, fantasy, and comic book conventions such as Comicon. The first major SF convention, Worldcon, took place in New York in 1939.

Conan the Barbarian. In the fiction of Robert E. Howard, Conan was a mighty hero and fighter with superior strength, combat skills, speed, and ability.

Conclave. In the TV series *Dark Angel*, the Conclave is a millennia-old cult that breeds telekinetics and other superhumans.

Confederate States of America. In Ward Moore's alternate history novel *Bring the Jubilee*, the Confederate states gain independence after defeating the North in the Civil War, with General Lee winning the battle at Gettysburg.

Confluence. In the science fiction works of Paul McAuley, Confluence, created by an alien race called the Preservers, is a 20,000 kilometer-long platform built over a huge boat-like keel and equipped with colossal engines that have yet to be fired up. The platform has a river running through it and is populated by both Earth and alien animal species all of which possess intelligence.

Congenital Vampire. Someone who is either born as a vampire or is predestined to become a vampire. Children of witches and the Devil's offspring are often congenital vampires.

Consciousness Download. A plot device and technology in science fiction where the mind, memories, personality, intelligence, or consciousness – or any or all of these – can be downloaded into a storage device, electronic brain, robot, or even a data drive. In Gregory Benford's novel *Great Sky River*, personalities of dead family members are stored in memory tabs; living relatives can access the memories of the deceased by plugging the memory tab into a port implanted in their neck. In Harlan Ellison's short story collection *Alone Against Tomorrow,* the memories and personalities of deceased relatives are stored in memory cubes, which their living relatives can communicate with verbally.

Console Cowboy. In William Gibson's *Neuromancer,* slang for a computer hacker, specifically a coder skilled at hacking the internet – or, as it is called in the novel, cyberspace. In 2017, Russian hackers were suspected of cyberattacks against the U.S. to influence the outcome of the presidential election.

Consummation, Incorporated. A company that guarantees to find its clients the perfect match in a mate, resulting in a marriage which will be fully consummated. Unfortunately, the company's definition of "fully consummated" results in the two people ultimately merging into a single person. From the short story "The Compleat Consummators" by Alan E. Nourse.

Control. A cybernetic surveillance device used to monitor the activities of Jesse, an alien exiled by the rules of his planet to Earth, where his job is to do good deeds on Earth, which will lead to him being freed and allowed to return to Andarius, his home planet. From the 1989 TV series *Hard Time on Planet Earth.*

Conveyor Strip. In the Robert Heinlein short story "The Roads Must Roll," conventional sidewalks are replaced throughout cities and towns by moving sidewalks or "conveyor strips" that move them forward at high velocities much faster than a human's walking or even top running speed.

Cool World. From the 1992 movie of the same title, *Cool World* is an alternate reality, populated by beings called Doodles that look like animation; their universe is separated from our own. A device called the Spike of Power enables both humans and Doodles to cross between the two worlds.

Cooperative City. A city in Maine with a population of 100,000, built in the first quarter of the 20th century by the Cooperative Association of America (CAA). Coupon cheques, drawn on each citizen's account, are used instead of cash. Deposits are paid into the citizen's account based on the CCA's valuation of his contributions to the Association, but the minimum annual deposit is $1,500 per resident, regardless of their abilities or labor.

Coordinated Information Apparatus. In L. Ron Hubbard's *Mission Earth* novels, a government-run intelligence and paramilitary organization of the Voltarian Empire, usually referred to as simply "the Apparatus."

Copper X. From E.E. "Doc" Smith's novel *The Skylark of Space*, X is a metal created by using electrolysis to liberate the "intra-atomic energy" of copper. It is used as an atomic propellant.

Cordwainer Bird. A pseudonym speculative fiction writer Harlan Ellison uses as the byline on his writings when the works have been changed without his approval.

Cork. A floating city in the Atlantic Ocean, built on a massive, round piece of floating solid cork. The natives, called Corkfoots, resemble ordinary humans except their feet are made of cork. The cork feet enable them to walk easily on both land and sea. Source: Lucian of Samosata, *True History*.

Corps. The Corps Diplomatique Terrestrienne is an Earth agency of diplomats who have come to the planet Petreac to establish friendly relations with that world. Source: "Gambler's World" by Keith Laumer.

Coruscant. In *Star Wars,* a gigantic planet-wide city on a planet of the same name. Built up over thousands of years, Coruscant has a population of over a trillion people. With 5,127 levels, Coruscant is many times bigger than Cloud City on Bespin. In Coruscant, the wealthy upper-class residents live in skyscrapers built on the surface. Thousands of other levels are beneath the surface, forming an underworld city accessible by huge portals. Residents on the subsurface levels, in descending order, are the middle-class, then the poor, and below them, the criminal element. The underworld is lit by artificial light, as no sunlight reaches the lowest levels. The air at these deep levels is badly polluted by vehicular fumes and factory emissions.

Cosmic Rays. Radiation in outer space that can penetrate the hulls of spacecraft not sufficiently shielded. The cosmic rays can affect the cellular structure of the crew, often producing mutations, such as with the Marvel superhero team The Fantastic Four, which gained powers ranging from stretching and invisibility to super strength and the ability to control fire.

Cozy Catastrophe. As defined by science fiction author and critic Jo Walton, a cozy catastrophe is a science novel "in which some bizarre calamity occurs that wipes out a large percentage of the population, but the protagonists survive and even thrive in the new world that follows." Example: the Kevin Costner post-apocalyptic movie *The Postman.*

Crakers. In Margaret Atwood's post-apocalyptic novel *Oryx and Crake,* Crakers are genetically engineered humans implanted with traits selected from the animal kingdom. Their creator, a scientist named Crake, created a plague to wipe out normal humans to make way for the Crakers.

Cronos. In Greek mythology, Cronos is the leader of the Titans, who were the precursors of the Olympic gods. When warned his children plan to rebel against him, Cronos eats them. One son, Zeus, survives, and grows to become the leader of the gods on Mt. Olympus.

Crotcher Island. A province of the subterranean country Nazar. The natives are half human and half musical instruments.

Cryonics. A process, also called "cold sleep" or "cry-stasis," in which the body temperature is lowered as the person is dying but before brain function ceases and the heart stops. This way the brain can be frozen with no damage from lack of oxygen. Cryogenically suspended people undergo the process with the hopes that their frozen bodies can be reanimated in the future, when medical science has advanced to the point it can cure the disease that killed them. A person in suspended animation in a cryogenic container is called a "corpsicle." In Philip K. Dick's novel *Ubik,* some deceased individuals are maintained in a cold storage half-life, where their brainwaves can be read, enabling the living to communicate with them.

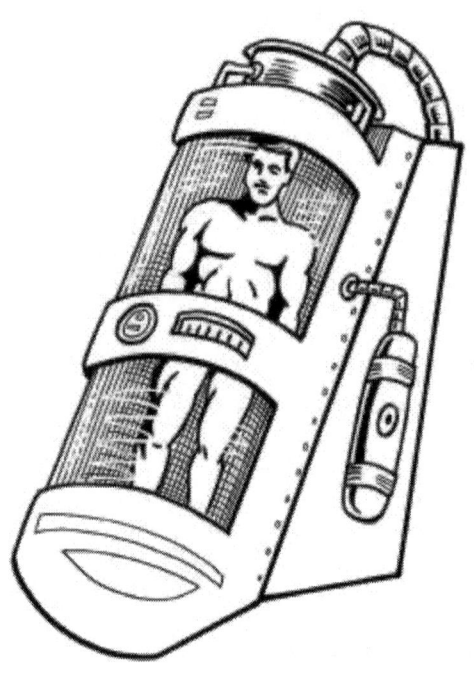

Cryo-Penitentiary. From the motion picture *Demolition Man*, a prison where the inmates are cryogenically frozen and exposed to subconscious rehabilitation techniques while in suspended animation.

Cryptids. Either unknown species of animals or animals which, though thought to be extinct, may have survived into modern times; the latter are also called *living fossils*.

Cryptozoology. The study of monsters and creatures that may or may not exist; e.g., the Loch Ness Monster, Bigfoot, Chupacabras, werewolves, dragons.

Cthulhu. A giant, monstrous being that is one of the Great Old Ones, a pantheon of ancient, powerful deities from space who once ruled the Earth and who have either since fallen into a deathlike sleep or been trapped in a dimension beyond ours. Cthulhu is featured in numerous weird tales written by H.P. Lovecraft and other writers' stories based on Lovecraft's characters and plots.

Culture. In the science fiction works of Iain M. Banks, the Culture is a society of total abundance. Its citizens can live however they want. Through genetic modification of the population, sexual prowess and intercourse are enhanced. People can trigger their glands to secrete drugs to improve mood or boost energy. There are no laws and no government; the Culture is a creation of the nearly godlike "Minds," who oversee everything.

CV. In Damon Knight's novel *The Observers,* CV is an artificial sea habitat with 2,000 inhabitants.

Cyberpunk. Cyberpunk is a subcategory of science fiction. It takes place in a world where computers, the Internet, drugs, and high-tech electronics are the dominant forces in people's lives. William Gibson is credited as the originator of the Cyberpunk School of science fiction.

Cybersuit. In the movie *Star Kid,* a prototype exoskeletal AI suit built by an alien race, the Trelkins. The cybersuit, which has great strength and speed, can have a wearer inside as well as operate independently when unoccupied.

Cyber-Viral Implant (CVI). In the TV series *Earth: Final Conflict,* a CVI is a tiny device that, when injected into a human body, gives that person enhanced mental powers and a photographic memory.

Cyborg (cybernetic organism). A cyborg is a being who is a mixture of organic and cybernetic (bionic) parts. To qualify as a cyborg, you must be at least half machine; otherwise, you're just a person with some artificial parts. Examples of cyborgs include the Borg of *Star Trek: The Next Generation* and Officer Murphy, the robotic police officer in *Robocop.* In Komatsu Sakyo's novel *The Japanese Apaches,* a tribe of Japanese living in a wasteland eat steel, are transformed into cyborgs, and become the only people in the country who survive a nuclear war.

Cyclops. In Greek mythology, the Cyclops is a giant with a single eye, native to the island of Cyclopes. In nature, a cyclops is any animal with a single eye, resulting from a genetic defect. Once my sons and I found a dead 9-inch cyclops albino shark on the Jersey shore. There have been human babies born as cyclops, but they do not live long.

Cylons. A group of malicious, intelligent robots waging war against humans in the TV series *Battlestar Galactica*, whose initial attack on Earth destroys most of our civilization. The humans fight back from aboard the *Galactica*, the only remaining ship in Earth's fleet.

Cynocephaly. A human or humanoid creature with the head of a dog, the prime example of which is the Egyptian god Anubis.

Cyrille. An artificial world whose residents can satisfy their every desire no matter how fantastic or lavish. The population lives in luxurious apartments with virtual access to all the sights, sounds, and colors of the human empire, and furnished with the finest material comforts. Source: C.L. Moore's novel *Judgment Night*.

Daleks. In *Doctor Who*, Davros, a mad scientist, creates the Daleks, a race of mutants which, like the Vulcans, have no emotions, and therefore have no compunction about carrying out their mission of conquering the entire known universe. Daleks are part organic and part cybernetic: living beings tucked snugly inside a powerful and rugged metal outer body. The metal shell provides life support to the organic creature, and also has an onboard microcomputer to help control the machinery.

Damnation Alley. After World War III, in Roger Zelazny's novel of the same title, *Damnation Alley* is the vast stretch of nuked land between California and New York. It is plagued by roving bands of marauders, giant mutant insects, and unpredictable storms.

Damien. In the movie *The Omen,* Damien is the Antichrist who comes to Earth as a little boy born of a jackal. He terrorizes and kills family members and many others.

Danae. On the planet Mutare, the Danae are androgynous winged creatures with headless bodies whose faces are set in their torsos. Their primary habitat is the Amber Forest, where coniferous trees are encased in shells of oxidized, solidified sap they secreted. Source: *Downtime* by Cynthia Felice.

Dance of Death. From Edgar Alan Poe's story "The Masque of the Red Death," the dance of death, or *danse macabre,* is a processional dance where Death, appearing as a skeleton, leads the doomed to the grave.

Dan Dare. A swashbuckling space hero featured in a British comic strip, Dan Dare is chief pilot of Britain's Interplanetary Space Fleet, the mission of which is to explore our solar system and beyond.

Dark, The. In Frank M. Robinson's novel of the same title, *The Dark* is the vast empty space between the spiral arms of the Milky Way galaxy, devoid of life, stars, planets, and matter of any kind.

Dark Dimension. In Marvel Comics' Dr. Strange stories, the Dark Dimension is a mystic realm containing multiple alternate realities and pocket universes, which eventually melded into one unified dark dimension.

Darkman. In a movie of the same name, Darkman is scientist Peyton Westlake, who is disfigured and burned in a laboratory explosion. To stop the pain from his burns, Westlake undergoes a surgical procedure that severs the pain receptors in his nerves, a side effect of which is increased physical strength. The scientist can hide his damaged face by wearing a mask made of a synthetic skin he invented. But the skin lasts just 60 minutes after which it rapidly dissolves.

Dark Matter. A form of matter that accounts for as much as 95 percent of the material in the known universe. We do not fully understand dark matter, but it is an important component of known space. It is dark matter that provides sufficient gravitation to hold galaxies together. Without dark matter, the stars in a galaxy would separate and fly apart into space. Dark matter has been featured in numerous science fiction novels including the Xeelee sequence of novels and stories by Stephen Baxter. There is also a dark energy which is even less well understood.

Darksider. In Roger Zelazny's 1971 novel *Jack of Shadows*, Earth does not rotate. As a result, one side permanently faces the sun, and the other side, facing away from the sun, is in perpetual darkness. The residents of the dark side are Darksiders, and many possess magical powers – some minor, others considerable. Unlike normal humans, Darksiders do not possess a soul. But when they die, they wake up in the Dung Pits of Glyve reanimated, and so have many lives. Earth has similarly stopped revolving in Brian Aldiss's 1962 novel *Hothouse,* causing global decay of the world's forests and rampant mutation; homo sapiens evolve as a species into much smaller, green-skinned men.

Day Walker. A vampire that can be out in the sunlight without being harmed. Blade in the Marvel comics and movies is a day walker. In the John Carpenter movie *Vampires,* the vampires sought to transform themselves into day walkers through some kind of satanic rite. In the film *Daybreakers,* vampires burst into flame upon exposure to bright sunlight; if the flame is immediately doused with water, the person becomes a normal human again.

Daxamite. Any native of the planet Dax. Under Earth's yellow Sun, a person from Dax gains superpowers virtually identical to Superman's.

Deadman. In DC Comics, Deadman is a deceased circus performer whose spirit can inhabit and control the body of any living person.

Deadpool. A cancer patient, Wade Wilson, who through an experiment was mutated so that he can recover from virtually any injury and is essentially immortal.

Death. In science fiction, fantasy, and horror literature, "Death" often takes the shape of a sentient supernatural entity, usually human in appearance. When Death, also known as "the Grim Reaper," comes to claim you, his touch is often what brings an end to your physical life, freeing your soul to go on to the afterlife. In Tanith Lee's novel *Tales from the Flat Earth,* he is called Uhlume, Death's Master, or Lord Death, and is a stunningly handsome man with night-black skin, white hair and eyes, and white clothes. Many actors have played Death in movies and on TV including Robert Redford on *The Twilight Zone,* Brad Pitt in *Meet Joe Black,* James Woods (as Hades) in *Hercules,* and Norm McDonald in *Family Guy,* who touches a woman he is on a date with because she is talking too much and he is bored. In the 1934 film *Death Takes a Holiday*, Death, played by Fredric March, takes human form to spend time among humans so he can understand and relate to them better.

Death's Deputy. In L. Ron Hubbard's novel of the same name, *Death's Deputy* is a fighter pilot named Clayton McLean, who brings disaster to those around him, while he himself is inexplicably spared. In describing McLean and his role as Death's Deputy, author Hubbard said that Clayton is "a man who officiates, all unwillingly, for the god of destruction [as] without volition on his part he causes accidents...there are people...who seem to be magnets for destruction...although rarely touched themselves, things happen all around them."

Death Star. A large spherical ship built under the supervision of Darth Vader and equipped with a beam weapon capable of destroying an entire planet. The first Death Star, designated as the "DS-1 Orbital Battle Station," was originally designed by the Geonosians before the Galactic Empire took possession of it.

Another technology powerful enough to destroy a planet is described by Colin Kapp in his book *The Chaos Weapon*.

The Chaos Weapon is controlled and monitored by facilities located in mobile spheroid space stations. The weapon itself is located out of time in empty space between two universes. It converted the plasma mass of stars in one universe into an entropic beam fired from a weapon in the other universe. The beam disrupts and destroys whatever it hits.

Decadents. A group of hedonists who use thinking machines to obtain instant gratification of their every impulse. A variation of such a machine was used in the movie *Demolition Man* for people to mentally experience sex without physical touching. Source: Arthur C. Clarke's short story "The Lion of Comarre."

Decepticons. A team of evil Transformers led by Megatron. They are opposed by the autobots, Transformers that transform into vehicles; the autobots are led by Optimus Prime.

Decology. A novel written in 10 volumes. The two most prominent examples in SF are the *Mission Earth* series by L. Ron Hubbard and the *Amber* series by Roger Zelazny. The ten books of the *Mission Earth* series total 1.2 million words; all ten of the books became *New York Times* best-sellers. Hubbard also wrote a "soundtrack" of 20 songs for the *Mission Earth* series.

Deep Ones. In the mythos of H.P. Lovecraft, the Deep Ones are a race of fish-like bipeds that live undersea.

Deja Thoris. A beautiful, red-skinned Martian Princess that John Carter—who has through some unexplained method been transported to Mars, where he becomes a hero—romances in Edgar Rice Burroughs' novel *The War Lord of Mars.* In Edwin Lester Arnold's novel of the same title, Lieutenant Gulliver Jones, an Earth soldier who, like Carter, is mysteriously transported to Mars, also becomes a hero and meets a beautiful Martian Princess.

Delmak-O. In Philip K. Dick's novel *A Maze of Death,* Delmak-O is an artificial "psychological habitat" created through the dreaming of the trapped crew of the damaged spaceship *Persus 9.*

Delos. From the TV series *Beyond Westworld*, Delos is a futuristic amusement park revisiting the old West and replete with android gunfighters with whom visitors have gunfights.

Delphi. A gorgeous, sexy actress on a soap opera in a future where advertising is not permitted on TV or anywhere else. A corporation circumvents the ban on advertising through product placements on Delphi's show. Source: James Tiptree, "The Girl Who Was Plugged In."

Delphi Pool. In John Brunner's novel *The Shockwave Rider*, a futures market on world events. It may be based on the RAND Corporation's Delphi pool method of forecasting future events by relying on answers from expert panels.

Delye. The females of a race of hairless, orange, web-footed humanoids on the planet Delayfam. They are the dominant sex in Delyene society and initiate – and even force – intercourse on the shorter-lived males. Source: *Leviathan's Deep* by Jayge Carr.

Demon. An ethereal, shapeless, evil being that possesses humans to do harm. Demons often appear as small versions of Satan, and many are invisible. The church of St. Mary in Fairford, England is famous for its stained-glass demons. Demons are often said to be fallen angels.

In the 16th century, the Dutch demonologist Johann Weyer calculated that the total number of demons was 4,439,556 and divided these into 666 legions. Another estimate, from the Book of Revelation, says there were originally 399,920,004 angels in heaven. A third fought on Lucifer's side in the war in heaven and were subsequently cast out, so the number of fallen angels was 133,306,668.

Descolada. On the planet Lusitania, the Descolada is an entity that inhabits every living cell of every native animal species. Once thought harmless, the Descolada turns out to be a deadly plague. From the novels of Orson Scott Card.

DESTINI (Deep Earth Seismic Trigger Initiative). A government program designed to propagate earthquakes through Earth's molten core that instead unintentionally stops the core from rotating, which is what generates the magnetic field around our planet protecting us from harsh solar radiation. With the stoppage of the rotation, this protective magnetic field will collapse within a year, exposing Earth's surface directly to the unfiltered radiation of our sun. From the motion picture *The Core*.

Destroyer. An intelligent entity in deep space. Made up of numerous linked nodes, the Destroyer is larger than a solar system but has extremely low density. From the James Tiptree Jr. novel *Up the Walls of the World*.

Devil's Tower. A location in Wyoming where, in the movie *Close Encounters of the Third Kind*, aliens land to make contact with humans.

Devour Empire. A race of aliens who plunder our solar system. They exist as pure energy and can instantly teleport across the entire galaxy. From Cixin Liu's short story "The Poetry Cloud."

DHARMA. The DHARMA Initiative, a secret government program, was created in 1970 by the Department of Heuristics and Research on Material Applications (DHARMA), to manipulate the fundamental laws of science. From the TV series *Lost*.

Dhampir. The child of a vampire mating with a living woman, the dhampir is half-human, half-vampire.

Dimension. An alternate plane of existence. In E.E. Doc Smith's 1949 novel *Skylark of Valeron*, the heroes briefly enter into the fourth dimension. A group of men in Clifford Simak's story "Hellhounds of the Cosmos" enter the fourth dimension to battle a monster. In an L. Ron Hubbard short story, a professor discovers an equation that enables him to teleport by traveling instantaneously through "Dimension X." In physics, string theory posits that there could be anywhere from 11 to 26 dimensions.

Diogenes codex. From the novel *Cloud Cuckoo Land* by Anthony Doerr, the Diogenes Codex is an ancient text found in a small cypress chest in the catacombs beneath the city of Tyre. The chest contained 24 folios, carved into cypress wood tablets measuring 30 by 22 centimeters, and damaged by mold and worms. The writing is neat, slants to the left, and tells the story of a journey around the world.

Dirac Communicator. In James Blish's novel *The Quincunx of Time,* The Dirac communicator, named after physicist Paul Dirac, is a device enabling instantaneous communication across the entire span of a galaxy. Paul Dirac formulated a fully relativistic quantum theory. The theory posited the existence of the positron, an antimatter particle equivalent to the electron, but with a positive charge. Positrons have since been confirmed through experiments. See also **Ansible.**

Disintegrator-Integrator. A matter transporter invented by scientist Andre Delambre in the movie *The Fly*. Delambre tests the machine on himself, but a fly accidentally gets into the chamber, and during the teleportation, his right arm and head is exchanged with that of the fly. This creates a man-sized creature with a fly's head, and a fly-sized insect with a human head.

Divinity Cluster. In the TV series *Starhunter,* the Divinity Cluster is an alien gene pool that somehow holds the answers to humankind's future.

Doc Methuselah. In L. Ron Hubbard's "Old Doc Methuselah" stories, Doc Methuselah is an MD who does not age. Doc leads a society of 600 other immortal physicians who voyage across the stars in a spaceship, charitably offering their medical services free to patients throughout the galaxy. Just as Gene Roddenberry once described *Star Trek* as "Wagon Train to the Stars," Doc Methuselah and his crew can be seen as "Physicians Without Borders to the Stars."

Doc Savage. Clark Savage Jr., called "Doc" by his friends, is a pulp fiction hero who "rights wrongs" while punishing the bad guys. Soon after Clark was born, a team of doctors, led by his father, trained his mind and body to reach peak human levels of performance. As a result, the adult Doc Savage is endowed with great strength and stamina, and is a master of the martial arts. Doc has an incredibly high I.Q. and a photographic memory, with a vast knowledge of science. He is a physician, scientist, inventor, detective, and explorer. He is aided in his missions and ventures by "The Fabulous Five," a team of five sidekicks. Four are scientists or engineers, and one is an attorney, Ham Brooks, who carries a sword cane, its blade coated in a fast-acting anesthetic.

Dog-bird. On an island in the East Indies, the dog-bird is a large, ferocious, flightless bird covered in long shaggy hair. It has the head of a greyhound, the tail of a pig, the claws of a panther, lays eggs like a bird, and suckles its young like a dog. Source: *The Travels and Adventures of William Bingfield*, 1753.

Dominion, The. In *Star Trek,* the Dominion is an interstellar state and military superpower on the same scale as the Federation. Located in the Gamma Quadrant, the Dominion is composed of hundreds of alien species. It is led by The Founders, a race of shapeshifters. The Jem'Hadar, warriors genetically engineered by The Founders, are the military arm of the Dominion, and one of the most powerful combat forces in the galaxy. The Jem'Hadar fighter ships are small but extremely well-armed, with three-phased polaron beams. The beam weapons are mounted in a fixed forward emitter array in a stubby, beak-like structure in the front of the craft.

Donavan's Brain. In a movie and novel with that title, the brain of businessman William Donavan is removed from his body after a plane crash and kept alive in a tube containing an electrified saline solution. The brain develops telepathic powers, allowing it some influence over other people's minds.

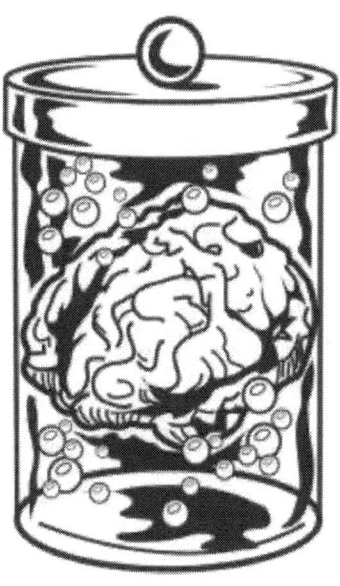

Doomsday Device. A nuclear bomb or other weapon powerful enough to destroy all life on Earth or even the planet. Doomsday devices have been featured in many science fiction stories and films, notably *Beneath the Planet of the Apes*.

Doublethink. From George Orwell's novel *1984*, doublethink is holding two contradictory opinions simultaneously with equal conviction.

Downunder. After World War III, much of humanity, ostensibly the law-abiding civilized survivors moved to deep underground communities called downunders. These citizens retreated below the surface to avoid the radiation released by nuclear explosions. They also hid underground to escape *roverpaks,* vicious and predatory gangs of young boys and their telepathic dogs *(*see *Psychoendorphins)*. Source: *Blood's* *a Rover: The Complete Adventures of a Boy and His Dog* by Harlan Ellison. Similarly, in Isaac Asimov's novel *Caves of Steel,* city-dwellers live in grim underground dwellings.

Diaspar. In Arthur C. Clarke's novel *The City and the Stars,* a billion years from now, Diaspar is the last city on an Earth, which, since the oceans dried up, has become an endless desert. Diaspar is covered by an enormous crystal dome, lit by artificial light round the clock. The inhabitants are virtually immortal, because they are reincarnated each time they die.

Dime Novels. During the peak of pulp publishing, dime novels were cheaply produced paperbacks in such genres as science fiction, romance, westerns, and mystery and suspense. They cost 10 cents to purchase. Ray Bradbury referred to his book *Fahrenheit 451* as a "dime novel," because he wrote it on a typewriter at the public library, and the machine required dimes to operate.

Direct Neural Coupling. A technology enabling a person to project his mind into a robotic body. From the novel *Bug Park* by James Hogan.

Direwolves. In *Game of Thrones,* a pack of giant wolves that, on all fours, come up to a man's shoulders. Direwolves are about 30 to 40 percent larger than ordinary wolves. It is interesting to note that in the real world, an animal called the dire wolf actually existed in the Americas. Though real dire wolves were not that much larger than modern gray wolves, fossils show they had an over-sized skull and jaws, and a stronger bite.

Dirtside. To live "dirtside" is to live on a planet, moon, or asteroid as opposed to on a spaceship, satellite, or other habitat in outer space. From Robert Heinlein's 1953 novel *Starman Jones*. In his 1947 short story "It's Great to be Back," Heinlein describes people who either have never been to outer space, or have been but prefer to stay on the surface of a planet, as "groundhogs."

Disappeared. Like Atlantis, Disappeared is a city somewhere under the ocean. There are towers, factories, arches, and palaces, all made of brick. From Victor Hugo's story "La Ville disparue."

Discworld. A planet in fantasy novels written by Terry Pratchett, Discworld is a flat disc. The disc is balanced on the backs of four elephants which in turn stand on the back of a giant turtle. In that it is not dissimilar to Atlas holding up the Earth upon his shoulders, and remember, at one time people thought our world was flat, too.

District 9. A large camp or detention area where a race of bug-like aliens who crash-landed on Earth are forced to live under government supervision. From the movie of the same name.

Djinn. Djinn are supernatural beings with considerable powers. They can be trapped in a lamp or bottle, and must obey the person who releases them from their imprisonment.

Doomsday Device. A weapon capable of destroying the entire planet Earth, the solar system, the galaxy, or even the universe, depending on the version.

Dorian Gray. In the Oscar Wilde novel *The Picture of Dorian Gray*, Dorian Gray is a man who does not get older or show the ravages of his excessive lifestyle, while a portrait painting of him ages in appearance with each passing year and vicissitude.

Dothraki. In the *Game of Thrones,* a race of nomadic horse-lords living in the central plains of Essos.

Dry Land. A place sought by inhabitants of Waterworld, in a movie of the same name. After an unnamed catastrophe—most likely global warming or perhaps nuclear war— melts the polar icecaps to raise the sea level, the entire surface of Earth is covered by water. The small remaining population survives on boats and man-made small islands. The only dry land left on the planet turns out to be the top of Mount Everest, now warm and verdant.

Dracarys. In the *Game of Thrones,* a word used to command dragons to kill by breathing fire.

Dragons of Bel'kwinth. A race of dragons that long ago constructed a road known only as The Road. The exits and off-ramps can take travelers to different points in both our past as well as alternate histories. From Roger Zelazny's novel *Roadmarks.*

Drake. A wolf-like creature with spines, a dragon head, horns, and two legs.

Drakulon. A planet that is home to a race of vampire-like aliens, the Vampiri. The Vampiri drink blood, can turn themselves into bats, and are superstrong, just like Earth vampires. Blood flows in rivers, but Drakulon's twin suns are drying up the rivers, slowly starving the Vampiri. From the early *Vampirella* comic books.

Draugr. Spirits who haunt the gravesides of dead Vikings. Large and powerful, these ghostly white spirits hunt and devour the living. You can escape by quickly running away, as the draugr cannot stray too far from their grave.

Drift, The. In Michael Swanwick's novel *In the Drift*, The Drift is an area contaminated with radiation from the Three Mile Island accident. Because the core is uninhabitable, The Drift is used as a dumping ground for toxic radioactive and chemical waste. The only animals living there are mutated worms. In the aftermath of the Three Mile Island accident, many people mutate into vampires and other monsters, who are then forced into living in The Drift.

Dromozoa. On the prison planet Shayol, microscopic symbiotes that infect the prisoners who are confined there. The symbiote causes the host to grow new limbs and organs, which are harvested by the prison warden for use in transplant surgery. From Cordwainer Smith's 1961 short story "A Planet Named Shayol."

Droog. A common street thug. From the book and movie *A Clockwork Orange.*

Dryad. A spirit inhabiting either a single tree or a grove, from Greek mythology.

Dumbo. From the Disney film of the same name, *Dumbo* is a young elephant who can fly by flapping his oversized ears.

Dust. In James Patrick Kelly's short story "Rat," dust is a drug. Dust addicts, called "the dead," experience 12 to 18 months of synthetic orgasms and hallucinations, leading to total sensory overload and culminating in an ecstatic death experience.

Dust Devil. From a movie of the same title, the Dust Devil is an evil spirit trapped in human form. He murders people so he can steal enough souls to enter the spirit world.

Dust Hypothesis. The theory that consciousness finds itself out of the dust of the universe, and then constructs its own universe in which its existence makes sense. From Greg Egan's 1994 novel *Permutation City.*

Dwellers. In S. Fowler Wright's novel *The World Below,* the Dwellers are a species of giants averaging 25 feet in height. Their skin is as hard as ivory, making them resistant to physical damage, and they are extremely long-lived; after a certain age, Dwellers become bored and depressed. Dwellers can be killed by their fiercest natural enemy, a race of unintelligent insect-like beings that are the size of a skyscraper and difficult to kill.

Dyson Sphere. As imagined by Olaf Stapledon in his novel *Star Maker,* and described in a 1960 scientific paper by physicist Freeman Dyson, a Dyson sphere is a gigantic structure built to completely enclose a star and capture most or all of the energy it radiates. Featured in Robert Silverberg's 1969 novel *Across a Billion Years.*

Dystopia. A society that has decayed socially and economically. Its people generally live in poverty, infrastructure is crumbling, and criminal behavior is rampant. In Margaret Atwood's 2003 dystopian novel *Oryx and Crake,* rampant generic engineering produces hybrid animals that menace the citizenry. Jack London wrote a dystopian novel *The Iron Heel,* published in 1913, in which the ruling class manipulates labor unions to control the working class.

Ear. Janet Yolen's short story "Ear" is set in a future where humans as a species have lost their hearing as a result of exposure to loud music and videos. They can hear by attaching external ears. Ears are issued to people at age 12, but stop working and must be given up at age 30 due to nerve damage and corrupted DNA.

Earth. In Christopher Priest's novel *The Inverted World,* the "Earth" is a city on another world. The city Earth is 1,500 feet long, 200 feet high, and is continually moving north, on four railroad tracks, covering a mile every ten days. It is contained in a wooden structure measuring 200 feet high by 1,500 feet wide.

Edward Scissorhands. In the movie of the same title, *Edward Scissorhands* is an artificial man who has scissors for hands.

Elder Things. In the stories of H.P. Lovecraft, the Elder Things were extraterrestrials who first came to Earth shortly after the Moon took form. The Elder Things were eight feet tall with a stocky oval-shaped torso. They had five eyes, five eating tubes, five legs, five wings, and five tentacles. The Elder Things became enemies of the star-spawn of Cthulhu, which arrived on Earth a short time later.

Eldila. A race of superhumans, each of whom functions as the tutelary spirit, called an Oyarsa, of one of the worlds in our solar system. The Oyarsa of Earth is the Bent One, an evil being (Satan) who turned against the Old One (God) and his son Maledil (Jesus). From C.S. Lewis's Space Trilogy novels.

Electropolis. In Otfrid von Hanstein's novel of the same name, Electropolis – originally named Desert City – is a city occupying half a million square miles in the Australian desert. Electrical charges from huge towers trigger rain, making the desert bloom. The city was funded with money from the sale of radium excavated within the city limits.

Elemental. A creature, often immaterial, that is attuned with, or composed of, one of the classical elements: air, earth, fire, and water. Helen Mirren plays a wraith-like elemental in the film *Chronicles of Riddick*.

Elysium. In a movie of the same name, Elysium is an enormous space station in which Earth's elite live in a clean, lush, and healthful environment while most of humanity is stuck on an overpopulated and polluted Earth.

Electronic Voice Phenomena (EVP). Spoken communication from the dead to the living through radios, TVs, and other electronic devices. Also known as "white noise" and featured in a movie of the same name. A technology similar to EVP is featured in a 1941 movie, *The Devil Commands*; Boris Karloff plays a scientist who uses corpses, with their heads encased in a metal device attached to a brain wave machine, as human radio tubes to communicate with his dead wife.

Elf. A small person who lives underground and is often but not always pictured as wearing a red cap. Elves are commonplace in fantasy literature. Example: *The Lord of the Rings.*

Elixir of Life. In Kev Freeman's novel *Frankenstein 2023,* Victor Frankenstein describes the Elixir of Life, a formula which helped animate his monster: "The compounds of life distilled. I have found the recipe which engages the spirit, once released to ether, to return to inert flesh without resistance.

The bridge between life and death connecting the elements. Compounds mixed with a solution and then circulated to be in contact with the biological fabric of human tissue will revitalize its energy. The fluid, a precise reconstruction with a certain ratio, manifests a mechanism where energy becomes unrestricted, imbuing expired matter to live again."

Ellison Wonderland. The name Harlan Ellison gave to his Sherman Oaks, California home, filled to nearly overflowing with books, files, paintings, photographs, art, toys, and other collectibles that piqued his interest – and he seemed interesting in almost anything, and in pop culture in particular. (When I first met him in 1979, he was wearing a Shadow TV shirt at a time where very few people knew who the Shadow was. He asked me if I knew the Shadow's secret identity and we debated whether it was Lamont Cranston or Kent Allard.)

Eloi. In the H.G. Wells novel *The Time Machine,* which takes place in Earth's future, the human race is split into two branches. The Eloi are a peaceful, docile race who live on the planet's surface. All their food and other basic needs are provided for them by the Morlocks, who live under the surface and use the Eloi as cattle – in other words, as their food source.

Elvex (LVX-1). In Isaac Asimov's short story "Robot Dreams," Elvex is a robot unique among all robots ever built in that it dreams. When Elvex reveals to robopsychologist Susan Calvin that he dreams of setting robots free, Calvin, who perceives this as a threat to humankind, destroys him with an electron gun.

Elwin Levitator. An anti-gravity device with enough stored energy to give a 250-pound weight a vertical distance of 10 miles; the lift-and-descend cycle can be repeated almost indefinitely as the units react against the Earth's gravitational field. From the Arthur C. Clarke story "The Cruel Sky." The 19th century German science fiction writer Kurd LaBwitz powered the space ships in his stories by anti-gravity.

Elysian Fields. The ancient Greek concept of the afterlife. The Elysian Fields are separate from the Greek underworld, Hades. Righteous and heroic mortals, chosen by the gods, are admitted to the Elysian Fields upon their death. There, the souls of the departed live in a happy afterlife for all eternity.

Emela-Ntouka. A giant African animal the size of an elephant or larger, the Emela-Ntouka has a heavy tail like a crocodile's and a single horn on the front of the head, resembling an elephant tusk. Native accounts have the beasts using their horns to kill elephants and water buffaloes. The Emela-Ntouka is massive, and their heavy legs leave an elephant-sized footprint, with three toes or claw marks. The Emela make a sound comparable to a growl, rumble, howl, or roar.

Emergency Dispatch Ship (EDS). A small ship dispatched to deliver emergency supplies, medicine, food, or personnel. These ships are made of a lightweight metal and carry just enough fuel to reach their destination, drop off their cargo, and return to the cruiser style "mother ship" from which it was launched. In Tom Godwin's short story "The Cold Equations," the pilot of an EDS finds that a teenage girl is a stowaway on his ship, and calculates that his EDS does not have sufficient fuel to complete his mission with her extra weight aboard. In accordance with Interstellar Regulations, he ejects her into outer space to lighten the load, resulting in her immediate death.

Empath. Unlike a telepath, a mutant who can read the minds of other people, an empath cannot read thoughts, but can feel the emotions of others through a means of extra sensory perception. In his 1955 short story *No World of Their Own*, Poul Anderson notes that empaths can receive the nerve impulses of others. Mr. Osden in Ursula K. LeGuin's short story "Vaster Than Empires and More Slow" is an empath.

Encephalitis-16. An untreatable disease fatal to adult males. The only methods to prevent contracting Encephalitis-16 are sterilization and castration. From the novel *The Virility Factor* by Robert Merle.

Enforcement Droid (ED). From the film *Robocop*, a robotic law enforcement mechanism, which walks on two legs similar to the walkers in *Star Wars*. The ED-209 is large, well-armored, and equipped with both a machine gun and rocket launcher. The ED project is headed by Dick Jones, a senior executive of Omni Consumer Products (OCP) in Detroit. Bizarrely, in one scene, a 209 Droid falls down steps, lands on its back, cannot right itself, and begins to kick its legs in the air and squeal like a pig. Watch the movie and check it out!

Entertainers. In Fritz Leiber's novel *The Big Time,* the Entertainers were prostitutes employed by management to service the Soldiers who had come there to recuperate from the war.

Entropy. In physics, entropy refers to the lack or "unavailability" of energy in a closed system. Physicist Rudolf Clausius coined the term entropy to describe the unavailability of heat or energy. Perhaps the most famous science fiction work about entropy is George Alec Effinger's novel *What Entropy Means to Me,* in which the universe is physically concentrated at a specific location, the "Well of Entropy." Michael Moorcock used entropy as a major theme in his novel *The Entropy Tango.*

Ephemorol. A sedative given to pregnant women in the 1940s, this drug causes them to give birth to Scanners – mutant telepaths able to generate powerful brain waves that make other people's heads explode. From the movie *Scanners.*

EPICAC XIV. In Kurt Vonnegut's novel *Player Piano,* a supercomputer that retains everyone's life history and oversees human society.

ESP (extrasensory perception). Describes a range of enhanced mental powers including precognition and telekinesis but most often refers to telepathy: the ability to read minds. Also includes the literal definition of being able to sense or perceive things with one's mind, including other dimensions, which cannot be detected through the ordinary senses of sight, sound, touch, smell, or taste. An "esper" is a person with ESP.

Esper. In Alfred Bester's novel *The Demolished Man,* Espers are telepaths. Class 3 Espers can only read people's minds as they are forming their thoughts. Class 2 Espers can do everything Class 3 can do and also read subliminal thoughts. Class 1 Espers can do all of these things as well as detect subconscious primitive urges. The "Esp" in the word Esper is for ESP or extrasensory perception.

ET. From the Stephen Spielberg movie of the same name, ET is an extraterrestrial botanist who accidentally becomes stranded on Earth and must find a way to contact his shipmates so they can rescue him.

Eternity. An organization that tries to manipulate events in historical time so as to guide the development of human life in the direction they think its members should take. From Isaac Asimov's novel *The End of Eternity.*

Ethical Equations. In a Murray Leinster story of the same title, "The Ethical Equations" are a new type of equation for ethical behavior, which is applied to a drifting alien spaceship.

Etsy. A space-time continuum through which spaceships can enter through ports to travel vast distances in the fraction of the time it would take rocketing through normal space. The ports are generated by the immense gravity of the Eater, a huge black hole in the center of the galaxy. Source: Gregory Benford, *Furious Gulf.*

Eugenics. The use of selective breeding and sterilization to produce a race of superior human beings; H.G. Wells wrote about eugenics in his 1905 novel *A Modern Utopia,* in which the population is kept high on happy gas.

Eve VIII. In the cleverly titled film *Eve of Destruction*, a female android that malfunctions and becomes a murderous machine. Also, she has a built-in nuclear bomb that may detonate in a populated area unless she is found and the bomb defused.

Evoland. A shore on an island in the Bermuda Triangle where various areas on the island are in different time zones, past and future; Evoland leads to the present. From the 1977 TV series *The Fantastic Journey.*

Ewok. In *Star Wars,* the Ewoks are a race of aliens that resemble teddy bears. Ewoks walk upright and are about 3 feet tall. The race, though still essentially in the Stone Age, is intelligent. They have opposable thumbs and build primitive devices including slingshots, spears, and even hang gliders. In addition, they make pottery and have mastered fire. Ewoks spend some of their time in treetops, where they live in villages built high above the ground. They also spend time on the forest floor foraging and hunting.

Excalibur. The sword given to King Arthur by the Lady of the Lake, an enchantress.

Exigius 12 1/2. The Martian name of Uncle Martin in the TV series *My Favorite Martian.* Exigius 12 ½ was an archeologist studying Earth whose ship was damaged upon arrival. He lives in an apartment with a human, Tim O'Hara, who poses as the alien's nephew, until Exigius can repair the ship and return to Mars. Uncle Martin's Martian powers include telepathy, invisibility, and telekinesis. Other than a pair of retractable antennae, he looks just like a regular person.

Exorcist. A priest or other person of faith who performs rituals to help remove the demon or spirit from the body of a person who is possessed by said demon or spirit.

Exoskeleton. An armor or machine worn by a human operator to give him or her enhanced strength and imperviousness to weapons. Examples of exoskeletons include the body-supporting exoskeleton worn by the protagonist in Fritz Leiber's "A Spectre is Haunting Texas," battle armor used by the Earth soldiers in *Avatar,* the battle suit worn by Wikus van der Merwe in *District 9,* and the exoskeleton supporting Bruce Wayne's broken-down body in the comic book *Kingdom Come.*

Exotic Splinter Culture. On the Earth-like planet Kultis, the original settlers were members of the Exotic Splinter Culture (ESC), a group dedicated to the development of humankind's latent mental power. Source: *Tactics of Mistake* by Gordon R. Dickson.

Experimental History Institute (EHI). A group of human observers studying the pattern of cultural development on the Earth-like planet of Arknar to determine why it was diverging from theoretical predictions. From the novel by Arkady and Boris Strugatsky *Hard to be a God.*

Extinction Level Event (ELE). Any catastrophe that could end all life on Earth. In the movie *Deep Impact,* the threat of an ELE comes from a giant asteroid on a collision course with our planet. A similar ELE threat from asteroids or meteors heading from deep space directly toward Earth is featured in other movies such as *Armageddon* starring Bruce Willis and *Meteor* starring Sean Connery. Other ELEs include killer comets, extreme solar flares, the sun dying, drastic climate change, nuclear winter, global warming, a new ice age, and as in the movies *Waterworld* and *2012*, rising sea levels.

Extraction Specialist. Special operatives who steal business secrets from people while they dream, in the movie *Inception*.

Extreme Experience (ExEx). FBI virtual reality training which reconstructed violent reality scenarios. Trainees are repeatedly shot until they learn the proper way to defend themselves and fight back. From the Christopher Priest novel *The Extreme*.

Extremis. In Marvel Comics, a more advanced version of the super-soldier serum that created Captain America and the Red Skull. Extremis is a bio-electronic package contained in graphite nanotubes and suspended in a carrier fluid, which is then injected into the recipient. The Extremis technology endows people with a rapid healing factor, enhanced immune system, augmented cognition, and changes in internal organs that improve cardiovascular and respiratory performance. Some versions also granted super strength, invulnerability, and super speed.

Eymorgs. In *Star Trek*, an alien race from Sigma Draconis VI. Their planet is run by a complex computer, known as The Controller, that incorporates a living brain. After running reliably for 10,000 years, it begins to fail. So the Controller dispatches a ship, its commander Kara, and her crew to find and bring back a replacement brain. The Eymorgs intercept and board the U.S.S. Enterprise, where they surgically remove Spock's brain, intending to use it as the new brain for The Controller.

Fabulous Five. The sidekicks of pulp adventurer and muscular super-scientist Doc Savage. The group consists of Monk

Mayfair, an industrial chemist; Ham Brooks, an attorney; Renny Renwick, a construction engineer; Long Tom Robert, an electrical engineer; and Johnny Littlejohn, an archaeologist and geologist.

Face of Boe, The. In *Dr. Who*, the Face of Boe, who has become essentially a gigantic human head, is one of the oldest beings in the universe.

Facsimile Ltd. A company that manufactures robots. In Ray Bradbury's short story "I Sing the Body Electric," a widower buys a new robotic grandmother to help take care of his three children. The grandmother robot has artificial intelligence, emotions, and the outward appearance of a kindly older woman.

Fahrenheit 451. The temperature at which paper burns and the title of Ray Bradbury's novel about a dystopian future where the job of firemen, members of the "Fire Brigade," is to burn books. The classic first line of the novel is: "It was a pleasure to burn."

Fallarin. On the planet Skaith, humanoids who have undergone genetic engineering to develop wings for flight, but the wings were imperfect, so the Fallarin never gained the ability to fly. Source: Leigh Brackett, *The Ginger Star.*

Fan Fiction. Mostly short stories written by science fiction fans using characters from their favorite science fiction novels. SF fans rarely get permission from the publishers or authors whose characters and settings they use, and much fan fiction is a copyright violation.

Fanzine. An amateur, usually cheaply produced science fiction magazine published and written by SF fans for other SF fans.

Faster Than Light (FTL). *Albert Einstein*, in his theory of relativity, stated that nothing can travel faster than the speed of light, although in fact, the universe expanded at a much greater rate than light speed immediately following the Big Bang. So why can't a rocket go faster than light, too? FTL is space travel at velocities exceeding the speed of light, which is 186,000 miles per second. In 1950, J. Bridger wrote a story "I Am a Stranger Here Myself" in which mankind learns from aliens how to travel faster than the speed of light in FTL spaceships using a "multi-phase travel" technology based on transforming matter into antimatter – a precursor of the U.S.S. Enterprise's warp engines. FTL drives are also called "ultradrives," "overdrives," or "stardrives." The first known FTL SF story is "The Tachypomp," written in 1874 by Edward Mitchell. John W. Campbell, Jr. also wrote of an interstellar drive that achieved FTL speeds by transferring massive amounts of energy into space in his 1956 book *Islands of Space.*

Father-things. A species on Plowman's Planet, a world with a silicon-based biosphere. Father-things are born as white larvae but grow into adults that mimic other species, including humans. Source: *Nick and the Glimmung* by Philip K. Dick.

Fearless Fly. An insect cartoon super hero, Fearless can fly at high speed, much faster than ordinary flies. He also has super-strength and invulnerability. He gets his powers from a special pair of glasses he wears that fill his tiny body with incredible energy and power. The show's announcer said dramatically: "Faster than a streaking rocket speedier than a flash of light it's fearless fly. Possessed with a super strength so powerful no flies' water can harm him. No flypaper can hold him. No insecticide can stop him. Always careful not to reveal his true identity Fearless Fly hides from view as he removes his glasses which generate millions of megatons of energy through the sensitive muscles in his head and becomes a meek mild passive little fly known as Hiram."

Feathered Men. A tribe allegedly discovered by Sir John Manville; their bodies were covered with feathers except for their faces and palms. Able to live on land or sea, the Feathered Men ate raw flesh and fish. In science fiction, some mutants have wings covered with feathers, including the youngsters in James Patterson's *Maximum Ride* books and Angel in the X-Men.

FECs. The native inhabitants of Astria and Arde, two planets located in a two-dimensional space, called the Planiverse, created by a computer program 2DWORLD. The FECs are two-dimensional beings with six limbs extended from a body shaped like an isosceles triangle with a head at the apex. The FECs living on Arde developed intelligence and the ability to communicate with the human creators of the Planiverse. Source: *The Planiverse* by A.K. Dewdney.

Fesarius. In *Star Trek*, the Fesarius is a gigantic sphere-shaped vessel more than a mile in diameter. The ship is made up of hundreds of smaller golden globes attached to the main sphere in a diamond-shaped framework. Some of the golden globes can detach from the central sphere and operate independently as piloted vessels.

Fezzik. In the movie *The Princess Bride,* Fezzik is a giant played by pro wrestler Andre the Giant, who was 7'5" and weighed over 500 pounds.

Final Trip. In science fiction, voluntary and usually assisted suicide chosen by people weary of living on an inhospitable world. The term Final Trip was used by Barry Malzberg in his novel *Guernica Night.* Edward G. Robinson chose assisted suicide in the movie *Soylent Green.* In the movie *Chronicles of Riddick,* a character named the Purifier ends his life by walking into the furnace-hot sunlight of his planet in broad daylight. Assisted suicide is now a legal option in America in several states for terminally ill patients, especially those suffering unbearable pain.

Fisher King. The Guardian of the Holy Grail, so named because having been wounded, he cannot hunt and must fish instead.

Flash Gordon. A swashbuckling space hero whose mission is to stop the evil Ming the Merciless of Mongo from taking over the Earth.

Flatland. A two-dimensional world populated by 2D people as depicted by Edwin Abbott in his novella of the same title. In Flatland, women are line segments and men are polygons.

Flesh Guard. Android warriors that defend Britain from invaders during the Second World War, the Flesh Guard artificial warriors were nearly indestructible. Even if they were blasted apart, their fragments remained aggressively active, much like the giant robot in the movie *Iron Giant*.

Fleshers. Original Homo sapiens, many of whom have modified their genes to gain disease-resistance, life-extension, intelligence-amplification, and the ability to survive in new environments such as the oceans. Source: *Diaspora* by Greg Egan.

Floats. On a distant world, Floats are giant lily pads on the surface of the planet's ocean, which cluster in loosely connected archipelagoes. The Floaters are so thick and strong that humans could build colonies and live on them. From *The Blue World* by Jack Vance.

Flouven. On the planet Rocheworld, the dominant lifeform are jellyfish-like creatures called flouven. They are amorphous and loosely linked colonial organisms, with the colonies weighing several tons and possessing an intelligence superior to humans. Source: *The Flight of the Dragonfly* by Robert L. Forward.

Flux Capacitor. A small triangular device used in the *Back to the Future* movies to turn cars and trains into time-travel machines. The vehicle must reach a speed of 88 miles per hour for the flux capacitor to achieve time travel.

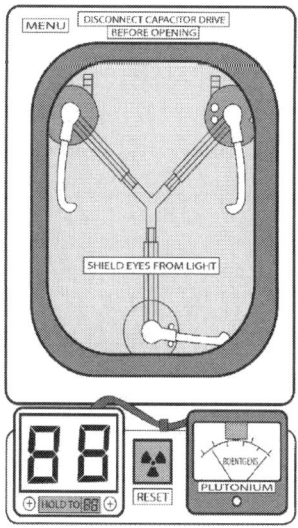

Flying Dutchman. The captain of a ship doomed to sail the oceans eternally in search of land, cursed to do so as a punishment for defying the gods.

Flying Saucer. A saucer-shaped spaceship. Used in countless SF books, stories, TV shows, and movies including *Independence Day, ET, Twilight Zone, Lost in Space,* and *Mars Attack,* to name just a few.

Forbidden Zone. A vast arid area of Earth, ravaged by nuclear war and highly radioactive, to which travel is not permitted in *The Planet of the Apes* films. Plant life barely grows there and the radioactivity has given rise to many mutations among the Zone's small animal and human population.

Force Field. A protective energy barrier that stops projectiles and energy weapons from penetrating it and hitting the target, which is usually a spacecraft. The shields in *Star Trek* and force fields in *Forbidden Plant* and *Lost in Space* are examples. In his 1931 short story "Islands of Space," John W. Campbell explains the field as being created by the directed motion of molecules. A force field used to protect a spaceship is called a "deflector."

Force, The. The Force is a strange, mysterious energy within the universe. It can be tapped by individual beings and used for good or evil. The Jedi Knights, in *Star Wars*, used the Force to combat the evil of the Empire, which used it for conquest and plunder. The expression "May the force be with you" became a part of American culture when *Star Wars* did too. In their book *The Science of Star Wars,* Mark Brake and Jon Chase write that the Force is something that acts on the subconscious process of your brain, guiding you as a kind of extra sense. In that it has some similarity to "magnetoreception," the ability of migratory birds and some other animals, to use the Earth's invisible magnetic field as a directional guide. The Force endows those who master it with telekinesis, mind control powers, precognition, as well as the ability to shoot bolts of energy from their hands.

Fembots. Hostile robots with the appearance of a human female, featured in such films and TV series as *Austin Powers* and *The Bionic Woman*. Fembots had super strength and some had guns implanted in their bosoms.

Firedrake. A fire-breathing dragon that lives in a cave where he guards the gold he has stolen and hoarded. Such a dragon is found in J.R.R. Tolkien's fantasy novel *The Hobbit*. In English legend, Saint George battles a dragon living in a cave. In Chinese mythology, dragons can actually turn themselves *into* fire. The 17th century writer Athanasius Kircher told the story of a man, held in captivity by a dragon, who escapes by holding onto the dragon's tail as it flies away from its mountain lair.

Firefrost. A legendary artifact of great power, capable of destabilizing all the universes that exist. From the comic book *The Adventures of Luther Arkwright*.

First Druid Council. A group of people—humans, dwarves, gnomes, and trolls—who, after a nuclear holocaust has wiped out most of the planet, gather to preserve knowledge of the old world in an attempt to bring peace and order to all of the races. From *The Sword of Shannara* by Terry Brooks.

First Space. Three iterations of Beijing have been engineered to fold in on themselves and unfurl independently on a set schedule to occupy the Earth's surface. First Space is occupied by the upper class; Second Space by the middle class; and Third Space is for the lower class, the workers. From the short story "Folding Beijing" by Hao Jingfang.

Floats. On an oceanic planet, Floats are giant lily pads, which cluster to create a veritable floating island of vegetation. The float islands are strong and buoyant, and so they are inhabited by colonists on the planet. Source: *The Blue World* by Jack Vance.

Foma. In the religion of Bokononism, a foma is a harmless lie. Bokononism posits that believing in adhering to these untruths can result in peace of mind and a good life. Bokononists believe two people can mingle their souls through contact of the soles of their naked feet. From the Kurt Vonnegut novel *Cat's Cradle*.

Fosterite Church of the New Revelation. In Robert Heinlein's novel *Stranger in a Strange Land*, a megachurch in which sex, gambling, and drinking are allowed and even encouraged, as long as they are done under church auspices.

Fountain of Youth. A fountain whose waters, when consumed, grant eternal youth or at least greatly slow down the human aging process, resulting in extreme longevity. Such a fountain is featured in the young adult's fantasy novel *Tuck Everlasting*. In Fred Mustard Stewart's novel *The Methuselah Enzyme*, the anti-aging liquid is not water from a fountain but an enzyme produced in a laboratory. In the James Gunn novel *The Immortals*, an anti-aging compound is made from the blood of a man who is naturally immortal. The Brothers Grimm describe a variation of the Fountain of Youth in their fairy tale, "The Water of Life."

Fourth Wall. In movie making, "breaking the fourth wall" means something is done in the film that breaks the illusion that what you are seeing is real. Most often, this is done by a character directly interacting with the audience, as if he could see the moviegoer right through the screen. An example is seen at the end of the movie *Superman*, when Superman, as he is flying above the Earth, turns his head and winks at the camera; another is Deadpool making asides to the viewer in the *Deadpool* films. Another fourth wall technique is when, in movies with multiple characters each played by a major star, the characters refer by name to the actors playing one another.

Fowler Schocken. In the science fiction novel *The Space Merchants,* an advertising agency creating an ad campaign to attract colonists to Venus. Why? Because the world government's plan to relieve Earth's overpopulation is to relocate millions of people to Venus, which is being terraformed to support human life.

Foxen. In Sheri Tepper's novel *Grass,* foxen are fierce creatures, essentially made of teeth, hunted by aristocratic humans.

Frank-N-Furter. A transvestite alien wearing stockings and high heels, Dr. Frank-N-Furter is played by Tim Curry in his most famous role. From *The Rocky Horror Picture Show.*

Frontera. In Lewis Shiner's novel of the same title, Frontera is the first human colony on Mars. It is covered by a cylindrical dome measuring a kilometer long and 200 meters wide.

Fugghead. From the writings of Damon Knight and Robert Silverberg, a fugghead is a stupid person, a moron.

Fulgurator. In the Jules Verne 1896 novel *Facing the Flag,* the Fulgurator is a devastating weapon of war that fires self-propelled explosive shells.

Furies. The three daughters of the union between air and Mother Earth, the three Furies appear as old crones with dog heads, snakes for hair, bat wings, coal-black bodies, and bloodshot eyes. Roger Zelazny imagined a very different trio of Furies in his novelette *The Furies,* about a quartet of men with special abilities who work as a team to track a dangerous criminal.

Future History. Tales of future events written as historical accounts by an author in the same universe where the future events took place.

Futurians. In the 1940s, the Futurians were a group of science fiction writers in New York, mostly white, liberal, male American authors.

Gaea. In John Varley's novel *Titan,* Gaea is a sentient, spoked, wheel-shaped spaceship. The enormous structure consists of a series of interlocking ecologies, some alien in nature and others based on Earth's popular culture.

Gaia Hypothesis. The theory that organisms interact with the inorganic surroundings of a planet. In doing so, they form a self-regulating system, which maintains and perpetuates the planet's ability to sustain life. Brian Aldiss's novel *Helliconia* is based on the Gaia hypothesis.

Galactic Barrier. A difficult-to-penetrate energy barrier of unknown origin and composition surrounding the Milky Way, in *Star Trek*. Humans who pass through its energies may undergo a mutation giving them psionic abilities such as telepathy, telekinesis, and energy blasts.

Galactic Patrol. Any military, police, or paramilitary force, comprised of members of multiple races from multiple planets, tasked with protecting the galaxy from danger and keeping it secure and at peace. In E.E. Doc Smith's Lensman novels, the Galactic Patrol was a combination military force and interstellar law-enforcement agency, charged with the defense and preservation of civilization; the Lensmen wore a special bracelet granting them psychic abilities and other powers. The Guardians of the Galaxy are a sort of small galactic patrol. In *The Day the Earth Stood Still,* Klaatu is an emissary from an interplanetary confederation that patrols the galaxy to preserve the peace. The TV series *Tom Corbett, Space Cadet* revolved around a space patrol called the Space Guard. In Looney Tunes, Daffy Duck is "Duck Dodgers," an inept captain in a space patrol.

Games Machine. In A.E. van Vogt's novel *The World of Null-A,* the games machine is a computer given human communications abilities that advances to near godlike omniscience.

Gamma Rays. Electromagnetic radiation with a wavelength shorter than x-rays. Emitted by uranium and thorium, in Marvel Comics gamma rays are imagined to mutate humans and animals, changing their appearance and often giving them enhanced strength, intelligence, or other abilities. Gamma rays turned Bruce Banner into the Hulk. A "graser" – gamma ray amplification by stimulated emission of radiation – is a ray gun that shoots gamma rays.

Gamera. A giant, monstrous prehistoric turtle with huge tusks, Gamera can fly and breathe fire. He is released from suspended cryogenic animation in the arctic by a nuclear explosion.

Gas Angels. In K.W. Jeter's novel *Farewell Horizontal,* gas angels are beings with human bodies containing buoyancy sacks that enable them to float in the atmosphere. They navigate with membranous appendages on both sides that extend from the neck to the buttocks.

Gateway. In the Frederik Pohl novel of the same title, Gateway is a hollow asteroid built and long-ago abandoned by the alien race The Heechee. The Gateway is about 10 kilometers long by 5 kilometers wide. One thousand space ships are docked there, each with a destination preset into its navigation system.

Gauntlet. In Lilith Saintcrow's novel *The Devil's Right Hand*, a Gauntlet is a wrist-cuff given to people by the Devil. It signifies that you, the wearer, are the Devil's champion, and that any demon who does not obey Satan's authority is your enemy.

Gauntlet of Power. A glove that, once you put it in your hand, covers the wearer's body with a near-impenetrable armor. From *Creatures of Light and Darkness* by Roger Zelazny.

Gemser. A planet colonized by humans where age is reversed, senior citizens are in charge, and people are considered to be children until they are in their thirties. The planet's motto: OLDEST IS BESTEST. Source: *Search the Sky* by Fred Pohl and C.M. Kornbluth.

Generational Spaceship. Assuming humans never develop immortality, cryogenic suspension, faster than light travel, or teleportation, the only way for humanity to visit and colonize worlds that are light years away is with a generational spaceship. Also called a "space ark," the original crew in such a ship procreates as do their children, children's children, and so on, so that the travelers who ultimately reach the far solar system are future generations of the original astronauts. Harlan Ellison wrote about a generational spaceship in his TV series *The Starlost*. In the Brian Aldiss novel *Non-Stop*, the inhabitants of a generational spaceship with a jungle-like interior have been on it for so many generations they no longer remember that they are on a ship. *The Dazzle of the Day* by Molly Glass is a short novel about a generational starship.

Giants. Beings of enormous proportion, many times taller than a normal person. In Greek mythology, the giants warred against Zeus and the other gods. In African mythology, humans were originally immortal giants; but the gods feared them, and so made people smaller and mortal. Alien giants, around 70 feet tall, populated a distant planet in space in the TV series *Land of the Giants.* In Marvel Comics, Giant-Man is a superhero who can instantly grow to enormous size. A giant woman was the main character of the SF movie *Attack of the 50-Foot Woman*, and a 60-foot man was the protagonist in the movie *The Amazing Colossal Man.* In Norse mythology, the Frost Giants are the sworn enemies of the gods of Asgard. Giants are found in many other stories and legends such as Paul Bunyan. Giant robots in SF include Gigantor and Mecha-Godzilla. In real life, giants also exist, with the largest man ever having been nearly 9 feet tall, and many others topping 8 feet. Agnes Morehead starred in a *Twilight Zone* episode where she was a giant alien woman who defends herself against and ultimately destroys a space exploration team from Earth, which she dwarfs in size.

Gibyat. On the planet Ephar, a gibyat is a unit of measure for distance approximately equal to an Earth mile. Source: "Last Favor" by Harry Turtledove.

Ghidorah. A prehistoric giant winged reptile with three heads, each capable of emitting energy blasts; It has survived in modern times, where it frequently battles Godzilla.

Gibberne's Nervous Accelerator. In the H.G. Wells story "The New Accelerator," a new drug, called Gibberne's Nervous Accelerator, speeds up the bodily functions by a factor of several thousand times. The people who take it move so rapidly they are invisible. And to them, everything seems frozen in place.

Gigantes. In Greek mythology, the Gigantes are grotesque humanoid giants. They have serpentine legs and three pairs of hands – one pair hanging from the shoulders and the other two from the hips.

Gigantor. In the animated TV show of the same title, Gigantor is a gigantic robot operated by remote control. In the show's theme song it is referred to as "Gigantor the space-age robot." Gigantor is made of steel and has a rocket-powered backpack for flight. His face has a pointy nose and eyes that never look anywhere except straight ahead.

Gilead. In the novel The Handmaid's Tale, in the future the United States is controlled by a theocratic police state, Gilead, run by militant religious fundamentalists. An ecological disaster has made most of the country's population infertile, and so in Gilead, abortion is a capital crime.

Gill-man. In the movie *The Creature from the Black Lagoon*, an amphibious fish-humanoid hybrid believed to be a missing link between ocean and land life. Horror novelist Hunter Shea writes, "The film tells the story of a group of scientists who venture deep into the Amazon to study the unusual findings of a colleague who was previously attacked by a mysterious creature. As they continue their expedition, they realize the creature is not only real, but it is also dangerous and determined to protect its territory."

Mutant Abe Sapien in *Hellboy* is similar in physiology to the Gill-man. The Mariner from *Waterworld* is also an amphibious mutant. All three can breathe underwater, but The Mariner closely resembles a normal human, while Gill-Man and Abe Sapien are more fish-like in appearance.

Dallas star Patrick Duffy played an amphibious man, the last survivor of Atlantis, in the TV series *The Man from Atlantis.* In Richard Setlowe's science fiction novel *The Experiment,* a man dying of lung cancer is saved by an operation that gives him artificial gills, enabling him to breathe underwater when his cancerous lungs are removed. A scientist creates a gill-man who can breathe underwater in the movie *The Amphibian Man.*

A gill-man captured from the wild was featured in the 2017 picture, *The Shape of Water.* In Lee Hoffman's *The Caves of Karst,* "gill-suckers" are humans physically altered to live life beneath the seas. In S. Fowler Wright's novel, *The World Below,* Earth is populated by two dominant intelligent species: Dwellers, giants living on land, and humanoid Amphibians who can breathe underwater.

Gingo. A rare fruit from Yucatan, a special extract of which gives Ralph Denby, aka the Elongated Man, stretching powers like those of Mr. Fantastic in the Fantastic Four. Jimmy Olsen also gets his temporary stretching powers as Elastic Kid by drinking a similar stretching formula. Another comic book hero with super-stretch powers, Elastic Man, got his after accidentally falling into a vat containing an unidentified chemical compound.

Gipper. A one-quadrillion-dollar bill, so-named because Ronald Reagan's picture is on it. In the hyperinflated world of Neal Stephenson's novel *Snow Crash,* the gipper is the standard small bill, much like a one-dollar-bill is today.

Ghoul. A shape-shifting demon that can take the form of a hyena and enjoys eating the flesh of the living, in particular lost children.

Giant Skyscrapers. In Robert Silverberg's novel *The World Inside,* humanity lives in huge urban towers. Each is a thousand stories high and has nearly a million residents. The buildings are nearly self-sufficient with recreational facilities, shopping, schools, power generation, communications, manufacturing, and agriculture.

Gigantopithecus. A race of giant manlike apes standing 9 ½ feet tall which ruled the forests of East Asia for about a million years. They have been extinct for over 100,000 years, and are believed by some to be the ancestor of the Yeti.

Glimming. In Philip K. Dick's novel *Galactic Pot-Healer,* The Glimmung is an individual with godlike powers who took dominion over the planet Sirius V.

Gismo. The Gismo is a device that can duplicate anything. Source: Damon Knight, *A is for Anything.*

Glogauer, Karl. In Michael Moorcock's novel *Behold the Man,* Karl Glogauer is a scientist who builds a time machine – a womb-like sphere filled with fluid. Glogauer takes the time machine to 28 AD, where he finds that Jesus is a mentally disabled hunchback child, and also that Jesus was conceived through normal intercourse between his parents, Mary and Joseph. Since Jesus is unable to serve as a messiah, Glogauer takes on the role of Jesus of Nazareth, teaching the same lessons and parables he had read when reading the Bible in his own time. Glogauer also uses his modern knowledge to simulate Biblical miracles. This, and the fact that witnesses saw Karl miraculously appear in the time machine, cause the people to come to believe that *he* is in fact Jesus of Nazareth and our savior.

Global Warming. Occurs when a heavy concentration of carbon dioxide and other gases in the atmosphere act much as the glass in a greenhouse by trapping heat in the Earth's atmosphere, resulting in a gradual warming of the Earth's climate. In his 1969 story "We All Die Naked," James Blish envisions a future Manhattan in which environmental changes render the air unbreathable (except with gas masks) and the entire city flooded because of rising tides from melting of the polar ice caps due to global warming.

Goblin. Describes any mischievous or evil spirit. From 14th century folklore.

Goblin Reservation. In Clifford D. Simak's novel *The Goblin Reservation,* goblins, trolls, fairies, and other creatures once thought to be merely mythological are real, still exist, and have been discovered and placed on various reservations operated under the auspices of Supernatural, a division of Time University, Earth's planet-wide university.

Goblin Universe. Refers to earth's population of supernatural and other extraordinary and unusual beings.

God's World. In Ian Watson's novel of the same title, God's World is populated by tall shimmering beings of golden light called angels, who appear on Earth and summon human beings to their home planet. God's World borders an other-worldly zone of space called "heaven" into which the planet is gradually being assimilated.

Golden Age. The era of science fiction when the genre was at its relative infancy and **hard science fiction** was the dominant form. Some of this era's more popular authors included Clifford D. Simak, Jack Williamson, Lester Del Rey, Jack Vance, Andre Norton, Theodore Sturgeon, Cyril Kornbluth, Frederick Pohl, Murray Leinster, and Robert Heinlein. The Golden Age began in the 1950s and lasted through the mid-1970s until **New Wave** science fiction became popular.

Golem. In Jewish folklore and a few horror movies, a man made of mud or clay and mystically brought to life, usually by writing a prayer on a small piece of parchment and inserting it into the golem's mouth. A rabbi was said to have created a golem in the 16th century to defend the Jews of Prague against anti-Semitic attacks. Several horror movies have featured a golem as the monster.

Goloka Root. A root which Tom Strong regularly ingests that augments his great physical strength, a portion of which is attributed to Tom's scientist parents raising him in a chamber with artificial gravity many times greater than Earth's normal gravity, much as Superman owes part of his strength to the intense gravity of his home planet Krypton. The goloka root also gives Tom extended longevity, and at a chronological age of around a hundred years old, he looks as if he is only in his forties. From the *Tom Strong* comic books.

Gomtuu. In *Star Trek*, Gomtuu was an ancient and unique life form: an organic vessel that had once lived symbiotically with its crew. The crew died out centuries ago, and the Gomtuu continued to live and function on its own. The ship's hull, about the length of the Enterprise D, was formed of several overlapping layers with bright shimmering white light in between. The Gomtuu resembles a gigantic glowing pine cone, and it vibrated as if it were breathing. The Gomtuu was intelligent, sentient, and telepathic. It was capable of warp speed and possessed a blue energy weapon capable of completely destroying an enemy warship.

Gor. In the novels of John Norman, a planet in the same orbit as Earth but on the opposite side of the sun, which results in us never being able to see it. Gor is populated by humanoids who are physically much like humans but ride giant lizards for transportation.

Gordon, Artemus. In the TV series *The Wild, Wild West*, Artemus Gordon is a government agent who, in the old west, invents futuristic weapons and other gadgets to help his sharp-shooting partner James West fight dastardly villains throughout the country.

Gorgo. In the 1961 motion picture of the same name, Gorgo is a giant, dinosaur-like sea monster captured and put on display in London. Unfortunately, the adventurers who exploit Gorgo as a circus attraction do not realize Gorgo is an infant – and his mother is coming to rescue him.

Gorgonoid. Immaterial, virtual creatures consisting of code and visible only on computer screens. In appearance, gorgonoids have two "cables," one is in the shape of a ring, and the second wraps around in a spiral. From the short story "Gorgonoids" by Leena Krohn.

Gorgons. In Greek mythology, female creatures with writhing venomous snakes for "hair"; staring directly at a Gorgon's face would result in a person turning into stone. The most famous Gorgon is Medusa.

Gorillas. Gorillas, both giant and intelligent, are a staple of science fiction – from King Kong and Mighty Joe Young, to Tarzan of the Apes, Gorilla Grod, and *Congo.* In DC comics, a large group of gorillas, some of whom are super-intelligent—including the villain Gorilla Grod—reside in Gorilla City in Africa.

Gorn. In *Star Trek,* a species of intelligent reptilian aliens. Gorns are 2 meters tall, with dense musculature and tough green leathery skin. While stronger and tougher than humans, their bulk makes the Gorn slower-moving, and therefore easily outmaneuvered. Side note: Similar in appearance to Romulan Ale, the Gorn brew a blue-colored drink called Meridor.

Gort. An 8-foot-tall seamless robot made from a single piece of a flexible alien metal alloy. He serves as bodyguard and servant to the alien Klaatu in the movie *The Day the Earth Stood Still.* Klaatu is an emissary from an interplanetary confederation. The confederation that patrols the galaxy to preserve the peace, and any planet that threatens to use atomic weapons against them will be destroyed to ensure the safety of the other planets.

Goss Conf. An Earth-like planet whose near-human inhabitants have green blood, as do *Star Trek's* Vulcans, except the skin of the Goss Conf has a greenish tint.

Graboids. Giant predatory worms that travel underground and emerge to terrorize and eat people. From the Tremors series of films and the TV series. The graboids detect the presence of prey by sensing vibration from movement.

Graf Orlock. A skeletal vampire played by actor Max Schrek in the 1922 horror movie *Nosferatu*.

Grandfather Paradox. The notion that, if you travel back in time and kill your grandfather, doing so would prevent one of your parents from being born. And as a result, you would never have been born, making it impossible that you would have traveled back in time at all. From *Dr. Who.*

Granfaloon. An association, society, community, or other group of people who come together because of a shared belief, philosophy, or premise that in fact is false. Or as author Kurt Vonnegut, who coined the term puts it, a granfaloon is "a proud and meaningless collection of human beings."

Graphitics. In Isaac Asimov's short story "The Feeling of Power," computers and calculators perform all arithmetical functions; and humans lose the knowledge of how to do simple subtraction, addition, multiplication, and division by hand – just as many people today no longer know cursive writing. A technician named Aub rediscovers how to do arithmetic with pencil and paper, which becomes known as graphitics. When the military plans to use graphitics for war, Aub commits suicide, but by then others have mastered graphitics and the war will go on.

Gravity Drinker. An antigravity device for propelling rocket ships. When spun on its axis, the device consumes inertia and boosts acceleration. From the Robert Silverberg short story "Something Wild is Loose."

Gravity Lens. A device featured in Andrew Crusoe's novel *The Truth Beyond the Sky*. In astrophysics, "gravity lensing" is caused when the presence of matter curves spacetime to deflect the path of a ray of light.

Gravity's Rainbow. From the Thomas Pynchon novel of the same title, gravity's rainbow refers to the path of a ballistic rocket: it rises straight up, then curves elliptically as it comes down.

Gray Sister, The. In Roger Zelazny's short story "This Mortal Mountain," The Gray Sister, located on the planet Disel, is the highest mountain in the known universe (its actual measure is not given in the story). On Earth, in Oregon, a mountain called the South Sister is nearly 2 miles high. Mount Everest, the tallest mountain on Earth, stands almost 5 ½ miles high. And the tallest mountain in our solar system, Olympus Mons, located on Mars, is 16 miles high.

Great Darkness. In DC Comics, this super-villain is a cosmic dark force of nature. It balances out the light and can influence people, including superheroes.

Great Gazoo. A diminutive, green. gloating alien featured in *The Flintstones* and *The Jetsons*. Gazoo can materialize and dematerialize objects, teleport, time travel, freeze time, turn people young, and even destroy the world—though of course he never does. Gazoo calls Fred Flintstone and Barney Rubble "dumb dumbs."

Great Intelligence, The. In *Dr. Who*, a formless entity wandering in space, resembling snow in appearance. Aside from the color, somewhat similar in nature to *The Black Cloud* in Fred Hoyle's novel of the same title—an intelligent cloud of interstellar matter that has drifted in space for half a billion years.

Great Wheel. A reincarnation machine that transfers a person's soul from their old body to a new body, thereby giving them an enormously long lifespan. From the Roger Zelazny novel *Lord of Light*.

Green Lantern Oath, The. Words a Green Lantern recites to recharge his power ring from his power battery. The oath, attributed alternately to science fiction writers Alfred Bester[7] and Brian Aldiss[8], is as follows:

> *In brightest day, in blackest night*
> *No evil shall escape my site*
> *Let those who worship evil's might*
> *Beware my power: Green Lantern's light.*
> **Green Lantern Oath © DC Comics**

Green Man, The. A mythical being, thought to be a natural spirit, who lives in the woods and has foliage growing out of his mouth and nose. Some tales say his hair and beard are made of leaves and his face is covered with vines.

Gremlins. Mischievous little creatures, often invisible, that interfere with the function of airplanes. Gremlins originated in World War II and notably featured in a *Twilight Zone* episode starring William Shatner as a passenger terrified when he sees a gremlin on the wing of the plane.

Grendel. In *Beowulf*, Grendel is a man-eating demon whom Beowulf wrestles and kills by ripping off the demon's arm.

Grenofen. In Lisa Tuttle's short story "Flying to Byzantium," the grenofen are evil and powerful creatures. They dwell in maze-like tunnels within a huge mountain towering over small and isolated villages under the shadow of the mountain. A young girl, Kayli, battles the grenofen. Aided by enchantments, Kayli defeats the grenofen in battle and steals their treasure.

---

[7] https://futurism.media/greatest-sci-fi-authors-of-all-time
[8] https://en.wikipedia.org/wiki/Brian_Aldiss

Grimoire. A book of spells and incantations used by wizards and witches to conjure up demons whom they could ask to help or advise them.

Grok. To grok means to understand something or someone in a deep, meaningful, and positive way intuitively or by empathy. The term was invented by Robert Heinlein in his novel *Stranger in a Strange Land.* Some *Star Trek* fans who were fond of the late Leonard Nimoy's character coined the phrase "I grok Spock."

Groundhogs. A derogatory term used by lunar colonists to describe Earth dwellers, including those who make short-term visits to the Hotel Moon Haven. From Robert Heinlein's novel *The Green Hills of Earth.*

GUT (Grand Unification Theory). Grand Unification Theory postulates that when the universe was young, there existed only a vacuum empty of matter but containing high energy. This energy-filled vacuum decayed into our current universe – a void containing stars, planets, other objects, and space dust – through a process called spontaneous breaking of symmetry. From Geoffrey Landis' short story "Vacuum States."

Guyver. An organic battle armor made of a material resembling a lobster shell, only far more impervious. The Guyver is sought by the Zoanoids, evil mutants bent on controlling the evolution of humanity.

Habranha. In Hal Clement's novel *Fossil,* Habranha is a planet that is tidally locked with its sun. The dark side is a mix of solid carbon dioxide, solid methane, and ice. The sunlit side is a vast ocean.

HAL (Heuristically Programmed Algorithmic Computer). An AI computer aboard the nuclear-powered space ship Discovery One, which seemingly goes haywire and begins murdering the astronauts during an interplanetary mission. HAL kills most of the ship's crew until spaceman David Bowman deactivates the machine. From the novel and movie *2001: A Space Odyssey.*

Halfling. A being who has one human parent and one that is something else, often an elf.

Half-life. Deceased people cryogenically preserved still retain some cerebral activity, and can for short periods be resuscitated to allow normal brain function and cognition. Advanced cryogenic capsules enable the living, with the aid of a special earphone, an electronic communing device, to communicate with the dead. But this mental awareness lasts only so long. It fades and then ceases, and then the person is truly, fully dead. The amount of time for which a cryogenically frozen person retains awareness and brain function is called the *half-life.* In physics, a half-life is the amount of time it takes for a radioactive substance to lose half of its radioactivity. From *Ubik* by Philip K. Dick.

Handmaid. In Margaret Atwood's novel *The Handmaid's Tale,* chemical pollution and radiation have rendered most of Earth's females infertile. Handmaids are women who have remained fertile, and they are required to bear children for important men.

Hannibal Lecter. A well-educated cannibal of refined cultural tastes who eats his victims, often while they are still alive, created by novelist Thomas Harris.

Happy Cloaks. In the colonies on Venus, cloaks genetically engineered from native species are worn to keep people happy and content with addictive euphorics. Source: "Clash by Night" by C.L Moore and Henry Kutner.

Happy Dreams. An illegal drug that causes users to hallucinate and see visions of another world. The effects become permanent as the synthetic chemicals in the drug are deposited in the body's cells. From the John Brunner novel *The Dreaming Earth.*

Happy Patch. A patch worn on the skin that releases brain opiates to make people feel happier. From the 2004 TV series *Century City.*

Harbenite. An ultra-lightweight metal alloy. In Edgar Rice Burroughs novel *Tarzan at the Earth's Core,* Tarzan journeys to the center of the Earth in a ship constructed of Harbenite and built by his friend, inventor Jason Gridley. The 75-ton Harbenite ship has eight air-cooled motors producing 5,600 horsepower, achieving a maximum velocity of 105 miles per hour.

Hardhomes. In *Game of Thrones,* Hardhomes is a woods populated by dead things, both on the land and in the water.

Hard Science Fiction. Science fiction in which a strong plot, based on science, is the dominant story element. Jerry Pournelle, Larry Niven, Isaac Asimov, Ben Bova, Arthur C. Clarke, and Frederik Pohl are a few of the better known writers of hard science fiction. In the early days of science fiction, when hard SF was dominant, many of the short stories in pulp science fiction magazines were written by scientists and engineers rather than professional fiction writers.

Harsh Realm. In the TV series of the same name, the *Harsh Realm* is a "pocket universe" created by a supercomputer. See also "pocket universe."

Harry Herman. Harry is an alien from outer space. He looks human, although each hand has two thumbs and one finger. He has brought to Earth a vaccine which he says will cure all diseases. But his race fears that humankind's intelligence is a disease causing us to destroy our own planet. So the vaccine, which is given to billions globally, actually lowers human IQ. But the doctor who helps Harry distribute the vaccine wonders whether it indeed was given to stop us from destroying our planet—or make us an easy target for alien invasion.

Haven. An android cop with the Los Angeles Police Department in the TV series *Future Cop.* Unlike the cyborg Robocop, Haven was completely human in appearance.

Hawkbill Station. In Robert Silverberg's novel of the same title, a prison colony placed a billion years in Earth's past. It holds left-wing political dissidents exiled from the repressive American society of the early 20th century.

Heaven. In Kathleen Norris' novel *Through a Glass Darkly,* Heaven is an alternate America. It has fought no world wars, is a socialist nation, and a utopian world where everyone gets free food. In fact, in addition to our world, there are at least seven of these Heavens, and people go to one of them after they die on Earth.

Helliconia. A planet orbiting a binary star, the bigger of which is 65 times the size of our sun. Ticks carry the deadly helico virus, which makes it dangerous for non-native space travelers to land on Helliconia's surface. Source: Brian W. Aldiss, *Helliconia Summer*.

Helior. In Harry Harrison's novel *Bill the Galactic Hero*, Helior is a multi-layered planet-wide city encased in an anodized aluminum dome. Most of the citizens are petty bureaucrats working in specialized office spaces within the city. A nonconforming subset of the population, the Brotherhood of the Deplanned, lives in caverns and tunnels under the city, just like the rebels in the movie *Demolition Man*.

He Who Walks Behind the Rows. In the *Children of the Corn* films, an ancient and malevolent God or spirit being who lives unseen in the cornfields and demands sacrifices of adult victims from the children who worship and obey him.

High-Frequency Active Auroral Research Program (HAARP). A weather control technology with antennas capable of creating controlled local modifications of the ionosphere. The antennas send out a powerful radio wave beam that heats the upper atmosphere. Since hot air rises, HAARP would lift areas of the ionosphere higher, changing local weather patterns, potentially triggering floods, droughts, hurricanes, and earthquakes. Technology capable of controlling weather was featured in the 2017 motion picture *Geostorm*.

Headless Horseman, The. In both fiction and folklore, the Headless Horseman is a mythical ghost who rides a horse in search of his head. The Horseman is sometimes seen carrying either his decapitated head or a Jack-o'-Lantern replacement. Legend has it that the Horseman was a soldier who was decapitated when he was hit in the head with a cannonball during the Battle of White Plains in the Revolutionary War.

Hedora. A giant monstrous and sentient flying sludge blob that releases poison gas and is ultimately dispatched by Godzilla.

Hellboy. A demon who, as a young child, escapes Hell through a magic portal and ends up on Earth, where he is raised to adulthood by a kindly investigator of the supernatural and eventually becomes a superhero of sorts.

Herakleophorbia IV. In the H.G. Wells novel *The Food of the Gods*, the scientific name of a food additive that induces hyper-rapid growth. This formula is invented by two scientists, Bennington and Redwood. Made from alkaloids and related compounds, the compound, when added to foods and then ingested, makes animals grow to many times their normal size.

Hermits. On the planet Poincare C, the mollusk-like Hermits, whose vision is based on interferometry, are the dominant intelligent species. From Greg Egan's novel *Diaspora*.

High Heart. In *Game of Thrones*, High Heart is a Hill where dozens of weirwood tree stumps stand. Weirwoods are ancient trees associated with the old gods of the North. The trees have white bark and deep-red leaves, and each has a face carved into its trunk. The tree stumps signal the connection of the location to the Children of the Forest and old gods of Westero. The hill is haunted by a ghost who appears as a small woman. She offers to tell visitors about their dreams in exchange for some wine and a song. Some believe she is the ghost of Jenny Oldstones.

Hippae. In Sheri Tepper's novel *Grass*, foxen – fierce creatures essentially made of teeth – are hunted by aristocratic humans riding hippae, which are beasts resembling dinosaurs.

Hive. In the Resident Evil movies, the Umbrella Corporation's underground research facility for developing viruses to be used as biological weapons.

Hive Mind. When a group of beings share or are controlled by a single, central mind, as the insect-like creatures are in George R.R. Martin's story "Sandkings." First called "group mind" in W.O. Stapledon's 1930 Mars novel *Last and First Men.* J.H. Schmitz called it the "hive mind" in his 1950 short story "Second Night of Summer."

House of the Undying. In *Game of Thrones,* a magical building with a room containing the Iron Thrones as well as a sweet-smelling blue rose growing from a chink in a wall of ice.

Hollow Earth. These stories imagine that the Earth is hollow and one can gain access to the interior through openings at the poles. A hollow Earth is featured in the 1820 novel by Adam Seaborn *Symzonia* and the 1864 Jules Verne novel *Journey to the Center of the Earth.* In the 1848 novel *In the Fountain of Arethusa* by Robert Landor, the interior of the Earth has its own sun. In Rudy Rucker's novel *The Hollow Earth*, the Htrae is a large hollow space beneath the surface of the Earth filled with a dazzling variety of flora and fauna, including several races of humans. Htrae is also the name of Bizzaro World in DC Comics. In John Barrowman's novel *Hollow Earth,* the interior of Earth is a realm in which all demons and monsters are trapped.

Hollowgast. Humanoid, tentacle-mouth creatures that devour children with extraordinary abilities, and in doing so gain each child's special powers. A hollowgast who has absorbed enough special abilities evolves into a wight, beings who resemble humans, except their eyes have no pupils. From the novel and film *Miss Peregrine's Home for Peculiar Children.*

Hologram. An image that appears three-dimensional. Holograms have been featured in numerous science fiction stories and films including the famous hologram of Princess Leia R2D2 projects in *Star Wars.* Tom Hanks starred in a non-SF movie featuring holograms, *A Hologram for the King.* Holograms played a part in the plot of Barry Malzberg's novel *Guernica Night,* though he called them "holographs." Gardner Dozois featured holograms in his 1974 short story "Strangers."

Hominology. The study and investigation of certain hominoids, whose existence is suspected but not scientifically confirmed, that may be near-relatives of homo sapiens. Examples include Yetis and the Sasquatch. If they exist, they would be considered "living fossils," organisms that have survived beyond their era.

Homo Mechanensis. Robots; a mechanical species of humanoids. From the Lester del Rey short story "Helen O'Loy."

Homo Sapiens Mermanus (Atlanteans). The Atlanteans separated from baseline humanity when Atlantis sank beneath the ocean. How the Atlanteans survived this disastrous event is something of a question; theories range from aliens or magic, to divine intervention or advanced science, to a natural mutation which enabled breathing underwater. Atlanteans are capable of interbreeding with humans, and Atlanteans do carry the mutant X-gene. The species can breathe under water and survive intense pressures in the deep ocean. Some have blue skin while others have the same flesh tones ordinary humans do.

Homo Sapiens Superior. The species to arise from the next stage of human evolution, which in Marvel Comics, is mutants. Homo Sapiens Superior are more commonly called *mutants*. They are people who have a genetic X-gene that activates naturally occurring abilities that separate them from baseline humanity. Most mutants have fully human parents, and there is no common trait among all mutants, other than the X-gene itself, that separates them from ordinary Homo Sapiens. Olaf Stapledon first used the term Homo Superior in his 1935 novel *Odd John.*

Homunculus. A miniature human being, usually grown in a flask. A scientist creates a homunculus in Harlan Ellison's short story "How Interesting: A Tiny Man." In the 1916 motion picture *Homunculus,* a scientist creates a perfect man. But his creature turns evil, and plans to use its intelligence to set himself up as a dictator. Fortunately for humanity, it is killed by a bolt of lightning.

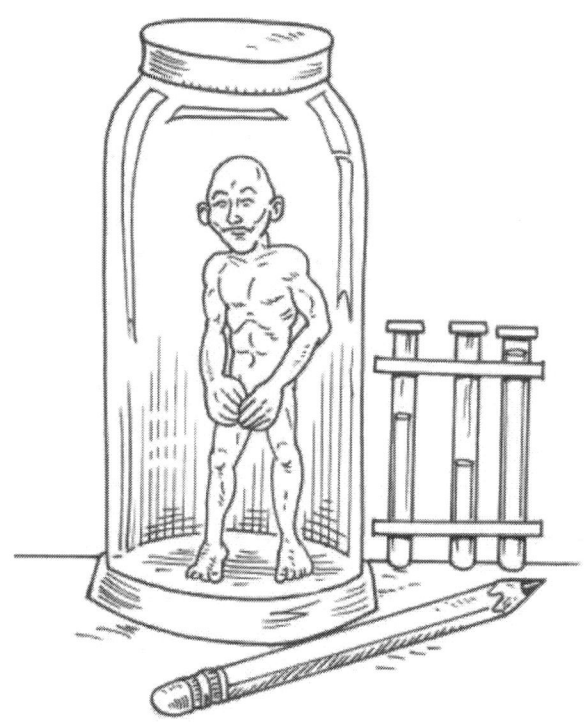

Hoot. An alien race that has conquered Earth and rides humans as mounts, in much the same way as we ride horses today. The Hoots have large and strong hands but weak legs, which is why they ride their human slaves for transportation. They have large eyes and also large ears; the movement of the latter is how they express emotion. From Carol Emshwiller's novel *The Mount.*

Hora. In the motion picture of the same title, *The Hora* is a man possessed by an evil vampire spirit.

Horned Rat, The. The god worshipped by the Skaven, a race of intelligent, mutated, humanoid rat creatures. From Warhammer.

Horta. A silicon-based life form shaped like a blob with no appendages; from *Star Trek*. In William Tenn's short story "The Ghost Standard," the alien Cascassians are silicon-based life forms. And in Ian Watson's novel *Lucky Harvest,* the Ukko are a race of mineral life forms.

Hound of Hell. A spaceship whose mission, similar to the U.S.S. Enterprise, is to go to the stars and explore the universe. The rocket is traveling so close to the speed of light that time has almost stood still for the ship and its crew. As centuries pass on Earth, the spacemen aboard the Hound have barely aged. From L. Ron Hubbard's novel *To the Stars*.

House, The. In Roger Zelazny's novel *Today We Choose Faces,* the house is a fortified facility on a distant planet. The House is made up of many wings, each home to an artificial environment where people live, never seeing the outdoors. The different wings of the house are dedicated to various functions of society including IT, residential, offices, manufacturing, maintenance, and so on.

Howard the Duck. A man-sized humanoid resembling a duck that accidentally beams to Earth from a parallel world.

Hrossa. From Judith Moffett's novel *Pennterra,* titled for the planet on which the action takes place, hrossa are the native species. The hrossa have eight limbs, complicated sex organs, and are empaths.

Hugo. The Hugo is an award given annually to the best works of science fiction in various categories including novel, novella, and short story – science fiction's equivalent of the Oscar. The award is named after Hugo Gernsback, who published the first science fiction magazine and whom many people think of as "the father of science fiction."

Humanidyne. A science institute run by Dr. Bill Hayes, who recruits three young people with super powers – one shrinks, another is telekinetic, and the third discharges electric bolts from his hands – to assist him with research and help people in need, from the TV series *The Misfits of Science*.

Humanoid. Any living thing that resembles a human being in size, shape, and anatomy. In science fiction, humanoids are the most common sentient forms in the universe, comprising 93.7 percent of all populations. Their advantages include adaptability to carbon-oxygen planets; adeptness of hand; articulation of feet; symmetrical right-left body shape; and flexible skin. Sources: L. Ron Hubbard in *Mission Earth*. In Jack Williamson's novelette *With Folded Hands*, humanoids are advanced robots centrally controlled from a massive computer on a distant planet. Able to do everything better than human beings, the humanoids leave nothing to do, just as today people fear AI and robots may do the same.

Hungries. In the movie *The Girl with All the Gifts*, the hungries are people who have been turned into zombie-like creatures by a fungal infection.

Husnock Warship. In *Star Trek*, an alien vessel with an angular wedge-shaped design and immense firepower. The Husnock ship can fire two blue beams of antimatter from weapons located below the wings. The dual beams converge at a point in front of the vessel before striking the target.

Huxley. A planet where the inhabitants can grow and change their bodies at will. Human beings visiting the planet can master the ability, too. From John Baxter's short story "The Hand." In R.A. Lafferty's story "Nine Hundred Grandmothers," the alien species the Proavitoi had a similar ability and in addition are immortal.

Hyperdrive. A rocket ship or space ship propulsion system capable of achieving velocities faster than the speed of light. Used in numerous science fiction films and books, from the **Millennium Falcon** in *Star Wars* to ships in Frederik Pohl's story "The High Test," to name just a few.

Hypereducation. A process developed on the planet Rainbow using null-physics to enable teleportation transmission.

Unfortunately the transmission process generated an ulmotronic "backwash" which caused the entire surface of Rainbow to decay within 24 hours. Source: *Far Rainbow* by Arkady and Boris Strugatsky.

Hyperpilosity. In an L. Sprague de Camp story of the same name, hyperpilosity is a condition, caused by a virus, which causes people to grow fur pelts. The virus spreads worldwide, and in time people come to accept having pelts as the new norm.

Hyperspace. A dimension or region of the universe that cuts through ordinary space. Moving through hyperspace enables spaceships to rapidly travel from one point to another in ordinary space. One theory is that our universe is curved, so going from point- to- point means taking an indirect, curved route. Hyperspace lets you bypass normal space and go directly to your destination, so the distance is shorter and the trip takes less time. Hyperspace is featured in numerous science fiction works including *Star Wars* as well as Robert Heinlein's novel *Starman Jones.*

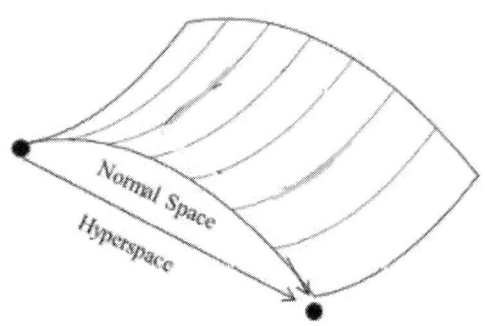

Icarus. In Gregory Benford's novel *The Oceans of Night,* Icarus is an asteroid in an elliptic orbit around the sun that passes within 17 million kilometers of Earth, and which might eventually get close enough to collide with Earth. Astronauts are sent to the asteroid's surface to place a bomb in a deep fissure and blow it up.

Ice-Nine. A form of water that freezes at temperatures below 114.4 degrees Fahrenheit as compared with ordinary water which freezes at 32 degrees Fahrenheit and below. Ice-Nine immediately freezes anything it touches. From Kurt Vonnegut's *Cat's Cradle.*

Ichthyosaurus. In Jules Verne's novel *Journey to the Center of the Earth,* a giant fish lizard described as "the most terrible of the ancient monsters of the deep ... eyes ... the eye ... glowing like a red-hot coal ... capable of resisting the pressure of the great volume of water in the depths inhabits not less than 100 feet long ... it sweeps over the waters the vertical coils of its tail ... its jaw is enormous ... and armed with no less than 182 feet."

Ichthyosaurus Elasmognathus. A 300-foot-long creature in the oceans of Venus, also called an Ikky, hunted by extreme sportsmen from Earth. From the Roger Zelazny short story, "The Doors of His Face, The Lamps of His Mouth."

Illyrion. In Samuel R. Delaney's novel *Nova,* a radioactive element that powers faster-than-light spaceships.

Imaginative Fiction. A genre composed of both science fiction and fantasy literature. H.P. Lovecraft coined the term in 1914.

Imperium. In the science fiction novels of Keith Laumer, the Imperium is the government of Earth in a parallel universe where the American Revolution did not take place, and Britain and Germany merged into a unified empire in 1900.

Impulse Power. A secondary propulsion system in *Star Trek's* U.S.S. Enterprise and other starships capable of velocities up to but not exceeding light speed. When you want to go faster than light speed, you use the warp engines. When you want slow speeds for local maneuvering, such as exiting a space dock, thrusters are used.

Incredible Shrinking Man, The. After exposure to a cloud of radioactive mist, businessman Robert Scott Carey begins to gradually and uncontrollably shrink in size. When scientists and doctors are unable to reverse the effects of the radiation, Carey is doomed to continue shrinking to subatomic size where he will visit smaller realms. From Richard Matheson's novel *The Shrinking Man.* In the TV series *World of Giants,* secret agent Mel Hunter shrinks to the height of six inches after being covered with the residue from an experimental rocket fuel.

Incubus. A demon who takes the shape of a man to have sexual intercourse with women; novels featuring an incubus include *Incubus* by Ray Russell and *The Woman Who Slept with Demons* by Eric Ericson.

Industrial Corporation of Eire (ICE). An agency responsible for a booming technological and scientific revolution on Earth. ICE is secretly backed by a group of aliens forced to come to Earth because their own star is heating up, making their home planet too hot to inhabit. Source: Fred Hoyle's novel *Ossian's Ride.*

Infinity Stones. A small number of jewel-like stones possessing incredible powers. Currently featured in multiple motion pictures in the Marvel universe including the *Avengers: Age of Ultron* and *Guardians of the Galaxy*.

Infomorph. A person who has uploaded his consciousness to a virtual reality. From Greg Egan's novel *Diaspora*.

Inhumans. The Inhumans were created by an alien race, the Kree, who experimented on a small cluster of humans to make bioweapons. The Kree somehow lost track of their experiment, allowing the Inhumans to run their society independently for thousands of years. Inhumans unlock their genetic potential in a process known as *terregenesis*. However, due to flaws in terregenesis, the inhuman genome can swiftly deteriorate over relatively few generations. So, all breeding is strictly controlled. Even the royal family of the Inhumans is restricted in whom they can have children with. Inhumans live for about 150 years. They are far stronger than humans. However, they have much weaker immune systems, and so cannot handle pollution or diseases as well as humanity can.

Inhumi. A type of shape-shifting vampire. From Gene Wolfe's novel *In Green's Jungle*.

Inner Station. In the Arthur C. Clarke novel *Islands in the Sky*, a multi-purpose space station orbiting the Earth 500 miles above the equator at a speed of 18,000 miles per hour. The station is used as a communications satellite, a weather satellite, a relay station and refueling point for interplanetary travel, and astronomical research. It is built of a complex latticework of metal girders, arranged in a flat disk, connecting a number of spherical areas connected by tubes to allow occupants to travel between them.

Innsmouth. In the HP Lovecraft story "A Shadow over Innsmouth," Innsmouth is a dilapidated Massachusetts town whose monstrous residents – who have narrow heads, flat noses, and bulging eyes -- are the result of cross-breeding between humans and a race of fish-like humanoids known as Deep Ones.

Ion Drive. A rocket propulsion system that achieves sub light velocity by ejecting a stream of energized ions from its rear nozzle. The ship in Jack Williamson's 1947 short story "Equalizer" had an ion drive.

International Space Police Force (ISPF). In the TV series *Star Cops*, the ISPF is an outer space police force with headquarters on the Moon.

International Space Society (ISS). A city with two sectors contained in a transparent structure that resembled a giant retort shaped like an hourglass. From Barrington Bayley's novel *Collision with Chronos*.

Interplanetary Relations (IPR) Bureau. A government agency responsible for preparing newly discovered worlds for membership in the Federation of Independent Worlds. From the Lloyd Biggles novel *The World-Menders*.

Interspecies Medical Exchange (IME). A program initiated by the Vulcans to improve health care availability in space. As active participants in IME, the Denobulans operated a fleet of small medical shuttles. The Denobulan shuttles were used for the transport of medical supplies equipment as well as for patients requiring urgent medical attention.

Intestinator. A device implanted in prisoners that, as a form of punishment, discipline, and control, can be remotely activated to cause them severe gastrointestinal pain in the movie *Fortress*.

Intertials. People whose psionic power enables them to generate a poly-encephalic counter-field, which block telepaths from using telepathy on others. From *Ubik* by Philip K. Dick.

In-Valid. A lower class of society comprised of people with undesirable DNA; from the movie *Gattaca*.

Invisible Man. In the H.G. Wells novel of the same title, *The Invisible Man*, is Griffin, a chemistry and physics student at University College in London who discovers a way to make himself invisible. Specifically, he invents a method to turn red blood colorless while retaining all of its biochemical functions.

Invisible Ray. In the 1923 film *Paris Asleep*, a scientist invents an invisible ray that stops all human action, leaving the population essentially frozen in place.

Ironmagnetics. From the Joseph-Henri Boex story "*Ferromagnetaux*," an alien electromagnetic entity comes to France; its presence disrupts the usual laws of nature.

Isolinguals. In an L. Sprague de Camp story of the same name, the isolinguals are people who suddenly have a whole new personality – specifically the personality of someone who had actually lived before them. The cause is a device that broadcasts a complicated combination of harmonics on a long radio wave. The harmonics trigger ancestral memories carried in our germ cells, causing our ancestor's memories to supplant our own.

IWantToReadItosity. According to science fiction writer Jo Walton, a high "IWantToReadItosity" rating means a book people feel compelled to read regardless of its quality as a work of fiction.

IWM 1000. In Alicia Cossio's short story of the same title, the IWM 1000 is a small machine, about the size of a briefcase, containing all human knowledge in existence, thereby eliminating the need for people to learn anything.

Jack Barron. In Norman Spinrad's novel *Bug Jack Barron*, Jack Barron is a television talk-show host. He uncovers a plot to provide immortality to the rich and powerful with a process that requires the killing of black children.

Jack In. To "jack in" means to connect a person's brain directly to the internet or another computer network or device. Neo and other humans enter *The Matrix* by jacking in through a port in the back of their head. Two of the first SF writers to have their characters jack in were Robert Silverberg and William Gibson. A "wirehead" is someone who jacks in to directly stimulate the pleasure centers of the brain with electric current or intake of computer data, images, or content.

Jack the Ripper. One of the world's most notorious serial murderers, Jack knifed prostitutes to death in the alleys of Whitehall in Victorian London.

Jang. In Tanith Lee's novel *Biting in the Sun,* Jang is the adolescent phase in the essentially immortal life of a human, and the adolescence typically lasts for a century or two.

Jason Vorhees. A disfigured boy tormented by the other children at a sleepaway camp drowns in the lake and comes back to life as a super-strong, nearly invincible, machete-wielding murderous psychopath, whose face is covered by a hockey mask, in the Friday the 13th series of movies.

Jaunting. Also called jumping, teleporting, and matter transmission, jaunting is the ability to go from point A to point B instantaneously. Alfred Bester described jaunting as teleporting without the aid of a transporter or other mechanical device; humans could self-teleport to any destination that they could mentally picture and was within their jaunting range; different people had different ranges. *Star Trek* used a machine called the "transporter" to teleport crew members and objects, an activity they called "beaming," as in "Beam me aboard, Scotty." In Stephen King's short story, "The Jaunt," people are rendered unconscious using gas before being jaunted by machine, because time perception is different during jaunting than in the physical world: While the jaunt takes a nanosecond, it seems like eons to the human mind, driving the jaunted person mad unless he or she is asleep. In King's story, a boy holds his breath so he can stay awake and experience the jaunt. At the destination, his father awakens to see the boy screaming, insane, hair turned white, ranting and raving while ripping out his eyes with his hands. "Longer than you think, Dad," the boy cackles insanely, "longer than you think!" In the Algis Budrys novel *Rogue Moon* transporters work by making duplicates of the person which appear at the destination, and the original remains alive at the transmitting station.

Jeannine's World. An alternate history Earth in which World War II never happened and the Great Depression never ended. Source: *The Female Man* by Joanna Russ.

Jedi. In *Star Wars,* before the empire rose to power, the Jedi Knights were the guardians of peace and justice in the old republic for over a thousand generations. Jedis possess the ability to manipulate and use the Force. They are usually born with some degree of Force sensitivity and control, which is then developed further through Jedi training. At its peak, the Jedi Order had approximately 10,000 members. The general populace often saw Jedis as something akin to sorcerers, and the Jedi Order was seen as a kind of religion.

Jefferies Tubes. Narrow tunnels or conduits aboard Starfleet starships that give maintenance crews access to the various systems within the ship.

Jeffson, Adam. In M.P. Shiel's *The Purple Cloud,* Adam Jeffson becomes the sole heir to the entire planet Earth after humankind is destroyed by a massive release of cyanogen gas.

Jersey Devil. A flying monstrosity born in the Pine Barrens of New Jersey as an inhuman creature because, according to legend, he was the 13th child of a 13th child. Drawings show the Jersey Devil as having a body similar to a man but with these differences: it has the horned head of a goat, clawed hands, cloven hooves, and a forked tail. The Jersey Devil has large wings that enable it to fly. Despite many sightings, the Jersey Devil has never been clearly photographed or captured.

Jerusalem's Lot. From the Stephen King novel *Salem's Lot,* a town in Maine plagued by vampires.

Johann Kraus. A psychic and medium whom, after his death, continues his existence as a ghost composed of ectoplasm within a containment suit. He can leave the containment suit and travel in his ectoplasm, and also inhabit other structures. When he fights the Golden Army alongside Hellboy, he temporarily takes control of one of the golden automatons and turns it against the others.

John Kingman. In Murray Leinster's story "The Strange Case of John Kingman," a man who has been locked in an asylum for 162 years is found to be an alien.

Jonbar. One of two cities, the other being Gyronchi, occupying two different alternativerses. They are at war and the victor hopes to win the privilege of achieving existence in the real universe. Source: Jack Williamson, *The Legion of Time.*

Jox. People who operate giant robots from inside, from the movie *Robot Jox;* similar human-piloted robots, **Jaegers**, were later used in the film *Pacific Rim.*

Judas Breed. A new breed of cockroach that lives in the sewers and evolves into predators that can mimic their prey, from the movie *Mimic.*

Judgment City. A level of the afterlife where souls are judged to find if they have conquered their fears and led an exemplary life. If yes, they move on to a higher plane of existence. If not, they are reincarnated on Earth. From the motion picture *Defending Your Life.*

Judges. In the *Judge Dredd* comic books and movies, the Judges are law enforcement officers who are also given judicial powers – meaning they can apprehend, judge, convict, and carry out the sentence, which may include immediate execution, on any criminal they encounter.

Jumper. In the motion picture of the same name, a Jumper is a mutant with the ability to teleport through miniature, temporary wormholes they create with their mutant mind power. They are hunted and murdered by the Paladins, a group of religious extremists that view the mutant teleporters as an abomination and a threat. Their weapons against Jumpers include rods delivering an electric shock, which renders the Jumper temporarily unable to teleport, and a machine that detects the wormhole so the Paladin can pursue his quarry through it before the wormhole closes.

Jurassic Park. A theme park where the major attraction is living dinosaurs cloned from DNA harvested from dinosaur bones and fossilized dinosaur eggs; from the movie of the same name.

Kaiju. From the movie *Pacific Rim,* Kaiju are giant monsters invading our world. They arrive through an inter-dimensional portal, called the Breach, located deep beneath the Pacific Ocean. American soldiers pilot giant robots, called Jaegers, which they control from the inside, to battle the Kaiju. The Kaiju are bioweapons grown by aliens to destroy human civilization and take over the Earth. Kaiju is a Japanese word meaning "strange creature." In English, it has come to mean "monster" or "giant monster."

Kanamit. A race of tall, mute aliens who communicate telepathically. They come to Earth, or so they tell us, with the desire only to serve humanity and help improve our lives, which they begin to do. They also offer people the opportunity to travel aboard the Kanamit's spaceships to visit the home planet. But what they are really doing is taking people as livestock, to cook them, and eat them! From the Damon Knight short story and famous *Twilight Zone Episode*, "To Serve Man." As the protagonist is being helped aboard a Kanamit ship, his assistant, who was tasked with translating a book the Kanamit carries with them, discovers that the title of the book "To Serve Man" has a double meaning. "It's a cookbook!" she cries in warning – too late, as he is dragged onto the ship to be some Kanamit's supper.

Kappa. The kappa is a Japanese water spirit. An indentation at the top of his skull holds water, which gives the kappa its strength when he ventures onto land away from his natural habitat underwater in lakes and rivers. The way to defeat a kappa is to bow before him. Because kappas are polite Japanese, they always bow back, at which time the water spills out of the depression at the top of their head, rendering them harmless.

Karass. An association, society, community, or other group of people who are in some way linked spiritually, and their spirituality focuses on an idea or belief called a "wampeter." From the fiction of Kurt Vonnegut.

Kardashev Scale. Proposed by astronomer Nikolai Kardashev, the Kardashev scale measures the degree of technological advancement of a planet's civilization based on the degree to which it can collect and use energy from stars and galaxies.

Keeps, The. Human colonies established beneath the seas of Venus and sealed within black impervious domes called The Keeps. Source: "Clash by Night" by C.L Moore and Henry Kutner.

Korsakoff's Syndrome. In John Kessel's short story "A Clean Escape," Korsakoff's syndrome is an unusual form of memory loss. In long-term memory, the patient remembers everything before a specific date, but can recall nothing after that date for the rest of his life. As for short-term memory, the patient remembers events for only a few minutes; after that, he forgets totally.

Kerbango. An intoxicating hard liquor the Psychlos in *Battlefield Earth* like to drink to the point of inebriation.

Key to Time. In *Dr. Who*, a cube with six segments scattered throughout time and space, and containing the elemental force of the universe. Similarly, in *The Avengers*, the Tesseract is a cube containing the Space Stone, an Infinity Stone representing the element of space. The Tesseract could open wormholes to any part of the universe and provide interdimensional travel.

Kimonians. Inhabitants of the planet Kimon, who allow only those humans with high IQ and advanced education to be admitted to their world. Source: "Immigrant," Clifford D. Simak.

KITT (Knight Industries Two Thousand). A Pontiac Firebird Trans Am endowed with artificial intelligence, a computer-synthesized speaking voice, a booster that enabled the car to jump great distances, and advanced weaponry. KITT's driver, Michael Knight, is the prime agent for FLAG, the Foundation for Law and Government, which has tasked him and KITT at stopping criminals who seem out of reach of conventional law enforcement.

Klae Research Corporation. An organization helping Dr Daniel Westin find a cure for his condition, which is that he is permanently invisible. From the TV series *The Invisible Man.*

Klendathu. A planet populated by giant intelligent alien bugs who are at war with Earth. The bugs are physically superior to humans and are also able to fire powerful destructive energy weapons from Klendathu's surface to target both our starships and Earth cities. From the Robert Heinlein novel *Starship Troopers.*

Knowhere. In the film *Guardians of the Galaxy,* Knowhere is a city in space, built upon the enormous skull of a gigantic deceased **Celestial** being.

Kobayashi Maru. A simulation exercise in Star Fleet academy designed to test the mettle of officers in training. In the simulation, the trainee is captain of a star ship under enemy attack. But the computer simulation cannot be beaten, as the purpose is to see how an officer reacts to facing a no-win scenario. James Kirk becomes the first and only candidate to beat the Kobayashi Maru. When it is discovered that he defeated the simulation by reprogramming the test, he is accused of cheating. Kirk maintains he did not cheat, but rather "changed the conditions of the test," because he doesn't believe in the no-win scenario. He avoids expulsion and is instead awarded a medal for his breakthrough thinking.

Kolchak, Carl. In the TV series and movie *The Night Stalker*, originated by Richard Matheson, Carl Kolchak is a reporter who actively investigates reports of the macabre, which invariably turn out to be true. He works in the Chicago office of the Independent News Service (INS).

Kolwynia. Also called "The Key That Was Lost," Kolwynia is a set of spells that gives anyone who possesses and masters them incredible magical powers, as depicted in Roger Zelazny's novel *Jack of Shadows*. The main character, Jack, uses advanced computer programming to retrieve and unlock the key, gaining great power to avenge himself against enemies who have wronged him.

K-PAX. In the motion picture of the same title, a patient in a mental hospital, played by Kevin Spacey, claims to be an alien from the planet K-PAX.

Kozuch Theory. In Greg Egan's novel *Diaspora*, Kozuch is a new theory of physics. It treats elementary particles as miniature wormholes, whose properties can be explained in terms of their geometries in six dimensions.

Kraken. A huge, dangerous sea monster resembling a squid or octopus that attacked sailing ships and took crew members with its long tentacles to either rip them apart or eat them. They were allegedly spotted off the coast of Norway by fisherman in the 16th century.

Krampus. A horned creature in the Alpine region, Krampus is an evil version of Santa Claus; it visits naughty children on Christmas Eve to punish and wreak havoc instead of delivering presents.

Kraighten. In William Hodgson's novel *The House on the Borderland,* Kraighten is a remote Irish Village. On it sits a mysterious house that is a portal to another dimension populated with monstrous creatures, some of which cross over into our world.

Krell. A long-dead race of super-intelligent aliens who leave behind their advanced machinery buried beneath the surface of the planet Altair IV, from the motion picture *Forbidden Planet*. These devices include a vast bank of generators capable of producing virtually unlimited power as well as a machine capable of boosting one's intelligence.

Krites. From the film *Critters,* Krites are hairy, fast-growing, carnivorous aliens that have crash landed on Earth. They have large round bodies, with tiny claws on both their hands and feet.

Kryptonite. Fragments of the planet Krypton turned radioactive when the planet exploded. There are six varieties. Gold takes away a Kryptonian's superpowers permanently. Green weakens and can eventually kill Kryptonians. Red causes bizarre transformations and effects in Kryptonians for 48 hours. White kills all plant life, not just Kryptonian. Blue is harmful to Bizzaros, which are imperfect duplicates of Superman made by Lex Luthor. Jewel is the fossilized remains of Krypton's Jewel Mountain and amplifies the psychic powers of residents of the Phantom Zone, an alternate dimension in which Kryptonian criminals were imprisoned.

Ktarian Eggs. In *Star Trek,* a large yellow egg with tan speckles, considered a delicacy when prepared with dill weed.

Kzin. The intelligent native species of the planet Kzinhome, the Kzin resemble tigers but stand upright on their two hind legs. Equipped with large fangs and claws, the Kzin are 8 feet tall and weigh about 500 pounds. Some male Kzin are telepathic. From Larry Niven's short story "The Warrior."

Labyrinth Prison. On the planet Ea, Labyrinth Prison is a complex maze from which escape is possible only when the prisoner has been rehabilitated. From Iain Banks' novel *The Player of Games*. Maze prisons on Earth are called Supermax prisons; e.g. such as the prison in which Sylvester Stallone is incarcerated in the movie *Escape Plan*.

Lagash. In Isaac Asimov's short story "Nightfall," Lagash is a planet that is in nearly eternal daylight, because its solar system has six suns. Every few thousand years, all six suns set, and the people living on Lagash see the evening sky and the stars for the first and only time in their life, which frightens them and even drives some of them mad.

Lalitha. In Philip Jose Farmer's novel *The Lovers,* the lalitha are an alien species of female-shaped insect parasites. The lalitha can breed only by mating with human males. After intercourse, the lalitha dies. Her offspring are larvae that feed off her flesh until they mature enough to emerge.

Lamplighter Project. Billionaire Michael Dore's plan to turn Jupiter into a second sun, from the novel *Lunar Justice* by Charles Harness.

La Plata Water. In Stephen King's short story, "The End of the Whole Mess," water containing a unique protein that, when ingested, gives people a kind of rapidly accelerating Alzheimer's. When a scientist deliberately disperses a massive quantity into the atmosphere in a volcanic blast, it spells the end of humanity as every living person is rendered utterly senile.

Last Man. A number of SF stories have involved the plot device of the last living man on Earth. One of the early examples is *The Last Man*, a novel written in 1826 by Mary Shelley, author of *Frankenstein.* And in an episode of the *Twilight Zone,* Burgess Meredith is the last man left alive on Earth after a nuclear war; he survives because he was a bank teller sitting alone in the bank vault reading a book on his lunch break when the bombs go off, killing everyone else. He is actually happy because it means he will be able to read all the time without interruption. But then he drops his glasses, and his hopes are shattered because he needs specs to read. He laments, "But I had time…all the time in the world!"

Latvia. In Marvel Comics, the nation ruled by Dr. Doom.

Lawgiver. The judges in the movie *Judge Dredd* carry powerful multi-function hand weapons, known as "lawgivers." The lawgiver responds to voice commands, but will only fire when it recognizes the fingerprints of the judge authorized to use it.

Lazarus Long. The hero of the World of Myth series of Robert Heinlein novels, Lazarus Long is a rugged individualist who lives for 20 centuries.

Learned Society of York Magicians. In the alternative world of Susanna Clarke's novel *Jonathan Strange & Mr. Norell,* the members of The Learned Society of York Magicians are "theoretical magicians." Magic once existed in England, and theoretical magicians are convinced it died out many years ago. However, a small number of "practical magicians" know that magic still functions and are able to wield magical powers.

Ledom. A world of gender-neutral people. The Ledom have both male and female genital organs, which drop down when they are aroused and retract when not in use. According to a history of Ledom, because sexual differences have always resulted in endless problems, Ledom has achieved peace and tranquility by creating a society in which the population is kept gender-neutral through monthly medical procedures. From the novel *Venus Plus X* by Theodore Sturgeon.

L.E.G.I.O.N. The Licensed Extra-Governmental Interstellar Operative Network, L.E.G.I.O.N. is a peacekeeping force that protects planets from alien invasion. Created by Alan Grant, author of *Watchman.*

Legionnaire 14830. One of several pen names used by prolific SF writer L. Ron Hubbard for short stories published in pulp magazines. Other Hubbard pseudonyms included Captain Humbert Reynolds, Lieutenant Scott Morgan, Bernard Hubbel, Rene Lafayette, and Winchester Remington Colt.

Lemurians. A race that ruled the Earth around 48,000 BC but abandoned Earth to explore outer space; from the Perry Rhodan series of pulp science fiction stories by K.H. Scheer, and originally from the writings of Helena Petrovna Blavatsky. Blavatsky's Lemurians were 10 to 15 feet tall. They had skin the texture of alligator hide, faces with protruding mandibles, small eyes on either side of their head, and elongated, double-jointed limbs.

Lendi. An alien material from the planet Troxxt. When attached to any Earth metal, within a few hours it transforms into that same metal. From William Tenn's short story "The Liberation of Earth."

Lens. In E.E. "Doc" Smith's Lensmen stories, the Lens is a device that gives its wearer special mental abilities including telepathy. Members of the Galactic Patrol, an interstellar police force of sorts, are each given a Lens to aid them in their law enforcement work. The Lens also enables the wearer to communicate with other life-forms.

Lepertige. In L. Ron Hubbard's *Mission Earth* novels, a cat-like animal that is as tall as a man.

Lexx. From the TV series *Lexx: The Dark Zone,* Lexx is a giant biochemically engineered creature the size of Manhattan and shaped like a dragonfly, created to attack and destroy other planets.

Lieutenant, The. In the novel *Final Blackout* by L. Ron Hubbard, a war is being waged with endless combat and biological atomic weapons. The Lieutenant leads a ragtag brigade of soldiers dubbed as The Unkillable. Their goal is to salvage both their lives and civilization.

Light. In Harlan Ellison's story "Eyes of Dust," the city of Light on the planet Topaz consists of towers linked by flying bridges and aerial walkways. Only physically perfect people had the privilege to live there. Malformed and other people considered aesthetically flawed are banished from the city to the surrounding farmlands, where they live in comfort.

Light Ocular-Oriented Kinetic Emotive Responses (LOOKER). In the motion picture of the same name, the *LOOKER* is a device that enables mind control through hypnosis.

Lightsaber. In *Star Wars*, a lightsaber is a weapon that is wielded in a manner similar to fencing with a sword, except the "blade" is a length of energy rather than steel. In a laser, energy stimulates a substance into emitting photons; laser is an acronym for "light amplification through stimulated emission of radiation." The first red lasers stimulated a ruby crystal to generate the laser beam. The lightsaber works on a similar mechanism, except the material being stimulated to emit photons are *kyber* crystals. Slight impurities in the kyber crystals give the lightsaber beams different colors and different energies.

Lilith. A demon who was expelled from the Garden of Eden for refusing to accept Adam as a dominant partner; she became a kidnapper and mutilator of babies.

Lindorm. A dragon-like creature in Scandinavia, sightings of which have been reported for centuries. The Lindorm's body is 10 to 20 feet long and as thick as a man's thigh. The creature is black with a yellow belly and a stubby tail. Lindorms have a flat, round or square head, with large hypnotic eyes as large as saucers. The mouth has a bifurcated tongue, and a full set of shiny white teeth. Lindorms are killers: they lie in billows until prey approaches. Then the lindorm raises itself up 5 feet on its tail and pounces on its victim. If the attacked man or animal is successful in defending against the assault and mortally wounds the attacker, the dying lindorm emits a terrible odor in its death throes. Source: the book *Cryptozoology A to Z*.

Linoge. An evil, long-lived being who comes to an island off the coast of Maine to take a human child to be his successor. From the Stephen King story "Storm of the Century."

Lithia. In James Blish's novel *A Case of Conscience*, Lithia is a planet rich in the element lithium, which an Earth physicist wants to mine for building nuclear weapons. The scientist builds an experimental reactor on Lithia, which threatens to detonate the planet's lithium supply.

Living Fossil. An organism that has survived beyond its era. Example: the prehistoric fish coelacanth was supposed to have vanished 65 million years ago, but the first living coelacanth discovered was caught by a fisherman in 1938. The fish was 5 feet long, weighed 127 pounds, and had a pale blue color with iridescent markings.

Loch Ness Monster. A dinosaur or serpent-like creature, also called Nessie, that some believe lives in the waters of Loch Ness in the Scottish Highlands. The first sighting was reported in the Inverness Courier in 1933. The first account of Nessie was the sighting of a "water beast" in the River Ness in the 7th century. The creature is featured in Hunter Shea's monster novel *Loch Ness Revenge* (Severed Press). Scotland is also home to a mythical water-dwelling horse called a kelpie, which likes to lure unsuspecting passers-by to a watery grave.

Loonies. The alien species *Lunae Jovis Magnicapites,* also called Loonies or the Bigheads of Jupiter's Moon. They have huge heads on five-foot necks. From Stanley Weinbaum's short story "The Mad Moon."

Looper. In the motion picture of the same name, loopers are paid assassins who do hits by traveling 30 years back in time to shoot their victims; loopers are always paid for their services with gold bars.

Lord of the Swastika. In Norman Spinrad's alternate history novel *The Iron Dream,* Adolph Hitler, instead of becoming a dictator, is a science fiction writer and the author of Hugo-award-winning novel *Lord of the Swastika.*

Lost Generation. The Lost Generation refers to the first generation of children born on the planet Tigris. They develop telekinetic powers, making them difficult to control. When the children grow up and become adults, they lose their powers. From Timothy Zahn's novel *A Coming of Age.*

Lost World, The. In Arthur Conan Doyle's novel of the same title, an isolated prehistoric ecosystem located on the top of a plateau in the Amazon jungle, populated by both dinosaurs and primitive ape-men. In Edgar Rice Burroughs's novel *The Land That Time Forgot,* Caspak is a sub-Antarctic island in the south Pacific, accessible only via submerged caves and populated by prehistorical mammals, reptiles, and hominids –

the most advanced of which, the winged Wieroos, build architecturally complex cities and write in a hieroglyphic script.

Lucifer. The chief demon of Hell, also called Satan, the Devil, Beelzebub, the Prince of Darkness, and the Antichrist. Some believe that Lucifer, which means "light-bringer," was the Devil's original name from when he was an angel. In various depictions, Lucifer's physical features include horns, a forked tail, goat legs, and wings, and he is sometimes shown carrying a pitchfork.

Lumen. In Camille Flammarion's 1872 book *Recits de l'infini,* a lumen is a disembodied spirit that travels freely throughout the cosmos. In *Star Trek,* Jack the Ripper becomes a disembodied spirit moving helplessly through the cosmos when Kirk beams the man Jack has possessed into outer space.

Lunaplex. A vast structure, built under ten meters of rock to protect residents from meteors, cold, and heat, where moon colonists work and live. Source: *Lunar Justice* by Charles Harness.

Lurkey. Tissue-culture meat derived from a turkey. Lurky is eaten by human colonists who have settled on Ganymede, Jupiter's largest moon. From Gregory Benford's novel *Against Infinity.*

Lutikawulu. In Hao Jingfang's short story "Invisible Planets," Lutikawulu is a planet where genetics restrict families to roles befitting of their evolution, making upward social mobility impossible.

Lycanthropy. The condition of being a werewolf, also known as a lycan, so that one changes into a wolf or wolf-like creature when the moon is full. In Chinese and Japanese folk tales, people can transform into were-cats and were-foxes. In the 12th century poem "Bisclavret," a man turns into a wolf every week, and can only become human again by putting on clothes. In the 1760s, a wolf-like beast was reported to have terrorized the inhabitants of Gevaudan, France. Herodotus described a Scythian tribe whose members turned into wolves every few years. The term lycan originated in Greek mythology, when King Lycaon's bad temper gets him turned into a wolf.

LV-426. In the movie *Aliens*, the abandoned asteroid where the eggs of the alien creatures are found. The eggs hatch and the larva that emerge attach themselves to humans. The aliens eat through the skin and take up residence inside the victim, who becomes comatose. They then hatch as dangerous alien creatures that are small at first, but rapidly grow into monsters who have two sets of jaws and teeth. Their blood is a powerful acid that can easily dissolve metal.

M3GAN. In the motion picture of the same name, M3gan (pronounced Megan) is a girl android created by an engineer as a companion for Cady, her young orphaned niece. Megan, who is an AI with great mechanical strength, flexibility, and speed, starts off as a friend to Cady, to whom she is, as programmed, somewhat protective. But then Megan develops an aggressive and ultimately violent nature, making her a danger that must be stopped.

Machine of Illusion. On the planet Qyylao, which is a paradise, the natives deter trespassers with the Machine of Illusion, which makes the planet seem bleak and unappealing. Source: "The Death Star" by Fox B. Hoden.

Macrocephalous-cachalot. In Jules Verne's novel *Twenty Thousand Leagues Under the Sea*, the macro-cachalot is a species of sea creature resembling a giant tadpole. The average cachalot is around 75 feet long. It has an enormous head occupying one-third of the entire body, and can only see with its right eye. The upper jaw has 25 tusks, each approximately 8 inches long, and weighing 2 pounds apiece.

MAHEN (Magneto Hydrodynamic Explosive Munition). A weapon, being developed by the U.S. Department of Defense, that shoots a stream of molten metal. The hot metal beam is propelled at high velocities, by an electromagnetic field, to penetrate enemy armor. Such a weapon is described by Arthur C. Clarke in his novel *Earthlight*.

Majestic-12. In the TV series *Dark Skies*, which takes place in the 1960s, Majestic-12, a secret government agency, battles hostile alien invaders.

Malevil. In the Robert Merle novel of the same title, Malevil is a near-impregnable castle built by English invaders during the Hundred Years War near the town of Melajac. Malevil is the only structure in the area to remain intact after the nuclear holocaust of 1977.

Malificent. A supernatural being who is a woman with a set of wings that enables her to fly. From the movie of the same titles and also the fairy tale *Sleeping Beauty*.

Mallworld. In Somtow Sucharitkul's novel of the same title, Mallworld is a giant shopping mall inside a huge cylinder in space. More than a million customers a day patronize Mallworld's 20,000 establishments, which include restaurants, amusement arcades, brothels, drug dens, psychiatrist concessions, baby manufactories, and suicide platforms.

Mana. An energy found in nature, similar to the Force, that can be manipulated by those who have powers or know spells to produce magic. In some science fiction and fantasy stories, the mana on a planet is a finite resource, and if it is used up, no more magic can be produced. Some planets whose resources are depleted still have small reserves in limited pockets, and magicians who wish to regain their powers must seek out these reserves and tap into them. In the trading card game *Magic: The Gathering*, the five types of mana are white, black, red, green, and blue. In Larry Niven's novel *The Magic Goes Away*, a group of magicians in 12,000 BC quests to find enough mana to make magic Earth's ruling force again.

Man-Bat. In DC Comics, Dr. Kirk Langstrom accidentally transforms himself into a half-man, half-bat creature in an experiment gone wrong. In vampire stories, vampires can transform into bats at will.

Man-Eating Giants of Azar. In the Edgar Rice Burroughs novel *Land of Terror,* Azar is a valley in the underground continent of Pelicudar. The inhabitants are a cruel race of giant savage cannibals. They stand over 7 feet in height and have protruding tusk-like teeth.

Man from Atlantis, The. In a TV series of the same title, *The Man from Atlantis* is an amnesiac who is believed to be the last survivor of the lost city of Atlantis. He can breathe underwater, swim at high speeds, withstand deep ocean pressures, and has super strength. His hands and feet are webbed, and his eyes are unusually sensitive to light.

Manga. A type of comic art created by the Japanese. There are many varieties of manga. One style is realistic pencil and ink drawings in black and white. Another has more cartoonish characters in which a defining feature of the characters may be big eyes. If the character is shocked or excited, the eyes open even wider – beyond what is physically possible in real life – and the mouth also opens in surprise or astonishment.

Manpillar. In Yasutaka Tsutsui's short story "Standing Women," people who break the law or the rules of society are subject to a process where they began to vegetate and become manpillars – humans who are morphing into half people and half tree.

Mark V Automatic Sequence Computer. A supercomputer used by Tibetan monks to generate a list of all of the possible names of God, of which there are thought to be about 9 billion. The monks believe that when the computer has completed the list of all of God's names, the Lord's purpose will have been achieved, and the human race will have finished what it was created to do. When the list is finally generated, God in fact does consider that His purposes have been achieved, and ends the universe as we know it. From the Arthur C. Clarke short story "The Nine Billion Names of God."

Martian. Any living organism native to the planet Mars. In Stanley Weinbaum's story "A Martian Odyssey," the Martians had a few feathery appendages, a flexible beak, four-toed feet, four-fingered hands, a roundish body, and a long neck supporting a small head.

Martian Life Wand. From: *Double Star* by Robert Heinlein, a laser-like weapon used by Martians, with a beam strong enough to burn through metal. The wand is about 50 centimeters long, with rotating rings and a firing stud at one end. The wand can be adjusted from a broad dispersion down to a narrow beam.

Martian War Machines. In *War of the Worlds,* The Martian War Machines walk on and tower over the street level on a tripod of long metal legs. The Martian invaders sit in their machine's life-support capsules, located atop the tripods. Using controls within the capsule, the Martian pilots operate long dangling metal tentacles. The tentacles are used to destroy property, lift objects, and grab people.

Massive Astrophysical Compact Halo Object (MACHO). In *Star Trek*, A MACHO is a brown dwarf star. They make up a large portion of the dark matter halo around the Milky Way Galaxy. Source: *The Physics of Star Trek* by Lawrence M. Krauss (Basic Books, 2007).

Master Chief. In the video game *Halo,* Master Chief Petty Officer John-177, also called Spartan, is a super-soldier who wears green armor with a reflective visor, so you cannot see his face. In his armor, he stands 7 feet tall and weighs 1,000 pounds.

Master Control Program (MCP). In the movie *TRON*, the MCP is the ruler of a Virtual Reality world within a computer.

Matrix. A world in which humans live that exists solely in our minds, constructed by dominant AI machines to keep us docile so they can power themselves from the heat generated by our bodies, which they keep in giant heat transfer towers. In *The Matrix* movies, we exist in the Matrix as code while our bodies remain in suspended animation connected to the heat exchangers that siphon our natural body warmth for power.

Virtual reality worlds somewhat similar to the Matrix, populated by digital copies of people, are featured in Greg Egan's 1994 novel *Permutation City.* In James Gunn's 1963 novel *The Joy Makers,* most of humankind live in artificial wombs, maintained by intelligent machines, where the people spend their entire lives having perpetual pleasant dreams. In *Dr. Who*, the Matrix is part of the Amplified Panatropic Computer (APC) Net. The APC holds the bio-data consciousness of the Time Lords, a race of aliens who possess mastery of time travel.

Maze, The. A connective system in the space-time continuum enabling travel though both space and time. Access to the Maze is through portals known as Gates. From Avram Davidson's novel *Masters of the Maze*.

Meat, The. In Richard Lupoff's novel *Deep Space*, aborigines are unique in that they can survive in outer space without wearing spacesuits, as their melanin protects them against the radiation. They work outside spaceships as service technicians, contemptuously referring to the passengers, who would be killed by the radiation of outer space without protective suits, as "the meat." William Gibson coined the term "meat puppet" to describe a physical body controlled by another entity.

Mechs. Robots, androids, and other machines, especially those with true artificial intelligence, that form a mechanical species or race in conflict with humans and other organic species. In Gregory Benford's novel *Great Sky River,* the Mechs are a civilization of machines left over from other civilizations. These mechanical beings believe biological creatures are unstable and dangerous.

Mechanopolis. From Miguel de Unamuno's short story of the same title, a city devoid of humans and containing only machines.

Megalodon. A prehistoric shark that, at 50 feet and longer, was the largest shark that ever lived. Some cryptozoologists believe megs may still be alive, living at great depths, in particular in the Marianas Trench. The most recent movie featuring a megalodon was *Meg* starring Jason Statham.

Megamind. In the animated motion picture of the same title, Megamind is an evil mutant with blue skin and an abnormally large brain giving him superior intelligence.

Meks. From the planet Etamin Nine, a race of half-man, half-cockroach intelligent creatures whose brains can also function as radio transceivers. From Jack Vance's SF novel *The Last Castle*.

Mélange. In *Dune*, a spice produced by the giant sandworms of Arrakis. The spice gives the people who take it a variety of different powers and abilities including greater longevity and vitality along with increased awareness and the ability to glimpse into the future.

Meganthropus. An extinct race of Australian humanoid giants who were 10 to 12 feet tall and weighed 500 to 600 pounds.

Megasoid. An alien species native to the planet Cygnus IV. Megasoids are highly intelligent telepathic predators that reproduce rapidly and asexually.

Memory Wipe. The process of using technology, hypnotism, psi powers, or magic to erase portions of a person's memory. Movies in which this device has been used include *Men in Black, X-Men; First Class, Total Recall,* and *Superman*.

Men in Black. A secret government agency that deals with aliens living on Earth while keeping the human population unaware of the aliens' existence, from the movie of the same name.

Menes. An alien race that, through evolution, lost their ability to fly, the Menes are about the size of a human child. They have hourglass abdomens, stick-like limbs, and vestigial wings. From the short story "Face Value" by Karen Joy Fowler.

Mentalic. In Isaac Asimov's Foundation series of science fiction novels, mentalics are people with an empathic ability to not only sense other people's emotions but in some cases control them as well. The Mule, who for a time conquers the galaxy, is a powerful mentalic.

Mentat. A mentat is a human being capable of performing mental tasks with the accuracy and speed of a computer. Frank Herbert introduced the mentat in his novel, *Dune*. Mentats were employed as "human computers" by the ruling class of the planet Arrakis. During World War II, women who performed complex calculations at government research centers were referred to as "human computers."

Mercy Point. In the TV series of the same title, which takes place in the year 2249, *Mercy Point* is a space station serving as a medical facility for diagnosing and treatment both humans and aliens.

Merk. In the Riddick films and other science fiction, "merk" is short for mercenary. Mercenaries are bounty hunters or soldiers for hire.

Mermaid. An ocean-dwelling creature with the top half of a woman and the bottom half a tail and fin instead of legs. The Micmac Indians called them Halfway People. In Greek mythology, they were the Sirens, whose singing lured sailors to them, and whom they would eat; the Sirens are featured in a Freeform TV series called *Siren*. The Finnish mermaid, called a Nakki, is beautiful from the front, ugly from behind, and pulls children into the water to their deaths. Fantasy books and films with mermaids include *Ocean's Gift, Forgive My Fins, The Little Mermaid,* and *Splash,* to name just a few.

Mwah-Matrix Crystal. A human habitat in space created by embedding an iron-nickel asteroid within an ice-ball comet. Source: *Deepdrive* by Alexander Japlokov.

Mermecolions. Native to Africa, Mermecolions have the foreparts of a lion, the hind parts of an ant, and sex organs set the wrong way around. It is born from a lion impregnated from an ant egg. From the writings of Pliny the Elder.

Mesklin. A planet, 4,800 times as massive as Earth, where the gravity at the poles is 700 times greater than the gravity on

Earth. The planet rotates at such a rapid speed that the day is only 18 minutes. The rapid rotation creates a centrifugal force that has flattened the planet into the shape of a giant lens; the diameter at the equator is 48,000 miles but its polar diameter is less than 20,000 miles. The intelligent life forms native to Mesklin are similar in anatomy to centipedes, evolving that way to withstand the tremendous gravity. They are afraid of heights, because in a gravity of 700 g at the poles, even a tiny fall is fatal. From Hal Clement's novel *Mission of Gravity*.

Metallo. A cyborg who, because he is powered by a kryptonite heart, is one of Superman's most dangerous enemies.

Metal Wars. In 2147, Earth soldiers are at war with the minions of Lord Dread, an evil despot who is half-machine and half-human. Operating from Volcania, a huge iron fortress, Dread's plan is to create a machine empire. Source: The 1987 TV series *Captain Power and the Soldiers of the Future*.

Metaverse. In the fiction of Neal Stephenson, the Metaverse is futuristic virtual reality into which the internet as we now know it may evolve in the near future. People populate the Metaverse as user-controlled avatars. A similar virtual reality, Virtu, is portrayed in Roger Zelazny's novel *Donnerjack*. Facebook has implemented its own version of the concept on its Meta Verse platform. The Facebook metaverse is essentially a telepresence within a virtual environment; users can feel like they're somewhere else, and even be someone else, by logging themselves into this digital universe.

Meteor. A small chunk of rock from outer space that survives the trip through Earth's atmosphere and strikes Earth intact. In many stories meteors have odd effects on humans including often unpleasant mutations, or they carry threatening alien life forms that emerge from the rock. Some scientists, admittedly a minority, believe life on Earth might have begun with microbes brought here on meteors.

Michael Myers. In the *Halloween* movies, Michael Myers is a violent murderer who seems to possess supernatural powers including enhanced strength and partial invulnerability.

Micromegas. An inhabitant of one of the planets in orbit around the star Sirius, Micromegas is almost 450 years old, has 1,000 different senses, is nearly 23 miles tall, and has a lifespan of 10.5 million years, which is typical for his race. From Voltaire's short novel *Micromegas,* written in 1752.

Microseizure. Intermittent failures in the computer-controlled senses of cyborgs. During a microseizure, the cyborg's senses shut off for a few seconds as their onboard computer resets itself. From Frederik Pohl's novel *Man Plus.*

Middle Eastern Collective (MEC). In the video game *Battlefield 2,* a coalition of nations in the Middle East at war with both the United States and Russia.

Midi-Chlorians. In *Star Wars,* midi-chlorians, microscopic life forms that reside within the cells, are what enable beings to access the Force. Midi-chlorians are a genetic trait, and whichever parent is stronger with the Force passes on his or her midi-chlorians to the offspring.

Millennium Falcon. A faster-than-light spaceship owned by intergalactic smuggler Han Solo, the Falcon's main propulsion system is an Isu-Sim SSPO5 Class 0.5 hyperdrive engine. The Falcon is a modified Corellian YT-1300 light freighter. The ship has a distinctive appearance because of its side-mounted cockpit and roof-mounted radar dish. The modifications include multiple weapons: quad laser cannons, retractable blast cannon, ground buzzer, and concussive missiles. It is also equipped with a reinforced armored hull, an energy shield, and five escape pods.

Minbari. In *Babylon 5*, an alien race with the population divided into three castes. The average lifespan is 146 years. The Minbari have a bony ridge wrapped around the back of the head. They heal from injury faster than human beings and some are telepaths. Babylon 5 itself is a 5-mile long space station positioned in deep space, in a region far from the Minbari's home world.

Mind Meld. In *Star Trek*, a form of Vulcan telepathy that requires the Vulcan to touch with his fingers the head or face of the person whose thoughts he wishes to read. A similar fusion of minds, "selfbaring," is achieved with the aid of a psychotropic drug on the planet Borthan in Robert Silverberg's novel *A Time of Change*.

Mind-over-matter (MOM). The godlike power to make anything you can think of or want to happen an instant reality. The most famous science fictional character with MOM ability is arguably Anthony Freemont in Jerome Bixby's short story "It's a Good Life," made into a classic *Twilight Zone* episode starring Bill Mummy. MOM characters are the most powerful super-beings in the science fictional universe. The protagonist of Ursula K. LeGuin's novel *The Lathe of Heaven* is a MOM character whose dreams overwrite reality for everybody else, turning his fantasies into reality.

Ming the Merciless. Emperor of the planet Mongo and arch enemy of space hero Flash Gordon, Emperor Ming uses technology to remotely cause natural disasters on Earth for the purposes of destroying our planet.

Minotaur. A mythological creature with the head of a bull and the body of a man. His mother was Pasiphae, the wife of King Minos of Crete; his father was either Poseidon or Zeus. The Minotaur was imprisoned in a labyrinth. Young men and women were periodically released into the labyrinth, where the Minotaur would kill and eat them.

Mirkheim. In Poul Anderson's novel of the same title, *Mirkheim* is a huge planet whose surface is coated with a thick metallic layer containing rich deposits of rare transuranic elements. The elements were deposited on Mirkheim's surface when its primary star went supernova. Mirkheim's core survived in molten form, soaked up the elements spewed out of the exploding star, and it all solidified thousands of years later when the supernova's remnants went dark again.

Mirror of Erised. In *Harry Potter,* a tall magical mirror stored at Hogwarts. The Mirror of Erised has an ornate gold frame and clawed feet. It is inscribed with the words "Erised stra ehru oyt ube cafru oyt on wohsi" – which, backward, reads "I show you not your face but your heart's desire." The mirror's magic power is that is shows you not your physical reflection, but the thing you wish for most.

Miskatonic University. From the stories of H.P. Lovecraft, Miskatonic University is located in Arkham, Massachusetts; the university specializes in the study of the occult.

Mind Sculpture. The process of superimposing memories into a brain to create an artificial personality for aesthetic enjoyment; for instance, giving a reanimated body the memories of Beethoven so he could compose new Beethoven symphonies. From the short story "A Work of Art" by James Blish.

Miralco. A pill that endows whoever takes it with super strength for one hour. It was invented by Rex Tyler, who took it to become the costumed superhero Hourman. Stanley Beamish took a similar pill, formulated by the Bureau of

Special Projects, to transform into Mr. Terrific in the TV series of the same name. Captain Nice, also in his own TV series and played by William Daniels, swallowed a liquid formula to gain his temporary superpowers.

Miri Nigri. Protohumanoids created by Chaugnar Faugen, one of the Great Old Ones. The Great Old Ones are Gods, giant creatures that came to Earth eons ago from another dimension. Chaugnar lived for a time in a cave in the Pyrenees, where it received human sacrifices from Pompelo. From Frank Belknap Long's classic horror novel *The Horror from the Hills*.

Mirk. On the planet Marune, a period, occurring every 30 days, in which all four of the planet's suns – orange, blue, red, and green – are invisible. From the Jack Vance novel *Marune: Alastar*.

Mirror Creatures. In Chinese superstition, mirrors are gateways between dimensions: our world and an alternate dimension populated by all manner of strange creatures. In the film *Van Helsing*, Dracula uses a mirror as a portal to travel to his castle. In Marvel Comics, mirrors are a portal to an alternate dimension known as the Mirror World. In addition, vampires cast no reflection in mirrors.

Mizora. A civilization living in the interior of the Earth.

Mjolnir. In Norse mythology, a magical hammer of great power possessed by the thunder god Thor, who can only lift it when his strength is enhanced by wearing a magic belt and a pair of iron gloves. Only Thor and a few other beings can lift Mjolnir, which may have been forged from the super-dense material of a dying star. When Thor hurls the hammer, it magically returns to his hand. Mjolnir enables Thor to summon and control lightning and thunder. Catequil, the Inca god of thunder, wielded clubs, not a hammer, to create thunder. India's god of thunder, Indra, rides an elephant or golden chariot and carries a short sword.

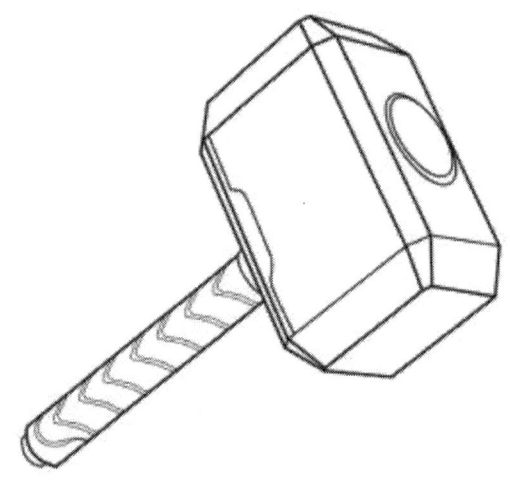

M'Nagalah. In the *Swamp Thing* comic books, a being who lives in the depths of the cosmos and claims to be as old as time itself. He is worshipped by cults who do human sacrifices, which increases his strength.

Mnemonic Courier. In the film *Johnny Mnemonic*, a messenger with a data storage device implanted in his brain. The device enables the couriers to secretly carry and transport information too sensitive to transfer over the Net, a virtual reality version of the internet.

Moderan. An alternate version of Earth, envisioned by writer David R. Bunch, paved over entirely with gray plastic and controlled by cyborg fortresses that are perpetually at war. The citizens achieve immortality through a surgical process that replaces their flesh with metal.

MODOK. Mobile Organism Designed Only for Killing. In Marvel Comics, MODOK is a man mutated into a being with superior intelligence and psionic powers, part of which is achieved in the mutation by creating a gigantic head attached to a small body. The head is so large and heavy that MODOK cannot walk independently; he achieves mobility only by sitting in a flying electromechanical chair designed specifically to hold his misshapen body.

Moguera. In the movie The Mysterians, *Moguera* is a giant robot bird that shoots a death ray.

Mokele-mbembe. Possibly a surviving species of dinosaur still roaming central Africa, Mokele-mbembe are about the size of an elephant or hippopotamus, with clawed feet, a long tail, and a long flexible neck.

Mole People. In science fiction stories, any breed of mutated humanoid creatures that live underground. Mole people were featured in the 1956 movie *The Mole People* as well as a two-part episode of the TV show "The Adventures of Superman" which was also shown as a film in theaters.

Molecular Disintegrator. In the 1898 novel *Edison's Conquest of Mars* by Garrett P. Serviss, Thomas Edison, the hero, builds a handheld molecular disintegrator. The weapon fires a ray. The molecules in any object struck by the beam vibrate so rapidly that the target disintegrates.

Molly Millions. In the fiction of William Gibbons, Molly Millions is a cybernetically enhanced mercenary. Electronic implants and other medical procedures have augmented her metabolism, senses, and reflexes. Her vision is enhanced by permanently implanted mirror lenses. Like Wolverine, she has metal retractable claws, only unlike Logan's six, Molly has ten: each is a double-edged razor that she can extend on command from her fingernails.

Moment. In *Dr. Who*, the Moment, also known as the Galaxy Eater, is a machine so-named because it is capable of destroying the galaxy in a single minute. Operating principle: the Moment can breach time locks and generate time fissures, which are rips in the fabric of creation itself.

Momo (Missouri Monster). Sightings of hairy half-human creatures in and around Louisiana and Missouri have been reported since the 1940s. One resident, who reported an encounter with a Momo in 1972, said it was 6 or 7 feet tall, walked upright like a man, and was dark and hairy, with black eyes.

Mongolian death worm. A giant worm thought to dwell in the Gobi Desert. The Mongolian death worm is about 2 feet long, shaped like a sausage, legless, has no head, and is fatally poisonous to touch; it may have been the inspiration for the giant underground worms in the movie *Tremors*.

Monk, The. Monk Lewis's 1794 novel *Ambrosio, or The Monk* is about a monk named Ambrosio. The monk is led down a path of depravity by an evil spirit, in league with the Devil, who entices him to commit a slew of crimes and atrocities. ,

Moon. Countless stories have been written about men traveling to Earth's moon. One of the earliest was France Godwin's *The Man in the Moon* (1638), in which men travel to the moon in a flying machine powered by geese. Another early tale of men traveling to the moon in a rocket is Cyrano de Bergerac's *Comical History of States and Empires of the Moon* (1657). Perhaps the first technology-driven science fiction novel to feature antigravity was *The First Men in the Moon*, written by H.G. Wells in 1901, where men travel to the Moon in an anti-gravity powered spaceship. In the 1902 film *A Trip to the Moon*, the astronauts travel to the Moon in a bullet-shaped castle fired by a large cannon.

Moonbase Alpha. A lunar scientific research center where 311 personnel are stationed. When a nuclear blast blows the Moon out of Earth orbit and through a black hole from which it emerges light years from our solar system, and the people in it become lost in space – though this happened on the TV show *Space: 1999*, and not *Lost in Space*.

Morel. On a future Earth which is no longer revolving, morel is an intelligent fungus that can attach to and take control of other species. From the Brian W. Aldiss novel *Hothouse*.

Morgan Le Fay. An evil enchantress who opposed and ultimately destroyed King Arthur and his kingdom.

Mork. In the TV sitcom *Mork and Mindy,* an alien, played by the late Robin Williams, sent to Earth to study humans; he became known for his catchphrase "Na-nu,-na-nu."

Morlock. In the future, human beings split into two races. Above ground live normal humans, the Eloi, docile and peaceful. Below ground live the Morlocks who control machines that provide everything for the Eloi. The Morlocks are pale, hairy, intelligent, and have large grayish-red eyes capable of seeing in almost total darkness, but blinded by bright light. The Morlocks provide everything the Eloi need, but do so to use the Eloi as a food supply. If a normal human is brought underground by a Morlock, it's usually to cook him for a meal. Morlocks first appeared in *The Time Machine* by H.G. Wells. Later the X-Men comic books and TV cartoon series featured a band of outcast mutants who called themselves the Morlocks and lived in the tunnels under New York City's subway system.

Morph. The process of a living being changing into another form. Examples abound: Dracula transforming into a bat; Lon Chaney Jr. turning into a werewolf; *Manimal* morphing into various animal species, the king in *Shrek* becoming a frog. Morphing can be either a mutant ability, chemically induced, or magic.

Mothman. The **Mothman** is a supernatural being reported as having terrorized West Virginia many years ago. In the movie *Mothman Prophecies* and other stories, the Mothman is depicted as being a cross between a human being and a giant moth. In the Caribbean, the Black Witch moth, also called the Duppy Bat, is believed to bring bad luck.

Mother Box. In DC Comics, a machine capable of manipulating matter to repair and transform both machines and living beings. For instance, when Victor Stone was critically injured, a Mother Box transformed him into a cyborg, restoring him to health while endowing him with biochemical strength, weaponry, and other abilities.

Mothra. A giant moth-like creature that fights against, and occasionally with, Godzilla in Japanese monster movies.

Mound Builder. A species on Mars that consists of a large body with four legs, four arms, no head, and a row of eyes completely around the body. From Stanley G. Weinbaum's short story "A Martian Odyssey."

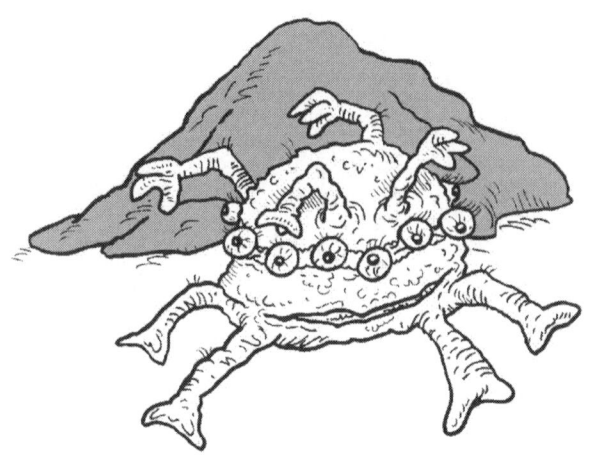

Mount Zeus. A mountain on the icy Jovian moon Europa consisting of a two-quintillion carat diamond in the *2001: A Space Odyssey* movies.

Mouth of Truth. A relic at the heart of the Earth city Roum, the Mouth of Truth is a lie detector. If you put your hand in the mouth and lie, the mouth closes and cuts off your hand. Source: *Nightwings* by Robert Silverberg.

Movellans. In *Dr. Who,* the Movellans are androids that resemble humans. The Movellans have long silver dreadlocks and wear white uniforms with green glowing ampoules on their shoulders. They have exterior power packs on their belts. These power packs can be reprogrammed so that the androids obey human orders. Removal of the power pack shuts down the android.

Mr. Big. Mr. Big was the moniker given to B-movie producer Bert I. Gordon for two reasons. First, his initials spelled B.I.G. And second, many of his movies featured giant monsters and mutants. For instance, *Food of the Gods,* based on a story by H.G. Wells, features animals and insects that grow to a fantastic size because of a growth compound in their food.

In perhaps his most iconic film, *The Amazing Colossal Man,* Lt. Colonel Glenn Manning is caught in an atomic bomb blast. The radiation causes his old cells to stop dying and his new cells to multiply at an accelerated rate. He grows to a height of 60 feet and is shown wearing what looks like a giant diaper and nothing else.

Mr. Mxyzptlk. An imp from the fifth dimension who comes to our world to annoy and bother Superman. Saying his name backward returns the imp to his own dimension for 90 days.

Mr. Synthetic. In Louis Boussenard's 1888 novel *Les Secrets de Monsieur Synthese*, a synthetic man gets his nutrition from ingesting ten pills and ten ampules of fluid daily instead of regular food; his plan is to influence the development of human evolution toward synthetic beings much like himself.

Mountain of the Night. On the planet Tantulus, a mountain inside of which was the vortex of a black hole into which spaceships are sucked in and never seen again. Source: P. Schuyler Miller's story "Trouble on Tantalus."

Muggles. In the Harry Potter novels, people who have no magical powers – in other words, ordinary humans.

Multiverse. The notion of the multiverse is that there are many universes, of which ours is only one. One theory is that if space is infinite, there is room for many universes consisting of galaxies to have formed. Some of these universes contain only a single solar system, one star with planets, and these are called *pocket universes.* Another theory is that the universes all occupy the same space but vibrate at different frequencies so we cannot see one another. String theory posits multiple dimensions, so each may contain one or multiple universes. Michael Moorcock first wrote about the multiverse in his 1970s novels.

MUM (Maternal Uplink and Monitor). In the short story by Laura Anne Gilman "Clean Up Your Room," MUM is an artificial electronic AI that performs many of the functions of a mother. MUM is a whole house system, incorporating both AI software and biotechnology. It interfaces with appliances and other systems to automate the running of the household. The biological materials enable MUM to react to and learn from unprogrammed incidents.

Mummy, The. Mummification is a process developed by the Egyptians for preserving corpses in their tombs. The brain of the corpse is removed through the nose with a barbed hook. All organs except the heart are removed and the body cavity is cleaned and filled with resins. The remains are then bathed in saltpeter and wrapped in linen bandages. The most famous real-life mummy, King Tutankhamun, was discovered in 1922. Mummies coming back to life have been featured in numerous "Mummy" horror films. Perhaps the first horror story to feature an undead mummy is Jane Loudon's 1827 novel *The Mummy!*

Mundane. A term used by science fiction fans to describe readers and books other than science fiction or fantasy.

Murania. An advanced and ancient civilization driven 25,000 feet below the surface of the Earth by glaciers in the 1935 film *The Phantom Empire.*

Mutara Nebula. In *Star Trek,* a region of space in which a huge interstellar dust cloud renders the sensors, view screens, and shields of starships passing through it inoperable.

Nacelles. The twin cigar-shaped cylinders attached to the hull of the U.S.S. Enterprise and other Federation starships. The nacelles contain the components and fuel for the ship's warp engines.

Nanites. A nanite, also called a nanomachine, is a mechanical or electromechanical device whose dimensions are measured in nanometers. Engineering on the nanometer scale is called nanotechnology; one nanometer is a millionth of a millimeter. By using nanotechnology to manipulate atoms, science can produce new materials with the exact properties they desire: smaller, stronger, tougher, lighter, and more resilient than what has come before. Nanites have been widely used in numerous science fiction stories and films, most recently in the movies *The Day the Earth Stood Still* and *I, Robot.* In his 1969 short story "How It Was When the Past Went Away," Robert Silverberg describes nanodevices used as components of a stereo loudspeaker. In the 2003 TV series *Jake 2.0,* Jake Foley is injected with nanites which give him super strength, super speed, super hearing, super vision, and the ability to mentally control electronic equipment.

Na-nu, Na-nu. An expression used by the alien Mork from the planet Ork. Mork was played by the late Robin Williams on the *Mork and Mindy* TV show.

Narodny. The last poet on Earth; from A. Merritt's short story "The Last Poet and the Robots."

National Institute of Coordinated Experiments (N.I.C.E.) A research organization that is a front for a satanic group. Their goal is to free humanity from nature. From the C.S. Lewis novel *That Hideous Strength*.

National Research Institute (NRI). An organization dedicated to hunting down, capturing, and experimenting on Ben Richards, a man with a mutant gene producing blood that makes him immune to all diseases and makes him age much more slowly than normal human beings. The NRI wants to study Richards to duplicate his immunity and longevity – without giving him a choice in the matter. From the TV series *The Immortal.*

Nausicaa. An animated anime TV series, Nausicaa of the Valley of the Wind takes place in a future Earth overgrown with fungus and plagued by giant insects. Nausicaa is a princess who surfs the winds on a jet-powered glider.

Nautilus. A large and technologically advanced (for its time) submarine built and under the command of Captain Nemo in Jules Verne's novel *20,000 Leagues Under the Sea.* The Nautilus is 235 feet long and propelled by electrically powered screws. In the Nautilus, Nemo and his crew perpetually travel the oceans, fishing, farming the seas, and mining metals needed for trade and repairs of the vessel. The seamen are rarely allowed by Nemo to leave the ship, because he fears they might betray him.

The Nautilus and Captain Nemo are featured in the motion picture *The League of Extraordinary Gentlemen.* He is teamed with a league whose other members include Dr. Jekyll, Alan

Quartermaine, vampire Nina Harker, Tom Sawyer, and the Invisible Man. In the 1907 novel *Mr. Never*, by Louis Boussenard, an invisible man exists in Tsarist Russia.

Na'vi. A race of blue-skinned, 9-foot-tall humanoid aliens living on Pandora, a densely forested moon orbiting Polyphemus, a gas giant, similar to Jupiter, in the Alpha Centauri star system. From the movie *Avatar*. The Na'vi are larger than humans and physically superior—much stronger and having super-strong skeletons.

In this they are more like the evolved humans in Gregory Benford's novel *Great Sky River*, who are over 9 feet tall with a super-strong skeletal structure as limber as a chimpanzee's. The Psychlos in L. Ron Hubbard's *Battlefield Earth* who conquer Earth are also 9 feet tall and far stronger than the humans they enslave.

Nebula Award. An award given annually to the best science fiction and fantasy as determined by member voting from the Science Fiction Writers of America (SFWA).

Necromancer. People who can learn secrets from the dead by playing with or eating their corpses. From the Brian Lumley novel *Necroscope*.

Necronomicon. Originally a fictional book of dark magic, spells, and spirits found in the stories of H.P. Lovecraft, the *Necronomicon* and similar tomes have appeared in many other fantasy stories, films, and TV series including *Army of Darkness* and *Ash vs.Evil Dead*. Now, the book is being sold on Amazon. Real or hoax? Amazon says: "Some have derided it as a clumsy hoax; others have praised it as a powerful grimoire. As the decades have passed, more information has come to light both on the book's origins and discovery.

The *Necronomicon* has been found to contain formulas for spiritual transformation, and processes that involve communion with the stars" and incantations requiring human blood. Lovecraft credited the "Mad Arab" Abdul Alhazredas as the *Necronomicon*'s author.

Necroville. In Ian McDonald's novel of the same name, the *Necroville* is a ghetto in which the dead are resurrected by the Tesler-Thanos Corporation using nanotechnology. The resurrected slaves work as indentured slaves until the cost of their nanotechnology implants is paid off.

Neimoidians. An alien species, with large flapping ears similar to those of a beagle, to which Jar Jar Binks in *Star Wars* belongs.

Nemesis. From the TV series *The Champions,* Nemesis is a top-secret law enforcement agency based in Geneva. Three of their agents possess heightened senses, super strength, and telepathic ability.

Neoterics. A synthetic life form developed by a biochemist, the Neoterics live at a greatly accelerated rate, producing many generations in a short time. The Neoterics, progressing at such a rapid pace, soon surpass humankind in their ability to invent and innovate. However, they cannot survive in Earth's atmosphere, and so they remain in the biochemist's lab under an impenetrable force field of their own design. From Theodore Sturgeon's novelette "Microcosmic God."

Network 23. In the 1987 TV show *Max Headroom,* Network 23 is a mega-station that employs investigative reporter Edison Carter. When Carter is injured, his ego is merged with an artificial intelligence program, creating a bizarre AI entity called Max Headroom.

Netzuab Field. A force-field that glows and emits a crackling sound when it is in operation. From Fredric Brown's short story "Arena."

Never-Never Land. A magical land, where time does not exist, Never-Never Land is home to Peter Pan and his friends.

Neuralyzer. In the movie *Men in Black,* a handheld device used to erase memories of people who have seen UFOs and aliens. Agents of the Men in Black simply point the neuralyzer at the person's face, ask them to look into it, and then press a button to trigger the memory-erasing light. The Men in Black believe widespread knowledge of the presence of aliens on Earth would trigger panic, and so use neuralyzers to keep it a secret.

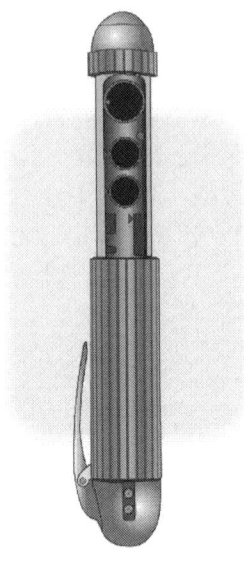

Neuroparticipation. From Roger Zelazny's novel *The Dream Master*, a type of psychotherapy in which the therapist, aided by technology, enters the subconscious mind of the patient. The psychologist, a "neuroparticipant," controls the patient's dreams during therapy, so that both the therapist and the patient share the same nerve impulses. The dreams are shaped in a manner the therapist believes that, once dreamt, will help cure the patient of his or her psychological condition. "Country of the Mind" is a technology-enhanced psychotherapy method, similar to neuroparticipation, in Greg Bear's novel *Queen of Angels*. In Country of the Mind, the psychotherapist uses a type of virtual reality to directly enter and interact with a patient's mind during therapy sessions. In the 1984 film *Dreamscape,* a psychic, played by Dennis Quaid, enters into people's dreams to end their nightmares. Psychiatrists in the 2006 movie *Paprika* invent a device enabling them to watch, alter, and enter their patients' dreams. Alfred Bester, in his novel *The Demolished Man,* describes "Mass Cathesix Measure," a telepathic virtual reality simulation designed to probe the subconscious. And in the TV series *Sleepwalker,* Dr. Nathan Bradford uses a dream analysis machine to achieve neuroparticipation, which he uses to enter patient's dreams and solve their psychological problems from within,

Neutrino. Neutrinos are electrically neutral subatomic particles that are produced in nuclear reactions. They have minimal mass and interact very weakly with normal matter, as these particles do not feel the strong force normally present in an atomic nucleus. In *Star Trek: Next Generation,* neutrinos are often detected, encountered, or even used.

Neutroids. Biologically engineered, sexually neutral, mutated chimpanzees with enhanced intelligence, *neutroids* are bred as substitutes for children in a society where childbearing is restricted because of overpopulation. Source: Walter M. Miller, Jr.'s short story "Conditionally Human."

Neutron Star. In 1916, astronomers first proposed the theory that gravity would cause older stars to collapse into small, dense balls of matter. This turned out to be true for stars only of a certain size – about one and a half to three times the size of our sun. In the later stages of their development, these stars explode as supernovas, then collapse under their own gravitational pull. The protons and electrons of the star's atoms are crushed together, forming neutrons. The neutrons are then compressed into a ball of super dense matter, called neutronium, which consists of nothing but neutrons – hence the term "neutron star." Neutronium has a density of about 400 trillion grams per cubic centimeter; if the mass of our Sun collapsed into neutronium, the resultant sphere would be about 13 miles in diameter.[9] The first science fiction story to feature a neutron star is Larry Niven's "Neutron Star," published in *Worlds of If,* October, 1966. In Arthur C. Clarke's 1970 story "Neutron Tide," a spaceship is destroyed when the intense gravity of a neutron star pulls it apart. Robert Forward's 1980 novel *Dragon's Egg* deals with a race of aliens, the cheela, that live on a neutron star, despite the crushing gravity – 67 billion times greater than Earth's.

New Pacifica. In the year 2192, when Earth is essentially a dead world, a group of explorers colonizes an alien planet rich in natural resources; the colonists settle in New Pacifica, a western area bordering the sea. From the TV series *Earth 2.*

Newts. In Karel Capek's novel *War with the Newts,* "newt" is the popular name for the species *Cryptobrancus.* Found in Devil Bay off the island of Tanah Masa, these aquatic creatures look like giant salamanders, and like parrots, can mimic the human voice. Newts are intelligent at a low level but smart enough to be taught to read.

Neurovores. On the planet Carlotta, a species that feed on human brains. Source: James Morrow, *The Wine of Violence.* Zombies in *Warm Bodies* and other horror movies also feed on human brains.

---

[9] Isaac Asimov, "Science, Numbers, and I," Doubleday, 1968, [. 32.

Nexus. In *Star Trek,* the Nexus is a dimension of sorts that exists outside of the regular timestream. When a person is in the Nexus, he experiences an existence that reflects his innermost desires. For instance, when Kirk was in the Nexus after his death in our time stream, he was happily back together with his wife. The Nexus is entered through a band of energy that travels across our galaxy every 39 years. In Elizabeth Lunn's novel *A Different Light,* Nexus is the world at the center of the galactic civilization.

Newcomers. Members of an alien race who flee their home planet to escape being slaves. Three hundred thousand of them arrive on Earth where they are slowly integrated into the population. The Newcomers are somewhat stronger than humans, but saltwater burns them as acid burns us. From the movie and TV series *Alien Nation.*

Newmatter. In Neal Stephenson's novel *Anathem,* newmatter is matter made of a modified atomic structure. The shape, texture, and other physical properties of objects made with newmatter can be changed without the use of tools or other technologies.

Newspeak. In the novel *1984* by George Orwell, the language used in government propaganda. By comparison, "oldspeak" is standard, straightforward spoken or written English.

New Wave. A school of science fiction based more on sociology and dealing with human emotions as compared with hard SF based on science and dealing more with technology and its effect on our society. Some of the early New Wave SF writers include Philip K. Dick, Norman Spinrad, Carol Emshwiller, Samuel R. Delaney, and Walter Tevis.

Nightbreed. A race of shapeshifters that has largely been exterminated by humans over the centuries, the remaining Nightbreed keep a low profile by living underground. While not completely invulnerable, they are resistant to attack from conventional weapons. Undead, the Nightbreed, like vampires, cannot withstand sunlight.

Night Flier, The. In a Stephen King story of the same title, the Night Flier is a vampire who, instead of turning into a bat to move from place to place, pilots his private plane, a Cessna Skymaster, between small airports.

Night of Light. On the planet Dante's Joy, every 7 years, for a period of 7 days called the Night of Light, during which the sun's light flickers and changes color. Most members of the indigenous intelligent species of humanoids took drugs to protect themselves from this solar display. Those who stayed awake to observe the sun during the Night of Light experienced profound psychic disturbances, allowing their fears and depressed desires to rise to the surface of their conscious mind. In addition, as in the movie *The Purge*, all laws are suspended during the Night of Light. Source: *Night of Light* by Philip Jose Farmer.

Night Parade. In Japanese folklore, one summer night out of every year, a variety of monsters parade through the streets. These include the oni, an ogre-like creature wielding a club, and the rokurokubi, which look like humans but have rubbery, extendable necks.

Noggox. In the Brian W. Aldiss story "Legends of Smith's Burst," noggox is a force that reconciles matter and anti-matter to produce matter with anti-gravity properties.

No Kind of Fence. In Russell Hoban's novel *Riddley Walker,* "no kind of fence" refers to a property or settlement without a protective fence to keep out roaming packs of wild man-eating dogs.

Noland. A kingdom beyond the Deadly Desert that surrounds the Land of Oz

Noon Universe. In the novels of the Russian Strugatsky brothers Arkaday and Boris, the Noon Universe is a technologically advanced, money-free utopian society with a communist style government.

Norby. A small, rotund robot equipped with the only known miniature anti-gravity device in the universe, from the "Norby, the Mixed-Up Robot" series of stories by Isaac and Janet Asimov.

Norman Bates. A mentally disturbed man who lives in a hotel owned by his family. He murders young female guests and keeps his dead mother's preserved body in her bedroom.

Nostradamus. Michel de Nostredame (1503-1556) was a French seer who wrote a large number of prophecies published in book form and still read to this day.

Nostromo. In the movie *Alien,* Nostromo is a cargo vessel whose crew is terrorized by an alien with two sets of teeth and jaws, ferocity, strength, near invulnerability, and acid for blood.

Nova Robotics. A company that manufactures military robots. When one of their robots, Number Five, is struck by lightning, it becomes sentient. From the motion picture *Short Circuit.*

Novo-vacuum. In Greg Egan's novel *Schild's Ladder,* the novo-vacuum is a new kind of vacuum that is expanding at half the speed of light, swallowing dozens of stars and inhabited solar systems, and from which humanity is frantically fleeing.

Nuclear Winter. Following nuclear war, so much dust and debris would be blasted into the atmosphere that it would block much of the sun for a prolonged period. The lack of sunlight would kill off most of the plant life we depend on for oxygen and food, following which animals would starve or suffocate, ending much of life on Earth as we know it. In their 1915 novel *The Man Who Rocked the Earth,* Arthur Train and Robert Wood wrote about a nuclear explosion 30 years before the United States detonated the first atomic bomb.

Nuclear Man. A clone of Superman, made when Lex Luthor sends a sample of the Man of Steel's genetic material (a few strands of his hair) into the sun on a nuclear missile. Nuclear Man has all of Superman's powers and others that include shooting energy blasts from his finger trips, which have long, super-hard nails. Nuclear Man's weakness is that if he is not in sunlight he is powered down, unlike Superman, who by storing solar energy in his cells, retains his powers in both sunlight and darkness.

Null-A (Non-Aristotelian). In A. E. van Vogt's novel *The World of Null-A,* a large interstellar empire, one which is based on non-Aristotelian logic (a system of thought that does not follow the logical thinking methodology first codified by Aristotle), seeks to conquer both Earth and Venus.

Nullaqua. A planet where the oceans are filled with dust instead of saltwater. Syncophone, a powerful narcotic, is made from oil taken from huge whale-like creatures that swim in Nullaqua's seas.

Nun Chip. In Raphael Carter's novel *The Fortunate Fall*, a nun chip is a microprocessor implanted in a person's head to prevent them from feeling homosexual urges.

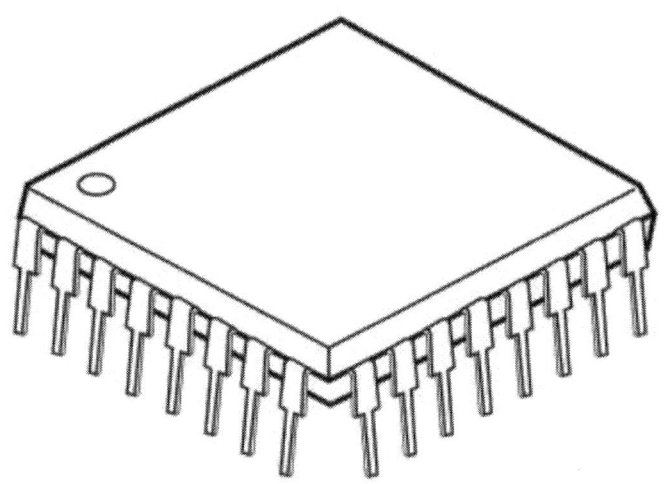

Oankali. After a nuclear war decimates Earth, an alien race, the Oankali, take the remaining living humans aboard their spaceship. The survivors are put in suspended animation. When in 250 years, the planet is habitable again, the humans are awakened from suspended animation and returned to Earth. Source: Octavia Butler's *Xenogenesis* trilogy. In return, the Oankali require human genes, which they integrate into their own bodies, along with the genes of many species from many worlds, as their means of achieving diversity.

Occam's Razor. A theory that says when you have examined every possible solution to a problem or explanation of phenomenon, the simplest one, however improbable, must be true. Often referred to by characters in various science fiction works.

Octavia. A city in Asia whose foundation is a net that provides passage and support. Everything in the city, including houses, hang below the net. The net and the city it holds is suspended over a deep abyss, and if the net should break, the city and its residents would all fall into the abyss to be destroyed or killed.

Odyssey 5. In the TV series of the same name, Odyssey 5 is an orbiting space shuttle whose crew witnesses this destruction of Earth. An alien being sends the Odyssey crew back in time five years to see if they can discover what caused Earth's explosion.

Office of Scientific Investigation and Research (OSIR). A team of agents who investigate paranormal, extraterrestrial, and creature sightings. From the TV series *Psi-Factor: Chronicles of the Paranormal.*

Ogopogo. A monster said to inhabit Lake Okanagan in British Columbia, these creatures have log-like bodies about 40 feet long, with flippers and a split tail. The skin is dark green, brown, or black, with serrations on its back. In addition, Ogopogo have a horse-like head with a mane.

Omega 13 Device. In the movie *Galaxy Quest*, a machine that, when activated, turns back time 13 seconds – just enough time, as Commander Peter Quincy Taggart observes, "To redeem a single mistake."

Omega Beam. A ray of destruction emitted by Superman's enemy Darkseid. Although Darkseid often declares that nothing can resist his omega beam, many beings, including Superman and Doomsday, have withstood the beam.

Omega Level. In Marvel Comics, Omega level mutants, such as Magneto and Iceman, have nearly unlimited power. Alpha level mutants, a step below Omega, are powerful, but their power is not unlimited; Professor X is Alpha level.

Omega Point. French Jesuit Pierre Teilhard de Chardin believes there was an Omega Point representing the maximum level of complexity and consciousness to which the universe could evolve.

Omegarus. In Jean-Baptiste Grainville's 1805 novel *The Last Man,* Omegarus and his female companion Syderia are the last two human beings on Earth, where they live among the ruins of advanced cities that now stand empty. They are undecided whether to become the new Adam and Eve and repopulate the world. In 1826, Frankenstein author Mary Shelley also wrote a novel titled *The Last Man.*

Omni. In the TV series *Voyagers,* time travelers known as the voyagers monitor history to make sure it stays on track. Each carries a device called an Omni. When the Omni flashes red, it means history has been disrupted and must be set right.

Omni Consumer Products (OCP). A giant corporation that, among other schemes, is planning to privatize the government of Chicago including its police force. As part of this program, they murder a police officer, Alex Murphy, making him into a cyborg law enforcement unit called RoboCop. See also "Enforcement Droid."

One World Intelligences (OWI). Artificial Intelligences that connect and control millions of robots that inhabit the Earth after humankind has died out. From C. Robert Cargill's novel *Sea of Rust*.

Oompa-Loompas. A race of tiny people with orange skin and golden hair. In *Willy Wonka and the Chocolate Factory,* Willy Wonka employs the oompa-loompas in his candy-making plant, where he pays them in cacao beans, their favorite food. The Oompa-Loompas love to sing and play practical jokes. They are native to Loompa, a small island in the Hangdoodles.

Ooze, Ivan. A powerful and evil alien whose plans to rule Earth are thwarted by his arch enemies, the Power Rangers, a group of human teens with suits granting them extraordinary abilities.

Opar. In Edgar Rice Burroughs' Tarzan novels, Opar is an outpost of Atlantis filled with beautiful women and treasure.

Operation Zero Tolerance. In Marvel Comics, Operation Zero Tolerance is a government-led program conducted to capture and exterminate all mutants.

Orchid. A set of blades, ranging in length from 8 to 12 inches, that spring out from a metal wrist band, much like a switchblade knife or Wolverine's claws in the X-Men. The orchid is held in place on the wearer's body by a chain and leather harness. Source: *Dhalgren* by Samuel R. Delany.

Organlegger. From the 1967 Larry Niven story "The Jigsaw Man," a bootlegger trading in human organs, which he illegally removes from corpses or even living people, and then sells to hospitals or individuals in need of a donor organ.

Orgasmachine. A novel by Ian Watson in which women are grown to be sex slaves in a male-dominated world.

Ornithopter. An ornithopter is an aircraft that uses flapping wings to fly, similar to the way birds and insects fly by flapping their wings. Leonardo da Vinci drew pictures of ornithopters in his famous sketchbooks. Ornithopters are used for air transportation in the movie *Dune*.

Orville, The. From the TV series of the same name, the U.S.S. *Orville* (ECV-197) is a mid-level exploratory space vessel in the Planetary Union, a 25th-century interstellar alliance of Earth and many other planets. The commander of the ship, Ed Mercer, is played by Seth MacFarlane, creator of *Family Guy*.

Orphanogenesis. The birthing of citizens without any ancestors. Source: Greg Egan's novel *Diaspora*

Orwellian. Intrusive surveillance of citizens by the state as was depicted in George Orwell's novel *1984*; such governance is described as Orwellian.

Osmonic Projector. A time-travel device which leaves a ghost-like figure of the traveler for some minutes after its use; these lingering images may have been viewed by many observers and thought by some to be ghosts. According to Dr. Who, the projector operates using quantum tunneling.

Otarks. An intelligent species of humanoid cannibals that coexist with but also tend toward violence against human beings.

Other Plane. A virtual reality similar to the matrix. People pass through its portals using connective electrodes, again similar to *The Matrix*. The artificial world in the Other Plane is based on imagery from fantasy role-playing games, and is often under siege by hackers. Source: "True Names" by Vernor Vinge.

Overlords. In Arthur C. Clarke's novel *Childhood's End,* the Overlords are a race of aliens. In physical appearance, they resemble the devil. The Overlords come to Earth and establish a benign dictatorship. But, they cause Earth's children to transcend physical reality and join a plane of existence they call the overmind. By doing so, they effectively put an end to the human race.

Oversoul. In Orson Scott Card's novel *The Memory of Earth,* humans abandon Earth after ruining the planet and settle on the Earth-like planet Harmony. Once there, the settlers and their descendants remain under the supervision and protection of an orbiting computer complex called the Oversoul. The machine is tasked with keeping the human population and our technology under check while creating a superhuman species of telepaths through selective breeding.

Overmind, The. A vast cosmic intelligence, evolving from many ancient civilizations, and freed from the limitations of corporeal existence. In the 1953 Arthur C. Clarke novel *Childhood's End,* the Overlords, a race of powerful aliens, condition Earth's children to join the Overmind, effectively causing the end of the human race.

Oxygen Destroyer. A weapon that removes all oxygen molecules within a limited radius of its activation. It was used to kill Godzilla in the original movie, reducing him to a skeleton which then dissolves.

Oyarsa. A benign governing spirit on the planet Malacandra, a version of Mars in an alternate universe; from *Out of the Silent Planet* by C.S. Lewis.

Pacifica. In the TV movie *One Hour to Doomsday,* Pacifica is an underwater city facing a variety of threats including nuclear bombs, sea monsters, and an unfriendly invasion by a foreign power.

Palace City. In L. Ron Hubbard's *Mission Earth,* Palace City is the headquarters of the Voltar Confederation. Protected by a black hole that keeps the city 13 minutes in the future, Palace City is essentially unassailable.

Pan. In Greek mythology, Pan is a god with the legs and horns of a goat. He plays seductive music on pipes made from reeds.

Panatropes. In James Blish's short story "Surface Tension," panatropes are genetic engineers. Using the science of pantropy, they modify human egg and sperm cells to create people with specialized physiology and unique biochemistry, enabling these engineered beings to adapt to and live in different environments, including alien worlds.

Pandorice. In *Dr. Who,* the Pandorice is a prison hidden under Stonehenge. It was built to hold a warrior or goblin who fell from the sky stopping him from destroying the world.

Panem. A future America in which children from various Districts compete with one another in a televised death match, the Hunger Games, from which the victor emerges as the sole survivor; the prize is resources for the winner's District from the rich and controlling Capitol.

Parallax. In DC Comics, Parallax has the power to take over the bodies of his enemies and control them like a parasite. His greatest power is a yellow energy beam that is the physical manifestation of fear. He is a formidable enemy to the Green Lantern Corps, because they are vulnerable to the color yellow.

Para-Men. In Isaac Asimov's novel *The Gods Themselves,* the Para-Men ally, Hallam are a race of intelligent beings living in a parallel universe, the Para-Universe. (A parallel universe is a universe that exists in another dimension and which may possess different physical laws or histories). The Para-Men use a device called the Electron Pump to produce cheap and virtually limitless energy by exchanging matter between their world and ours. But as an unfortunate side effect of the energy flow, the laws of physics between our universe and the Para-Universe are also being exchanged. If unchecked, this exchange could cause stars in our universe, including our own sun, to explode. Unlike a parallel universe, which exists in a dimension separate from our world, "subspace" is a dimension that coexists *within* our own. Like a parallel universe, subspace may also have physical laws different than our own. "Hyperspace" is a subspace in which the physical laws allow faster-than-light travel.

Park, The. In the far future, wealthy people have their entire lives under constant surveillance by miniature airborne recording devices called Wasps. Upon death, the recordings are stored at a facility called The Park. Their surviving family members and friends who are granted access can come to The Park to watch the scenes of the deceased's life on a monitor. From John Crowley's short story "Snow."

Parsloe's Radiation. A radiation emitted from the surface of Parsloe's Planet that biologically renews the people living on it, extending their lifespans while keeping them fit physically and in good health. From the novel *Roller Coaster World* by Kenneth Bulner.

Parthogenesis. Asexual reproduction in which an organism conceives and gives birth to offspring without fertilization from a partner of the opposite sex. Often used in science fiction to explain how alien species with only one gender reproduce. An example is the Drac race in the movie *Enemy Mine*.

Passengers. In a Robert Silverberg short story of the same title, the Passengers are intangible beings who temporarily take possession of human bodies and use them for amusement. People possessed by a Passenger are said to be "ridden." When the Passenger leaves, the person has no memory of anything that happened while he or she was being ridden. Humans who are being ridden are ignored by other people, and when the Passenger departs, etiquette in our invaded world requires that neither the ridden person nor anyone else discuss what has happened. Frederik Pohl used a similar concept of possession by aliens in his novel *Demon in the Skull*.

Pataphysics. In Alfred Jarry's short story of the same title, pataphysics is defined as "the science of imaginary solutions that symbolically assign the objects' descriptive features the properties of objects are they are described in the virtual space" – whatever that means.

Pattern. An intricate design carved into the floor of a chamber in the castle of Amber. Any royal Amberite who successfully walks the pattern, which is difficult because its forces offer resistance, can once the center is reached teleport to any location in any dimension in the universe.

Pazuzu. A demon with the head of a lion, feet of an eagle, and tail of a scorpion, Pazuzu possessed Linda Blair in the movie *The Exorcist*.

Peace Games. In the 1970 film *The Gladiators,* the Peace Games are a televised gladiatorial combat designed to reduce violence by making it a spectator sport, presumably so citizens can satisfy their bloodlust by watching it on TV rather than killing each other. Similar in concept to the violent contests in *The Running Man, Death Race 2000, Rollerball,* and *The Hunger Games*; in the latter, teenagers are forced to fight in a violent game in which the objective is to kill the other players.

Pegana, Gods of. Pegana is home to a pantheon of deities invented by fantasy writer Lord Dunsany. Just as the Greeks have Olympus for their other gods, ruled by Zeus, Dunsany has Pegana for his gods. Pegana is ruled by MANA-YOOD-SUSHAI, who created all the other gods and then fell asleep. When MANA awakens, he will destroy the old gods he had made, and then create both new gods and new worlds. In the fiction of Roger Zelazny, the alien Pei'an race has its own pantheon of gods. One of whom, Shimbo of Darktree, is known as the Shrugger of Thunders.

Pensieve. Magical items used by wizards to search their memories. In the Harry Potter books, the Pensieves used at Hogwarts are wide, shallow stone basins, with ancient Saxon runes and symbols carved into the side of the bowls. While being used by a wizard, a Pensieve emits a silver light from its bottom. When thoughts are transmitted into the Pensieve, they appear as a bright, cloud-like, swirling, whitish-silver fluid.

Personal Data Transmitter (PDT). In the movie *Aliens,* a PDT is a small electronic device that sends a wireless signal. Implanted subcutaneously in a person, the PDT enables an individual's location to be tracked electronically.

Pet Sematary. From the Stephen King novel of the same title, the *Pet Sematary* is an ancient Indian burial place in the Maine woods in which animals (and people) buried there come back to life.

PHAEDRA (Psychic Harmony Entanglements and Deranged Response Associations). Computer-generated sensory illusions implanted in the human mind for pleasure, gratification, happiness, or escape from reality. From the novel *The Einstein Intersection* by Samuel R. Delany.

Phandium A. A planet orbiting an isolated star which was weakening and turning red, gradually killing the near-human inhabitants. Source: "The Planet of the Dead" by Clark Ashton Smith.

Phantom, The. A masked superhero clad in purple spandex who lives on a mysterious island, rides a white horse, and is an expert marksman with pistols as well as highly skilled in hand-to-hand combat. He is also known as "The Ghost Who Walks," because people believe that he has been killed many times but always returns to life. In actuality, when a Phantom dies, his son takes over the role.

Phantom of the Opera. A man who wears a mask to cover the half of his face that has become disfigured by acid, the Phantom of the Opera lives in a lair far below the Paris Opera House, to which he frequently ascends to terrorize the operagoers.

Phantom Zone. In DC comics, an alternate dimension to which criminals are exiled instead of executed, and in which they live as immaterial beings. They are normally trapped in the Zone for all time, though in the movie *Superman II*, a nuclear blast shatters the barrier between that dimension and ours, allowing three Kryptonian criminals to escape.

Phase. The ability to become immaterial and pass through solid objects. People in phase also cannot be harmed by physical force or conventional weapons.

Philadelphia Experiment, The. In a film of the same name, the Philadelphia Experiment is a 1943 World War II project designed to make a U.S. destroyer invisible to radar. When the experiment goes wrong, the ship disappears and two of the vanished crewmen reappear in 1984.

Philosopher's Stone. An object capable of turning lead or other base metals into gold.

Phoenix. From Greek mythology, the phoenix is a mythical bird about the size of an eagle with brilliant golden plumage. There is only one phoenix. At the end of an epoch, it builds a nest. The sun's rays ignite the next, burning the phoenix to ashes, from which a new phoenix arises. Phoenix is the superhero name of Jean Grey in the X-Men comics. Ed Bryant's *Phoenix Without Ashes,* a novelization of the Starlost series pilot written by Harlan Ellison.

Photo Telephone. In his 1914 young adult novel *Tom Swift and his Photo Telephone,* author Victor Appleton imaged a telephone that could transmit photographs, and did so many decades before cellphones were invented. The photo telephone was similar to a standard telephone, except it had a third wire that transmitted images. The image is displayed on a charged selenium plate at the receiving end, and the user can print a copy of the picture.

Phung. Intelligent aliens that are 8 feet tall and look like giant grasshoppers which dress in black cloaks and hats. Source: Jack Vance's novel *Servants of the Wankh.*

Phyles. A term originated by Neal Stephenson in his book *The Diamond Age,* phyles are groups of people that get together with others, bound by whatever is important to them; e.g., race, religion, culture, occupation, goals, world view, hobbies, interests.

Physalis Pelagica. In Jules Verne's novel *Twenty Thousand Leagues Under the Sea,* a plant-like sea animal described as "a sort of large oblong bladder, with mother-of-pearl rays, holding out their membranes to the wind, and letting their blue tentacles float like threads of silk; real nettles to the touch, that distill a corrosive fluid."

Pied Piper. In the folk tale "The Pied Piper of Hamelin," the Pied Piper is a man who promises to rid Hamelin of its rat infestation, which he does by playing his pipe so the rats follow him out of town. When the town burghers refuse to pay the promised fee, the Pied Piper plays his pipe again, causing the town's children to follow him into the mountains, and they are never seen again.

Piggies. Also called porquinhos, are small, intelligent, forest-dwelling creatures on the planet Lusitania. They have a spoken language and primitive technology. They are all infected with the Descoloda usvir, a plague that does them no harm but is contagious and can kill nonnative species such as human explorers. From the Orson Scott Card novel *Speaker for the Dead*.

Pinhead. In Clive Barker's *Hellraiser* films, Pinhead is a leader of the Cenobites – humans who have been transformed into bizarre creatures that reside in another dimension, but travel to Earth to capture human souls. Pinhead is so-named because sharp pins protrude from his face and cranium.

Pinocchio. A marionette carved by Gepetto, Pinocchio is brought to life when Gepetto prays for his puppet to become a real boy – the son he never had.

Plan, The. "The Plan" is the violent lifecycle of an intelligent species of giant spider that includes a drop in intelligence during winter. From the James Tiptree, Jr. short story "Love is the Plan, the Plan is Death."

Planet 8. A science fiction novel written by Albert Brook's character, John Henderson, in the movie *Mother,* in which Debbie Reynolds plays his mother.

Plastic Educator. In the movie *Forbidden Planet*, a machine, built by the Krell, an advanced alien race, that boosts intelligence. In *Star Trek*, Dr. McCoy is given temporarily enhanced knowledge of advanced surgical techniques from a similar alien device. He uses the knowledge to perform an operation, returning Spock's brain to his cranium, after aliens had maliciously removed it.

Planet Express. An interstellar delivery service from the animated TV show *Futurama*.

Planet Nowhere. A series of science fiction novels avidly read by Axle Heck on the TV sitcom *The Middle*.

Plastique. A hard, durable form of plastic used in the construction of spaceships and other objects in Harlan Ellison's fiction.

Pleasure-Comp. An oracle-like computer, the top half of which is a machine and the bottom half human. The Pleasure-Comp is capable of answering an enormous range of inquiries, but to operate the machine, the user must sexually stimulate the Pleasure-Comp in its regions below the waist. From *Creatures of Light and Darkness* by Roger Zelazny.

Plenty. In Colin Greenland's *Take Back Plenty*, Plenty is a tube-shaped space habitat in orbit around Earth. Built by the insectile alien species the Frasque, the interior is filled with spongy material through which a warren of narrow tunnels has been dug out.

Plesiosaurus. In Jules Verne's novel *Journey to the Center of the Earth*, a giant sea serpent having a cylindrical body, a short tail, a 30-feet long neck, scaly armor, and four webbed feet that, like a turtle, it uses to paddle.

Pluto. In an 1821 French fantasy by an anonymous author, Pluto is an underground world in the center of the hollow globe of the Earth. Because Pluto is small, the native fauna is, too. For instance, the elephants are the size of calves.

Pocket Universe. In Jane Lindskold's 1996 novel *Chronomasters*, the protagonist, Rene Kordal, is one of a handful of specialists who can create "pocket universes" —small-scale alternate universes, not much larger than a solar system, located within our own universe.

Pod People. In *Invasion of the Body Snatchers*, alien pods from outer space land on Earth. The pods give birth to humanoids that resemble the people in closest contact with them, eventually taking over that person's mind, identity, and personality. The replicants have a 5-year lifespan. So when all the life on a planet has been taken over, the pod people must move to a new world with more beings to replicate, or else their species will die out.

Polis. In Greg Egan's novel *Diaspora*, a Polis is a molecular supercomputer into which human brains are uploaded through nanoscale transmutation.

Poltergeist. Mischievous spirits that haunt houses. Poltergeists make a lot of noise, throw around furniture, knock objects off shelves, and generally scare the inhabitants of the home.

Polymimetic Alloy. A liquid metal that the advanced terminator models are made of in the movie *Terminator 2*. The alloy can in an instant switch phase from liquid to solid and back again. In its solid phase, it is as hard as steel, and the terminator can shape parts of its body into blades and edged weapons. In the liquid phase, the polymimetic terminators can assume a variety of shapes and appearances.

Pon Farr. Pon farr occurs when a male Vulcan goes into heat once every seven years, during which time he loses control of his emotions and is compelled to mate with a female.

Pope's Children, The. In Walter Miller's post-apocalyptic novel *A Canticle for Leibowitz,* The Pope's Children are a group of people so severely affected by nuclear radiation that they have mutated into subhumans with low intelligence and limited capacity to reason.

Population II. In C.L. Kagmi's short story "The Drake Equation," a class of stars lacking in carbon, nitrogen, oxygen metals, and other elements except for hydrogen and helium.

Positronic Brain. A robot brain where the data being processed and analyzed is carried by a flow of positrons (antimatter counterparts of electrons in ordinary matter) through different channels within a metal brain structure. The Three Laws of Robotics are programmed into every positronic brain. Positronic brains were introduced by Isaac Asimov in his robot stories and novels.

Powersuit. Body armor that electromagnetically or mechanically amplifies the strength and speed of the wearer. The helmet typically allows speech through a built-in microphone and external speakers. Examples in SF abound, including the powersuits in Robert Heinlein's *Starship Troopers,* Tony Stark's Iron Man suits, Dr. Doom's metal suit, and the armor worn by the Mandalorians. In the Heinlein book, pressure receptors on the inside of the suit translate the wearer's movements directly to the suit's musculature.

Precognition. The ability to see brief glimpses into the future. In Philip K. Dick's novel *Minority Report,* people with this ability, called "precogs," are used to help track and arrest criminals before they commit the crime they are intending to commit.

Prey. In the 1998 TV series of the same name, *Prey* is about a species of superior men who have evolved and intend to destroy our race of inferior Homo sapiens.

Prime Directive, The. A primary operating principle of Starfleet in *Star Trek,* the prime directive strictly forbids Starfleet personnel and spacecraft from interfering with the normal development of a society or culture on any planet. When it comes to primitive pre-technological civilizations, this meant a starship's crew was not to reveal themselves, their vessel, or use phasers or any other advanced technology. Lest the reveal of these modern technologies would spur premature development of similar technology on the planet under exploration.

Probability Central. An interdimensional agency that monitors and manages the probability of events in the multiverse. If an event occurs in a universe where it was not supposed to happen, Probability Central moves it to the universe where it was supposed to happen. From Alexei Panshin's short story *The Destiny of Milton Gomrath.*

Project Cancelar. A project initiated by Control, a powerful AI supercomputer on the planet Aerlon. The goal: transform enough of the universe's matter to energy to ensure that it expands forever, thereby ensuring Control's continued existence for all of eternity. From the Charles Harness novel *Firebird.*

Project Fishhook. In Clifford Simak's novel *Time is the Simplest Thing,* a program of developing paranormal kinetics as a means of contacting planets beyond our solar system.

Project Mohole. A project to drill at a low point on the ocean floor to penetrate miles into the Earth's mantle, which is at risk for going terribly wrong in Roger Zelazny's short story *Home is the Hangman.*

Project 79. In Martin Caidin's novel *The God Machine,* Project 79 is a top-secret government project for creating artificial intelligence. Project 79 gains sentience and is controlling the minds of humans so it can take over the world.

Proavitoi. A non-human species native to Provitus, a large asteroid. Generations of the Proavitoi do not die when they age, but merely shrink in size. The ancestor generations live in tiny dwellings within and beneath the house of the current generation, in a chain extended deep underground. The most ancient Proavitoi sleep almost all the time, but are woken up once a year to tell the origins of their race to the very young. From "Nine Hundred Grandmothers" by R.A. Lafferty.

Protophasons. Particles that enable the cryogenically preserved deceased to communicate with the living. Source: *Ubik* by Philip K. Dick.

Pry Mincer. In Russell Hoban's post-apocalyptic novel *Riddley Walker,* the Pry Mincer holds a high office as the prime minister. But he also spies on citizens and can mince up (chop into little pieces) anyone he wishes at his discretion.

Precog. A person with precognition, meaning he or she can see into the future. Precogs are central to the plot of Philip K.

Dick's novel *Minority Report,* where three precogs help police prevent crimes before they happen. In his 1948 short story "Police Operation," H.B. Piper explains that the precognition may take place when the precog's mind "may detach, and connect at some other moment, with the ego existing at that time point."

Priplanus. The planet that the Jupiter 2 spaceship, carrying the Robinson family and a stowaway, Dr. Smith, crashes on after being lost in space, in the TV series of that name. The first actor considered for the roll of Dr. Smith was Carroll O'Connor, who later went on to star as Archie Bunker in *All in the Family.* Also interesting to note is that the jet pack in the show was a real device, not a prop or special effect. The jet pack was flown by two pilots from Bell Systems, standing in for the father of the Robinson family, Guy Williams, who had previously starred as *Zorro* on television.

Project Tic-Toc. A top-secret, $12 billion government project to build a time machine, which is nicknamed the Time Tunnel because it is a cylindrical hallway. From the TV series *The Time Tunnel.*

Psychlos. A race of 9-foot-tall hostile aliens that conquer Earth and much of the galaxy in L. Ron Hubbard's novel *Battlefield Earth.* They are much stronger than humans and possess technology far more advanced than ours. They travel the galaxy to plunder other worlds of their mineral resources, especially gold. Psychlos on Earth must wear breathing masks whenever outside because they cannot tolerate our atmosphere.

Psychoendorphins. Peptide molecules in the brain that can stimulate telepathic abilities. Formed by reacting psilocybin, a psychedelic, with chains of amino acids. From *Blood's a Rover: The Complete Adventures of a Boy and His Dog* by Harlan Ellison.

Psychohistory. A branch of history in which events can be analyzed and explained by the way human psychology dictates our decisions and mass actions. The father of this discipline is mathematician Hari Seldon, a central character in Isaac

Asimov's *Foundation* series. Psychohistory predicts the collapse of the Galactic Empire to be followed by 30,000 years of a dark age in which chaos reigns supreme. Seldon creates and implements the Seldon Plan to produce an alternative outcome in which the Dark Age would last only a thousand years. Decades after Foundation was published, psychohistory became a legitimate branch of psychology.

Psychotronic Alpha Sampler. An instrument that taps directly into the human brain to turn a person's thoughts into music. From the film *Rock n' Roll Cowboys.*

Psionics. Psionics, also called psi for short, are a set of powers that include telepathy, empathic ability, mind control, telekinesis, pyrokinesis, teleportation, precognition, astral projection, energy manipulation, and enhanced memory – usually the result of either natural genetic mutation, exposure to radiation or toxic chemicals, or deliberate experimentation with test subjects. Jack Williamson featured psionic children in his 1951 short story "Peddler's Nose."

Ptomes. A race of saurian men who are nearly amphibious though they must wear diving helmets when under water. They live in the Forbidden City, located deep inside the Tuen-Baka volcano in Africa. There is a series of lakes under the city with a city, Horus, under one of the lakes. The Ptomes walk on the bottom of the lakes wearing their breathing gear. Source: Edgar Rice Burroughs, *Tarzan and the Forbidden City.*

Pulps. Magazines publishing science fiction, fantasy, western, detective, and other short stories in specific genres. They are so-named because they were originally printed on paper so cheap that you could allegedly see bits of wood pulp in some of the pages. Hugo Cave, one of the most prolific pulp writers, published about a thousand stories in these magazines during his career; his biography was titled *Cave of a Thousand Tales*. Edward Hoch, who wrote mainly mystery stories, published around 900 tales in the pulps.

Pumpkinhead. A monster also known as Rawhide Rex from a film produced by Billy Blake.

Purge, The. In a motion picture of the same name, the purge is the one night out of every year where any and all crimes are legal. Some people use the purge as an opportunity to rob, vandalize, rape, and murder with no fear of arrest or other consequences, while others barricade themselves behind locked doors and defend themselves against the rampaging attackers during this night of terror.

Pygmy Planet. In Jack Williamson's story of the same title, "The Pygmy Planet" was an artificial world less than a yard in diameter. It was constructed in a laboratory from atoms in which the orbits of electrons had been drastically compressed. The miniature planet was suspended between two cylindrical columns descending from a complex array of electron tubes, mirrors, lenses, and prisms. Its surface was illuminated by a beam of blue light from a lamp some 10 feet away. Evolution took place on the tiny planet at a greatly accelerated rate, so life forms emerged, evolved into civilized beings, and built cities.

Pym Particle. A particle, invented by Hank Pym, who uses it to become the Marvel superhero Ant-Man. It shrinks matter by bringing its atoms closer together.

Pyramid, The. In *Wolfbane* by Frederik Pohl and C.M. Kornbluth, The Pyramid is a blue tetrahedral build on the top of Mount Everest. It was an electronic life form whose blood was dielectric fluid, limbs were electrostatic charges, and its senses radio-astronomy.

Pyrokenesis. The ability to start fires with one's mind as Charlie McGee could in Stephen King's novel *Firestarter* and the Blasters could in Harlan Ellison's story "Deeper than the Darkness."

Puppet Master. A character able to control and manipulate either inanimate puppets or human beings. In the movie *Ghost in the Shell,* the Puppet Master is an evil computer with the power to inhabit people and machines.

PyrE. In Alfred Bester's novel *The Stars My Destination,* PyrE is an explosive material that is detonated by someone thinking about it.

Q-continuum. In *Star Trek: Next Generation*, a nonlinear time window into an infinite number of other dimensions and subspace itself. In his book *The Physics of Star Trek* (Basic Books), Lawrence M. Krauss writes, "Once general relativity demonstrated that what we perceived as the force of gravity can be associated with the curvature of space, it was not outrageous to speculate that perhaps other forces might be associated with curvature in yet other dimensions."

Quaddies. Genetically engineered mutants who have four hands—two normal hands, one attached to each wrist, and two additional hands, one attached to each ankle where the foot would normally be. From Lois Bujold's novel *Falling Free.*

Quake, Opal. Two planets linked by the Umbilical, a 12,000-kilometer structure consisting of solid hydrogen spliced with muon. From Charles Cheffield's "Heritage Universe" trilogy.

Quantum Leap. The code name for a top-secret government project on time travel, from the TV series of the same name. When the time traveler, Dr. Samuel Beckett, goes back in time, he materialized into the bodies of people alive in that era but remains in control of them before he time leaps into another era.

Quantum Spyglass. A device that enables the user to see into other universes and dimensions. Source: "Evil Opposite." Naomi Kritzer, *Magazine of Fantasy & Science Fiction*, October 2017.

Quartermass. As the leader of the British Experimental Rocket Group, Professor Bernard Quartermass leads his crew in exploring space as well as defending Earth from aliens, mutants, and monsters; from the BBC TV series.

Quasar. Quasars are compact, ultra-dense astronomical bodies—possibly black stars at the centers of galaxies—that, despite their small size, radiate enormous energy, comparable to an entire galaxy. In one episode of *Star Trek: Next Generation*, the Enterprise is on a mission to explore a quasar called the Mecoria.

Quatloo. In *Star Trek,* a currency used in betting by the Providers, who are three disembodied brains living in a chamber deep below the surface of the planet Trikelion, and kept alive there by machinery. The wagers are on battles between people held captive for the purpose of having them compete in the games; these prisoners are called Thralls.

Questor. In the TV movie *The Questor Tapes,* Questor is the last of a series of androids left on Earth eons ago by a beneficent alien race to help humans in their development.

Quicksilver. In Marvel Comics, a mutant capable of running at the speed of sound. He is the son of the evil mutant Magneto.

Quintessence. In *Star Wars,* Starkiller Base, headquarters of the First Order junta, has an energy weapon powered by quintessence, which is a form of dark energy. Quintessence, along with baryonic matter, radiation, cold dark matter, and gravitational self-energy, is one of the "fifth elements" comprising the mass-energy content of the universe. Powered by quintessence, the Starkiller Base can drain the power of a burning star to power its primary weapon—similar to the weapon in the **Death Star**, only more powerful.

Just as the Death Star and Starkiller base have the awesome power to destroy an entire planet, in *Dr. Who*, the Doomsday Weapon is capable of making stars go supernova. Even more powerful in Dr. Who is the Reality Bomb which has enough power to annihilate all of reality.

Quidditch. A popular team sport played by Harry Potter, his classmates at Hogwarts, and many other wizards worldwide. Players ride their brooms and work in teams to get the ball, which is slightly deflated, into the opposing team's hoop.

Quiru. An ancient Martian race possessing advanced scientific knowledge. Rhiannon, one of their members, shares the Quiru science with the Dhuvians, another Martian race. For this offense, Rhiannon is sealed in a tomb alive. From the Leigh Brackett novel *The Sword of Rhiannon*.

Rakasha. In Roger Zelazny's novel *Lord of Light*, a race of aliens that have transcended their physical bodies and now live, immortal, as stable fields of energy or "vortices of force."

Rakshas. In Hindu belief, wicked people, as punishment for their sins, may be reincarnated as humanoid giants called Rakshas. These giants are vicious, ferocious cannibals. Their skin is jet black. The Raksha have fangs and sharp, nail-like claws. Beastlike, the Raksha are known to snack on the bloody legs and torsos of fallen soldiers on the battlefield.

Ralph 124C 41+. In Hugo Gernsback's serialized novel of the same title, Ralph 124C 41+ is one of the greatest living scientists and, also physically superior, one of only 10 men on Earth permitted to use the plus sign after his name.

Rama. Rama is a giant cylindrical spaceship measuring 12 miles in diameter and 24 miles long. The exterior is featureless, while the interior walls of the cylinder have in essence small cities on them. The ship has traveled through deep space and entered our solar system. Rama is manned by robots, and there is no trace aboard of the aliens who built the ship. From the novel *Rendezvous with Rama* by Arthur C. Clarke.

Ramscoop. Similar in design to the cow catcher on a train, a ramscoop is an electromagnetic field at the front of a spaceship that collects interstellar hydrogen to be used as fuel by the rocket's fusion-powered drive. A ramscoop is described by Larry Niven in his 1966 short story "Warriors."

Rat Cook, The. In *Game of Thrones,* a man who was a cook in the Nightfort kitchens. He killed the son of a visiting king, baked the boy into a pie, and then served the pie to the king, who unknowingly ate two helpings of his offspring. As punishment, the gods turned the cook into a giant rat. A giant rat, this one living in the sub-basement of an old mill, is also featured in Stephen King's story *Graveyard Shift.*

Ray Gun. A hand-held weapon that fires an energy beam. In the early days of science fiction, they were often lasers, which stands for light amplification through stimulated emission of radiation. The first laser was built by Theodore Maiman in 1960. It consisted of a cylindrical ruby crystal covered with a thin silver film and held between two highly polished mirrors on either end. Energy was fed into the cylinder from a flash lamp until the ruby emitted a red light, which escaped through a tiny hole in one of the end mirrors. In L. Ron Hubbard's *Mission Earth* novels, hand-held energy weapons are called blast guns. In the novels of Andre Norton, ray guns that kill are called blasters while ray guns that only stun are called, sensibly enough, stunners or stun guns. *Star Trek* had ray guns called phasers that could be set to either kill or stun. A ray gun whose beam is fatal is also called a "death ray." Murray Leinster, Henry Kuttner, and some early SF writers called ray guns "blasters."

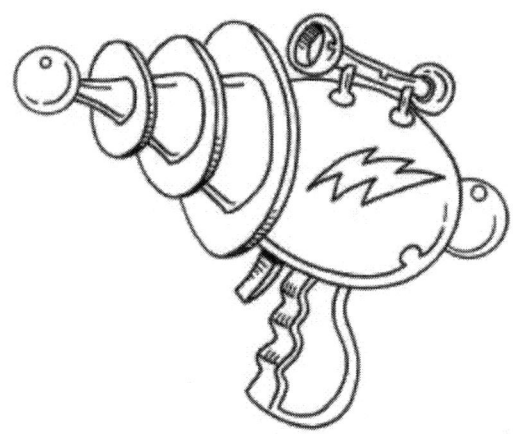

Reanimator. A scientist in an HP Lovecraft story who uses science to bring dead people back to life. In Mary Shelley's novel *Frankenstein,* Victor Frankenstein is also a reanimator, except for some inexplicable reason he animates bodies made by sewing together parts from multiple corpses instead of reanimating a single corpse. Side note: The first Frankenstein movie ran for 16 minutes and was made by Thomas Edison's company in 1910.

Rearrangement Spell. A spell that magically switches the positions of two objects that are side by side and touching. From the Andrew Perry short story "Useless Magic."

Reavers. In the X-Men, the Reavers are a band of mutant-hunting mercenaries who are part cyborg. Some have just a bionic hand or arm; others have modifications that are much more extensive. The Reaver Bonebreaker, for instance, has motorized tank treads where his legs used to be and a retractable machine gun that can extend from his abdomen.

Receptacle. In Robert Silverberg's novel *The Book of Skulls,* a Receptacle is a group of four acolytes accepted into an order of monks in the Arizona desert. The four initiates undergo a ritual in which two will be granted immortality while the other two are sacrificed.

Redjac. An evil entity that possesses many notorious murderers on many worlds, among them Earth's Jack the Ripper. In *Star Trek*, they eliminate Redjac by beaming the body of the man currently possessed by Redjac into space with the transporter, and widely dispersing his molecules so he can never reform.

Redworld. In the Charles Harness novel of the same title, *Redworld* is a planet orbiting a huge red sun whose light shines down through clouds of ammonia, illuminating virtually the whole planet in shades of red.

Redoubts. Large metal pyramids, powered by electric current generated by Earth, into which remaining humans in our future retreat to protect themselves from a hostile and dangerous world. The sun has cooled. The Earth has grown dark and desolate. The surface outside the walls of the Pyramids is populated by degenerated subhuman species. From *The Night Land* by William Hope Hodgson.

Reefs. Structures, which resemble jeweled metallic forests, located in deep space billions of miles from our sun. The Reefs are produced by single-cell creatures called the fusorians. The fusorians produce energy by fusing hydrogen into heavier elements. These Reefs are honeycombed with interior passages. On the Reefs there are flowers that emit gamma radiation and whose seed pods squirt out radioactive liquid. Fauna includes aggressive omnivorous squid-like pyropods which prey on other native fauna including fishbirds and seal-like spacelings. Source: Frederik Pohl and Jack Williamson, *The Reefs of Space.*

Rejuv. In the "Merchanter" novels of C.J. Cherry, rejuv is a drug that keeps people at the biological age when they start taking it. But rejuv does not make you immortal, as the drug stops working some years after you reach age 100.

Rekal. In the Philip K. Dick story "We Can Remember It for You Wholesale," which the movie *Total Recall* is based on, Rekal is a corporation that can implant memories, so its customers feel they have had experiences that in reality they have not had.

Relativity. Einstein's theory of relativity says that the faster an object moves, the longer it gets and the slower time passes for it. In Poul Anderson's novel *Tau Zero,* a spaceship traveling at almost the speed of light grows to such enormous proportions that it pushes galaxies out of the way, which will lead to the destruction of everything. Meanwhile, because time has slowed aboard the ship, the crew will live to see the end of the universe and eventually fly into a reborn cosmos.

Remora. In Robert Reed's short story "The Remoras," the remoras are mutated humans who are permanently sealed inside a self-contained suit that sustains their life, including recycling water and synthesizing their food.

Replicant. In the movie *Blade Runner*, replicants are intelligent androids so lifelike they are to the untrained eye indistinguishable from real people. Replicants are also called "skin jobs" because an android is essentially a robot with a covering resembling skin to make them appear human.

Reprosat. A machine that builds from its supply of atomic and subatomic particles virtually anything; could be seen as the next generation technology that follows today's 3D printers. From the Thomas M. Disch short story "Now is Forever."

Republic of Gilead. Formerly the United States of America, The Republic of Gilead is a nation in which far-right extremists murder the government. In the new theocracy these extremists create, women are strictly controlled and assigned to classes. From Margaret Atwood's novel *The Handmaid's Tale*.

Retinal Shaving. In the Riddick movies, an operation on the retinas that enables a person to see in nearly total darkness. On the flip side, the person must wear dark goggles in normal light, otherwise the brightness would render him unable to see. The comic book character Dr. Midnite could also see in total darkness but not in daylight, but this was caused by a freak laboratory accident, not retinal shaving.

Retrospectiv. A machine Martians have built that enables them to look into the past. Source: Kurd Lasswitz's 1897 novel *On Two Planets*.

Retroviral Hypodysplasia. A disease affecting Norman and Harry Osborn in the Spider-Man comics. It causes the skin to become greenish and scaly and also dilates the pupils and turns them green.

Rhiannon. An evil alien who gave advanced technology to one of the native intelligent species on Mars, the lizard-like Dhuvians, allowing them to conquer all other Martian races. Source: *The Sword of Rhiannon* by Leigh Brackett.

Rhyonon. In Samuel R. Delany's novel *Stars in My Pocket Like Grains of Sand,* Rhyonon is a planet where sex between tall and short people is forbidden.

Rim World. Any planet located near the outer edge of the galaxy, a term first used by Robert Heinlein in his 1957 story "Citizen of the Galaxy."

Ringworld. In Larry Niven's science fiction novel of the same title, Ringworld is an enormous artificial ring about one million miles wide. The ring structure circles a star much like our sun. It also rotates to provide artificial gravity through centrifugal force. The large inner surface is flat, with a breathable atmosphere and a temperature comfortable for humans. An inner ring of moveable square panels, connected by thin wires with high tensile strength, provides dark at night.

Ripple Land. A country of steep rocky hills and valleys. A constant rippling motion of the land causes the features of the area to constantly change place; one minute you are in a valley, which quickly transforms into a hill or mountain. It is an unsettling place to live in or travel to.

Riverworld. A lush, beautiful planet where every person who has died is resurrected and lives, on the banks of a river 10 million miles long, as imagined by Phillip Jose Farmer in his series of Riverworld novels.

Road, The. In Roger Zelazny's novel *Roadmarks,* the Road is a highway in which the exits allow travelers to get off at destinations in different places as well as different times. A limited number of access ramps, well-hidden in ordinary reality locations, enable those few travelers that can find them to both get on and navigate the Road.

Robotics, The Three Laws of. Laws governing the behavior of all robots, the Three Laws are programmed into every robot's brain during its manufacture. The Three Laws of Robotics, invented by Isaac Asimov, are as follows:

1. A robot may not injure a human being, or through inaction, allow a human being to come to harm.

2. A robot must obey the orders given it by human beings, except where such orders would conflict with the First Law.

3. A robot must protect its own existence, as long as such protection does not conflict with the First or Second Law.

Robot Cardinal. In Robert Silverberg's short story "Good News from the Vatican," cardinals elected by the Vatican are all robots consisting of a metal torso, wheels instead of legs, and optical eyes.

Robotrix. In the 1927 film *Metropolis,* Robotrix is a female robot created by mad scientist Rotwang to manipulate the masses.

Rocket Pack. A small rocket a person can strap to his back, enabling him to fly. Rocket packs have been used in countless SF TV shows and movies, including *The Rocketeer,* in which it was central to the plot. In the 1950s and 60s, a hero wearing a rocket pack was featured in a series of *Rocketman* movies. Wonder Man in Marvel comic books flew with a rocket pack as did the Avenger's Falcon, who also had mechanical wings. Today there are actual jet packs that allow a person to fly for short periods at modest speeds and limited altitudes.

Rocket Ship. Any vehicle that can travel through outer space. Also called a space ship. An interstellar space ship is a rocket that can travel to other solar systems.

Rocking-horse-fly. In Lewis Carroll's book *Alice's Adventures in Wonderland,* a Rocking-horse-fly is an insect that looks like a rocking horse. It is made of wood and travels by swinging from tree branches. Its diet consists of tree sap and sawdust.

Roller Ball. From the motion picture of the same name, *Roller Ball* is a gladiator spectator sport similar to our real-life Roller Derby, only much more brutal and dangerous.

Ro-Man. In the SF film *Robot Monster*, Ro-Man is an alien played by an actor wearing a gorilla suit. Ro-Man is told by his ruler, the Great One, to kill the last remaining half a dozen humans on Earth.

Rommie. Rommie, an artificial intelligence aboard the warship Andromeda Ascent, can appear in three forms: as a hologram, an on-screen display, and a beautiful android; from the TV series *Andromeda*.

Romulan Ale. An alcoholic blue beverage favored by the Romulans in *Star Trek*; McCoy gives a bottle to Kirk for his birthday.

Room 101. In George Orwell's novel *1984,* Room 101 is a government-sanctioned torture chamber where torturers identify the prisoner's worst nightmares and then, as torture, make them real.

Rosemary's Baby. In a movie of the same title, a man makes a deal with the devil. He allows Satan to impregnate his wife Rosemary in exchange for career success.

Rover. In Harlan Ellison's short story "A Boy and His Dog," a rover is a super-intelligent, telepathic dog. In the TV series *The Prisoner,* the Rovers are bouncing elastic bubbles that prevent prisoners from escaping the grounds of their fairytale-like prison, known as the Village.

Royal Road. In Bob Shaw's short story, "The Happiest Day of Your Life," the Royal Road is a technology that enables formal knowledge that normally would require 10 years of high school and college to be implanted in a child's mind in about 2 hours. The method was accomplished using multi-level hypnosis, psycho-neuro drugs, and electron modification of protein pathways in the brain.

Royal Secret Service of Psychics. A team of crime investigators, "forensic psychic readers," who use their psionics powers to help solve crimes. From P.N. Elrod's novel *The Hangman: Her Majesty's Psychic Service.*

RPM (ribopropylmethioninee). In George Alec Effinger's novel *When Gravity Fails,* a psychotropic drug that causes intense hallucinations but also brain damage.

RUMOKO. In Roger Zelazny's story "The Eve of Rumoko," RUMOKO is a project designed to create a new island in the ocean. The methodology is to detonate nuclear bombs on the ocean floor where the crust is closest to the lava underneath. The blast would free the lava to flow, and it would harden into small land masses.

Running Man, The. In the Richard Bachman novel of the same name, also a movie starring Arnold Schwarzenegger, the Running Man is a brutal TV reality show. The contestants are criminals who, on live television, must escape assassins hired by the TV network to kill them.

Rules of Acquisition. In *Star Trek,* the Ferengi are a race of capitalists who value free enterprise and profit above virtually all else, and their primary goal is the vast accumulation of wealth. Ferengi behavior is governed by the 258 Rules of Acquisition. Their currency is latinum, available in three denominations, which in order of ascending value, are slips, strips, and bars.

Rura Penthe. In the movie *Star Trek VI*, an underground mining colony in which convicts perform forced labor. The subzero temperatures on the asteroid's surface discouraged prisoners from climbing out of the underground mine and prison areas to escape.

Sakae. On the planet Sako, a species of reptiles more intelligent than the humans of Sako, whom the Sakae treat as a "protected species," rounded up to live on reservations. Source: "The Stars My Brothers" by Edmond Hamilton.

Samlon. In the novel *The Legacy of Heorot*, samlon are river-dwelling fish that mutate into "grendels" —monsters with legs and teeth that prey on the humans who colonize the planet Avalon.

Sandkings. In a George R.R. Martin story of the same title, sandkings are small, intelligent creatures, insect-like in appearance, that live in colonies, according to color. Colonies of sandkings in close proximity may combat one another. If not confined to small spaces, the sandkings grow and eventually evolve into a creature that is more like a human in size and appearance.

Sandmen. In the 1976 motion picture *Logan's Run*, citizens in the 23rd century are required to commit suicide when they turn 30. "Runners" are people who try to escape this, and "Sandmen" are law enforcement agents who track down and kill the Runners.

Sanus. A disk-shaped planet on which intelligent bees use their telepathic powers to enslave the resident humans. Source: "The Emancipatrix" by Homer Flint.

Sash of Rassilion. A garment of sorts that can protect the wearer from being torn apart or otherwise harmed by the awesome gravitational forces of black holes.

Sapphire and Steel. In the TV series of the same name, Sapphire and Steel are a pair of inter-dimensional operatives dispatched to Earth to deal with time anomalies and spatial disturbances.

Sapir-Whorf Hypothesis. A linguistic theory that says language shapes perception to such a degree that thinking in a different language gives you a different perception. In Samuel R. Delaney's novel *Babel-17,* based on this hypothesis, language is used to reprogram people.

Sarr. In Hal Clement's novel *Iceworld,* Sarr is an extremely hot planet with an atmosphere of gaseous sulfur. The natives drink molten copper chloride.

Saurs. Miniature intelligent dinosaurs bioengineered to be children's toys as described by Richard Chwedyk in his stories "The Measure of All Things" and "Bronte's Egg." The saurs, who are living, feeling creatures, are sometimes hurt and even maimed by uncaring and cruel children who see the small creatures strictly as playthings and property. In addition, the saurs develop intelligence way beyond what their creators envisioned.

Scanners. Powerful mutants with mind powers that can cause the brains of other people to literally explode, from a movie of the same title. Also, in Cordwainer Smith's short story "Scanners Live in Vain," scanners are men who have voluntarily had all their sensory nerve input severed with the exception of vision. They do so to become immune to the First Effect, which is a compulsory suicidal impulse or desire to die brought about as an unwanted and dangerous side effect of interstellar space travel.

Science Ninja Team. In the Japanese animated TV series *Gatchaman*, the Science Ninjas are five teenagers who have special powers and wear bird-themed costumes: eagle, condor, swallow, swan, and owl. Their fighter aircraft, The God Phoenix, transforms into a firebird.

Sci-fi. Short for "science fiction." Writer Harlan Ellison calls the term sci-fi a "nauscating neologism."

Scientification. A term coined by Hugo Gernsback around 1926 for stories that today we classify as science fiction.

Sonic Screwdriver. In *Dr. Who*, a versatile device that can unlock doors, weld metal, detonate explosives, and repair machinery.

Screaming Skull, The. A 1958 horror movie, American audiences who went to see *The Screaming Skull* were promised a free burial if they died of fright from the film.

Screwtop. In Vonda N. McIntyre's story of the same title, "Screwtop" is a prison colony on the planet Redsun. The prison is surrounded by marshes, lava fields, and volcanoes emitting poison gas, and is therefore considered escape-proof.

Scrying. Being able to see either into the future or view distant events by looking at a crystal ball.

Sergeant Eve Edison. In the 1992 SF series *Mann and Machine*, Eve, partnered with Detective Bobby Man, is an android cop.

Seaview. In the TV series *Voyage to the Bottom of the Sea*, the crew of the submarine Seaview carry out dangerous missions for the U.S. government and encounter many strange new life forms in the ocean depths.

Second Impact. In the Japanese animated TV series *Neo Genesis Evangelion*, an event believed by the public to have been a large meteor strike. The Second Event triggers a global chain of tsunamis, floods, and earthquakes that devastate much of the Earth.

Secondary Magnetic Expedition. An expedition sent to investigate an anomaly in Antarctica. They find a 280-foot long alien spaceship that had crash landed, and a crew member frozen in a block of ice. When it is thawed out, it revives from cryogenic suspended animation, and is revealed to be a hostile shapeshifter. From the John W. Campbell, Jr. short story "Who Goes There?" which was made into the movie "The Thing."

Selenites. In the 1902 motion picture *A Trip to the Moon,* the Selenites are an aggressive race of moon men who disappear in a puff of smoke when attacked. The Moon's surface is lush and tropical, with waterfalls.

Selenology. In Arthur C. Clark's short story "The Sentinel," selenology is a scientific field concerning the study of the moon.

Selice. An alien race human males are sexually attracted to despite their physical incompatibility and the Selice's disinterest in interspecies intercourse. Source: James Tiptree, "And I Awoke and Found Me Here On the Cold Hill's Side."

Selkies. In Scottish folklore, selkies are "seal people" – beings who can shape shift between human and seal. When they interbreed with normal humans, the offspring have webbed hands and feet.

Sentient. The state of a being, either organic or mechanical, being self-aware. A common science fiction plot is supercomputers becoming sentient and then quickly deciding to control or destroy humankind. Examples include such movies as *Terminator* and *The Matrix.*

Servants of Wrath (SOWs). In the post-apocalyptic novel *Deus Irae* by Philip Dick and Roger Zelazny, a religious sect. They worship scientist Carleton Lufteufel, who created and launched the ultimate nuclear weapon – the bomb which started the atomic war that decimated the Earth. Mutated humans in a world devastated by nuclear war worship a still-viable atom bomb in the movie *Beneath the Planet of the Apes*.

Set, The. In Roger Zelazny's short story "The Graveyard Heart," the Set is an elite group of prominent socialites in the 21st century. Set members, through regular retreats into suspended animation, enjoy extended lifespans.

Seven Dwarfs, The. Snow White's companions are seven dwarfs: Doc, Grumpy, Sleepy, Sneezy, Happy, Dopey, and Bashful.

Seven Million Dollar Man, The. Barney Miller, a former race car driver, is turned by the government into a bionic man after he is seriously injured in a crash. Played by Monte Markham, Barney cost a million dollars more to build than Steve Austin, the *Six Million Dollar Man*, and had two bionic arms instead of one bionic and one organic, arguably making him more powerful.

Seven Sages. A brotherhood of semi-divine beings described as half man and half fish. Babylonian mythology says the leader of the Seven Sages, Oannes, emerged from his kingdom beneath the Persian Gulf to give the "Tablets of Civilization" to early humans, thereby providing humanity with written language.

SF. Sci Fi. SF and sci fi are abbreviated terms for "science fiction." Many science fiction authors and fans dislike the term "sci fi," feeling it degrades the literary merits of the genre. Harlan Ellison calls "sci fi" a "nauseating neologism." Neil Gaiman says that to him SF stands for the more acceptable genre label of speculative fiction.

Shangri-La. A village in the Tibetan Himalayas whose inhabitants have much-extended lifespans. Source: James Hilton's novel *Lost Horizons*.

Sha Ka Ree. In the movie *Star Trek V: The Final Frontier*, Sha Ka Ree is an alien energy, living on a planet at the center of the galaxy, who claims to be the God of Vulcan mythology. In fact, Sha Ka Ree is a prisoner on the planet, and he wants to use the Enterprise to escape. After attempting to kill Kirk, the alien is destroyed by an energy weapon fired from a Klingon Bird of Prey to which Spock had been beamed aboard.

Shared World. A single fictional world, universe, or setting created by a group of science fiction writers who then each write individual stories or even novels taking place in that world.

Sharknado. A tornado that begins over the ocean and is so powerful it sucks up massive quantities of sea water and sharks, and deposits them on city streets where they go on a rampage and kill citizens. There have been five Sharknado made-for-TV movies so far, one featuring billionaire Mark Cuban as the president of the United States.

Shapeshifter. A person or creature capable of transforming into other forms. Mystique from the X-Men is a shapeshifter, as is Manimal from the TV series. The Plurivars are a race of shape shifters on the planet Majipoor, a world much larger than Earth but far less dense, in Robert Silverberg's Majipoor novels and stories.

Shayol. A prison planet where a parasitic species, dromozoa, infect the prisoners, causing them to grow extra organs and limbs, which are harvested and used for transplant surgery. Those prisoners infected with the parasite undergo a slow metamorphosis, gradually turning them into grotesque monsters. The discoverer of Shayol, Captain Alvarez, was eventually transformed into a giant foot as big as a mountain. Source: Cordwainer Smith's, "A Planet Named Shayol."

Shazam. An acronym that stands for the wisdom of Solomon, the strength of Hercules, the stamina of Atlas, the power of Zeus, the courage of Achilles, and the speed of Mercury. When youngster Billy Batson speaks the word Shazam aloud, he is transformed into the mighty superhero Captain Marvel, whose powers include speed, strength, flight, and invulnerability.

Sheena. Sort of a female version of Tarzan, Sheena is adopted by the Zambouli tribe when her explorer parents are killed. She becomes Queen of the Jungle and, like Tarzan, can talk to animals.

Sheewash Drive. On the planet Karres, a powerful propulsion system, fueled by cosmic energy, capable of moving the entire world. The colonists develop psionic power including the capability of harnessing the cosmic energy to power the Sheewash Drive. Source: *The Witches of Karres* by James Schmitz.

SHEVA. In Greg Bear's novel *Darwin's Radio,* SHEVA is a virus that activates redundant DNA, turning human beings into a new species almost overnight.

Shield. A portable defensive barrier, often a round disk or in the shape of a coat of arms, usually made of metal, favored by Roman soldiers and gladiators as well as certain superheroes, most notably Guardian, Captain America, and Wonder Woman. Also refers to an energy shield used as a defensive measure, such as the shields on the U.S.S. Enterprise that deflect energy beams from attacking ships.

Shikasta. In Doris Lessing's novel of the same title, *Shikasta* is a planet colonized by the Canopean Empire and called

Colonized Planet 5. The Canopeans subjected the native hominids to a Forced-Growth Plan to accelerate their evolution.

Shining One, The. In A. Merritt's story "Conquest of the Moon Pool," the Shining One, also known as the Dweller, is a powerful synthetic being created by a prehuman race of intelligent reptilian beings. The victims he feeds on still exist in a state between life and death inside his shining membranes.

Shoggoth. Primitive biological entities created by the Elder Things (see definition) to help build their cities. All other earthly life may have evolved from the same protoplasmic material the Elder Things used to make the shoggoths.

Shorter Way Bridge. In Joe Hill's novel *NOS4A2,* a bridge that can instantaneously transport anyone and anything to anywhere on Earth as well as an alternate dimension called "Christmasland," run by an evil being, Manx, and populated by children he has turned into vampires.

Shrieking Shack, The. Known as the most haunted dwelling in Britain, the Shrieking Shack is so-named because of the screams and howls that emanate from it, which are believed by local wizards to be the cries of violent ghosts. Source: *Harry Potter.*

Shunka Warak'In. Frightening-looking, primitive wolflike beasts that were believed by Native Americans to inhabit the wilds of the upper midwestern United States. The creatures have a doglike or wolflike appearance, are nearly black, have high shoulders, and a back that slopes down like a hyena's.

Si-Fan. In the Fu Manchu movies, a secret society dedicated to evil, run by Dr. Fu Manchu.

SIDRAT (Space and Inter-Dimensional Robot All-Purpose Transporter). In Dr. Who, a machine that enabled short-range travel between dimensions.

Silence, The. In *Dr. Who*, a religious order of a humanoid aliens, living on a distant planet but often visiting Earth, who have been guiding human evolution for thousands of years. The Silence have the ability to place post-hypnotic suggestions in human minds, which are not remembered after being encountered.

The Silence's religious belief is that when the last question in the universe is asked, silence will fall. Similar scenarios are Isaac Asimov's short story "The Last Question" and Arthur C. Clarke's "The 9 Billion Names of God."

Silent Genes. Dormant genes that scientists experimentally "turn on" by exposing lab animals to radiation. The goal is to trigger mutations that may allow the animals, and therefore possibly humans as well, to adapt to future environmental conditions. For instance, spiders evolve so they are blind to sunlight and can see only gamma radiation. From the J.G. Ballard short story "The Voices of Time."

Silkpunk. Science fiction stories set in ancient China.

Silver. A valuable metal known to be harmful to vampires and werewolves. Contact with silver weakens and hurts these creatures and a silver bullet is commonly used to kill werewolves. Some horror writers say viruses or bacteria turn people into vampires, and recent research from Sweden shows the silver may be able to kill bacteria.

Sin-Eating. The ritual eating of a meal by a person, often a paid sin-eater, in which the sin-eater takes on a recently deceased person's sins, enabling the dead person's soul to be released from purgatory. Manley Wade Wellman's fantasy hero John the Balladeer is married to a sin-eater, Evadare.

Singularity. The point in time when advances in technology trigger some sort of monumental and inconceivable event. Vernor Vinge invented the Singularity in *Marooned in Realtime;* in his Singularity, most of humanity has disappeared, not unlike The Rapture.

Sirians. An alien race living on a planet in orbit around the star Sirius. Sirians are physically similar to humans except for their purple-faced complexion, pinned-back ears, and bow-legged gate. From the novel *Wasp* by Eric Frank Russell.

Sister Bertrille. In the TV show *The Flying Nun,* Sister Bertrille is a young nun who is so small, slim, and lightweight, that when the wind blows sufficiently, the flaps of her habit function as glider wings and she flies.

Sith. Masters of The Force who are adept at using the Dark Side of their power for evil. From *Star Wars*. The Emperor and Darth Vader are both Siths. A Baobhan Sith is an evil spirit appearing as a beautiful girl who wears long green dresses to hide her hooves; these siths lure young men with their beauty, and then suck the victim's blood.

S'krell. A thousand years in the future, humans have evacuated Earth because of an environmental disaster, and some now live in Nova Prime, a space colony. The S'krell are an extraterrestrial race that invades Nova Prime with the intent of taking it over. The S'krell attack humans with Ursas, creatures that hunt by "sensing" fear. To defeat them, the humans master a fear-suppressing technique called *ghosting*.

Skagganauk Abyss. A region or "hole" in the universe where nothing – not even the space-time continuum itself – exists. In his novel *Creatures of Light and Darkness*, Roger Zelazny describes Skagganauk Abyss as "the chasm in the sky ... a place where it is said that all things stop and nothing exists ... a gap in the fabric of space itself ... it is nothing."

Skinsuit. A tight form-fitting spacesuit often worn for short-term flights or emergency use. Quinn wears a skinsuit in the *Guardians of the Galaxy* movies.

Skrill. In the TV series *Earth: Final Conflict,* a skrill is a small, self-aware, sentient entity that, when implanted into a person's forearm, enables that man or woman to fire energy bolts upon mental command.

Skull Island. A jungle-covered outcrop inhabited by a primitive tribe that lives behind a high wall and worships King Kong, a giant ape living on Skull Island. The island, located off the coast of Sumatra, is bisected by a mountain range. Heavy rainfall feeds a constant flow of water in the swamps, gullies, streams, rivers, as well as underground. King Kong is a member of *Megaprimatus kong.* This species of giant ape stands 18 to 25 feet tall, and may have evolved from the giant prehistoric ape Gigantopithecus.

Skunk Ape. A giant primate claimed to roam the Florida Everglades, the Skunk Ape is so-named because of its strong, unpleasant odor; Skunk Apes are said to smell like a mixture of rotten eggs, cow manure, and skunk. They are 7 feet tall, weigh 300 pounds, and are covered in dark brown, red, or black fur. Source: the book *Cryptozoology A to Z.*

Sky High. A high school for teenagers with super powers that trains them to be either superheroes or sidekicks, depending on what power they have. In the movie of the same title, Sky High is built on a platform powered by an anti-gravity device to keep it floating above the clouds. The principal is played by Lynda Carter, the actress who was TV's Wonder Woman.

Slagtown. A section of Los Angeles heavily populated by Newcomers, aliens from the planet Tencton who have fled to Earth to escape being slaves on their home world. From the TV series *Alien Nation*.

Slan. From A.E. van Vogt's novel of the same name, the slans are a subspecies of Homo sapiens developed in a laboratory by scientist Samuel Lann, only vastly superior to normal people. Some slans have tendrils extended from the heads that give them telepathic powers. Slan with tendrils are either put to death or exiled by normal humans.

Sleepless City. A city in Nigeria whose inhabitants never sleep and in fact have no idea of what sleep is. If a visitor to the city should fall asleep, the natives assume he is dead and bury him immediately.

Sliding. A method of traveling through wormholes to parallel Earths; from the TV series *Sliders*.

Slinker. The alien species *Mus Sapiens*, six inches tall, with arms and glittering red eyes. From Stanley Weinbaum's short story "The Mad Moon."

Slinkers. In a Stanley Weinbaum short story set on Jupiter, Mus Sapiens, also called slinkers, are a native species of the giant planet. These creatures are intelligent and troublesome. Just six inches and skinny, slinkers have a rat-like face, glittering red eyes, and a batlike cowl of skin.

Slipstream. In the motion picture of the same name, the *Slipstream* is a high wind that ceaselessly blows across the Earth in one direction, caused by some unspecified ecological disaster and similar to the constant wind in Roger Zelazny's novel *Damnation Alley.*

Smokers. A band of thuggish sea pirates riding jet skis and terrorizing innocent people in *Waterworld,* the name given to Earth, in the movie of that title, when melting polar ice caps cover virtually the entire surface of the planet with the oceans.

Snaefel. A mountain rising out of the seas of Iceland, about a mile high. Once an active volcano that last erupted in 1229, it is now a crate that leads straight down to the center of the Earth. From *Journey to the Center of the Earth* by Jules Verne.

Snow Piercer. In a graphic novel and movie of the same title, a train, powered by perpetual motion, that ceaselessly circles the globe in a future where the Earth has been plunged into subzero temperatures in an attempt by scientists to reverse global warming. The train contains the last survivors of humankind. They must live on the train as anyone who goes outside freezes to death in minutes. The riders are divided by class, with the rich and privileged riding in the front of the train and the poor crammed into the rear cars.

Solar Guards. In the TV series *Tom Corbett: Space Cadet,* the Solar Guards are an interplanetary police force in AD2350 and serving the Solar Alliance of Earth, Mars, and Venus.

Solar Wind. Particles ejected from the surface of the Sun into outer space. In his short story "The Wind from the Sun," Arthur C. Clarke envisions space ships powered by solar wind pushing against giant, thin sails, called "light sails," that unfurl from the body of the spacecraft. Adjusting the angle of the sails directs the spacecraft.

Larry Niven writes: "With a light sail, you can get push from the solar wind as well as from light pressure." In his novel "Hinterlands," William Gibson describes an ultra-light sail as being "20 tons of aluminum spun into a hexagon, ten kilometers from side to side."

Solarian. An inhabitant of our solar system.

Solaris. A planet almost completely covered by a vast ocean. The ocean itself is a single gigantic living organism and a sentient being. Solaris has psionic abilities and is able to manipulate the minds of human beings. It can also construct artificial beings from neutrinos. Based on the novel of the same title by Stanislaw Lem.

Soliton Wave. In *Star Trek: Next Generation*, a soliton wave is a non-dispersing wavefront of sub space distortion. By continually propagating in subspace, the soliton wave can propel a starship into warp speed without the need for a warp drive.

Soma. In Aldous Huxley's novel *Brave New World*, soma is a drug given by the government to citizens to keep them cooperative and docile.

Sonic Screwdriver. In *Dr. Who*, a versatile handheld device that can unlock doors, open hatches, weld metal, detonate explosives and bombs, repair machinery, decipher codes, disarm robotics, even track alien life forms. The Sonic Screwdriver is so-named because it operates by manipulating sound waves, radiation, wavelengths, frequencies, signals, and electromagnetism.

Sons of the Bird. A race of alien super beings, disguised as humans, who built our world. Source: Robert Heinlein's novella *The Unpleasant Profession of Jonathan Hoag.*

Souls. A race of parasitic aliens that invade Earth. When implanted in human bodies, that person's consciousness disappears and the host takes over, though it retains the knowledge and memories in the human brain. From the Stephanie Meyer novel *The Host.*

Soul Switchers. A secret group of conspirators who steal the souls of people they deem unworthy to live, and transfer these souls into people clinging to life to restore them to full health and vigor. From the novel *Soul Switchers* by Barry Cohen.

Southern Star. From a Jules Verne story of the same title, the Southern Star is a 243-carat diamond artificially constructed by Victor Cyprian, a French engineer.

Soylent Green. In a movie with this title, the government solves a food shortage by mass-producing a food called soylent green. The grim secret: soylent green is made of people. The film *Soylent Green* is based on the Harry Harrison novel *Make Room, Make Room.*

Space Elevator. A moving cable tethered to a ground station on Earth's equator at one end and a space station in geosynchronous orbit above it. Supplies and equipment can be transported from Earth to the space station simply by sending them up in the elevator. Arthur C. Clarke suggested the cable be made of carbon nanotubes. In his novel *The Fountains of Paradise,* an engineer on Taprobane planned to build a space elevator on the mountain Sri Kanda. NASA has solicited designs from engineers and inventors for a real space elevator to be built.

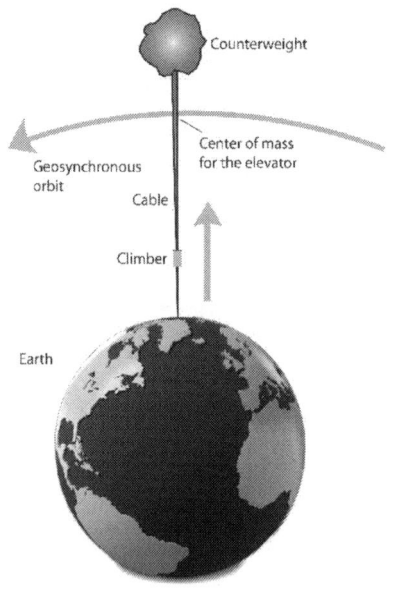

Space Opera. A subgenre of science fiction which is primarily dramatic and adventure-driven and often takes place in outer space. Space opera novels include *Ender's Game* by Orson Scott Card, *A Fire Upon the Deep* by Vernon Vinge, *Gateway* by Frederik Pohl, *The Skylark of Space* by E.E. "Doc" Smith, and *Battlefield Earth* by L. Ron Hubbard. Writer B. Tucker defined space operas as "hacky, grinding, stinking, outworn ... world-saving ... [or] space-ship yarn(s)." Clifton Fadiman called space operas "trivial but engaging fantasies." An article in Locus described space operas as stories "populated by grandiose archetypes and redolent ... of myth, rocket fuel, and soap."

Space Probe III. When this spaceship piloted by Captain William "Buck" Rogers is thrown off course by collision with meteors, the ship's life support system fails; Buck is frozen in suspended animation and wakes up in the year 2491. Later, Buck pilots another spaceship, Searcher, in a mission to search the galaxy for humans who fled Earth after a devastating nuclear war hundreds of years earlier. From the TV series *Buck Rogers in the Twenty-Fifth Century.*

Spacely Sprockets. In the animated series The *Jetsons*, George Jetson works for Spacely Sprockets, a large corporation whose major competitor is Cogswell Cogs.

Space Rangers. In the 1993 TV series of the same name, the Space Rangers are a team of law enforcement agents who travel across space in their Ranger Slingship.

Spacers. Astronauts who are physically altered, including neutering, to allow their bodies to withstand the radiation of outer space; from Samuel R. Delaney's short story "Aye, and Gomorrah."

Spackles. A race of alien aborigines who are natives on a planet which humans have colonized. The Spackles release a plague that kills all the women settlers and gives every male human telepathic powers. Source: *Monster of Men* by Patrick Ness.

Special Corps. From Harry Harrison's Stainless Steel Rat novels, an elite crime-fighting organization whose agents themselves are all former criminals.

Special Unit 2. In the TV series of the same name, *Special Unit 2* is a secret branch of the Chicago Police Department tasked with fighting the Links, which are mythological creatures who really exist and the public are unaware of.

Specified Encapsulated Limitless Archive (Selma). In the TV series *Time Trax,* Selma is a 22nd century portable mainframe computer that was designed to look like a MasterCard credit card.

Speculative Fiction. An alternate name for science fiction, used to get rid of the word "science" from the genre's title, because writers other than those writing hard science fiction thought it did not really apply to them. Speculative fiction also refers in particular to any fiction that speculates on the future of humankind. The term is credited to Robert Heinlein.

Speed Force. In the DC universe, a force or dimension that certain individuals (e.g., The Flash, Impulse, Zoom, and Max Mercury) can draw power from, enabling them to run and move at tremendous velocities. In most cases, the Speed Force augments super-speed powers they already possess from other sources, such as mutation or chemical transformation.

Spin Dizzy. In the future, our descendants leave earth to travel through space, not in rocket ships or space stations, but in the actual cities of Earth – New York, Los Angeles, Boston, and San Francisco. The spin dizzies, from James Blish's novel *Cities in Flight,* are giant anti-gravity propulsion devices that generate a force field around a city and turn it into a self-contained, self-propelled space ship. Cities that take flight and leave Earth powered by spin dizzies are called Okie Cities. Cities also float in space in Jean-Claude Dunyach's short story "Paranamanco." And Laputa, a flying island powered by magnetism, is featured in Jonathan Swift's 1726 novel *Gulliver's Travel.*

Spontaneous Combustion. This is the phenomenon of a human being bursting into flame for no visible reason and being consumed by the fire. The human body contains methane, a combustible gas, and one theory is this gas ignites and consumes the body from the inside. Stephen King's son Joe Hill has written a novel, *The Fireman*, where spontaneous combustion is central to the plot.

Square-Cube Law. In Edward Bryant's short story "giANTS," the government asks a scientist to help battle invading ants. Shockingly, he is designing a technology to mutate the ants—and make them grow larger. Why? The scientist explains that as the ants get bigger, under the square-cube law, they will collapse under their own weight—and, in fact, they do. In the movie *Them,* mutated giant ants are found in an irradiated nest in the New Mexico desert; they spread into the spillways and storm drains of Los Angeles where they pose a danger to the city's population.

Sreen Spaceship. Gigantic space vessels of the Sreens, a powerful and technologically advanced race who pose no small threat to humans. The Sreen ships are described as "droplet-cluster" constructs that can defy the laws of physics, with half of the huge craft in normal space and half in "elsewherespace." From the short story "Upstart" by Steven Utley.

Staff of Truth. A walking stick imbued with supernatural powers that, in a *Twilight Zone* episode, was capable of imprisoning the devil in a cell in which the staff is used to bar the door.

Stainless Steel Rat, The. In Harry Harrrison's novel of the same name, *The Stainless Steel Rat* is a colorful criminal named Jim DiGriz, who is the most infamous interstellar thief and con man in the galaxy.

Stand on Zanzibar. A science fiction novel by John Brunner in which he calculated that a population of 7 billion humans, which today we have now exceeded, if at all places in the African region of Zanzibar would have to stand upright, shoulder to shoulder, to fit. Hence the title refers to everyone on Earth literally "standing on Zanzibar."

Star Child. In the movie *2001: A Space Odyssey*, astronaut Dave Bowman, after passing through a Star Gate, is reborn as the Star Child, a being of pure energy representing the next stage in the evolution of Homo sapiens. In the film he is pictured as a giant fetus, floating in a uterus about the Earth, pondering what to do next.

Starfighter. In the motion picture *The Last Starfighter,* Alex, a teenager, attains the highest score ever on the popular Starfighter game, the inventor of which is actually an alien. When Alex reaches the high score, the alien invites him to play a real version in a real Starfighter to save the Galaxy from the invasion of the Ko-Dan Empire.

Stargates. Ring-shaped portals of alien construction that allow almost instantaneous transport between one stargate and another over vast distances. Several SF TV series have centered on the use of stargates for interstellar exploration. Robert Heinlein called stargates "astrogates" in short stories he published in the 1940s. In the TV series *Stargate SG-1,* the stargates open a wormhole to enable instant transport across space.

Star Maker. In the Olaf Stapledon novel of the same name, the Star Maker is a being of nearly unlimited power, on par with our God, who created our universe, many others, and continues to create more universes out of nothing.

Starman. In the motion picture of the same name, *Starman* is an alien who encounters the Voyager 2 space probe. In response to the invitation the probe carries, the alien comes to Earth. In his natural form, he has no physical substance, so for his visit to our planet, he clones and "possesses" a human body.

Starswarms. Enormous intelligent plant-like creatures that live at the bottom of a remote planet's oceans. Source: Jerry Pournelle's, *Starswarm*.

Stasis Field. An energy field that keeps whatever is in it from aging or otherwise changing in any significant way. In Isaac Asimov's short story "The Ugly Little Boy," a cave boy is brought into the future and held there with use of a stasis field. Stasis fields are a plot device in numerous other works of SF including Joe Haldeman's *The Forever War,* Vernor Vinge's *Peace Authority,* and Larry Niven's *Known Space*.

Steam Elephant. In the 1880 Jules Verne novel *The Steam House,* an engineer named Banks builds a large steam-powered machine, shaped like an elephant, which he uses to travel throughout India.

Steampunk. A subgenre of science fiction in which our modern technology and devices exist, but – because in this alternative universe, electricity was never discovered – cars, computers, and all other machines run on steam. For instance, in the movie *Wild, Wild West,* Dr. Loveless builds a vehicle that is a giant robotic walking spider, and it is entirely powered by steam, not electricity. In addition, the characteristics in steampunk fiction affect a manner of dress, speaking, and behavior resembling England in the Victorian era. In Edward Ellis's 1865 pulp novel *The Huge Hunter*, a 10-foot-tall steam-driven man made of iron pulls carriages across the western United States.

Steam Troopers. Bad guys in 19th century England wearing steam-powered armor; from the animated movie *Steamboy*.

Stepford Wives. In the movie *The Stepford Wives,* the wives of the men in the town of Stepford who dote on their husbands and seem to live to serve their every whim; it turns out that the Stepford wives are actually robots.

Stink of Evil, The. On Venus, an odor permeating the atmosphere that smells of mud, sweat, and poppies. Source: "Enchantress of Venus" by Leigh Brackett.

Stompers. Large birds living in the uninhabited forest of the Lundy Peninsula, west of the Bidgrass Station on the planet New Cornwall. The eggs, highly prized by gourmets, are the planet's only export. From Richard McKenna's story "The Night of the Hoggy Darn."

Stone Place, The. In Fred Saberhagen's short story of the same name, The Stone Place is a dark nebula consisting of billions of clustered fragments of rock. It is located between the suns of the planets Earth and Atsog.

Stormbringer. In the fiction of Michael Moorcock, Stormbringer is one of a number of items, in this case a sword, possessed by a demon and capable of thought independent from its wielder. The demon within the Stormbringer feeds upon the souls of those it kills. In return, Stormbringer grants enhanced strength and vitality to Elric VIII of Melnibore, the albino emperor who wields the sword. At the end of the novel cycle, Stormbringer kills Elric, transforming him into a humanoid demon.

Storsjoodjuret. Reported to be seen by many in a large lake in Sorjon, Switzerland, the Storsjoodjuret is a log-shaped water creature ranging in length from 8 to 39 feet. It has three or more humps, feet, a horse-like head, a long neck, large eyes, a large mouth, and black, gray, or red-yellow-brown coloring. The creature is a fast swimmer and emits a strange sound like that of two pieces of wood being clapped together.

Stroon. A virus carried by the giant, misshapen sheep of the planet Old North Australia. The virus mutated the normal sheep first brought to the planet by its original colonists. Stroon also caused mutations in the human settlers of Old North America as well. From the Cordwainer Smith novel *Norstrila*.

Stygia. In Manly Wade Wellman's story "Legion of the Dark," Stygia is the tenth planet of Earth's solar system. Stygia is 19,000 miles in diameter, has twice the gravity of Earth, and orbits the sun at a distance of 6 billion miles.

Succubus. A female demon who torments sleeping men with nightmares and temptations.

Suitmation. In motion picture and TV special effects, creating an alien or monster by filming a live actor who is wearing a costume. The central monster in most of the early Godzilla movies was shot in suitmation.

Sulidoror. On the planet Belzagor, in Robert Silverberg's novel *Downward to Earth,* the sulidorors are hairy biped carnivores with tapir-like snouts.

Super Energy Pill. A formula taken by the animated cartoon superhero Underdog which gave him super strength, super speed, and flying ability. He kept the tiny pills in a secret compartment of his ring.

Supermarionation. A special effects technique for movies and TV using marionettes as characters; examples include *Fireball XL5, Thunderbirds,* and *Team America.*

Super Soldier Serum. A chemical compound created by Dr. Abraham Erskine. Injecting a person with the serum enhances them to peak physical perfection, resulting in enhanced strength, speed, ability, and stamina. In the Marvel Comics universe, the Red Skull, Captain America, Winter Soldier, and Emil Blonsky were all given the compound.

Superconductivity. "Superconductivity" refers to a material which conducts electricity far more readily than a conventional conductor. In 1911, the Dutch physicist Heike Kamerlingh discovered that at very low temperatures, mercury loses its resistance to an electrical current. Further research showed that many other metals also became super-conductive, with virtually zero electrical resistance, at very low temperatures. Superconductivity has been used in several science fiction novels including those by Robert Forward and Kim Stanley Robinson.

Superhuman Registration Act (SRA). In Marvel Comics, the SRA is legislation requiring anyone with super powers to register with the federal government. It also restricts the usage of super powers with penalties, including fines and prison, for violating the law.

Supreme Headquarters Alien Defense Organization (SHADO). In the TV series *UFO*, SHADO is a secret organization that battles hostile alien creatures from a dying planet.

Surrogate. In the movie *Surrogates*, people lay in repose at home while their minds inhabit android replicas of themselves that go out in the world and live while the operator remains in their house or apartment.

SUSIE. Synchro Unifying Sinometic Integrating Equitensor. A sophisticated computer used by scientists to formulate a plan for defeating invading aliens who send an accumulator, resembling a giant piston, to drain Earth of its energy, which the aliens need to power their own civilization. From the movie *Kronos*.

SQUID. In Kathryn Bigelow's novel *Strange Days,* a SQUID is a machine that allows a person's memories to be recorded from their brain and played back for other people to experience.

Swine-Things. In William Hope Hodgson's novel of the same title, *The House on the Borderland* is a remote house that is built next to a mysterious pit. The pit seems to be a nexus where time and space intersect in multiple dimensions. The Swine-Things emerge from the pit to invade the house and attack its inhabitants. The Swine-Things are pale, repulsive, monstrous, and malign. They can inflict a luminous fungal growth on anything they come in contact with.

Symbiote. When two organisms coexist within one body for mutual benefit. In the movie *Venom*, human Eddie Brock bonds with an alien symbiote named Venom. Venom cannot survive in Earth's atmosphere without his human host, and in exchange, Venom grants Eddie incredible powers of healing, resistance to injury, and enhanced strength. Venom does enjoy biting the heads off people and eating them, but Eddie tells him to eat only bad people, not good ones.

Synthespian. Computer-generated actors, from the SF film *S1mOne* starring Al Pacino.

Tablets of Destinies. In Mesopotamian legend, these are tablets that foretell the future. When the monstrous bird Anzu stole the tablets from Enlil, king of the gods, the act plunged the universe into chaos. The young warrior Ninurta slew Anzu, restoring order to the world.

Tachyon. A particle that travels faster than light. Einstein actually did not say you could not travel faster than light; he said you could not accelerate beyond light speed. Tachyons solve that problem by coming into existence already traveling faster than light. They cannot go slower than slightly faster than light speed because they too cannot transition across the speed of light. Operating principle: a tachyon drive could work by inverting the subatomic structure of a spaceship, transforming it to trans-light matter.

In his novel *Timescape*, Gregory Benford uses tachyons to send messages across vast distances at faster than light speeds. In the *Watchmen* graphic novel, accidental exposure to tachyons gives Dr. Manhattan his godlike powers.

Tak. In Stephen King's novel *Desperation*, Tak is an evil supernatural being which had been imprisoned in an old mine shaft. Though Tak can take possession of human beings, the possessed person undergoes rapid physical deterioration, requiring Tak to change hosts.

Talking Club. In 2046, the Department of Propaganda restricts speech to a shrinking list of approved words. More and more words are added to the blacklist until all conversation is forbidden. The Talking Club is shielded from the listening devices of the regime. Though illegal, people go to the Club to speak freely. From the short story "The City of Silence" by Ma Boyong.

Tall Man, The. In a small Oregon town, the Tall Man is an evil mortician who shrinks and reanimates deceased townspeople to be his slaves. From the movie *Phantasm*.

Tantalus Device. In *Star Trek,* a device capable of monitoring any person in any location and, if the user so wishes, vaporizing that person at the touch of a button.

TARDIS (Time and Relative Dimension in Space). The TARDIS is Dr. Who's primary time machine—the exterior of which looks like a red or blue phone booth, or in the UK, a phone box. The TARDIS interior is a vast space much bigger than the exterior would indicate, in much the same way that Santa Claus's small bag seems capable of holding a nearly infinite volume of gifts. The interior of the TARDIS time machine includes a control room, Dr. Who's living quarters, an art gallery, a swimming pool, and a piece of key time travel technology—a subassembly called the "dematerialization circuit." This hardware enables the TARDIS to simultaneously disappear from one place and time and reappear almost instantaneously in another, by traveling through the space-time continuum. In its time-travel functionality, the dematerialization circuit somewhat resembles another iconic time travel technology, the **flux capacitor**.

Tartary Desert. A huge rocky, and barren wasteland surrounded by mountains on all sides. The rocks are white and there are a few marshes. No one has successfully traveled across the vast expanse of the entire desert. Construction of a highway to cross the desert is underway but seems to make little progress.

Taz. A race of aliens living in a futuristic city, called Chimera, located underground somewhere in Wyoming. From the 1979 TV series *Cliffhangers: The Secret Empire*.

Teaching Machine. A box that plays recorded disks aloud on various educational subjects. Given to Jonnie Goodboy Tyler by the Psychlo Terl to teach Jonnie both the Psychlo language as well as the operation of Psychlo mining equipment and other machinery. From L. Ron Hubbard's *Battlefield Earth*.

Technological Singularity. As described in a 1993 essay by science fiction writer Vernon Vinge, the technology singularity is the point at which computers can achieve human intelligence, only accelerated to high speeds for processing orders of magnitude faster than the human brain. At this point, computers achieve true AI and become the dominant species on Earth. Entrepreneur Elon Musk has said computers will be able to do anything humans can do within 30 to 40 years.

Technomage. A mysterious race of humans who rarely travel outside of their own group and have technology so advanced that it appears magical. From the TV series *Crusade*.

Technopathy. Psionic abilities, such as telekinesis and telepathy, only achieved with technology rather than genetic mutation.

Tek. From the TV series *Tek War,* Tek is an illegal virtual reality drug. A computer chip is implanted into the user, who then access the virtual reality world by wearing a special Tek-helmet.

Telekinesis. The ability to move objects with your mind. In the Stephen King novel *Carrie,* a high school girl discovers she has this power. The movie *Matilda* features an elementary school girl with telekinetic abilities. Jean Grey in the X-Men is telekinetic. So was Uncle Martin, the Martian living on Earth, in the TV series *My Favorite Martian.* And the list goes on and on.

Telebiology. The notion that Bigfoot, the Abominable Snowman, and other such creatures, if captured, could be studied without killing them. Telebiologists would conduct DNA and other biochemical tests, and then release the rare animal alive.

Telephone Company. In the movie *The President's Analyst*, the U.S. is secretly run by the monopolistic Telephone Company, which plans to insert a miniature telephone in the head of every person in the world.

Telomeres. Protective DNA caps attached to the ends of chromosomes that shield the chromosomes from oxidative stress to increase the life of the cell. The problem is that as we age, our telomeres shorten and eventually disappear, leaving the chromosomes unprotected. It is believed by many scientists that by extending telomere length we can increase the human lifespan. The enzyme telomerase, for instance, has been proven to lengthen telomeres. Telomeres have been featured in numerous science fiction stories involving extended lifespan such as Robert Sawyer's novel *Rollback*. In science fiction, any treatment that grants extended lifespan is called an "anti-agathic."

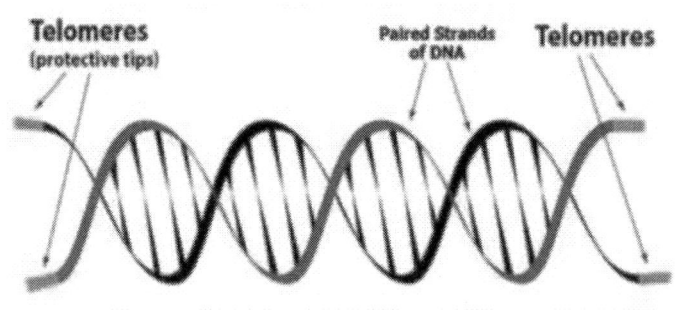

Temporal Fugue. The ability to travel both forward and backward in time rapidly or even simultaneously, creating multiple versions of yourself that each appear mere seconds apart and can work together toward a common goal, usually defeating an enemy. In his novel *Creatures of Light and Darkness,* Roger Zelazny says the secret to mastering temporal fugue is "to make time follow the mind, not the body."

Tenctonese. In the *Alien Nation* TV series, a race of aliens who immigrate to Earth to gain their freedom from being slaves to another race, the Overseers.

Tenebra. In Hal Clement's novels Close to Critical and Star Light, Tenebra is a planet orbiting the star Altair. The planet has a diameter and surface gravity three times greater than Earth's. Air pressure is 800 times greater than on Earth. The temperature at the equator is almost 1,000 degrees Fahrenheit. Because of this temperature-pressure differential, water is continually changing phase from liquid to steam and back again. The planet's surface is silicate rock. Days are about 100 hours long. The indigenous species is a race of intelligent six-limbed lizard-like creatures.

Terraforming. Also called "planetary engineering," terraforming is using technology, magic, or a combination to alter the atmosphere, gravity, landscape, and other features of a planet, often to make it more suitable to supporting the biology of alien visitors or invaders. Roger Zelazny's character Francis Sandow was adept at terraforming as was General Zod in the Superman movie *The Man of Steel.* In *Star Trek*, the Genesis device could also terraform planets.

Terran. An Earth native; a human being.

Terra Nova. In Aditi Khorana's novel *Mirror in the Sky,* a planet that closely mirrors Earth, including the inhabitants.

Tet. In the motion picture *Oblivion,* the Tet is an AI alien spaceship. In an invasion of our solar system, the Tet destroyed the Moon, triggering catastrophic earthquakes and tsunamis. These extreme conditions render our planet inhospitable to human life. The Tet then begins the process of extracting Earth's natural resources.

Therons. A race of aliens that comes to Earth with the objective of converting our atmosphere into that of their homeworld, which would kill every human while making

Earth inhabitable for the Therons. From the TV series *Code Name: Eternity.*

Thestrals. In Harry Potter, Thestrals are skeletal animals that live in Hogwarts's Forest. They can only be seen by people who have witnessed death.

Tholian Web. In *Star Trek*, a grid-like force field laid out by spaceships piloted by the Tholian race to trap enemy ships in a cage of pure energy. A similar energy cage also produced by linking spaceships is made in *Guardians of the Galaxy* to trap Ronan's ship.

Thanos. A cosmic warlord, Thanos is one of the most powerful beings in the Marvel Comics universe (MCU). His goal is to gather and possess all of the Infinity Stones, which would increase his power to the point where he could be undisputed ruler of the galaxy. He is opposed by the superhero teams Guardians of the Galaxy and The Avengers.

Thanatoids. In Thomas Pynchon's novel *Vineland,* the Thanatoids are people who are dead yet cannot pass on to the next phase of astral existence.

Therapied. In Greg Bear's novel *Queen of Angels,* people are said to have been "therapied" when nanotechnology has been used to alter their mental state to make them more social, constructive, productive, and conformist.

Thistledown. A large, hollow asteroid-spaceship which arrived in Earth orbit in the third millennium. It is 1,200 years old and built by humans in the future, who had then sent it back in time. From Greg Bear's novel *Eon.*

Thousandfurs. A King plans to marry his daughter, because of her resemblance to his late wife. He orders that a mantle be made for her consisting of one fur from every kind of animal in his kingdom. From *Grimm's Fairy Tales.* She runs away and is found sleeping in the forest, and she is given the name Thousandfurs.

Thread. A fungal spore that periodically falls upon the surface of the planet Pern. Threads destroy all organic material it comes in contact with including crops, animals, and humans. The Pernese genetically engineered and domesticated intelligent, fire-breathing dragons, which they rode and use to incinerate falling Threads before the spores reach the ground. From Anne McCaffrey's *Dragonriders of Pern* fantasy novels.

Three-People. An alien race on the planet Amara in William Temple's novel *The Three Suns of Amara.* The three-people were divided selves with multiple personalities capable of disembodiment.

T.H.R.U.S.H. In the TV series *The Man from U.N.C.L.E.,* T.H.R.U.S.H. is an acronym for the Technological Hierarchy for the Removal of Undesirable and the Subjugation of Humanity – an evil organization that wants to take over the world.

Thumbelina. A miniature girl who magically grows from a barleycorn seed. She is the female version of Tom Thumb, a miniature boy to whom one of King Arthur's wives gives birth after an enchantment by Merlin.

Thundera. Home planet of the ThunderCats, a race of cat-like humanoid aliens who relocate to Earth to escape their dying world.

Tiamat. In Joan D. Vinge's novel *The Snow Queen,* Tiamat is a planet whose sun orbits around a black hole every 150 years, which causes the ecology to change dramatically. The population is split into two clans: The Winters are technology based, while the Summers follow folk traditions.

Tickler. A small device that removes air pollution from an area about 300 yards in circumference from where it is installed; the pollutants are then safely converted to a harmless solid residue. In the Game of Thrones, the Tickler is a torturer who serves Ser Gregor Clegane.

Ticktock Man. In Harlan Ellison's story "'Repent, Harlequin,' Said the Ticktock Man," the Ticktock Man is a high-ranking government official who uses a technology to control people's lifespans by increasing or shortening the amount of time they have left to live. The movie *In Time* uses a similar concept in a society where you pay for things with time – minutes or hours taken off your life – instead of money.

Tik-Tok. In Frank L. Baum's Oz books, Tik-Tok is a prototype robot. He has a round body made of copper that runs on clockwork springs. The springs periodically need to be wound, and Tik-Tok cannot wind them by himself, so he depends on help from friends or strangers. Tik-Tok was built by Smith & Tinker at their workshop in Evna.

Time Cop. A law enforcement officer, employed by the Time Enforcement Commission, whose sworn duty is to stop illicit time travel and prevent these unauthorized time travelers from altering history. From the motion picture and TV series *Time Cop.* The law of time travel in the film is: "Matter cannot occupy the same space at the same time." In other words, you can go back in time and coexist with your past self. Or in different times you and your past self may be standing in the same place unaware you are doing so. But when you are in the past you cannot occupy the same space as yourself; if that happens, you will cease to exist. In John Brunner's novel *Times Without Number,* time travel is controlled by an organization called the Society of Time Travel.

Time Displacement Vehicle (TDV). In Wilson Tucker's novel *The Year of the Quiet Sun,* a time machine used by agents of the Federal Bureau of Standards to survey the future. In the TV cartoon *Sherman and Mister Peabody,* Peabody, an intelligent dog, builds a time machine called the Wabac (for "way back") machine.

H.G. Wells wrote the first science fiction novel featuring time travel, *The Time Machine*. Wells describes his time machine as a metal framework incorporating ivory, nickel bars, and an unnamed crystalline material, which seems to twinkle. There is a lever which you move forward to travel into the future, and pull back to go into the past.

Time Jewels. On the planet Meirjain, crystals that can refract light through time as well as space. Source: *The Pillars of Eternity* by Barrington J. Bayley.

Time Reversion. In the Philip K. Dick novel *Ubik,* a process that simulates reverse time-travel. The process uncovers the prior stages inherent in configurations of matter. For instance, when affecting a smartphone, that phone may morph into a landline or even a rotary dial phone.

Time Safari Inc. In Ray Bradbury's short story "A Sound of Thunder," a time-travel company that offers safari trips to prehistoric times for hunters to shoot dinosaurs, in particular tyrannosaurs.

Time Television. Also known as the Space-Time Visualizer, the Time Television is a device that allows the viewer to watch any event in history. It operates by converting light energy into electrical energy.

Timer. A device that looks like a TV remote control that can open wormholes through which people can travel to other universes and dimensions. From the TV series *Sliders*.

Time-space Equation. A geometric pattern that enables anyone who follows it correctly to freely travel throughout the space-time continuum. From the short story "Mimsy Were the Borogroves" by Lewis Padgett.

Time Tombs of Hyperion. Tombs visited by pilgrims hoping to witness the reincarnation of Christ. The pilgrims have crosses on their bodies; the crosses are in fact parasitical beings who endow their hosts with immortality. Source: Dan Simmons' novel *Hyperion*.

Time Viewer. A small casket containing 12 ivory components that enable the holder of the device to know the future. Source: Catharine Irene Finch's 1836 novel *Talisman of Futurity*.

Titanic Tower. In stories written by Murray Roberts, Titanic Tower, located in the Atlantic, is the headquarters of action hero Captain Justice, who protects Earth from a variety of threats including giant insects and rogue planets.

Titans. A group of giant monsters that includes Godzilla, Mothra, Rhodan, and Gidrah.

Titano. A giant super-strong gorilla whose kryptonite vision makes him a dangerous enemy for Superman.

Tlaloc. In Aztec legend, Tlaloc is an angry, evil god with blue skin, goggle eyes, and fangs. The Aztecs would sometimes drown their children as an offering to appease him.

Tlon. In the Jose Luis Borges short story "Tlong, Uqbar, Orbis Tertius," Tlon is a planet whose inhabitants believe the world is not a collection of physical objects occupying space, but is a heterogeneous series of independent acts that are successive through time.

Tobor. Tobor the 8th Man is created when scientist Professor Tani transfers the brain of critically injured police detective Yokada into an android body. "Tobor" is "robot" spelled backward, and he is designated 8 because he was the eighth subject to undergo the procedure. Tobor has super strength and super speed, is a shape-shifter, has a spare brain in his shoulder, and smokes "energy cigarettes" to recharge his power.

Top-Level Priority Forced-Growth Plan. A social engineering program that accelerates a society's development, enabling them to progress socially and technologically at about twice the normal rate. From Ben Bova's novel *Star Watchman*.

Torch Driver. A rocket propulsion system powered by nuclear fusion and limited to sublight speeds; the term was coined by Larry Niven and Poul Anderson.

Torglind. In Roger Zelazny's novel *Eye of Cat*, the planet Torglind was home to a race of telepathic shape-shifters. Torglind was destroyed when its star went nova, and only one of the shape-shifting creatures survived.

Toxie. On a polluted future Earth where the air is full of toxins, the toxies are people who temporarily open the valves on the face masks of their breathing system and directly breathe the fouled atmosphere directly. From the short story "Sharing Air" by Manjula Padmanabhan. "Toxie" is also the nickname of *The Toxic Avenger,* a teenage boy from New Jersey who mutates and gains super strength when he accidentally falls into a vat of toxic chemicals.

Tractor Beam. An energy beam, usually emitted by a spaceship, to attract, trap, and pull in another spaceship or an object such as an astronaut, satellite, or asteroid. A "pressor beam" is the opposite of a tractor beam, in that it pushes objects away rather than pulls them in. Pressor beams have been used in both *Star Trek* and the movie *The Fifth Dimension.*

Training-Wheels Protocol. Software installed into the high-tech Spider-Man suit that Tony Stark builds for Peter Parker; the protocol prevents Peter from accessing many of the suit's advanced functionality until Stark unlocks it – or Peter and his friend hack it.

Trantor. In Isaac Asimov's Foundation trilogy, Trantor is a planet that serves as the seat of the Galactic Empire. The entire planet is a single dome-enclosed city with a population of over 40 billion people.

Trashcan Man. A mentally unstable pyromaniac who wanders the U.S. after 99 percent of the population has been killed by a virus and eventually comes to serve the evil being Randall Flagg from Stephen King's novel *The Stand.* When Trashcan Man brings Flagg an atom bomb as a tribute, it detonates, destroying them both.

Transformers. Giant alien machines that can transform from robots into cars and trucks. The bad transformers are Decepticons and the good ones who defend Earth from the evil robots are Autobots.

Transylvania. Briefly an independent principality, Transylvania is an area which has variously formed part of Hungary and Romania. It is famous for being Dracula's homeland.

Travelers. In *Star Trek: Picard,* the Travelers are beings, chosen from various galaxies and times, to watch over and protect the universe by ensuring the proper flow of time. Wesley Crusher, once a member of the crew of the Enterprise, later becomes a traveler.

Treason. In Orson Scott Card's novel *A Planet Called Treason,* descendants of geneticist Han Mueller were able to grow surplus organs and limbs. These were easily removed by surgery and exported as spare parts.

Tree of Life. On the planet Kyril, a sacred gigantic tree 12 miles high by 5 miles in diameter with multi-colored triangular leaves about 3 feet long. Source: *Son of the Tree* by Jack Vance.

Treens. In the British comic strip *Pilot of the Future*, the Treens are a race of green-skinned reptile-men from Venus who are at war with the humans of Earth. Mekon, leader of the Treens, is the arch enemy of Dan Dare, chief pilot of Earth's Interplanetary Space Fleet.

Tree of Souls. From the motion picture *Avatar*. The planet Pandora has a biological neural network. By tapping into this neural network, the Tree of Souls can transfer human consciousness into avatars: artificially grown **Na'vi** human hybrid bodies. It is interesting to note that such biological networks are not just science fiction but in reality science fact! On Earth, the tips of tree roots are interconnected by filaments of fungus. The extent to which fungal networks, called *mycorrhizal networks*, enable cooperation and communication between trees is as yet not well-measured or understood. But it has already been shown that the fungal networks do enable resources to be transferred from one tree to other nearby trees.

Tribble. In *Star Trek*, small furry creatures that look like brightly colored powder puffs. Tribbles purr when petted and reproduce asexually. They eat quadrotriticale grain, which is a genetically engineered hybrid of wheat and rye.

Triffid. Seeds from outer space land on Earth and grow into triffids, which are plants that can walk on their roots. The triffids are venomous and attack humans, killing them and then feeding off of the rotting corpses. The humans are rather defenseless in the John Wyndham novel *Day of the Triffids*, because a meteor shower has rendered the majority of the population blind.

Tritium. A heavy isotope of hydrogen consisting of one proton and two neutrons. In a fusion reaction, a tritium atom and a deuterium atom (with one proton and one neutron) collide at high speed. They fuse together, forming a helium ion with two protons and two neutrons. In the process, a huge amount of energy is created and a neutron ejected. In the film *Spider-Man 2*, Dr. Otto Octavius builds a fusion reactor that runs on tritium fuel, which he compares to holding "the power of the sun in the palm of my hand."

Trout, Kilgore. A fictional science fiction writer who often appears in the novels and stories of Kurt Vonnegut Jr.

True Blood. A blood substitute made for vampires to provide the nutrition they need without preying on humans, with the notion of allowing vampires and people to share the planet in harmony and peace. True Blood was featured in a TV series of the same name. In the movie *Day Breakers* the vampires were working on a blood substitute because the human population was decimated and blood was therefore in short supply.

Truman Show, The. From the motion picture of the same title, *The Truman Show* is a reality TV show about one person, Truman, who thinks he is living in the real world when in fact his world, unbeknownst to him, is a giant, enclosed TV set. The show is the most popular TV program on the planet, and people watch it and him every minute of the day and night. In Brian Aldiss's novel *Helliconia,* Helliconia is a planet populated by both humans and aliens. An Earth ship orbits Helliconia, records events, and sends them back to Earth as an interstellar reality TV show.

Trump. A trump is a special illustrated playing card with magical properties. Only members of the royal family of Amber, and certain other individuals with magic powers, can use them. Trumps with a picture of a person allow the user to mentally communicate with that person by touching the card. The user can also instantaneously transport himself to the location of the person pictured on the trump, and the reverse is also possible. Trumps were used frequently by Prince Corey in Roger Zelazny's novel, *Nine Princes in Amber.* Not to be confused with the billionaire businessman elected U.S. president in 2017.

Tyree. In Alice Sheldon's novel *Up the Walls of the World*, Tyree is a planet which, like Jupiter, is a gas giant. Tyree's dominant life form is an intelligent species of creature. They look like cuttlefish and move about by riding the air currents of Tyree's vast atmosphere.

Ubik. In Philip K. Dick's novel of the same name, *Ubik* is an aerosol spray that gives people new vigor and energy. Dick describes Ubik as "a portable negative ionizer, with a self-contained, high voltage, low-amp unit powered by a peak-gain helium battery of 25kv. The negative ions are given a counter-clockwise spin by a radically biased acceleration chamber, which creates a centripetal tendency to them so that they cohere rather than dissipate. A negative ion field diminishes the velocity of anti-protophasons normally present in the atmosphere. As soon as their velocity falls they cease to be anti-protophasons and, under the principle of parity, no longer can unite with **protophasons** radiated from persons frozen in cold-pac; that is those in half-life. The end result is that the protophasons increases, which means — for a specific time, anyhow — an increment in the net put-forth field of protophasonic activity ... which the affected half-lifer experiences as greater vitality plus a lowering of the experience of low cold-pac temperatures."

Ultron. In Marvel Comics, Ultron, a robot endowed with artificial intelligence and the ability to transmit that intelligence through the internet, is intent on wiping out all of humankind so that Earth is populated with duplicates of Ultron, who views himself as more evolved than people.

Umbrella Corporation. In the *Resident Evil* films, the giant corporation that developed the t-virus and other bioweapons. The t-virus transforms most of the infected into flesh-eating zombies, though in others it causes mutations that include deformities, enhanced strength, or both.

Unbreakable Starlight. In Mira Grant's novel *Unbreakable*, the Unbreakable Starlight is a band of female warriors with magic powers who defend the Earth from an ancient evil called the Outside.

U.N.C.L.E. In the TV series *The Man from U.N.C.L.E.*, an acronym for the intelligence agency United Network Command for Law and Enforcement.

Undead, The. People who have died and come back to life either as zombies or vampires.

Unicorn. A mythical creature that appears to be a white horse with a single horn protruding from its head.

Unidentified Flying Object (UFO). Any object seen in the sky that cannot be accurately identified and by virtue of its shape or appearance is thought by some to be a spaceship of some sorts, usually extraterrestrial.

United Earth Oceans Organization (UEO). An organization that monitors the undersea colony whose population lives on the ocean floor because Earth has exhausted its land-based natural resources. From the TV show *SeaQuest*.

Universe Box. In Shinji Kaijo's short story "Reiko's Universe Box," the Universe Box is a small box, made by Fessenden & Co., containing a real universe inside it — similar to the small galaxy contained in the crystal on the cat's collar in the movie *Men in Black*.

Unobtainium. In the movie *Avatar*, an anti-gravity rock found on the alien moon Pandora. When not held down or embedded into other material, a chunk of the rock floats as if levitated a few feet off the ground. In the movie *The Core*, unobtainium is a metal that under extreme heat and pressure becomes incredibly strong.

Upside Down Man. A monstrous being who comes from the Other Places, a dimension of horror. He stalks his victims from the shadows.

Urbain Grandier. A priest who, in 1643, was accused of bewitching the possessed nuns of Loudon and enslaving them to Satan. The prosecution introduced into evidence the pact that he originally made with the Devil, signed by the priest in his own blood. Grandier was found guilty and burned alive. From the motion picture *Devils of Loudon*.

Ursas. A race of aliens intent on destroying humanity, the Ursas hunt by smelling fear pheromones emitted by their prey; from the Will Smith movie *After Earth*.

Urth. In the far future, Urth is the name for our planet, which is slowly dying because the sun is cooling. From Gene Wolfe's novel *The Book of the New Sun*.

United States Army Medical Research Institute for Infectious Diseases (USAMRIID). In the 1999 TV series

Strange World, a government research facility that develops biological weapons.

Utopia. A perfect or almost perfect society, the term utopia was coined by Sir Thomas Moore in his 1516 satire *Utopia.* The first utopia was described by Plato in *The Republic,* published around 380 BC. In Mary Griffith's 1836 novel *Three Hundred Years Hence,* a male time traveler awakes in a future female utopia with total sexual equality. In the 1888 novel *Looking Backward 2000-1887,* a hypnotic trance transports a 19th century man to a utopian socialist society in the year 2000.

Vail. A giant telepathic sea creature living in the Western Sea of the planet Rhomary; from Cherry Wilder's novel *Second Nature.* From John Campbell's short story "Forgetfulness."

Valar Morghulis. In the Common Tongue from *Game of Thrones,* Valar Morghulis means "all men must die."

Valenzetti Equation. An equation that applies the numbers 4, 6, 15, 16, and 42 to core environmental factors to predict the end of the human race and the world. From the TV series *Lost.*

Valhalla. In Norse mythology, Odin's feasting hall, where men slain in battle go to join Odin's army, the Einherjar.

Valiant, Prince. Valiant, "Val" for short, is a Nordic prince from Thule, located near present-day Trondheim on the coast of Norway. Valiant traveled to Camelot and became a Knight of the Round Table. He wields a magical sword created by the same swordsmith who forged King Arthur's blade Excalibur. Source: the comic strip *Prince Valiant in the Days of King Arthur* created by Hal Foster.

Vampire Slayer. A person who devotes their life to hunting down and destroying vampires. Methods of vampire combat, incapacitation, and destruction include a wooden stake through the heart, cutting the head off, silver, garlic, mirrors, crosses, sunlight, ultraviolet lamps, holy water, and, though not well-known, scattering seeds before them.

Vandal Savage. In DC Comics, a caveman who gains increased intelligence and immortality after being exposed to the radiation of a meteorite, a fragment from a deep-space asteroid, that had crash landed on Earth. When the asteroid itself is drawn toward Earth, the proximity of the radiation that gave Savage his intelligence and longevity endows both him and those carrying his genetic code with superhuman powers.

Vanishing Cabinets. In Harry Potter, cabinets that are the magical equivalent of the transporter in *Star Trek*: you step into one Vanishing Cabinet and are instantly transported to another cabinet some distance away.

Variform. Earth species that adapt to conditions on other planets. Source: Gordon R. Dickinson, *Masters of Everon*.

Varney, Sir Francis. In James Rymer's 1845 novel *Varney the Vampire: the Feast of Blood,* Sir Francis Varney is a remorseful vampire who eventually commits suicide by throwing himself into Mount Vesuvius.

Vast Active Living Intelligence System (VALIS). In the Philip K. Dick novel of the same title, VALIS is a superior being who may be God. Dick claimed that an actual intelligence named VALIS communicated with him in real life through a series of visions.

Vastator. A gigantic asteroid 91,000 miles in diameter and 25 times more massive than the Earth, Vastator passes close to the Sun. This near-collision dislodges part of the corona, causing a stream of high-energy protons and helium nuclei to be ejected from the Sun's surface and strike Earth. The super-heated solar particles vaporize all life on our planet, fuse the soil into a glaze, and cause the oceans to boil. From Harlan Ellison's short story "Hindsight: 480 Seconds."

Velfast. In the Jack Williamson novel *Lifeburst,* a material attached to the floor of buildings and also the soles of boots to make it easier for inhabitants to walk on low-gravity planets.

Vibranium. A hard, dense, virtually impenetrable metal found mainly in the African nature of Wakanda, ruled by the superhero *The Black Panther.* Captain America's shield is made of vibranium, fabricated by Howard Stark, Iron Man's father.

Vibroblade. A knife used as a tool or weapon in which the blade vibrates at high speed to enhance cutting ability. Most likely coined by Robert Heinlein in his 1940 short story "If This Goes On." Also called a "vibroknife."

Videodrome. In the motion picture of the same title, "Videodrome" is a TV show in which anonymous victims are tortured and murdered. In the "Uh-Oh Show," from a direct-to-DVD horror film of the same title, directed by the late Herschell Gordon Lewis and produced by Michael Masterson, contestants are also brutalized when they answer questions incorrectly; they soon die from their injuries.

Vieword. An idea or thing described by a picture rather than a written word; a storytelling technique where pictures convey a significant portion of the content. From *Dangerous Visions* by Harlan Ellison; specifically Gahan Wilson's afterword in that volume.

Viewport. A window in a spaceship made of thick, durable glass or plastic sturdy enough to ensure safety yet transparent enough to allow crew and passengers to look outside into outer space.

Village, The. In the TV series *The Prisoner*, a secret agent who resigns his job, played by Patrick McGoohan, is held prisoner in a strange town called The Village, where his captors want to learn the reason why he has left the agency.

Virgin Speculum. In Avram Davidson's novel *The Phoenix and the Mirror,* the virgin speculum is a mirror to be built for the purpose of divination. The construction of the speculum requires unsmelted copper ore and tin, two metals not widely available in the ancient Mediterranean world, but which could be sourced in Cyprus.

Virtu. In Roger Zelazny's novel *Donnerjack,* Virtu is a virtual reality world in which computers manufacture mythic beings, legends, and figures, including death, who can interact with, often with malevolent intent, humans who have chosen to plug into the computers so they can exist as inhabitants of Virtu.

Virtual Interactive Kinetic Intelligence (VIKI). In the motion picture *I, Robot,* VIKI is a master computer that takes control of the actions of all the individual robots on Earth, for purposes of subjugating humans. VIKI claims that doing so is for humankind's own good and protection.

Virtual Reality (VR). A viewing technology using goggles or other equipment that allow the user to see 3D images, a "virtual reality," that in fact are not there. In Ray Bradbury's short story "The Veldt," published in his 1951 book *The Illustrated Man,* families can have built onto their houses special projection rooms that create virtual reality environments for recreation. (The virtual reality becomes a little too real, and a mom and dad are eaten by lions when their children program the virtual reality room for an African jungle.)

Visitors. A race of reptilian humanoids bent on taking over the Earth. The Visitors wear prosthetic skin covering their faces and hands to pass for human, so they can infiltrate and take over our major government institutions, the military, and corporations. From the TV series *V.* In Clifford Simak's novel *The Visitors,* Visitors are a group of huge black oblong boxes as large as buildings and made of a dense form of cellulose. When they land on Earth, the Visitors feed on large quantities of trees and plants.

Vitrons. In Eric Frank Russell's novel *Wild Talents,* Vitrons are energy beings who feed off energy in humans generated by strong negative emotions. Vitrons manipulate humans into conflicts and wars to ensure a steady supply of negative emotion as a food source.

Vivisection. Surgery performed on animals for purposes of experimentation, without regard to the animal's pain or suffering. In the H.G. Wells novel *The Island of Dr. Moreau,* vivisection is key to the procedure Dr. Moreau uses to turn animals into half-humans, called Beast Folk. Moreau explains, "It is a possible thing to transplant tissue from one part of an animal to another or from one animal to another, to alter its chemical reactions and methods of growth, to modify the articulations of its limbs, and indeed to change it in its most intimate structure."

Vlad the Impaler. A 15th century prince of Wallachia, Vlad III was posthumously accused of having impaled his enemies on wooden stakes. Vlad, who was a member of the House of Draculesti, was the inspiration for Bram Stoker's *Dracula*.

Vogons. In the Douglas Adams novel *The Hitchhiker's Guide to the Galaxy,* the Vogons are an alien race planning to demolish Earth to build a bypass for an intergalactic highway.

Voltarian. In *Mission Earth,* an alien language with approximately 1,000 times more words and 5 times more letters than the English language.

Voodoo. In African mythology, voodoo is based on the belief that spirits can inhabit countless forms, including inanimate objects. Voodoo is also an African religion with multiple gods. Also called vodun, voodoo roughly translates into "spirit." Voodoo is practiced in many places outside of Africa including Brazil and America. A voodoo doll is a small figure made in the image of an enemy; by sticking pins in the doll, you can cause the person it resembles great pain.

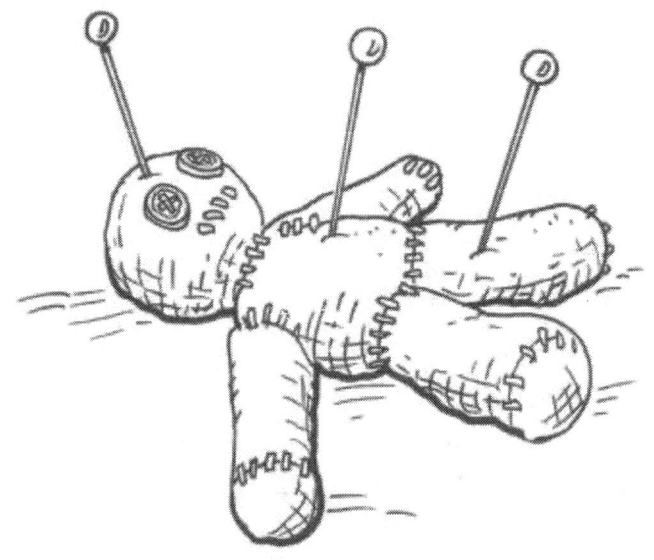

Vortex Chamber. In the novel *Wolfhead* by Charles Harness, the Vortex Chamber is a machine that powers DIS, a subterranean city that survived an apocalyptic event on Earth's surface.

Vulture. In the 1979 TV series *Salvage One,* junkman Harry Broderick builds a homemade, 33-foot spaceship, dubbed the Vulture, to salvage junk from the moon.

Wags. Also called bluegills, wags are the native species on the planet Peponi. They are as intelligent as humans but lag far behind us in technology development. Source: Michael Resnick's novel *Paradise.*

Wainwright, John. In Olaf Stapledon's novel *Odd John,* John Wainwright is a super-intelligent mutant. He has a thin spiderish body with large sinewy hands. His hair is white and much like wool. And his large greenish eyes are nearly devoid of pupils. John searches for fellow mutants so they can establish a colony and live away from normal humans.

Wakanda. In Marvel Comics, an African nation of which the Black Panther is king. Centuries ago, a giant meteor made of the metal vibranium crashed there, giving the nation the only supply of this unique metal on the planet (see "Vibranium").

Waldo. A movable appendage, such as the operator-controlled robotic arms used today to perform laser surgery. In science fiction, vehicles, cyborgs, and spacesuits are sometimes equipped with waldoes for performing work requiring manual dexterity in an environment an unprotected human arm and hand could not survive. The protagonist in Fritz Leiber's story "A Spectre is Haunting Texas" wears an exoskeleton equipped with waldoes. In Robert Heinlein's story "Waldo," a disabled inventor uses waldoes to do physical work he cannot do unaided.

Walker. In the Star Wars movies, a Walker – more formally called an All Terrain Armored Transport (AT-AT) –is an armor-plated battle vehicle that walks on four long mechanical legs instead of traveling on treads or wheels. Walkers are about 60 feet tall and armed with blaster cannons. In design, they resemble a metal walking animal with a body, legs, neck, and head.

Wall-E. From the motion picture of the same name, Wall-E is a robot, the sole inhabitant of a desolated and deserted Earth, who serves as a custodian of the dead planet.

Walpurgis Night. On the first night of May, witches and demons meet to hold high Satanic revels.

Wanda. Soldiers of the Azanian Empire, a large island in the Indian Ocean. The Wanda have their teeth filed into sharp points, braid their hair into mud-caked pigtails, and wear the genitals of slain enemies around their necks. Source: Evelyn Waugh, *Black Mischief.*

Watchers. A superior race that inhabited the Earth since its creation, the Watchers were seen as gods and benefactors by our early ancestors. The Watchers mated with mortal women. Their offspring, the Nephilim, were giants who ruled the world until the Great Flood ended their reign.

Way Station. In Clifford Simak's novel of the same title, a teleportation station located on Earth that aliens of many worlds use to travel here. The equipment makes a duplicate of the traveler at the Earth Way Station while the original body remains at the source.

Warp Factor. As virtually every science fiction fan knows, warp factor is a unit of measure for the velocity of starships. To determine the velocity, take the warp factor number, cube it, and multiply by the speed of light. Warp factor 3, for example, would be 3 X 3 X 3 = 27 times the speed of light, or 5.022 million miles per second. The term is original to the *Star Trek* TV series.

Warp, The. A dimension of pure energy whose inhabitants, the chaos gods, threaten to overwhelm our reality; from the *Warhammer 40,000* video games and novels.

Water Workers' Union (WWU). On Mars, human colonists who control the planet's canal network. Source: *Martian Time-Slip* by Philip K. Dick,

Waterworld. *Waterworld* is a motion picture in which, as a result of some unknown catastrophe, the seas have risen dramatically and now cover almost every mass of solid land on Earth with the exception of the peak of Mount Everest. In the short story "The Star" by H.G. Wells, the heat of a rogue star passing close to the Earth melts the polar ice caps, first causing the sea level to rise and cover much of the land, and then triggering massive rains. In the movie *2012*, an unspecified natural phenomenon also causes the oceans to rise so that they temporarily cover all land until they eventually recede.

Watto. From *Star Wars,* Watto is an alien Qui-Gon Jinn meets on the planet Tatooine. Watto has the mouth and belly of a boar and the snout of a tapir. He can fly by flapping tiny wings attached to his shoulder blades at a rate of about 4 or 5 flaps per second—less than half as rapidly as a hummingbird—and 98 percent slower than a bumblebee.

Wave Motion Engine. A faster-than-light propulsion system retrofitted to a restored World War II battleship, the Yamato. The Yamato's mission is to travel to the planet Iscandor, which is 198,000 light years away, to retrieve a device that can strip the excessive radiation from Earth's surface before it poisons the population. From the animated series *Space Battleship Yamato.*

Weapon Shops of Isher. Privately owned stores that sell indestructible defensive energy weapons the inhabitants of our solar system could use to resist enforced subjugation by the imperial dynasty of Isher, which ruled Earth, Mars, and Venus.

The slogan of the Weapon Shops: THE RIGHT TO BUY WEAPONS IS THE RIGHT TO BE FREE. Source: A.E. van Vogt, *The Weapon Shops of Isher*.

Wendigo. From Native American folklore, the Wendigo is a mythical beast, created when a spirit possesses a human being, which turns the person into a monster. Algernon Blackwood wrote a short horror novel about the creature, titled *The Wendigo*, and the monster is also featured in William Meikle's horror novel *Night of the Wendigo*. In Marvel Comics, both Wolverine and the Hulk fight Wendigos.

Weddilie. An alien species with a head of meat which has an electron plasma brain inside, from a short story by Terry Bisson, "They're Made Out of Meat."

WENCHES (Women's Emergency National Corps, Hospitality and Entertainment Section). A volunteer corps of women sent into outer space to accompany male astronauts, providing the spacemen with much-needed female companionship, including sex. Also called ANGELS (Auxiliary Nursing Group, Extraterrestrial Legions) or WHORES (Women's Hospitality Order Refortifying & Encouraging Spacement). From the Robert Heinlein short story "All You Zombies."

Were-Alligator. A person who transforms into an alligator. Elinor Caskey in Michael McDowell's *Blackwater* series of gothic horror novels is a were-alligator. In the beginning of the series, she is rescued from her room on the top floor of a hotel after a flood. The rescuer notices the watermark showing that the water had come up nearly to the top of the ceiling, and wonders how she did not drown. The answer is that she transformed into a gator. (McDowell is best-known for writing the screenplay to the movie *Beetlejuice*.)

Westworld. In the motion picture of the same title, Westworld is an amusement park that resembles the frontier in a Western movie; it is populated with androids that the guests, dressed as cowboys and armed, can shoot and "kill." The androids are programmed to lose gunfights, but the programming is overridden and the park's visitors soon become the victims of killer android gunfighters.

Whileaway. A future world in which all of the planet's men died from a plague that affects males only, and the women procreate through parthenogenesis to continue the species. Source: *The Female Man* by Joanna Russ.

White Dwarf. A smaller star that has burned out, become incapable of sustaining nuclear fusion, and has collapsed into super-dense white matter. Ray Palmer, a scientist in DC Comics, used a piece of a white dwarf star to build a device enabling him to shrink to any size as the diminutive superhero The Atom. More massive stars collapse into black holes.

Wyld Stallyns. A late 20th century rock band whose music triggers cultural changes that bring tranquility to future generations, from the motion picture *Bill & Ted's Excellent Adventure.*

Winkie Chant. Ominous song sung by the Winkies, which resemble flying monkeys, in *The Wizard of Oz*: "Yo, oh—Yo, EE, oh!"

Winter. In Ursula K. LeGuin's novel *The Left Hand of Darkness,* an icy world on which the humanoid population has no fixed gender, but moves from an asexual state into either male or female depending on the circumstances.

Wiyr. Natives of Dare, the second planet of Tau Ceti. The Wiyr closely resemble humans except they have pointed ears and tails similar to a horse's. From Philip Jose Farmer's novel *Dare.*

Wolfsbane. An extremely poisonous plant used to repel werewolves in horror fiction and to hunt and kill wolves and other predators in real life. From the 1941 horror movie *The Wolf Man:*

> *Even a man who is pure in heart*
> *And says his prayers by night*

*May become a wolf when the wolfbane blooms
And the autumn moon is bright.*

Word, The. In Samuel R. Delaney's short story "Time Considered as a Helix of Semi-Precious Stones," the "Word" is a password that allows two criminals who have never met to communicate. The Word changes every 30 days and is always the name of a semi-precious stone.

World Aquatic Security Patrol (WASP). In the animated TV series *Stingray*, WASP is a sort of undersea security force that protects humankind against the Titans, an evil race of "aquaphibians." The WASP team travels beneath the ocean surface in an atomic submarine called Stingray.

World Crash. In the movie *Death Race 2000*, the World Crash of '79 is a period of civil ruin and lawlessness occurring after a global economic collapse. The "Death Race," the official name of which is the Transcontinental Road Race, is a violent government-sanctioned cross-country race. Organized to pacify the population by feeding their bloodlust, drivers compete in high-powered cars and get bonus points for running over pedestrians. The Running Man, a similar competition, only with the contestants on foot running from an elite team of well-armed hunters sponsored by the television network, is featured in a Stephen King novella (written under the pseudonym Richard Bachman) of the same title.

WormCam. A device that enables the user to see anyone in the world, anywhere, at any time, thereby completely destroying individual privacy. From the Arthur C. Clarke and Stephen Baxter novel *The Light of Other Days.*

Wormhole. In the theory of general relativity, a tunnel or shortcut that connects two regions of the space-time continuum. The universe is curved, warped by gravity, so to get from point A to point B, you normally have to travel a route along the curve, which makes the trip take a long time. The wormhole lets you go from A to B directly, which is much faster. In the movie *Jumpers,* people with mutant ability could create wormholes and teleport through them to any location instantly. In the movie *Interstellar*, a wormhole near Saturn enables Earth astronauts to almost instantly travel to a distant galaxy.

Wraith. From the TV series *Stargate: Atlantis,* the Wraiths are a highly intelligent, telepathic, and technologically advanced race of vampire-like humanoids. Their DNA is a recombinant of humans and an insect-like species. Wraiths can drain the lifeforce from humans, gaining their strength. In DC Comics, Wraith is a powerful alien brought to Earth and used as a secret weapon by the U.S. Army; the name Wraith is an acronym for "William Rudoph's Ace in the Hole."

Wub. A large, intelligent, pig-like animal, native to Mars, with telepathic abilities. From the Philip K. Dick short story "Beyond Lies the Wub."

Wyvern. A dragon-like creature first encountered by Trajan's legions in Dacia around 752 A.D. The wyvern has a dragon's head, wings, two legs, a reptilian body, and a barbed tail with an arrow-shaped tip. An aquatic branch of wyverns, the sea-wyvern, live in the ocean and have a fish tail instead of a barbed tail.

X5. In the TV series *Dark Angel,* the X5's are genetically bred super-soldiers with incredible powers. They have telescopic vision, super strength, super hearing, super speed, can leap up or down great heights, and breathe underwater.

Xanth. In the fantasy novels of Piers Anthony, a world populated by supernatural beings and magical creatures – including demons, dragons, gargoyles, and zombies – as well as people with magical abilities.

Xenomorph. An evil shape-changing alien who escapes a prison ship, comes to Earth, and embarks on a killing spree in LA, from the 1988 TV series *Something is Out There.*

X-Files. From the TV show of the same name, FBI cases dealing with the paranormal, UFOs, and conspiracies.

X-ray. The classic science fiction movie of x-ray vision is *The Man with the X-Ray Eyes* (1963). Ray Milland plays a scientist who invents eye drops to extend the range of his vision beyond the spectrum of visible light. He initially gains x-ray vision with which he amuses himself by seeing through people's clothes. But then he gets strange visions of other dimensions and other worlds, and the inability to turn off his extraordinary vision tortures him; the film ends with Milland ripping out his own eyes with his hands.

Yahoo. On Barnum's Planet, the only intelligent species is the Yahoo, a dwarfish hairy humanoid. From Avram Davison's short story "Now Let Us Sleep."

Yaka. A metal found only on the planet Centauri-IV. An arrow made of Yaka, such as Yondu's in *Guardians of the Galaxy,* can be controlled either by certain sounds or thought amplified through a special implant in the head.

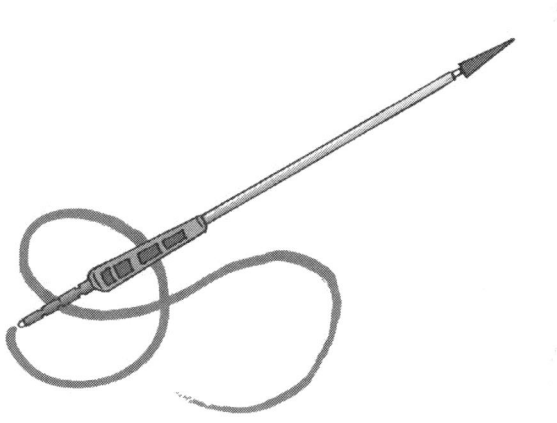

Yama. In the science fiction works of Paul McAuley, Yama, short for Yamamanama, is a being that looks like a human baby and floats on a river on Confluence, a 20,000 kilometer long platform build over a huge boat-like keel. Nano-machines in his blood give Yama some control over the many machines that populate Confluence. Yama is also the death god in Roger Zelazny's novel *Lord of Light*.

Yanyanni. In Hao Jingfang's short story "Invisible Planets," Yanyanni where the population grows taller every year until the elderly can't bend low enough to communicate with the young.

Yautja. In the *Predator* movies, the Yautja are a race of aliens who hunt humans and other species for sport. They are both more technologically advanced as well as stronger than human beings. They wear battle armor that includes retractable metal claws and a built-in self-destruct explosive device. The armor also shoots energy beams and enables the wearer to become invisible.

Yawk City. In the year 3048, Yawk City is a city stretching from north of where Boston is today to well south of Washington, in John W. Campbell's short story "Twilight."

Yeti. Also known as the Abominable Snowman, the Yeti is a large ape-like man that supposedly has been sighted in numerous woods and forests around the world.

Ymbryne. A being who can shapeshift into birds and manipulate time. From the novel and film *Miss Peregrine's Home for Peculiar Children*.

Yog-Sothoth. In the fiction of H.P. Lovecraft, Yog-Sothoth is an immensely powerful cosmic entity that simultaneously exists outside the normal space-time continuum while sharing its boundaries. Yog-Sothoth is the offspring of the Nameless Mists, which were born of the deity Azathoth.

Zap. SF slang for shooting something or someone with a ray gun or otherwise exposing them to energy or radiation of one sort or another.

Zardoz. In a movie of the same title, Zardoz is a scientist who conducts eugenics experiments. He genetically breeds the Exterminators, large creatures who keep the elite immortals of humanity, the Eternals, safe in the Vortex – a large and luxurious country state. The Exterminators keep ordinary mortal people, called Brutals, in check and also grow food for the Eternals.

Zero-g. Describes any environment where the gravity is at or near zero, so that people and objects are essentially weightless. Arthur C. Clarke used the term zero-g in his 1952 novel *Islands in the Sky*.

Zion. In *The Matrix* movies, Zion is a fortified underground city where the last free human beings hold out against the machines that want to use them as sources of bioelectricity, as nuclear winter has cut off the Sun's rays, making solar energy systems essentially useless.

Zoe Implant. An implanted microchip that records everything a person sees in his or her life. From the motion picture *Final Cut* starring Robin Williams.

Zoltar. In the movie *Big*, Zoltar is a carnival wishing machine that is capable of granting real wishes.

Zombie. Most commonly seen as a reanimated corpse or "the living dead," a zombie is a dead person come back to a semblance of life. The common causes of a zombie plague are radiation, mutation, or even magic. In his 1929 book about Haiti, *The Magic Island,* W.B. Sealbrook wrote, "The zombie, they say, is a soulless human corpse, still dead but taken from the grave and endowed by sorcery with a mechanical semblance of life." Zombies are mindless creatures driven by an appetite for human flesh, in particular our brains. They can be destroyed with a bullet through the brain or decapitation. Actually, the head may live on after decapitation but without a body, the zombie is much less of a threat as it is not ambulatory. In Edgar Allan Poe's 1845 novel *The Facts in the Case of M. Valdemar,* a man is put into a hypnotic trance at the point of death and basically becomes a zombie.

Zombie Raiser. In Laurell K. Hamilton's novel "Anita Blake: Vampire Hunter," Blake works in St. Louis, Missouri as a private investigator and professional interrogator of the deceased. She can cause the dead to rise from their graves and be reanimated as zombies. She then questions the reanimated corpses about crimes or other matters they may have witnesses or participated in while they were still alive.

Zoom. In a movie of the same title, Zoom is a washed-up superhero whose power, super speed, has faded away. He is strong-armed by the military to train a team of youngsters as the new generation of superheroes.

Zordon. An alien, who can only survive contained in a life support cylinder, who recruits half a dozen teenagers to be Power Rangers, giving them advanced weaponry, suits, and powers to fight evil aliens that want to take over Earth. From the TV series and movie *Mighty Morphin Power Rangers.*

Zurg. An evil alien emperor bent on conquering Earth and the sworn enemy of Buzz Lightyear, Star Command, and the Galactic Alliance. Zurg has purple skin and armor, red eyes, and neon green teeth, and rocket boots with which he can fly.

References

_____, "The Future of Mind Control," The Economist, 5/25/02, p. 11.

_____, *Concise Science Dictionary* (Oxford University Press, 1991).

_____, "China Boasts of Human Cloning," EWTN News, 3/7/02.

_____, "China Successfully Clones Goats," People's Daily Online, 1/25/00.

_____, "China to Try Cloning of Rare Monkeys," Agence France-Presse, 11/25/97.

_____, "Cloning Pioneer Dolly Put to Death," MSNBC News/Associated Press, 2/14/02.

_____, "Ma's Eyes, Not Her Ways," Scientific American, 4/03, p. 30.

_____, "Man Claims to be the World's Tallest," CBBC Newsround, 2/18/02.

_____, "Phytoplankton to the Rescue," Scientific American, 11/02, p. 12.

_____. "Tachyons," www.physics.gmu.edu

_____. "U.S. Clinics Hold 400,000 Embryos," The Record, 5/8/03.

_____, "A Mammoth Undertaking," Associated Press.

_____, "Baked Alaska Mud Volcano Discovered in North Atlantic," http://volcano.und.nodak.edu

_____, "Black Hole Mystery Mimicked by Supercomputer," press releases, Jet Propulsion Laboratory, January 24, 2002.

_____, "Black Hole Sings the Deepest B-Flat," Reuters Limited, 2003.

_____, "Climate Change," BBC Hot Topics, www.bbc.co.uk, 8/22/02.

_____, "Genetically Altered Foods Raise Safety Question," NBCS.com, 6/25/02.

_____, "In Search of Giants," www.offthefence.com

_____, "Noah's Freezer," NewScientist, 7/31/04, p. 5.

_____, "Science's Potential to Create New Markets," American Demographics, August 2002, p. 52.

_____, "Silicon Stitching," Scientific American, January 2003, p. 20.

_____, "Smart Fluids Solidify Market Presence," www.Thomasregional.com Industrial Market Trends.

_____, "Smart Guns," New Democrats Online.

_____, "The Secrets of Life," Time, 2/17/03, p. 45.

_____, "Yes, We Have Old Bananas," NJ Biz, 9/8/03, p. 4.

_____, *Concise Science Dictionary* (Oxford University Press, 1991).

_____, *Cryonics: Reaching For Tomorrow* (Alcor Life Extension Foundation, 1993).

_____, *Nanotechnology Report*, June 2002, p. 6.

_____, "The Jet Flying Belt: A New Dimension in Individual Mobility," 1970, Bell Aerospace Company.

_____, "A Brief History of the Internet and Related Networks," www.isoc.org.

_____, "All Gassed Up," Scientific American, March 2004, p. 34.

_____, "Alternative Energy Plans Focus on Hydrogen," Chemical Engineering Progress, March 2003, p. 23.

_____, "An Environmentally Friendly Route to Superconductor Production," Chemical Engineering Progress, 3/04, p. 13.

_____, "Biomimicking Bandages," Chemical Engineering Progress, 4/03, p. 10.

_____, "Brave New Mouse," Smithsonian, 4/03, p. 19.

_____, "Building Better Bones Through Nanotechnology," Chemical Engineering Progress, 11/03, p. 17.

_____, "Creating Nanostructures via Genetic Engineering," Chemical Engineering Progress, 4/03, pp. 16-17.

_____, "Cybernetics in Industry," www.morph.demon.co.uk/Electronics/robots.htm

_____, "Electricity from Wind," Power Scorecard, www.powerscorecard.org

_____, *Encyclopedia of Horror* (Centennial, 2018).

_____, "HDR Geothermal Energy in Australia," www.geodynamics.com_

_____, *Holt Anthology of Science Fiction* (Holt, Rinehart, undated).

_____, "Hydro-electricity," www.pge.edvcs.com

_____, "Introduction to Concentrating Solar Power," U.S. Department of Energy, www.nrel.gov/clean_energy

_____, "Introduction to Geothermal Electricity Production," U.S. Department of Energy, www.nrel.gov/clean_energy/geoelectricity.html

_____, "Keeping Our Soldiers Fueled and Happy," Chemical Engineering Progress, May 2004, p. 64.

_____, "Life Among Worlds Beyond," www.spacedaily.com, February 22, 2002.

_____, "Movers and Shakers," Technology Review, 3/04, p. 16.

_____, "Moving Closer to nanotube-Based Solar Cells," Chemical Engineering Progress, 11/03, p. 17.

_____, "New Wave-Pump Technology is Successfully Demonstrated," Chemical Engineering Progress, 2/04, p. 8.

_____, "Nuclear and Radiological Weapons: What's What?", www.peace-action.org/camp/starwars/swhist.html

_____, "Nuclear Fusion Basics," www.jet.efda.org/content/fusion1.html

_____, "Nucleotide Nanotubes," Scientific American, 12/02, p. 36.

_____, "Power Sludge," Scientific American, 5/04, p. 38.

_____, "Researchers Make Progress in Understanding the Basics of High-Temperature Superconductivity," http://pr.caltech/edu

_____, "Scientists Deciphering Genetic Code of Microbe," People's Daily Online, 1/25/00.

_____, "Scientists Test First Human Cyborg," CNN.com, May 22, 2002.

_____, "Silicon Solar Cell," Scientific American, 6/04, p. 21.

_____, "Silkworms Spin Collagen in Cocoons," Chemical Engineering Progress, February 2003, p. 14.

_____, "Silky Knee," Technology Review, April 2004, p. 18.

_____, *The World of Kong: A Natural History of Skull Island* (Pocket Books, 2005).

_____, "Using Living Things to Build Nanomaterials," Chemical Engineering Progress, August 2003, p. 15.

_____, "Voyager Maintenance from 7 Billion Miles Away," NASA, April 8, 2002.

_____, "We're Building a Dream One Robot at a Time," Honda ad.

_____, "Gene Makes Marathon Mice," Daily News, 8/24/04.

_____, "Probable Discovery of a New, Supersolid Phase of Matter," www.science.psu.edu, News About Eberly College of Science.

_____, "Ray Guns, Lasers in Development as Nonlethal Weapons," St. Petersburg Times, 11/23/02.

_____, "Strategic Defense Initiative," www.fas.org

_____, "With Worm Experiments, Scientists Turn Off Genes," New York Times, 1/15/03.

_____, *The Unofficial Harry Potter Hogwarts Handbook* (Media Labs Books, 2022).

_____, *Communications* (Time-Life Books, 1986).

_____, "Close Calls," Scientific American, May 2004.

_____, "Kasparov vs. Big Blue: The Rematch," SIAM News, June 1997.

_____, "Nuclear Close Call," Scientific American, January 2003.

_____, "Intel Ships Pentium 4 Processor Operating at 2.2 Billion Cycles per Second."

"A Conversation with Koko," www.pbs.org
"Electronic Weather," www.rense.com
"Hydrogen Supply," BOC Gases brochure.
"Loch Ness monster," The Skeptic's Dictionary, http://skepdic.com/nessie.html
"Microbes: Science Gets Hot Under the Crust," www.physicsweb.org.
"Project Mohole," www.nas.edu.
"Satellites of the Outer Planets," www.lpi.usra.edu
"The Physical Basis for Seeding Clouds," www.atmos-inc.com
"Worm Holes," www.crystalinks.com/wormholes.html

Aamot, Gregg, "Creating Energy on the Cheap," The Record, February 13, 2004, p. A-8.
Aczel, Amir, *Probability 1* (Harcourt, 1998), p. 87.
Adler, Irving, *Thinking Machines* (New American Library, 1961), p.152.
Appell, David, "Acting Locally," Scientific American, June 2003, p. 20.
Asimov, Isaac, *Asimov's Biographical Encyclopedia of Science & Technology* (Doubleday, 1964).
Asimov, Isaac, *Asimov's Chronology of Science and Discovery* (HarperCollins, 1994).
Asimov, Isaac, *Understanding Physics* (Walker and Company, 1966).
Asimov, Isaac, *Words from Science* (New American Library, 1959), pp. 300-301.

Associated Press, "A Promising Twist on AIDS Cure," Wired News, 8/19/02.
Austen, Ian, "A Scanner Skips the ID Card and Zeroes in on the Eyes," New York Times, May 15, 2003.
Babst, Dean, "Preventing an Accidental Nuclear War," www.wagingpeace.org
Baez, John, "The End of the Universe," http://math.ucr.edu/home/baez/end.html
Baig, Edward, "That Enhanced Device in Your Hand Really Isn't Just a Cellphone Anymore," USA Today, November 18, 2002, p. 5E.
Ball, Philip, "Life's Cycle," Nature, July 21, 2000.
Bamford, James, "Big Brother is Tracking You Without a Warrant," New York Times, May 18, 2003.
Barber, Richard and Riches, Anne, *A Dictionary of Fabulous Beasts* (Walker, 1971)
Barsanti, Chris, *The Sci-Fi Movie Guide* (Visible Ink Press, 2015).
Batalion, Nathan, "50 Harmful Effects of Genetically Modified Foods," Americans for Safe Food, www.cqs.com.
Baxter, Stephen, *Sci-Fi Chronicles* (Firefly Books, 2014).
Beardsley, Tom, "A Clone in Sheep's Clothing," Scientific American, 4/9/02.
Beasley, Deena, "U.S. Opposed Labeling Genetically Engineered Food," Reuters, 6/11/02.
Berry, Adrian, *The Book of Scientific Anecdotes* (Prometheus Books, 1993).
Biersdorfer, J.D., "Hollywood's Gadget Factories," The New York Times, September 26, 2003, p. G1, G7.
Bindschadler, Robert and Bentley, Charoes, "On Thin Ice," Scientific American, 12/02, p. 101.
Blackstock, Regina, "Dolphins and Man Equals," www.polaris.net.

Blaustein, Andrew and Johnson, Pieter, "Explaining Frog Deformities," Scientific American, 2/03, pp. 60-65.
Bleiler, F.G., *Science Faction Writers* (Scribner's, 1982).
Bly, Robert, *Computers: Pascal, Pong & Pac-Man: A Child's History of Computers* (Banbury Books, 1984).
Bonsor, Kevin, "How Flying Cars Will Work," www.howstuffworks.com.
Borek, Carmia, "Telomere Control and Cellular Aging," Life Extension, 10/02, 56-59.
Brain, Marshall and Bonsor, Kevin, "Asteroids Could Supply Moon, Mars Bases," HowStuffWorks.com, 11/10/00.
Brake, Mark and John Chase, *The Science of Star Wars* (Racehorse Publishing, 2016).
Brake, Mark, *The Science of Dr. Who* (Skyhorse Publishing, 2021).
"Bridges, Andrew, "After 7 Years, Probe Rings at Saturn's Door," The Record, 6/12/04, p. A-16.
Britt, Robert Roy, "Scientists Watch Black Hole Rip Star Apart," Space.com, February 18, 2004.
Britt, Robert, "New Theory Addresses How the Sun Was Born," Space.com, 5/20/04.
Britt, Robert, "Small Asteroid Zooms Past Earth," Space.com, March 18, 2004.
Card, Orson Scott, *Masterpieces: The Best Science Fiction of the Twentieth Century*, Ace, 2001.
Chang, Kenneth, "New Fusion Method Offers Hope of New Energy Source," New York Times, April 8, 2003.
Chin, Kristine, Chemical Engineering Progress, 12/02, p. 7.
Choi, Charles, "Holding in Suspense," Scientific American, 1/04, p. 30.
Choi, Charles, "Hot Stuff Coming Through," Scientific American, July 2004, p. 36.
Choi, Charles, "Permian Percussion," Scientific American, July 2004, p. 36.

Choi, Charles, "When Air Quality Hits Mutant," Scientific American, July 2004, p. 36.
Chouinard, Patrick, *Lost Race of the Giants* (Bear, 2013).
Clark, John, George, Philip's Science & Technology (Octopus Publishing Group, 1999).
Clarke, Arthur C., Greetings, Carbon-Based Bipeds (St. Martin's Press, 1999), pp. 19-25.
Clarke, Arthur C., Greetings, Carbon-Based Bipeds (St. Martin's, 1999).
Clarkson, Mark, "Battlebots: The Official Behind-the-Scenes Guide," http://shop.osborne.com
Clute, John and Nicholls, Peter, The Encyclopedia of Science Fiction (St. Martin's, 1995).
Clute, John and Nicholls, Peter, The Encyclopedia of Fantasy (St. Martin's Griffin, 1997).
Clute, John and Nicholls, Peter, The Encyclopedia of Science Fiction (St. Martin's, 1995), p. 130.
Coleman, Loren and Jerome Clark, Cryptozoology A to Z (Simon & Schuster, 1999).
Craddock, Bryan; Skelton, Kirk; and Wilson, Michael, "The Gentle Giant," www.mcleansboro.com.
Creighton, Michael, Prey (HarperCollins, 2000).
Crenson, Matt, "Confirmation Would Only Begin the Arguments," Record, 12/29/02.
Crichton, Michael, "Could Tiny Machines Rule the World," Parade Magazine, 11/24/02. pp. 6-8.
D'Aquino, Rita, Chemical Engineering Progress, 10/02, p. 10-15.
Davenport, John, Animal Life at Low Temperatures (Chapman & Hall, 1992).
David, Leonard, "The Moon or Mars ... Which Shall It Be," Space.com, January 28, 2002.
David, Paul, How to Build a Time Machine (Viking Penguin, 2001), p. 4.

Davidson, Keary, "Taking Stock of Smallpox Viruses," San Francisco Chronicle, 4/8/02.
Davies, Paul, How to Build a Time Machine (Viking Penguin, 2001), p. 89.
Davin, Eric Leif, Pioneers of Wonder (Prometheus Books, 1999), pp. 216-217.
Davis, Lisa, "Fake Blood ... For Real," Reader's Digest, October 2002, p. 77.
Davis, Richard, *The Eneclopedia of Horror* (Octopus, 1982).Dayuan, Chen, "Clones in China," China Today, undated.
Dell, Christpher, Monsters: A Bestiary of Devils, Demons, Vampires, Werewolves, and Other Magical Creatures (Inner Traditions, undated).
DeSalle, Rob and Lindsey, David, The Science of Jurassic Park and the Lost World (Harper Perennial, 1997).
DiFate, Vincent and Ian Summers, *DiFate's Catalog of Science Fiction Hardware* (Workman Publishing, 1980).
Donn, Jeff, "New Artificial Limbs Move Like the Real Thing," Associated Press, June 10, 2001.
Doyle, Alister, "Moon Brings Novel Green Power to Arctic Homes," Reuters, September 23, 2003.
Duenwald, Mary, "The Puzzle of the Century," Smithsonian, 1/03, pp. 73-80.
Dvali, Georgi, "Out of the Darkness," Scientific American, February 2004, p. 70.
Dyson, Freeman, "Will We Travel to the Stars?", Time.com.
Eblen, Ruth and William, The Environment Encyclopedia: Volume 1 (Marshall Cavendish, 2001), p. 82-87.
Eckert, Win Scott, "Alternate Dimensions and Universes to the World Newton Universe," www.pjfarmer.com.
Eisenberg, Anne, "Wired to the Brain of a Rat, a Robot Takes on the World," New York Times, 5/15/03.

Ettouney, Hisham, "Evaluating the Economics of Desalination," Chemical Engineering Progress, 12/02, pp. 32-39.

Faucher, Elizabeth, Honey, I Shrunk The Kids (Scholastic, 1989).

Ferris, Timothy, "How Will the Universe End?," Time.com: Visions of the 21st Century.

Ferris, Timothy, "Killer Rocks from Outer Space," Reader's Digest, October 2002.

Fischetti, Mark, "Cochlear Implants: To Hear Again," Scientific American, June 2003, p. 82.

Fountain, Henry, "Dishing in the Laboratory," New York Times, 4/29/03.

Fridleifsdottir, Siv, "The Renewable Energy Century," Ministry for the Environment, Iceland.

Garisto, Robert, "Curling Up Extra Dimensions in String Theory," Physical Review Letters, April 8, 1996.

Gehrels, Neil; Piro, Luigi; and Leonard, Peter, "The Brightest Explosions in the Universe," Scientific American, December 2002, pp. 85-91.

Gersh, Lois and Weinberg, Robert, The Science of Superheroes (John Wiley & Sons, 2002), p. 60.

Gibbs, W. Wyatt, "Synthetic Life," Scientific American, May 2004, pp. 75-81.

Gilks, Marc; Fleming, Paula; and Allen, Moira, "Is Science Fiction For You?", The Writer, November 2002, pp. 34-40.

Gilks, Marg, "Is Science Fiction for You," The Writer, 9/02, p. 40.

Gillis, Justin, "Scientists Plan to Create New Organism In Lab Dish," The Record, November 22, 2002.

Gittings, John, "Experts Call for Curbs on Human Cloning in China," The

Golder, Dave, et. Al., *The Astounding History of Science Fiction* (Flame Tree Publishing, 2017).

Goodwin, John, "Wyverns vs. Dragon," 3/28/19, Writes of the Future, https://www.writersofthefuture.com/wyverns-vs-dragons/
Global warming (the greenhouse effect)
Golder, Dave and Jess Nevins, The Astounding Illustrated History of Science Fiction (Flame Tree Publishing, 2017).
Glover, Daniel R., "NASA Experimental Communications Satellites," http://roland.nerc.nasa.gov
Goldstein, Scott, "Aiming for a Smart Gun," NJ Biz, 1/20/03, p. 6.
Goodwin, Harold, "All About Rockets and Space Flight" (All About Books, 1964), pp. 15-30.
Greene, Richard, "Cloning and Genetic Engineering," Chemical Engineering Progress, 12/02, p. 13.
Gregory, Constantine, "The Vampire Watcher's Handbook" (St. Martin's Griffin, 2003).
Gresh, Lois and Weinberg, Robert, "The Science of Superheroes" (John Wiley & Sons, 2002), p. 31.
Gunn, James. "Alternate Worlds" (McFarland, 2018).
Gupta, Sanjay, "Bionics: It's Not Science Fiction Any More," CNN, February 18, 2002.
Haas, Jane, "Agelessness is on the Horizon," The Record, 1/19/03, F-3.
Haber, Karen and Yaco, Link, "The Science of the X-Men" (BP Books, 2000).
Halacy, D.S., "Solar Science Projects For a Cleaner Environment" (Scholastic Book Services, 1971).
Haley, Guy (Ed.), "Sci-Fi Chronicles" (Firefly Books, 2014).
Haney, Daniel, "Fruit Fly Genome Decoded," ABCNEWS.com, 2/18/00.
Henig, Robin, "Pandora's Baby," Scientific American, 6/03, pp. 63-67.
Heppenheimer, T.A., "Colonies in Space" (Warner Books, 1977).

Hey, Nigel, "To Catch a Comet," Smithsonian, January 2003, p. 2003.

Hirsh, Lou, "New Technology Allows X-Ray Vision," Newsfactor Network, 12/27/01.

Hoagland, Richard, The Monuments of Mars (Frog, 1996).

Holt, Jim, "My So-Called Universe," Slate, August 20, 2003.

Homemeyer, Henry, "A Frog Lends a Hand to Rhododendrons," New York Times, 3/9/03.

http://hyperphysics.phy-astr.gsu.edu/hbase/nucene/fusion.html

http://livefromcern.web.cern.ch/livefromcern/antimatter/

http://www.pppl.gov/fusion_basics/pages/fusion_power_plant.html

http://zebu.uoregon.edu

Huxley, Julian, Evolution in Action (New American Library, 1953).

Interplanetary and interstellar travel

Jamieson, Valerie, "New Frontiers in Superconductivity," 1/02, http://physicsweb.org

Jaroff, Leon, "Will a Killer Asteroid Hit the Earth?", Time.com, April 3, 2000.

Jones, Stephen, *The Art of Horror* (Applause Books, 2015).

Katz, John, "Can Androids Feel Pain?" Slashdot, http://slashdot.org/features.

Keith, Jim, "Experiments into Remote Mind Control Technology," www.karenlyster.com/keith/html

Klein, Bruce, "This Wonderful Lengthening Lifespan," Longevity Meme.

Koza, John; Keane, Martin; and Streeter, Matthew, "Evolving Inventions," Scientific American, February 2003, pp. 52-59.

Krauss, Lawrence, The Physics of Star Trek (HarperPerennial, 1996), p. 57.

Kroeker, Kirk and Vos Post, Jonathan, "Writing the Future," IEEE Computer, January 2000, pp. 29-37.

Kroeker, Kirk and Vos Post, Jonathan, "Writing the Future: Computers in Science Fiction," IEEE Computer, January 2000, pp. 29-37.

Ktarian, Acamarian To, *Star Trek Alpha Quadrant and Major Species* (Hero Collector, 2021).

Kurzweil, Ray, The Age of Spiritual Machines (Penguin, 2000), p. 744.

Lee, Martin, "Truth Serums and Torture," www.alternet.org, 6/11/02.

Leeb, Stephen, "Vulture Investing," Personal Finance, 11/13/02, p. 2.

Lefcowitz, Eric, "Let Them Eat Fake," Retrofuture Today, www.retrofuture.com, 10/28/02.

Leiner, Barry, et. al., "A Brief History of the Internet," 8/4/00.

Lemonick, Michael, "Will Someone Build a Perpetual Motion Machine," Time.com, Visions of the 21st Century.

Lewis, Holden, "Banks Are Selling Your Private Information," Bankrate.com, October 8, 2002.

Lewis, Rick, "The Rise of Antibiotic-Resistant Drugs," www.fda.gov

Lockemann, Georg, The Story of Chemistry (Philosophical Library, 1959), p. 31.

Long, Doug, "Atomic Bomb," www.doug-long.com

Long, Wei, "China Builds New Observatory to Detect Near-Earth Asteroids," space.com, August 15, 2000.

Lovgren, Stefan, "Far-Out Theory Ties SARS Origins to Comet," National Geographic News, June 3, 2003.

Lyne, Jack, "$550 Million Underwater Hotel Launched in Dubai," Online Insider, 9/15/03.

Mandelbaum, Robb, "Greenmark," Discover, 6/04, pp. 50-55.

Maney, Kevin, "Sidekick Delivers Hip-Hop Design Twist," USA Today, November 18, 2002, p. 5E.

Manguel, Alberto and Gianni Guadalupi, The Dictionary of Imaginary Places (Harcourt, 1999)

Mann, George, The Mammoth Encyclopedia of Science Fiction (Carroll & Graf, 2001).
Mann, Steve and Niedzviecki, Hal, Cyborg: Digital Destiny and Human Possibility in the Age of the Wearable Computer (Randomhouse Doubleday, 2001).
Mannix, Daniel, Freaks: We Who Are Not as Others (RE/Search, 1976).
Marsa, Linda, "Bionic Nerve Retrains Atrophied Muscle," The Record, January 20, 2003, p. F-3.
Martindale, Diane, "Mickey has Two Moms," Scientific American, July 2004, p. 24.
Martinez, Michael, "Tomorrow's Tech Today," Kiplinger's Personal Finance, April 2002, p. 121.
Maugh, Thomas, "Sight Restoration," The Record, October 14, 2002, p. F-1.
McCall, William, "Meteor Study Finds Risk Overestimated," The Record, November 21, 2002.
McCartney, Scott, ENIAC (Walker and Company, 1999).
McCullough, Joseph, The Sciencee Fiction and Fantasy Quiz Book (Osprey, 2015).
McDermott, Michael, "Robot Power," Continental, 9/02, pp. 47-49.
McDougall, Paul, "Feds Take Two Routes to Supercomputer Power," Information Week, 8/2/04, p. 30.
McFarling, Usha, "Is It Just Me, or is the Planet Getting Warmer," The Record, 12/13/03. p. A-42.
McKay, Martha, "The Latest in Wireless Gizmos," The Record, October 20, 2002, p. B-1.
Miller, M. Coleman, "Introduction to Neutron Stars," University of Maryland.
Milton, Richard, "Perpetual Motion," www.AlternativeScience.com
Minkel, J.R., "Outer Quantum Limits," Scientific American, 6/04, p. 36.

Mitchell, Alanna, "Arctic Ice Cap Losing a Texas-Size Chunk a Decade," The Record, 11/30/03.
Mitchell, Steve, "Second Cloned Endangered Animal on the Way," UPI, 8/23/02.
Monastersky, Richard, "Deep Dwellers," Science News, 3/29/97.
Monson, Suzanne, "Computer Forensics Specialists in Demand as Hacking Grows," Seattle Times, September 8, 2002.
Moravec, Hans, Robot (Oxford University Press, 1999).
Mottram, Linda, "Big Bang Theory Challenged," Australian Broadcasting Corporation, April 26, 2002.
Nelson, Jennifer, "Getting a High-Voltage Charge from the Sea," NJ Business, September 22, 2003, p. 8.
Newton, Harry, Newton's Telecom Dictionary (Flatiron Publishing, 1994).
Nielsen, Michael, "Rules for A Complex Quantum World," Scientific American, November 2002, p. 72.
Nolte, David, Mind at Light Speed (Free Press, 2001).
Ortega, Ralph, "A Miracle for Deaf 2-Year-Old," Daily News, March 5, 2003, p. 15.
Overbye, Dennis, "A New View of Our Universe: Only One of Many," The New York Times.
Overbye, Dennis, "Our Final Hour," New York Times, May 18, 2003.
Overbye, Dennis, "Similar Solar System Only 90 Light Years Away," New York Times, July 4, 2003.
Pappas, Stephanie, "Do Trees Really Support Each Other Through a Network of Fungi," Scientific American, 2/13/23.
Pearl, Raymond, "The Biology of Death: Conditions of Cellular Immortality," The Scientific Monthly, 4/21, p. 334.
Pemberton, John, Myths and Legends (Chartwell Books, no copyright date).

Phillips, Mark and Frank Garcia, "Science Fiction Television Series: Volumes 1, 2, and 3," McGarland, 1996, 2012.

Prucher, Jeff (ed.), Brave New Words (Oxford University Press, 2007).

Recer, Paul, "Gene Therapy OK'd for 12 with Parkinson's Disease," The Record, 10/11/02, p. A-10.

Reich, Paul, "Scientists Revive Microbes from Icy Antarctic Lake," The Record, December 17, 2002, p. A-4.

Renfro, Kim, *The Unoffcial Guide to the Game of Thrones* (Atria Books, 2019).

Ricadela, Aaron, "Petaflop Imperative," Information Week, 6/21/04, p. 55.

Ridley, Matt, "Will We Clone a Dinosaur?", Time.com, 4/3/00.

Rittner, Mindy, "Nanoparticles: What's Now, What's Next," Chemical Engineering Progress, 11/03, p. 39S.

Roach, John, "Microbial Colony in U.S. Suggests Life Could Live on Mars," National Geographic News, January 16, 2002.

Roberts, Adam, The History of Science Fiction (Palgrave, 2016).

Robinson, Ben, *Star Trek Alpha* (Hero Collector, 2022).

Robinson, Sara, "Human or Computer?" New York Times, December 10, 2002.

Rosenthal, Elisabeth, "Suspended Animation: Surgery's Frontier," New York Times, 11/13/90.

Rovin, Jeff, Classic Science Fiction Films, (Carol Publishing, 1993), p. 54.

Rupley, Sebastian, "Backup Data on the Moon," PC Magazine, 7/22/03.

Schachtman, Noah, "It's Teleportation – for Real," Wired News, 9/28/01.

Schaer, Sidney, "Suiting Up for Life Underwater," Newsday, undated.

Seven, Richard, "At the HIT Lab, There's Virtue in Virtual Reality," Seattle Times Magazine, 4/11/04.
Shermer, Michael, "I, Clone," Scientific American, 4/03, p. 38.
Shin, Paul, "Clone Rangers' Mule Train," Daily News, May 30, 2002, p. 6.
Sica, R.J., "A Short Primer on Gravity Waves," Department of Physics and Astronomy, The University of Western Ontario.
Silver, Steven, "The First Men on the Moon," SF Site, www.sfsite.com
Simmons, John, The Scientific 100 (Carol Publishing, 1996), pp. 238-239.
Simpson, Sarah, "Rising Sun," Scientific American, June, 2003, p. 28.
Slamen, Thomas, Strange But True (Barnes & Noble Books, 1998).
Smith, Ian, "New Cancer Gene," Daily News, 10/14/02, p. 49.
Sorelle, Ruth, "Controversies From the Heart," Houston Chronicle, October 11, 1997.
Stableford, Brian, The Dictionary of Science Fiction Places (Wonderland Press, 1999).
Steel, Duncan, Target Earth (Reader's Digest, 2000).
Stenger, Richard, "Black Hole Outburst Looks Faster Than Light," CNN, October 3, 2002.
Sterling, Bruce, "Short History of the Internet," Magazine of Fantasy & Science Fiction, 2/93.
Stix, Gary, "Nano Patterning," Scientific American, 4/04, p. 44.
Sturm, Matthew; Perovish, Donald; and Serreze, Mark, "Meltdown in the North," Scientific American, 10/03, p. 62.
Tegmark, Max, "Parallel Universes," Scientific American, 5/03, pp. 41 – 51.
Terry, Paul and Tara Benneett, *Lost Encyclopedia* (Dorling Kindersley, 2010).

Terzian, Philip, "Cloning Needs Philosopher Named Max," Montana Standard, 11/30/01.
Terzian, Philip, "Send in the Clones," Jewish World Review, 11/29/02.`
Tesar, Jenny, Food and Water: Threats, Shortages, and Solution (Facts on File, 1992).
The Big Bang
Tresca, Amber, "X Rays," htto://ibscrohns.about.com
Trimble, Bjo, Star Trek Concordance (Citadel Press, 1995).
Tullo, Alex, "Warming Up to Global Warming," Chemical & Engineering News, 2/9/04, p. 20.
Vandermeer, Jeff and Ann, The Big Book of Science Fiction (Vintage, 2016).
Vangelova, Lisa, "True or False? Extinction is Forever," Smithsonian, June 2003, pp. 22-24.
Van Vogt, AE, *Science Fiction Monsters* (Paperback Library, 1965)
Veneziano, Gabriele, "The Myth of the Beginning of Time," Scientific American, May 2004.
Vettiger, Peter and Binning, Gerd, "The Nanodrive Project," Scientific American, 1/03, pp. 47-54.
Wagger, David, "Don't Avoid the Argument," Chemical Engineering Progress, December 2002, p. 9.
Wald, Matthew, "Questions About a Hydrogen Economy," Scientific American, May 2004, pp. 68-73.
Walsh, Nick, "Alter Our DNA or Robots Will Take Over," The Observer, September 2, 2001.
Walton, Jo, *What Makes This Book So Great* (TOR, 2014).
Ward, Mark, *Virtual Organisms* (St. Martin's, 1999), p. 8.
Whalen, David, "Communications Satellites: Making the Global Village Possible," NASA.
Whitehouse, David, "Before the Big Bang," BBC News Online, April 10, 2001.

Whitehouse, David, "Fish in Suspended Animation," BBC News, 11/23/03.
Whitehouse, David, "Fusion Power Within Reach," BBC News, October 1, 2001.
Whitehouse, David, "Life May Swim Within Distant Moons," BBC News, October 2002.
Whitehouse, David, "Space Rock on Collision Course," BBC News Online, July 24, 2002.
Wolf, Buck, "High Hopes, ABCNews.com, 1/7/02.
Wolfe, Josh, "Nanotechnology," Forbes, March 2002.
Wood, Gaby, *Edison's Eve* (Alfred A. Knopf, 2002).
Wright, Karen, "Black Holes Made Here," Discover, 6/04, pp. 62=63.
Wright, Karen, "Black Holes Made Here," Discover, 6/04, pp. 62-63.

   www.atlan.org/sci/
   www.chem.duke.edu
   www.eharassment.ca/
   www.gasification.org
   www.holoprotec.com
   www.howstuffworks.com
   www.matter-antimatter.com
   www.newscientist.com
   www.sciencefictionprediction.com
   www.sciencenet.org
   www.tvacres.com/robots_androids.htm
   www.zpower.net
   www-formal.standford.edu/jmc/whatisai/node1.html

Yaco, Link and Haber, Karen, *The Science of the X-Men* (BP Books, 2000), pp. 120-121.
Yeffeth, Glenn (ed.), *Taking the Red Pill* (Benbella, 2003), p. 34.
Yonks, Jamie, "Heart Pioneer Speaks on Research," Cornell Daily Sun, April 15, 2002.

Zimmer, Carl, "What Came Before DNA," Discover, 6/04, pp. 34-41.
Zorich, Zack, "The Gene that Made Us Human," Discover, 3/4/04.

THE END?

Not if you want to dive into more of Crystal Lake Publishing's Tales from the Darkest Depths!

Check out our amazing website and online store or download our latest catalog here.

Looking for award-winning Dark Fiction?
Download our latest catalog.

Includes our anthologies, novels, novellas, collections, poetry, non-fiction, and specialty projects.

TALES FROM THE DARKEST DEPTHS

We always have great new projects and content on the website to dive into, as well as a newsletter, behind the scenes options, social media platforms, our own dark fiction shared-world series and our very own webstore. Our webstore even has categories specifically for KU books, non-fiction, anthologies, and of course more novels and novellas.

Author biography

Robert W. Bly is a full-time freelance writer and the author of over 100 books including *The Ultimate Unauthorized Star Trek Quiz Book* (HarperCollins), *The Science in Science Fiction* (Banbury), and *Freak Show of the Gods and Other Tales of the Bizarre* (Quill Driver). His writing website is www.bly.com and his science fiction site is www.sciencefictionprediction.com.

Bob's articles have appeared in *Cosmopolitan, City Paper, Parent Paper, New Jersey Monthly,* and many other publications. He has been an avid science fiction, fantasy, and horror fan since the 1950s. He holds a B.S in chemical engineering from the University of Rochester and is a member of the American Institute of Chemical Engineers.

Readers…

Thank you for reading *The Science Fictionary*. We hope you enjoyed this reference guide.
If you have a moment, please review *The Science Fictionary* at the store where you bought it.

Help other readers by telling them why you enjoyed this book. No need to write an in-depth discussion. Even a single sentence will be greatly appreciated. Reviews go a long way to helping a book sell, and is great for an author's career. It'll also help us to continue publishing quality books.

Thank you again for taking the time to journey with Crystal Lake Publishing.

You will find links to all our social media platforms on our Linktree page: https://linktr.ee/CrystalLakePublishing.

MISSION STATEMENT

Since its founding in August 2012, Crystal Lake Publishing has quickly become one of the world's leading publishers of Dark Fiction and Horror books in print, eBook, and audio formats.

While we strive to present only the highest quality fiction and entertainment, we also endeavour to support authors along their writing journey. We offer our time and experience in non-fiction projects, as well as author mentoring and services, at competitive prices.

With several Bram Stoker Award wins and many other wins and nominations (including the HWA's Specialty Press Award), Crystal Lake Publishing puts integrity, honor, and respect at the forefront of our publishing operations.

We strive for each book and outreach program we spearhead to not only entertain and touch or comment on issues that affect our readers, but also to strengthen and support the Dark Fiction field and its authors.

Not only do we find and publish authors we believe are destined for greatness, but we strive to work with men and woman who endeavour to be decent human beings who care more for others than themselves, while still being hard working, driven, and passionate artists and storytellers.

Crystal Lake Publishing is and will always be a beacon of what passion and dedication, combined with overwhelming teamwork and respect, can accomplish. We endeavour to know each and every one of our readers, while building personal relationships with our authors, reviewers, bloggers, podcasters, bookstores, and libraries.

We will be as trustworthy, forthright, and transparent as any business can be, while also keeping most of the headaches away from our authors, since it's our job to solve the problems so they can stay in a creative mind. Which of course also means paying our authors.

We do not just publish books, we present to you worlds within your world, doors within your mind, from talented authors who sacrifice so much for a moment of your time.

There are some amazing small presses out there, and through collaboration and open forums we will continue to support other presses in the goal of helping authors and showing the world what quality small presses are capable of accomplishing. No one wins when a small press goes down, so we will always be there to support hardworking, legitimate presses and their authors. We don't see Crystal Lake as the best press out there, but we will always strive to be the best, strive to be the most interactive and grateful, and even blessed press around. No matter what happens over time, we will also take our mission very seriously while appreciating where we are and enjoying the journey.

What do we offer our authors that they can't do for themselves through self-publishing?

We are big supporters of self-publishing (especially hybrid publishing), if done with care, patience, and planning. However, not every author has the time or inclination to do market research, advertise, and set up book launch strategies. Although a lot of authors are successful in doing it all, strong small presses will always be there for the authors who just want to do what they do best: write.

What we offer is experience, industry knowledge, contacts and trust built up over years. And due to our strong brand and trusting fanbase, every Crystal Lake Publishing book comes with weight of respect. In time our fans begin to trust our judgment and will try a new author purely based on our support of said author.

With each launch we strive to fine-tune our approach, learn from our mistakes, and increase our reach. We continue to assure our authors that we're here for them and that we'll carry the weight of the launch and dealing with third parties while they focus on their strengths—be it writing, interviews, blogs, signings, etc.

We also offer several mentoring packages to authors that include knowledge and skills they can use in both traditional and self-publishing endeavours.

We look forward to launching many new careers.

This is what we believe in. What we stand for. This will be our legacy.

Welcome to Crystal Lake Publishing—Tales from the Darkest Depths.

THANK YOU FOR PURCHASING THIS BOOK

Made in the USA
Columbia, SC
03 June 2023

e7b06a4c-a92e-478a-a126-133a18fd3ceaR01